ONCE UPON A HIGHLAND SUMMER

Also by Lecia Cornwall

The Secret Life of Lady Julia
How to Deceive a Duke
All the Pleasures of the Season
The Price of Temptation
Secrets of a Proper Countess

Once Upon a Highland Summer

Lecia Cornwall

AVONIMPULSE
An Imprint of HarperCollinsPublishers

Excerpt from *What a Lady Most Desires* copyright © 2014 by Lecia Cotton Cornwall.

Excerpt from *The Secret Life of Lady Julia* copyright © 2013 by Lecia Cotton Cornwall.

Excerpt from *Rescued by a Stranger* copyright © 2013 by Lizbeth Selvig.

Excerpt from *Chasing Morgan* copyright © 2013 by Jennifer Ryan.

Excerpt from *Throwing Heat* copyright © 2013 by Candice Wakoff.

Excerpt from *Private Research* copyright © 2013 by Sabrina Darby.

EPub Edition NOVEMBER 2013 ISBN: 9780062328434

Print Edition ISBN: 9780062328441

10 9 8 7 6 5

To Griffin, my own Scottish lad, and to the people of High River, Alberta, where part of this book was written before the flood. Stay strong!

ONCE UPON A HIGHLAND SUMMER

"Angus MacNabb!"

Was there no peace in his own grave?

He'd been tormented enough in life. He squeezed his eyes shut and tried to ignore the soft voice calling him, drawing him, pulling him back into the world, even knowing she was the one and only person who could.

"MacNabb, I know you can hear me. Stop being stubborn and come out. We wouldn't be here if it wasn't for your foolish curse, and you're going to help me fix it."

"Stubborn!" Angus snapped, unable to resist the goad. "Isn't that a case of the pot calling the kettle—" He stopped and stared. Georgiana stood shimmering in the air before him.

He blinked, wondering if he was seeing a ghost, then recalled that he was.

Even dead, Georgiana had the power to steal his breath away—if he'd had any breath to steal. She tilted her head and smiled at him, just the way he remembered. It had been nearly sixty years since he'd seen that smile, but he'd never forgotten it. It smoked through him now like life itself, filled him with passion and pain.

Georgiana Forrester, the late Countess of Somerson, raised her eyebrows as if she was waiting for him to finish his comment, but he didn't. How could he speak while her eyes roamed over the plaid he'd been buried in? He'd looked his best when they'd laid him out, and he straightened his shoulders proudly now, and pushed the laird's bonnet back on his brow.

"That's a fine gown ye're wearing. You still look like a lass." His lass.

Georgiana looked down at the silver satin with a moue of distaste. "I detest this gown. I married Somerson in it, and they chose it for my burial. The only good thing I can say about it is that it still fit perfectly after all those years. I don't know how they found it. I ordered my maid to burn it."

MacNabb frowned, and one of the eagle feathers in his bonnet fell over his eye. The three feathers proclaimed him laird of his clan, chief over every rock, tussock of grass, and starving child as far as the eye could see from the crumbling tower of old Glenlorne Castle, where they stood now. It had been their trysting place until— The old, familiar anger flared.

"Somerson!" he spat the name, filling it with sixty years of hatred. "Only a cheap fool would bury his wife in her wedding gown."

Georgiana's chin came up. "You said you liked it. Besides, the day of my marriage and the day of my burial were equally sorrowful. I think it was a most appropriate choice."

MacNabb sighed, and a breeze moved restively through

the treetops beyond the tower's crumbling walls. "Aye, well, that's not why we're here, is it, to debate our grave clothes?"

He looked around the tower, open to the sky now, the roof long gone. The rotting stones of the windows framed a view of the glen, the loch, and the new castle of Glenlorne at the opposite end of the valley. The new keep, already over a hundred and fifty years old, looked near as decrepit as this tower, older by four centuries. He sighed again.

If he turned and looked away to the east, he'd be able to see Georgiana's uncle's cottage, Lullach Grange, but he kept his back to it. He'd spent sixty years watching the empty house for her candle in the window, the signal that she'd meet him here, at the tower, but that light had gone out when their families tore them apart forever. The familiar bitterness of loss filled him again, still, and he turned to glare at her.

"What do you want of me, woman?" he asked gruffly.

Her eyes remained soft, unafraid. "You cursed us, Angus."

"I had cause enough!"

She shook her head, her smile wistful. "We were in love, and they would not let us marry, but your curse has echoed through two generations of both our families. It must end. I want my granddaughter to know the kind of happiness we shared, Angus."

"Was it happiness? It made the rest of our lives unbearable. Well, mine anyway. I canna speak for you, of course." There wasn't a day he hadn't thought of her. Her name had been the last word on his lips.

She looked down at her hand, where her wedding band had once sat. The family heirloom now graced the hand of the present countess. It was another ring she missed, the one

Angus had given her to seal their love, a promise ring with a small ruby. "Neither of us had joy in our marriages." She waved her hand to indicate the tower. "The last true happiness I felt was here, that last night, in your arms."

Angus could see the place she meant right through her transparent body, the sheltered spot where they'd lain together, wrapped in his plaid, alternately making love and whispering about the future, pledging themselves to each other. His hands coiled, aching to touch her. *Could* they touch? He didn't know, but to reach for her and close his arms on empty air yet again would be too much to bear.

"Ye've come at a bad time, *gràdhach*," he said, the Gaelic term for "beloved" slipping off his tongue. He could have bitten that tongue in two when she smiled sweetly at him. "My son just died, and my clan's left leaderless. My daughter-in-law is trying to sell out to Engl—"

"Not leaderless. You have a grandson, don't you?"

"I do. But Alec left Glenlorne years ago, swearing he'd never return. Mayhap it's better he doesn't."

"You don't believe that."

"What's left for him to come home to?" he asked, his mouth twisting bitterly.

She floated over to stand beside him. "There's the land, Angus. And there's love. Love can rebuild anything."

He stared at her, saw the foolish hope in her eyes. That look, that hope had made him fall in love with her, made him believe anything was possible. He shut his eyes against the feeling stirring in his breast. "Ye can't truly think I believe in *love*, do ye?"

She reached out a hand, laying it on his arm. He couldn't

feel it, but light flared where their shadows touched, glowed. "You did once—an Englishman's daughter and a Scot—who would have imagined it in those terrible times? It was almost impossible."

"It *was* impossible."

She laughed, and the sound echoed through the tower, startling a bird to flight. It flapped into the night with a frightened cry. Georgiana ignored it. "It was only impossible for them, not for us. I doubt we'd be here now, together in this place again, if our love had died too."

No, his love for her had never died. Not even here, on the other side of death. He loved her still, yet what point was there in that? Was it to be an eternity of pain instead of a mere lifetime? "What has any of this to do with Alec?" he demanded. Was it his imagination, or could he smell her perfume?

"My granddaughter's name is Caroline." Her voice was soft, fond, gentle.

"Caroline? You want to match her to my grandson? How can you be sure they'd even suit? Wouldn't the current Earl of Somerson object to a match with a penniless Scots laird o' nothing?"

"Leave him to me. We need only bring my Caroline and your Alec together, remind them, perhaps, of—" She cast a meaningful look at their trysting place.

"Has she any money?" he asked ruthlessly, trying to ignore the tender memory. "He needs to marry a lass with a bloody fortune if he's to save this place!"

She dismissed his concern with a wave of her hand. "She has a respectable dowry, of course, but that hardly matters.

They'll find a way, but not because of money—love, Angus, love." The sound of the word swirled in the air around him. It softened his heart.

"I'm not against trying, *gràdhach*, but we can't force them to fall in love, or be sure it'll last."

She smiled sweetly and sighed, and the white heather growing under the walls shivered restively. "'Tis almost summer, Angus. Remember how easy it was to be in love in the summer? All we need do is bring them here. The rest will take care of itself."

Angus frowned, still dubious that anything to do with love or marriage could ever be that simple.

Beyond the sanctuary of the tower, belligerent clouds covered the moon, and thunder muttered a dark warning.

A storm was about to descend on the peaceful valley of Glenlorne.

CHAPTER ONE

"I'll have your decision now, if you please."

Lady Caroline Forrester stared at the carpet in her half brother's study. It was like everything else in his London mansion—expensive, elegant, and chosen solely to proclaim his consequence as the Earl of Somerson. She fixed her eyes on the blue swirls and arabesques knotted into the rug and wondered what distant land it came from, and if she could go there herself rather than make the choice Somerson demanded.

"Come now," he said impatiently. "You have two suitors to choose from. Viscount Speed has two thousand pounds a year, and will inherit his father's earldom."

"In Ireland," Caroline whispered under her breath. Speed also had oily, perpetually damp skin and a lisp, and was only interested in her because her dowry would make him rich. At least for a short while, until he spent her money as he'd spent his own fortune on mistresses, whist, and horses.

"And Lord Mandeville has a fine estate on the border with Wales. His mother lives there, so she would be company for you."

Mandeville spent no time at all at his country estate for that exact reason. Caroline had been in London only a month, but she'd heard the gossip. Lady Mandeville went through highborn companions the way Charlotte—Somerson's countess—devoured cream cakes at tea. Lady Mandeville was famous for her bad temper, her sharp tongue, and her dogs. She raised dozens, perhaps even hundreds, of yappy, snappy, unpleasant little creatures that behaved just like their mistress, if the whispered stories were to be believed. The lady unfortunate enough to become Lord Mandeville's wife would serve as the old lady's companion until one of them died, with no possibility of quitting the post to take a more pleasant job.

"So which gentleman will you have?" Somerson demanded, pacing the room, his posture stiff, his hands clasped behind his back, his face sober. Caroline had laughed when he'd first told her the two men had offered for her hand. But it wasn't a joke. Her half brother truly expected her to pick one of the odious suitors he'd selected for her and tie herself to that man for life. He looked down his hooked nose at her, a trait inherited from their father, along with his pale, bulging eyes. Caroline resembled her mother, the late earl's second wife, which was probably why Somerson couldn't stand the sight of her. As a young man he'd objected to his father's new bride most strenuously, because she was too young, too pretty, and the daughter of a mere baronet without fortune or high connections. He'd even objected to the new countess's red hair. Caroline raised a hand to smooth a wayward russet curl behind her ear. Speed had red hair—orange, really—and spindly pinkish eyelashes.

Caroline thought of her niece Lottie, who was upstairs

having her wedding dress fitted, arguing with her mother over what shade of ribbon would best suit the flowers in the bouquet. She was marrying William Rutherford, Viscount Mears—*Caroline's* William, the man she'd known all her life, the eldest son and heir of the Earl of Halliwell, a neighbor and dear friend of her parents. It had always been expected she'd wed one of Halliwell's sons, but Sinjon, the earl's younger son, had left home to join the army and go to war rather than propose to Caroline. And now William, who even Caroline thought would make an offer for her hand, had instead chosen Lottie's hand. Caroline shut her eyes. It was beginning to feel like a curse. Not that it mattered now. William had made his choice. Still, a wedding should be a happy thing, the bride as joyful as Lottie, the future ripe with the possibilities of love and happiness.

Caroline didn't even *like* her suitors—well, they weren't really *her* suitors—they were courting her dowry, and a connection to Somerson. They needed her money, but they didn't need her.

"Is it truly such a difficult choice? You are twenty-two years old. Time is of the essence." Somerson said coldly. "Surely one gentleman stands out in your esteem. Do you find Speed handsomer, or perhaps Mandeville's conversation is more enjoyable?"

No and no!

She looked up at her half brother, a man twenty-four years her senior, and one of the most powerful earls in the realm, ready to plead her case, but saw at once that was pointless. He'd married the daughter of an equally powerful earl, had nine children, and seemed happy enough with his wife, though Charlotte was a virago, a gossip, and a glutton. She weighed eighteen stone, and was never without a plate of sweetmeats close to hand.

Speed was the male version of Charlotte. Somerson was just like Mandeville, obsessed with his own importance.

No, there would be no point in arguing, or refusing. Somerson had decided, even if she had not, could not. Caroline's stomach turned over, and she closed her mouth. Her half brother's face was hard, and without the slightest bit of sympathy. She was simply a matter he wanted settled as quickly and quietly as possible. Caroline was an unwanted burden now her mother was dead. She knew he'd choose for her if she refused to do so, and it was impossible to say which gentleman would be worse. She shifted her feet, which made him stop pacing to regard her like a bird of prey.

"Caroline?" he prompted.

The curling vines in the carpet threatened to rise up and choke her, though her own misery was already doing the job well enough.

She forced a smile. "I promised Lottie I'd help her choose a gown for her wedding trip. There really has been so much to do for *her* nuptials that I have not had a moment to think about my own," she said as lightly as possible, twisting the ruby ring, her mother's legacy, on her finger.

"It's been two days," Somerson admonished. "How much time could it possibly take to make such a simple choice?"

Caroline shut her eyes. It was hardly simple. She'd been a sentimental child, and had grown up to be a young woman with starry-eyed ideas of what romance and marriage ought to be. She'd always thought she'd know the moment she set eyes on the man she wanted to marry. She'd feel a surge of love that would warm her from her toes to her crown, and angels would sing. She felt only horror when she looked at Mandeville and Speed. Her skin crawled and crows croaked a warning.

Flee.

The idea whispered in her ear.

She swallowed, and met Somerson's eyes, steeling her courage to refuse, but the ice in his expression chilled her. She had been raised to be obedient, even when the yoke chafed. "Tomorrow—I'll give you my decision tomorrow."

His eyes narrowed as if he suspected a trick. She widened her smile till it hurt. "At breakfast, is that clear?" he said at last.

"Perfectly," she murmured. "May I go?"

But he'd already turned away, as if he had more important things to think about and she'd taken up too much of his time. She curtsied to his back and left the study.

Upstairs, Charlotte was shrieking at the modiste, berating the poor woman because the lace wasn't sitting properly at Lottie's bosom. Caroline felt sorry for the dressmaker—it was past midnight, and this was the third time Charlotte had changed her mind about her daughter's wedding gown. Caroline had no doubt Charlotte would let her half sister-in-law get married wearing a burlap sack if it got the matter done faster, and got Caroline packed off, out of sight and out of mind forevermore.

A distant door slammed, and a maid rushed down the steps, nearly colliding with Caroline.

The poor girl was flushed, and she nearly tripped trying to curtsy and run at the same time. "Oh, excuse me, my lady—

more treacle tarts are needed upstairs at once." She bolted
down the kitchen hallway like a frightened rabbit.

Caroline set her hand on the banister. She lifted her foot,
held it over the first step, and stopped.

There was another loud objection upstairs, and Lottie
burst into noisy tears.

Caroline stepped back. She should go up to help soothe
her niece, or go to bed and think about her choice, but there
was no point in that. She could never bring herself to pick
Speed or Mandeville.

Flee.

She turned, wondering if someone had spoken, but there
was no one there, just the modiste's cloak and bonnet, hanging on a peg beside the front door.

Flee.

Caroline grabbed the cloak and swung it over her shoulders, and clapped the bonnet onto her head. The brass door
latch was cold under her palm. Her heart pounded. Another
shriek of rage echoed down the stairs, and she opened the
door and stepped out, shutting it behind her, cutting off the
dreadful sound. For a moment she stood on the front step,
looking up and down the dark street, wondering which way to
go. It was yet another choice—and one she couldn't wait until
morning to make. Taking a breath, she pulled the hood close
to her face and turned right.

She hurried away from the lights of Somerson House,
moving into the shadows. If anyone bothered to look for her
tonight, they'd find her gone. If not, then even Somerson
would understand her choice when he sat down for breakfast
tomorrow.

Chapter Two

Alec MacNabb pulled the collar of his coat up to hide his face as he opened the door to Countess Bray's bedchamber. He slid inside the dark room and shut the door, pausing a moment with his hand on the latch, both to let his eyes adjust to the darkness, and to see if the lady was going to sit up in her bed and scream. He held his breath, listened to the tick of a clock, as loud as hammer blows.

The mounded shape under the eiderdown covers didn't move, except to utter a soft snore. He exhaled, and smiled. The countess was clearly exhausted, having danced half the night away at Lady Elsley's ball. He scanned the room, looking for a place to start.

The delicacy of the white furnishings made him aware of the fact that he was too tall, too dark, too male for such a space. If she opened her eyes, she'd probably think the Scots were invading, pillaging, raping, and killing women in their beds. He looked at the bed wryly. Countess Bray would be the last lady on earth he'd wish to ravish. Pillaging, though, was another matter.

He crossed to her dressing table. The jewels she'd worn to the ball had been carelessly left to glitter among her perfume bottles and combs, but he ignored them and opened the drawer, pushing past the lace handkerchiefs, searching for the hidden panel he suspected would be at the very back. What lady with secrets like Countess Bray's wouldn't have such a hiding place? She was smug enough that she would hardly suspect anyone would come to steal those secrets, and that the thief would know exactly where to find them. Every lady had the same hiding places for their billets-doux, their diaries, the trinkets their lovers gave them, and every lady thought no one would ever find them. The wood shifted under his fingers and gave with a slight but satisfying click. The lady on the bed sighed, turned over, and he froze where he was, waiting until her breathing grew deep and even again.

Carefully, he removed the panel, and set it atop the dressing table. A necklace glinted maliciously and would have slipped and fallen to the floor if he hadn't caught it. The gems warmed in his hand like a lover, sparkled up at him. He recognized the stone—the famous Bray ruby. The flawless jewel flashed like a drop of noble blood, the pearls glowed, and the diamonds winked at him coquettishly. For a moment, he was tempted. The necklace would fetch a fortune—enough to buy books and new gowns for his sisters, and keep their larders full for weeks. He could probably rebuild the crumbling family castle, and refurnish it too. He frowned and set the necklace aside as if it burned. By his own choice, Glenlorne was not his concern, and he had a job to do. He reached back into the dressing table's hiding place, and closed his hand on what he'd come for, a bundle of letters, bound with ribbon.

He drew them out with a smile. He was good at this, and it really was becoming almost too easy . . .

His elbow knocked against a perfume bottle, and he watched in horror as it teetered on the edge of the dressing table for a split second before it fell to the floor and shattered. The scent of roses filled the air as the countess stirred and sat up in bed. Alec froze in the shadows with the letters in his grip, silently cursing his clumsiness and the room's paucity of hiding places for a six-foot Scot.

At first, she didn't look to see what had disturbed her. She reached for a vial on the bedside table, and opened it with sleepy fingers, and added a few drops to a glass of water and drank deeply, sinking back on her pillow.

The bitter scent filled the air. Laudanum. Alec let out a silent breath, and ran a shaking hand through his hair. All he had to do was wait for the drug to work and make his escape when the countess fell asleep again, but she turned to lie on her back, and he was directly in her line of sight.

Her first sound was a mere grunt of surprise, but Alec knew a scream would follow now she'd seen him. His only choice was to get the hell out as fast as possible. He ran for the door.

He would have made it if it hadn't been for the broken glass and the spilled perfume. It made the floor slick, and he slipped, landed hard on his hands and knees, and dropped the letters. The ribbon broke, and they fell to the floor like leaves around him.

As the countess's shrieks gathered power, he scrambled for the envelopes in the dark, cursing in Gaelic as the perfume soaked into the knees of his breeches, stung the places where the shards of glass bit into his flesh like sharp-toothed guard dogs.

By the time he'd regained his feet, the countess was sitting up, staring at him, her mouth wide in the darkness, the sheets clutched to her bosom, her screams ear-splitting. He had no idea a lady could shriek so unceasingly, without even pausing to draw breath. He threw open the door, and her alarm followed him down the hall as he ran toward the window at the end, his point of entry, and his escape route. He heard footfalls behind him, pounding along the corridor, and hoped they'd pause to check the countess first, and buy him precious seconds. The window was just ahead, and he hunched his shoulders, made ready, and jumped. He tumbled through the opening, cracking his shoulder on the frame, tasting the night air. He ignored the pain and rolled down the slate roof of the porch, and fell heavily to the ground. There was glass in his knees, and in his hands too, and he grunted as shards renewed their assault.

He could still hear her screams as he fled. Surely the entire household and half the neighboring ones had woken by now.

He heard the cry from the window, a male voice, baritone to the lady's soprano in a very bad comic opera. "Stop, thief!" But Alec was running over the greasy cobbles, praying he didn't slip, hoping Countess Bray hadn't gotten a good look at him. He didn't stop until he was well away, and sure he wasn't being followed. He ducked into the blackest alley he could find, and flattened himself against the wall, his heart slamming against his ribs, his lungs burning, and sent up a prayer that whoever might be lurking in the alley wasn't worse than those pursuing him.

Nothing. The only rats were the four-legged kind, the only cats the hopeful moggies searching for food.

He stepped out under a streetlamp, looked at the blood on his fingers, saw the glitter of glass. He used his teeth to pluck the shards from the cuts, and spat them out. He patted his pocket, making sure the letters were still safe against his pounding heart, and took a flask of whisky out of his coat and drank. There was more blood on his knees, but that would have to wait until he was home.

He was back at his lodgings within a half hour, a dozen streets and a whole social class away from Lord Bray's fashionable Mayfair town house. He poured himself a tumbler of whisky and emptied his pockets, dropping the crumpled, bloodstained letters on the table, letting his heartbeat slow. He dropped his breeches and grimaced as he plucked the glass out of his knees.

He cursed aloud. He wasn't usually clumsy. In fact, he was the best "retriever" the Crown had, the one they called upon for the most sensitive, important missions. But he knew there was always a chance of being caught. It took just one small mistake. Like knocking over a perfume bottle. He shut his eyes as he tossed the last bit of rose-scented glass into the chamber pot. He crossed and splashed cold water over his face, and stared into his own hollow eyes in the small oval mirror. He looked like what he was, a hard, desperate creature of the night, dark-haired, gray-eyed, muscular; a thief, a man with no home, no family, no honor. He turned away, stared instead at the letters on the table. There was no need to worry. Even if the mission hadn't gone exactly according to plan, it hadn't failed. He had the letters he'd been sent for. It had been a close call, but he hadn't been caught.

He glanced at the letters, eight billets-doux that were important enough to the Crown to ask a man to risk life and limb to retrieve. He wondered what was in them that could be so damaging, but it wasn't his job to ask questions. He was expected to steal them, not read them. Tomorrow he'd deliver them, and the problem the letters represented, whatever that might be, would be resolved. He looked at the clock. It still lacked several hours until dawn. He didn't want to sleep. He never slept after one of his excursions. He sat and drank whisky and wished he were in Ceylon, where his family believed he was. He'd left Glenlorne eight years ago, bragging how he intended to make a fortune as a planter in the South Seas. He'd never made it farther than London, and he wasn't a planter. He was a thief.

He turned back to the letters, and stacked them as neatly as possible given their tattered condition—his fault entirely. He'd even gotten blood on the edges of the vellum. He noted the royal seal on the envelopes, the gold edges of the expensive stationery. Important letters indeed. He'd been told there were eight letters in all, a collection of indiscreet romantic thoughts carelessly put to paper, irrefutable evidence of a royal affair, now long over. The contents of the letters had become a threat to someone important, a potential source of embarrassment or scandal for the Crown, perhaps, or even blackmail—which was why he was sent to fetch them back, before any mischief was done that could not be undone. He counted the letters as he stacked them. His throat closed and he counted again.

And again. *Seven.*

He searched his pockets, looked on the floor. It wasn't there.

He sat heavily in the chair and ran a hand over his face. He'd dropped one—lost it in the street, or left it behind in Lady Bray's bedchamber.

That, of course, meant disaster. His stomach turned to water, and he swore, cursing his carelessness.

He pulled on his coat and headed out into the night once again.

He had to find the missing letter.

CHAPTER THREE

Caroline ran smack into a wall that seemed to have appeared out of nowhere in the middle of the dark sidewalk. She bounced off the hard surface as if she weighed nothing. If not for the hands that grabbed the front of her cloak, she'd have toppled backward into the dirty street.

For an instant she hung in the grip of the dark, terrifying figure as he dragged her into the light of the closest streetlamp and loomed over her. The bitter taste of fear dried her throat, and she scrabbled at his gloved hands uselessly with shaking fingers. He could see *her*, but with the light behind him, he was just a shadow, huge and sinister. Her heart began to pound, and she almost wished she'd stayed safely at home.

Almost.

She tried to pull away, to run, but he held her as easily as if she were a child with no strength at all. Real fear coiled through her like smoke, making her weaker still. Had Somerson seen her leave the house, and sent him after her? If he was a footman, he wasn't one she knew, nor was he wearing Somerson livery. He was dressed in black from head to toe, part of the night. Terror turned her knees to jelly, and she sagged, but he hauled her up and set her on her feet without letting her go. One fist held her cloak under her chin.

"What the devil are you doing, careering around the streets in the dark?" he demanded. "I might have cut your throat, thinking you a pickpocket!"

Hysterical laughter bubbled in her throat. He thought *she* was someone to be afraid of? "I'm not!" she protested, stepping back, pulling out of his grip. He let her go and she backed into another wall, a real one this time. She shrank against it, laid her palms flat on the rough bricks. "I didn't see you. I must have tripped on my cloak. It's borrowed, you see, and—"

"Borrowed?" he growled. She detected a burr in his voice, an accent of some kind. She felt his eyes scanning her, assessing her, and knew what he must be thinking. A lady on the street alone was unheard of in Mayfair, especially at night, in clothes that weren't her own. Her cheeks heated despite the damp chill in the air.

She pushed farther back into the wall, fearing the gentleman was about to hook his fingers into her borrowed cloak once again and frog march her back to Somerson House.

If, of course, he *was* a gentleman. Her heart leaped into her throat and cowered there, making speech impossible. She could not scream or plead or reason with her captor.

"Where are you going at this hour of the night?" he demanded.

Caroline's mouth worked soundlessly as her mind searched for an answer to that. Where *was* she going? She hadn't even thought of that when she raced out of Somerson House.

"North." The word popped into her head and out of her

mouth before she knew she was going to say it. "I'm going north," she said again, testing it, liking it. The Somerson estate in Northumbria where she'd grown up was north. But it would be the first place he'd look for her.

"Scotland? Gretna Green, perhaps?" the shadow demanded.

"Scotland?" she croaked as if she were an idiot who'd never heard of the place.

"To marry in secret? You're eloping, aren't you?"

"Eloping?" she gasped. If he only knew it was quite the contrary!

"I beg you to reconsider your plans. You shouldn't be wandering the streets alone, and if your intended was any kind of man at all, he wouldn't put you in such danger. You'd do better to go straight back home and forget—"

"No!" she cried. He tilted his head, and the lamplight caressed the right side of his face, revealing a strong jaw, a high cheek, a broad brow, and a lock of dark hair. One gleaming eye gazed at her, sharp as a raven's. She swallowed. "No, I can't go home. I am going to meet—him—at the Ram's Head Inn. Is that not where the stagecoaches leave from?"

The one dark eyebrow she could see shot into his hairline. "You're taking public conveyance? A stage? The bas—groom—could have at least agreed to pay for a seat on the Royal Mail," he growled. His hand gripped her elbow so suddenly she flinched. "Oh, lass, he's not worthy of you! I have three sisters of my own, and if any man dared to—"

She plucked her arm out of his grip. She couldn't turn back now. If he knew what she was facing, if he could imagine for just one instant what his own sisters would do if faced with such a choice, he'd let her go on her way, but there was hardly time to explain. "Please, just tell me the way!" She glanced back down the street, half expecting to see a gang of Somerson footmen coming after her, carrying torches and toasting forks, leading Charlotte's dreadful little dog on a string to sniff out her trail.

He shifted his booted feet on the cobbles, and the sound made her jump. She swallowed, clenched her fists inside her cloak, took a grip on herself.

"You're certain you won't change your mind and let me escort you home? You haven't even got any baggage," he mused. "Or gloves."

"Sent on ahead," she said breathlessly. She would have to step around him to flee, but in the dark, he looked as wide as he was tall. He could stop her easily. He could probably break her in half if he wanted to. She began to edge along the wall, making ready to pick up her skirts and run, should wits fail her, and it was beginning to look as if she'd left those behind at Somerson House along with everything else.

"Have you any money?"

That stopped her. She felt the blood drain from her limbs. She couldn't get on a coach or even take lodgings without money. She felt hot blood flood her face. She must have glowed as brightly as the streetlamp, for he sighed.

"Never mind, I can see you haven't."

He picked up her hand and turned it over in his own, the leather of his glove cool against her skin, and dropped a purse into her palm and folded her fingers over it. "Since you are determined to pursue this foolish and dangerous course of action, allow me to ensure you reach your intended as safely as possible. Take the mail coach, not the stage. It's faster, and less likely to be troubled by highwaymen, though you've nothing to steal. Only board if there's another woman on the trip, is that clear?"

Her cheeks blazed all the hotter. What must he think of her, a foolish girl running away from home to an uncertain future? She must look far younger than her twenty-two years, and as dim as an unpolished apple. She swallowed, raised her chin, and nodded, trying to appear a woman of the world. He was crushing her mother's ring against her finger with his grip. It reminded her she had one item of value on her person. She could not bear to think of it in the hands of a common thief or a highwayman. This man had shown her kindness, and a lady paid her debts.

She pulled her hand out of his and took the ring off. It glittered like a drop of blood in the yellow lamplight. "Allow me to repay you, sir. I assure you I am not in the habit of taking money from gentlemen I don't know." He didn't touch it, and she pushed it toward him. "Take it. Better you than a highwayman."

He took it from her hand, held it carefully between his thumb and forefinger and studied it. Was he wondering if the stone was real? She didn't dare wait for him to decide. She began walking, moving as quickly as she could without running. She held her head confidently, proudly, but her ears were pricked for the sound of his footsteps behind her, but there was only silence.

Caroline turned once, but the street behind her was empty. She swallowed, and felt a shiver of fear race up her spine. She was truly alone, then. She slowed for an instant,

wondering if it was too late to turn around, to go back, and . . .
It began to rain, the heavy drops slapping against her hood.

Scotland. Would Somerson look for her there? Would
he look for her at all, or be glad she was gone, an unwanted
burden removed from his shoulders?

Caroline swallowed. Whatever her future held, it did not
include Viscount Speed or Lord Mandeville.

She felt the reassuring weight of her benefactor's purse
in her pocket, and tightened her cloak around her shoulders against the rain, and resumed the long walk toward the
coaching inn.

Alec felt a surge of annoyance. He had things to do, more
important things than protecting some chit on a fool's errand.
He should be searching the streets for the damned letter, as
he had been doing when she almost knocked him over.

He followed her instead, staying in the shadows, because
she was beautiful and alone and needed someone's protection.
Her face—what he'd seen of it under the shadow of her hood
and bonnet—had been white in the lamplight, her fear as pal-
pable as her determination to see her mission through.

She reminded him of his half sisters, especially since she
was about the same age as Megan, the eldest, would be by
now. He fervently hoped none of his sisters would ever do
anything as stupid as this woman was about to do. In all
likelihood, she'd end up unmarried, ruined by her worthless lover, and forced to return to her family once she realized
she'd been duped. She would spend the rest of her life hidden
away, an embarrassment to her kin. Would this adventure be

enough to sustain her for the years of regret to come? Her family would likely do nothing to find the bastard, since that would only add to the scandal. Alec clenched his fists. He'd hunt down any man who dared harm anyone he loved.

But he didn't love this woman. He didn't even know her, had barely gotten a good look at her in the dark. So why was he following her? Curiosity, perhaps—or guilt, because he'd never be there to protect his sisters if they needed him, might never see them again at all. He wondered who this woman might be, if she had a brother who'd failed her when she needed him. Maybe she was a servant, he decided. The ruby ring she'd given him was valuable. A maid might take the chance of stealing such a jewel before she fled her employer. He felt a momentary twinge of guilt at his own almost-theft of Lady Bray's necklace. He frowned, wondering if he was abetting a robbery now. But why would she give her ill-gotten prize to him? The ring was worth far more than he'd given her in coin.

He studied the slender figure ahead of him, walking with determination toward the inn, set on her path. She was brave, he'd give her that. Most of the ladies he knew would melt like sugar at the mere mention of rain, and none of the ladies he knew would ever be found walking the streets of London at night, rain or no. Yet he decided she wasn't a servant. Her bearing declared her nothing less than a lady born and bred, and her nervousness said that despite her bravado now, she was unused to being out alone. He hugged the shadows and watched her, and kept an eye out for signs of trouble.

She reached the inn safely, and Alec slipped out of the rain and into the stables to wait. He watched the coach pull up, saw her get in. There were two other women and a pair of men on the journey, all of them respectable-looking folk. She'd be safe enough for the moment.

The coach pulled away as dawn lit the sky, turning the wet streets of London pink for a few brief moments. The color of hope, and love.

He turned away, banishing the ridiculously sentimental thought. Instead, he wished the young lass well, whoever she was.

He had his own problems to face. He retraced his steps until he stood in front of the grand façade of Bray's elegant town house.

But the letter was nowhere to be found.

Chapter Four

Thomas Ellison, Earl of Bray, thundered along the hallway that led to his wife's apartments. Her maid ran behind him, running to keep up, no doubt terrified by the string of curses he'd let fly when she came to his study to summon him.

He'd been reading a rather interesting letter when she knocked. There had been an unusual break-in the night. A perfume bottle had been broken, but the magnificent Bray necklace had been left untouched on her dressing table. According to the footman who reported the incident to Bray when he rose this morning—since no one would dare to wake the earl unless the house was about to burn down around his bed as he slept—a thin plank of wood was found in the countess's chamber, the exact width of the drawer in the little table, along with a single letter bearing the Prince of Wales's seal. It hadn't taken Ellison long to figure out what had occurred. He had a number of drawers with secret panels himself, though none had been touched. Whatever the thief had wanted had been in his wife's possession. The footman presented the letter to him on a silver tray, along with a tattered length of blue ribbon. Once he read the letter, addressed to his wife, and written in the kind of intimate language that left no doubt of an affair, Bray realized there must have been other letters, tied with the ribbon, perhaps from different lovers.

He read this letter over again, and yet again, scanning the tender lines written in the prince's all too familiar hand. How many times had he received notes from Prinny, written on the same gold-embossed stationery, inviting him to come to a rout, or a dinner party, or an evening of gaming?

Bray's first impression had been awe. Elizabeth had attracted the Prince of Wales? After the second reading, he'd realized he'd been cuckolded. After rereading the letter a dozen times, he was furious at the betrayal of his wife, and the royal prick who professed to be his friend. He wasn't the only lord the prince had put in this position. Other powerful men had been made fools by the prince in the same way. Those men had never been able to hold their heads up quite as high after their cuckolding. Nor were they able to demand satisfaction from the prince for his sins. They simply had to live with it. Bray was not that kind of man. He would have his revenge, somehow. He'd been plotting it when Elizabeth's maid arrived.

The girl opened the door of his study nervously, and dipped a deep curtsy and stayed there, not daring to rise. "Her Ladyship has taken too much laudanum, my lord. May I send for the doctor?" she asked.

He stared at the letter in his fist. "No."

She looked up, her country cornflower blue eyes wide. "But—" Her argument died on her lips as he abruptly got to his feet, let the chair of his desk crash to the floor behind him. How dared she argue with him? It wasn't as if this was the first time Elizabeth had drugged herself insensible with laudanum. She used the drug with such frequency that Bray had forbidden the servants to send for the doctor when the countess had one of her "spells," as they called them. The doctor had been coming every week for the past six months, and each time he brought more laudanum with him. It was Bray's opinion that it was the medicine that was causing his wife's problem. When the quack diagnosed the countess with a condition he called "frantic dyspepsia," Bray had thrown the man out of the house with his own two hands.

He pushed past the cowering maid and strode down the hall, and now the maid was running behind him to keep up. Was she afraid he might hurt her mistress? She should be.

He didn't bother to knock when he got to his wife's bedroom. He simply threw open the door. He slammed it behind him, right in the maid's face, probably taking the skin off her nose, if her squeal was any indication. Good. If he found the chit had been gossiping about his wife's addiction, he'd do worse. He couldn't abide gossip. And now there was the letter, or letters, perhaps. How many people knew the truth?

He came to a stop beside the bed, his mouth twisting in disgust at the sight of his countess. "Elizabeth."

She barely seemed aware of his presence, a lolling of her head the only indication that she'd heard him at all.

"Elizabeth!" he bellowed, and her eyelids cracked open to reveal glittering, unfocused eyes. The black pupils drifted upward, exposing the whites as her head dropped back onto the pillow.

He slapped her. She cried out and raised slack arms to

shield herself from another blow, but he picked up the laudanum bottle instead and threw it against the wall where it shattered, the brown liquid staining the silk wallpaper with long copper ribbons.

"Please, Ellison, my nerves—" she whimpered.

"There's nothing wrong with your nerves!" he growled. "Sit up and explain yourself at once, or I'll pour cold water on you. Your maid wants me to send for a priest since I won't allow the doctor to come."

"My letters—did she find them? Oh, where could they have gone?" She threw her wrist over her eyes, her mouth twisting in ugly paroxysms of anguish.

He felt no pity. "Is this what you mean?" he demanded, holding up the crumpled letter. Her face flushed, and he could see that she knew exactly what it was.

"It was a long time ago," she pleaded, her fingers scrabbling uselessly over the pink satin counterpane. "I only wanted Sophie to have the very best—"

"What did you do?"

She sobbed, turning her face away from his. "I was seduced. I had no choice!"

He felt disgust rise in his gorge. "You're my wife, Elizabeth, my countess. I married you to get an heir, a *legitimate* heir. You dared to betray me with the Prince of Wales, Fat George, a man I considered my friend? Did the two of you laugh as you cuckolded me, when you lied to my face? A horrible thought struck him. "Is Sophie even my child?"

She didn't answer his question, but he knew by the way her eyes widened and her face reddened.

"No," he managed, his throat closing.

She reached for his hand. "I did it for you, to gain his favor!" He pulled away before she could touch him. She sank back on the bed and shut her eyes, her hand falling limp by her side. "You didn't love me, Ellison, but he made me feel wanted. He wrote me love letters and poems. He *wooed* me. You never wooed me."

"Wooed you?" He stared at her in bafflement. She was an earl's daughter, had come with land and a huge dowry. He'd married those facts as much as the woman before him. The land and money brought him comfort that she had never offered.

"I just wanted to be loved, but he was as cold as you, once I'd—" She had the grace to blush. "Once I'd submitted to his desires. It was only once, just one time, I swear. I kept his letters, read them over and over, knew that someday—"

He felt his head start to buzz. "*Letters?* There's more than one? How many?"

"I don't remember!" she pleaded.

"You do," he insisted. "How many letters?"

"Eight!" she sobbed.

"All like this one?" he asked, horrified, imagining the intimate details of his cuckolding spreading like plague, being read aloud in salons all over London, discussed by gentlemen in the clubs and gaming hells.

She forced herself up. "I did it for you, Ellison. He wouldn't acknowledge her, wouldn't answer my letters after she was born. But I had these"—she reached for the page in his hand, but he held it away from her. "I wanted to make him pay, wanted to force him to acknowledge her, to marry her to royalty. Surely you can see how advantageous a royal marriage would be for us?"

He stared at her. "You tried to blackmail the Prince of Wales?"

She ran a hand through the tangles of her hair, preening. "I gave him what he wanted. Now he must pay."

"You're a fool," he whispered. "He was my *friend*. How he must have laughed all these years, knowing his cuckoo was in my nest. He danced with Sophie at her come-out ball—oh, what an honor, what a jest!" Bitter acid filled his mouth. He turned away to spit in the chamber pot. When he turned back, Elizabeth was watching him. She had the gall to look proud, even in her drugged state.

"You didn't think I was beautiful, but he did. He wrote me poems. He swore he couldn't live without me, would harm himself if I did not submit to him—"

"And he wrote this down?" Bray demanded. "In letters?" Oh, the stupidity! He rubbed his eyes with his thumb and forefingers. "Does Sophie know?"

"Of course not. I wanted to wait until Prinny arranged a suitably important marriage for her before I told her—"

He laughed bitterly. "I have raised her to the highest consequence, insisted on the best tutors, the finest modistes, the most esteemed company. I had no idea I was raising a princess."

She raised her chin. "And now you do. Perhaps *you* could convince His Highness to see that Sophie must be married as befits her station in life," she said.

"Her station in life is the bastard product of a roll in the hay between two of the stupidest people in England!"

Her face fell, her slack jaw dropping to her chest. He had no more to say. His anger had been spent, and the bottom had dropped out of his world in the space of a morning. He turned away from the bed, unable to look at her.

"Your maid will pack your things. You're leaving at once."

"Where am I going?" she whined.

"Carswell Park for the time being. I will decide where you'll go more permanently later."

"Ellison, please!" she begged, trying to rise from the bed. She was a ruin, a parody of a lady turned whore. He let his gaze move over her, taking in her eyes, red and bleary from drugs and tears, her expensive lace nightdress, rumpled and stained, and the tangled mass of hair falling around her like the locks of a madwoman.

Perhaps he'd send her to a madhouse as part of his revenge.

He crossed to the door, opened it. Her maid jumped back from the keyhole, nearly knocking over the footman crouching behind her. Both servants regarded him with wide-eyed expressions of feigned innocence, but he knew they'd heard everything.

"Pack her things," he said to the maid. "She's to be ready to leave for Carswell Park within the hour. You will accompany her, and so will you." He included the footman. Let them rot with their secret on the Welsh border for a while. There'd be no one to gossip with on the wild edge of civilization. "You are to speak to no one before you go, is that clear? I will know if you say even one word of what has occurred here," he said menacingly.

They both nodded, fear in their eyes now, wordlessly obedient, suitably terrified.

He stalked down the hall, passing Sophie's apartments.

He could hear the dissonant clatter of a pianoforte being badly played. She was having her lesson. He paused outside the door. He usually liked to go in and listen, play the indulgent father. His fist clenched. Not today. He wasn't sure he could ever look at her again. For a moment he considered sending her away with her mother. But questions would be asked. Sophie was the Season's most popular debutante. People would want to know why she'd left Town so suddenly. What if the prince asked him about her? Would he have the gall? And the stories the *ton* would make up for themselves would be every bit as ruinous as the truth.

He cringed as she played another wrong note. She was still his daughter in the eyes of the law, his to dispose of as he wished. Elizabeth expected him to marry the girl to royalty, did she? He'd do the opposite. He'd marry the girl off quickly and quietly, to the most minor lord he could find—anyone who'd take her, so long as he took her far, far away.

CHAPTER FIVE

The butler who opened the door of Westlake House was crisply dressed and wide-awake, as if it were noon instead of barely dawn. If he was surprised to see Alec on the doorstep, he gave not the slightest indication. He simply stepped back and let him enter the cavernous hall, assuming that Alec had been summoned, and had come at once, the hour notwithstanding.

"Good morning, Northcott," Alec said, stepping over the threshold into the Earl of Westlake's home, and handing Northcott his hat as he did so.

"Good morning, sir. I'll see if His Lordship is in, if you'll be so kind as to wait."

Alec waited, though he knew that the Earl of Westlake was not only in, he'd probably been working for hours, delving into the secrets and sins of society, raking through the lives of his fellow peers with a fine comb, scrutinizing private correspondence, examining wicked billets-doux, and analyzing wills, dinner menus, laundry lists, and dry documents of sale for hidden meanings. Alec wondered if the Crown's spymaster ever slept, and rubbed a hand over his own face, realizing he'd not been to bed himself since yesterday.

He'd delivered the letters yesterday, admitting one was missing, and within hours, he'd received the summons to appear first thing this morning. His stomach had been churning ever since. Mistakes were costly in this business. Alec assumed there'd be a dressing-down, and a stern warning to be more careful. At worst, he'd be sent back to search the Countess of Bray's chamber. He tugged on his earlobe. His ears were still ringing with the good woman's screams.

"His Lordship will see you in the study, sir," Northcott said, interrupting Alec's thoughts. He led the way down the hall.

Adam De Courcey, Earl of Westlake, rose from his desk as his guest entered. "Ah, MacNabb. How very intuitive of you—I was just writing you another note."

Alec frowned. "Another? When have I ever failed to answer your call the first time?"

The earl's eyebrow twitched. "This is another matter, and hence, another note. Coffee, please, Northcott," Westlake said, dismissing his servant. He indicated a seat across the desk from his own, and picked up an open letter on the polished mahogany surface. "You inherited your father's title recently—you are the Earl of Glenlorne." Westlake said, making the fact that he hadn't heard it from Alec first an unspoken accusation.

Alec hadn't known. The surprise caught him in the gut, but he hid it, and continued to regard Westlake evenly.

How could he have known? He had as little contact as possible with his family. They believed he had left England some years ago, and was in Ceylon. The bitter tang of shock filled Alec's mouth. So his father had died young, just as Alec had feared, after a useless life of drink. He had not left Scotland on good terms with his father—or his stepmother, which had more to do with why he left. Alec had objected when his father began to sell off land, to make changes to old ways that had existed for centuries, and had written letters and decrees while he was in his cups that had destroyed old alliances. Alec suspected it hadn't all been the MacNabb's own doing. He could not prove it, of course. It had been better to leave than to watch the clan destroyed further. He tightened his hands on the arms of the chair. It galled him that Westlake should somehow know before he did.

Of course it hardly mattered. No doubt there was nothing to inherit except a worthless title, a crumbling castle, and a mountain of debt. With each generation there was a little less worth inheriting. It was as if the clan was cursed with ill luck. His great-grandfather, knowing war was coming, had hedged his bets on the outcome of the Jacobite rebellion by dividing his eight sons, placing half on the royalist side, and half in Bonnie Prince Charlie's camp. The battle and the terrible aftermath had taken the flower of the clan, along with the laird and seven of his fine sons—all save the youngest. The lad had been away from home, took no side at all, and the English had let him keep what little was left of Glenlorne. Throughout Alec's grandfather's lifetime, and his father's lifetime, things had only gotten worse for the once proud and prosperous clan. Soon, Glenlorne would be gone altogether, and all that would remain would be tired legends of MacNabb glory, told around smoky fires in tumble-down huts by men in rags—the kind of stories his grandfather used to tell Alec when he was a boy. He couldn't help. He was no leader. He'd left home eight years ago, full of bright plans, and failed. He was Earl of Glenlorne? Yes, the clan was cursed indeed.

"Yes," he said in answer to the earl's pronouncement of his new circumstance, as if they were discussing the weather, as if he'd known but simply didn't care. He had no intention of returning to Scotland for the burial, or of acknowledging the title. He wondered how his half sisters were faring, and the folk of the clan, and felt a prickle of guilt. He pushed it away. What could he have done if he'd stayed? He'd only cause more pain. He met the question in Westlake's sharp gaze with disdain, telling the earl silently to mind his own business. Westlake smiled.

Alec supposed he shouldn't be surprised that Westlake knew before he did. There was damned little Westlake didn't know.

"Actually, it isn't all that recent. It was almost a year ago," the spymaster said.

A year? How had his stepmother and his sisters managed since? Alec gritted his teeth and remained stubbornly silent, ignoring the prompting of the earl's raised eyebrows to explain himself.

"Is that all you wished to see me about? There's nothing you need purloined, no one you want followed?" he growled.

Westlake smiled coolly. "I have a letter here from Countess Devina—"

"Who?" Alec asked.

Westlake's articulate eyebrows twitched in surprise and annoyance. "Your stepmother, I believe?"

"Devorguilla?" Alec blurted.

"It appears she's styling herself as Countess Devina now."

Warning bells sounded in Alec's head over more than the alteration of her name. Devorguilla had always had a penchant for things English. She would never have dared to change her name while his father was alive. It meant she was up to something.

"Now why on earth would she write to you?" Alec asked. Surely Devorguilla—Devina—had no idea Alec was in London. His family believed he was in Ceylon, didn't they? He shifted in his seat, a familiar froth of guilt and failure stirring in the pit of his stomach.

"She didn't," Westlake said. "She wrote to your man of affairs here in Town, Richard Waters. I have someone in his employ who keeps me informed of interesting developments."

Alec frowned. She wanted money—probably needed it desperately. Not that he had any to spare. He thought again of Countess Bray's necklace, and wondered how much—

"She wants you dead," Westlake said without emotion, as if Devorguilla had written to ask Waters for the funds to buy a bolt of cambric, or a length of ribbon.

Alec felt his jaw drop. "Dead?"

"Since you've been missing for quite nearly the requisite seven years, and haven't acknowledged your inheritance of the title, she's wondering if Waters can advise her of the rules of law that will allow her to have you declared legally dead, so she may claim your estate."

"Claim my estate?" Alec blurted. "There's nothing to bloody claim!"

"Still, she wishes to use any available funds to provide suitable dowries for her three daughters, Megan, Alanna, and Sorcha."

Dowries. Of course the girls would need dowries to marry well. He hadn't considered that it was now his responsibility.

"Can she do this?" Alec asked.

The earl's brows twitched again, indicating amusement, if Westlake was capable of such an emotion. "You appear very much alive to me, Glenlorne," he replied, using Alec's new title. "I expect you'll want to go north and deal with this yourself, in person."

Alec stared at him. "No."

Westlake's brows took wing for his hairline. "No?"

Alec got up and paced the length of the carpet. "I shall direct Waters to send her a letter." Was that the correct thing to do? He might be an earl by inheritance, but he had no idea how to be an earl. What should he say to Devorguilla, what commands should he give, beyond confirming the fact that he was indeed still alive?

Westlake didn't speak for a long moment. He seemed to be considering something. "In truth, Glenlorne—"

"MacNabb will do just fine, thank you," Alec growled.

"I need you in Scotland—or at least out of London. The missing letter has turned up. Lord Bray has it, and I've been assured he knows the whole truth. He packed Countess Bray off to the country yesterday afternoon, and he refused an invitation to dine with the Prince Regent."

"What does that mean?" Alec asked. He had no idea what the letters contained.

"It means that I can no longer use your services."

Alec gripped the back of the chair until the leather squeaked. "Because of one mistake in seven years?"

Westlake remained calm—he was never anything but calm. "No, not entirely, though I do recall I warned you that mistakes could not be allowed to happen. No, you've got a title now. You've become visible, a gentleman. Someone might recognize you if you began to frequent the kind of society functions your new status allows."

"Now why would I do that?" Alec demanded.

Westlake opened a drawer, took out a book, and held it up.

Alec read the title. "*Waverley*? Walter Scott's novel?"

Westlake riffled the pages. "Yes. The whole *ton* is reading it, my wife included, and mainly because the Prince Regent is fascinated by it. He invited Scott to London, and his interest is now making all things Scottish quite fashionable. He has Scottish ancestry, of course, and he'll be the King of Scotland eventually."

Alec chuckled. "I doubt he'll be inviting me to tea to chat about my homeland, my lord."

"No, but as a Scottish earl, you'll be in much demand by the rest of the *ton*, the fashionable folk who wish to emulate His Highness's interest. Why, my own wife has suggested we summer in Scotland, give a ball with a Scottish theme. I have put her off, of course, but you can see why you must go."

Alec folded his arms over his chest. "And if I refuse?"

"I trust you remember an English earl still has precedence over a Scottish one?" Westlake asked calmly. "Did you know that Bray has offered a reward regarding the robbery of his home the other night? It seems a valuable necklace was stolen, his wife terrorized so badly she had to retire to the country. His footman saw a tall man with dark hair," he mused.

"I didn't take the necklace," Alec said.

"Of course not, but it would be most inconvenient if you were identified—perhaps even hanged—for a crime you did not commit. You *did* terrorize Her Ladyship, if nothing else. She might be able to identify you."

Alec's lips twisted bitterly, and he cast a glance around the luxurious room. There was nothing at Glenlorne to compare with this. Not even the coffee that Northcott had silently delivered at some point during the conversation. Westlake crossed to the tray, and poured out. The rich fragrance reminded Alec that he wasn't in Ceylon, living the life of a rich planter. He was a penniless thief, and his life, his secrets—they all belonged to Westlake. He left his coffee untouched and gave Westlake an exaggerated bow.

He grabbed Devorguilla's letter off Westlake's desk and shoved it into his coat for good measure. "If you don't mind my lord earl, I'll handle my own affairs from now on," he said, and strode toward the door.

CHAPTER SIX

The heavy coach jolted and flew like a child's toy over yet another deep rut in the road. Caroline winced and clutched the window ledge until the vehicle righted itself.

"That was a bad one!" The gentleman in the green hat, a certain Mr. Brill from Hampshire, chuckled. Caroline refrained from rolling her eyes. He'd made that same pronouncement about every single pothole between London and—well, wherever they were now.

"Yes indeed, Mr. Brill," the woman in blue said, fanning her flushed face with her glove. "All this rain has made the roads a dreadful mess. I have no hope at all of reaching my destination with my bones intact!"

"And where is it you're bound, Mrs. Hindon?" asked the second gentleman, a clergyman named Scroop. He had stuck his long nose into a book of Latin history as the coach set out from London, and left it there for most of the trip. After hours with nothing to do, Caroline envied him the prize of something, anything—even Latin history—to read. Mrs. Hindon preened under his attention.

"I'm going to Berwick, sir. My sister lives there, and she's been poorly. Her husband died not a month past, and she's in the family way. I hope to be a comfort to her however I can."

"I daresay a nice stipend would ease her grief, what with another mouth to feed coming along! These are trying times." Mr. Brill put in.

"Poor lass," murmured the young woman beside Caroline, who had shyly introduced herself as Miss Louisa Best. Caroline had yet to see Miss Best's face around the broad brim of her plain straw bonnet, since she kept her eyes downcast. Her brief comment marked the first time she'd spoken since she'd murmured her name to her fellow passengers by way of introduction.

"I myself am bound for York," Brill declared, offering no further details. He fixed Miss Best with a curious stare, like a magpie sighting something shiny. "And where are you traveling to, Miss Best?"

"Scotland," she replied. "I'm going to be governess to three young ladies of quality, to teach them English manners."

Mrs. Hindon gasped, and Mr. Scroop coughed. Brill chuckled. "Manners, eh? You'll be hard-pressed to do that, I daresay."

"Barbarians!" Mrs. Hindon said, pressing a hand to her vast blue bosom in horror. Caroline swallowed the lump that rose in her throat. Hadn't the gentleman who'd assisted her been a Scot?

"Scotland is no place for a decent Englishwoman," Scroop pronounced, like God giving a commandment.

"Why? What have you heard?" Miss Best squeaked out the question that hovered on Caroline's own lips.

Mrs. Hindon made a frightened mewl and widened her eyes as she looked to the men to explain.

Mr. Brill leaned forward. "They don't wear clothes, for a start. Well, not clothes as you and I know them." He held up a hand as Mrs. Hindon gasped. "I know 'tis an indelicate topic, but it's the truth. They dress in rags, and eat their meat raw, or they eat oats, like horses."

Caroline frowned. Her grandmother had told her stories of Scotland. Though she'd died when Caroline was very young, Caroline didn't remember any mention of raw meat or naked savages. Her grandmother had spoken of meadows blooming with heather, fast-flowing rivers filled with salmon, and—

"If we English had not put down Bonnie Prince Charlie's rebellion all those years ago, and forced a modicum of civilization on the Scots, I daresay they'd be completely wild by now," Mr. Scroop said, shutting his book, and concentrating on giving Miss Best the benefit of his opinion.

"But I have a letter from a countess, a real countess, who lives in the Highlands. She writes well enough." Miss Best opened her reticule and fumbled for a folded letter, which she held out like a talisman.

Scroop sniffed, declining to touch it. "She likely had a proper English cleric write it for her. The Scots can't read and write like we do. They don't even speak English outside of Edinburgh, and even there, they maul and molest our language until it's nearly gibberish!"

Caroline recalled her rescuer's soft Scottish burr. He'd been perfectly understandable, and he was certainly kinder than either of these men. She noted the hard light of malice in Scroop's eyes, the dull ignorance in Mr. Brill's. Indignation heated her skin. They were frightening Miss Best. She watched the young woman put the letter away with shaking fingers.

In fact, they were frightening *her*. Caroline bit her lip. Had she made a terrible mistake? She should have stayed in London. Perhaps she could have talked Somerson out of making her choose a husband yet, pleaded for time. Her Scottish rescuer hadn't said anything about the terrors of Scotland. Of course, he was expecting her to have an escort, a bridegroom, who would marry her quickly over the anvil, then bring her straight home again to England.

She bit her lip and stared out the window at the passing scenery. She'd made an impulsive decision that could affect the rest of her life, something that could result in a far more tragic future than she'd face as wife to Speed or Mandeville. She'd trusted a stranger on the street and rejected the counsel of her own half brother, an earl and a gentleman. She held her breath. She should turn back, go home, apologize, and marry as she was expected to. She considered her choice again, and shuddered.

She shut her eyes, wondering what her Scot truly looked like, trying to conjure a kind face out of a shadowed cheek, a fragment of dark brow, and a single gleaming eye. He *had* been kind, and she was determined that he should look so, and be exceedingly handsome as well. She imagined a smiling countenance with blue eyes and auburn hair—or perhaps brown eyes and dark hair?

Beside her, Miss Best swallowed audibly, holding back tears. Caroline laid a hand on her arm. "Surely it isn't as bad as they say. The Rebellion of '45 was long ago, and Bonnie Prince Charlie is gone," she soothed. "My grandmother used to tell me stories about Scotland, and there wasn't a single mention of—"

Another gasp of horror filled the coach. "You're a Scot?" Mrs. Hindon warbled, as if she feared Caroline was about to produce a claymore from under her cloak and murder everyone present, starting with her.

"No, I'm English!" Caroline said quickly.

"And where are you traveling to?" Mr. Brill asked.

Caroline swallowed. "To Sc-Scotland." This time the word rolled awkwardly off her tongue, and a tidal wave of doubt swept through her belly.

Mr. Scroop's brows lowered suspiciously. Mrs. Hindon gasped. Mr. Brill laughed coldly.

Miss Best turned to stare past her bonnet at Caroline. "Have you been there before?"

Caroline swallowed. "No."

"Then why go now?" Mrs. Hindon demanded. Everyone looked at Caroline, fixed their eyes on her like hungry vultures eyeing prey, someone weak, vulnerable, and far from home, where she should have had the good sense to stay.

But her future, whatever it might be, lay ahead. Of that she was certain. The tidal wave receded. She could hardly admit that to her fellow travelers, or tell them the truth.

"I'm going . . ." Caroline racked her brain for a story they'd believe. "I'm on my way to—" Another hard jolt cut off her words.

"That was a bad one!" Brill said, but the passengers were watching Caroline, waiting for her to answer. She felt a bead of sweat slip between her shoulders. "I'm going to a wedding!" she managed. Hadn't her rescuer assumed she was eloping?

"A wedding!" Curiosity replaced the suspicion in Mrs. Hindon's pale eyes. "Bride or groom's side?"

"Um, bride," Caroline managed. "In Edinburgh. My sister is marrying an English soldier stationed there, you see—a captain." The romantic story sprang fully formed to her mind. "He's very handsome, and my sister is so very happy." Everyone was staring at her with rapt fascination. She took a breath, ready to add the next chapter, but the coach hit another bump.

"That was a bad one!" Brill and Scroop said together, and Mrs. Hindon giggled.

"You'd best pick flowers for the wedding on this side of the border. Nothing grows in Scotland. Scots eat mutton, and the mutton eats everything else. It's a barren place where the sun never shines," Brill said.

"God's blight upon a heathen land," intoned the clergyman.

Miss Best whimpered again and clasped her gloved hands together tightly, as if she were praying.

The coach pitched like a ship on stormy seas as the horses turned into a muddy inn yard. Mrs. Hindon whooped as she was thrown against Miss Best. Scroop grunted as Mr. Brill's elbow knocked his Latin history to the floor. Caroline clung to the seat.

The passengers sighed as the coach came to a halt, righting bonnets and hats as they descended from the vehicle, blinking at the late afternoon sun and stretching cramped muscles.

Miss Best picked up her skirts and hurried into the inn,

and Caroline followed, with Mrs. Hindon coming behind, picking her way through the mud like a fussy hen, complaining loudly about the ruination of her half boots.

Caroline's stomach growled. She hadn't eaten a proper meal since supper the night before last at Somerson House. How far away it seemed now, a place just as foreign as Scotland. Was her half brother looking for her? She glanced around the low-ceilinged inn, scanning the faces of the inhabitants, but they stared back dully, with little interest in who she might be.

"When is the next mail coach going south?" Miss Best was asking the innkeeper. "I wish to purchase a ticket!" she said.

"But you just got off the London Mail!" he said in surprise.

"I've changed my mind! I want to go back to London this very minute," she said desperately, an edge of panic in her voice.

Caroline caught her sleeve. "Oh, Miss Best, I'm sure Scotland isn't nearly as bad as they say!"

Miss Best blinked away tears, and snatched her arm out of Caroline's grip. "How would you know? You said you've never even been there!"

"But—" Caroline began.

"Do you want the ticket or not?" the innkeeper said.

"What do *you* know of Scotland?" the girl asked him.

"It isn't England," he said cryptically.

"Then I'll take the ticket!" Miss Best opened her reticule to retrieve her money. The letter fell out, and Caroline stared at it, white paper against the aged black boards of the floor. Coins rang on the wooden bar, and Miss Best snatched up her ticket and turned away.

"Wait, your letter!" Caroline said, bending to pick it up.

The girl backed away from it as if it were poisoned. "I don't want it!" she said. "Burn it!"

With that, Miss Louisa Best fled into the ladies' waiting room without a backward glance.

Caroline felt the letter tingle in her gloveless fingers. She glanced down at the cracked seal. Was that a lion or a bear? She couldn't read the name, or the motto. She unfolded it.

I am pleased to offer you the post of governess at the sum of seven pounds per year, plus your room and board here at Glenlorne Castle. You will be responsible for teaching English to my three daughters, aged eighteen, seventeen, and twelve, as well as advising them on English manners and dress. We shall expect you at Glenlorne by the first of the month.

The letter was signed by the Countess of Glenlorne.

"Glenlorne," Caroline whispered. It was a destination, a respectable paying job with a mother and three daughters. The countess wanted someone to teach English and manners. Who better than an English earl's daughter?

She opened the Scotsman's purse, and reached for a coin to pay for a meat pie and a cup of tea, feeling hope soar in her breast. She silently thanked her unknown benefactor once again, and the imaginary face in her mind's eyes smiled, his hazel eyes twinkling as his red-gold locks floated on a fresh Highland breeze.

Her heart lifted a little. This was an adventure, an opportunity, a true tale to tell her children and grandchildren, and Caroline wasn't about to be as foolish as Miss Best and turn back now.

In her mind, her Scottish hero chuckled, a warm, low, seductive sound. His blue eyes twinkled and a lock of blond hair feathered across his broad brow as he held out his hand to her.

CHAPTER SEVEN

Alec stared into the amber depths of his whisky, ignoring the denizens of the modest gentlemen's club. Devorguilla's letter sat in his pocket, and he'd read it a dozen times.

She needed money. The estate needed repairs, and all her meager funds were going to care for her young daughters. Her late husband, the seventh earl, had left numerous debts to be settled, she pleaded. If she could find a way to declare Alec dead and sell Glenlorne, she could make arrangements that would provide dowries for her girls. She wanted nothing for herself—or so she said. She said not one word of Glenlorne's people, or the fact that the land beneath the crumbling castle represented four hundred years of MacNabb history— her daughters' history, and his own.

"Good evening, Glenlorne," a fellow patron greeted Alec by his new title as he passed, heading for the gaming rooms. Alec gritted his teeth, but didn't acknowledge the man. Within hours of meeting with Westlake, a dozen men had greeted him as Glenlorne instead of plain MacNabb. He silently cursed Westlake, and Devorguilla too. How long would it take for news to spread that his earldom was penniless, and his family would prefer it if he were as dead as his father? There was no doubt that Devorguilla wanted to sell whatever there was left to sell. Alec wondered how much the castle and the land might be worth. He'd come to one conclusion in the hours since his meeting with Westlake—when he returned to Scotland, if he returned at all, he'd need money. It was now up to him to provide for his half sisters, at the very least. He'd probably be forced to do exactly what Devorguilla intended to do and sell Glenlorne. Or—he looked at the door to the gaming room—he could go home with at least a little brass in his pocket, perhaps, if he was luckier than he'd been recently. If he was far luckier than that, he might even win enough to fool them into thinking he really had been in Ceylon. He had to try at the very least. He swallowed the last of his whisky and rose from his seat.

An hour later, Alec stared down at the worthless cards in his hand.

"Well, my lord earl?" Jasper Kendrick asked.

Alec ignored the use of his title. The balance of his coin already lay before Jasper, and the man was about to win yet again. Alec felt a thin trickle of sweat crawl down his spine. He forced himself to grin, as if he'd inherited a rich dukedom instead of a penniless Scottish ruin, and laid down his cards, and tossed his remaining few guineas onto the table. "I'm leaving Town for a few weeks, so I'll save you the trouble of carrying my vowel till I come back."

"You're leaving in the middle of the Season?" Jasper's pale blue eyes bulged. "Now? You must know a title improves a man no end in the eyes of potential brides. You're bound to be the talk of every hen party in London now you've inherited. The ladies won't be happy to see a handsome, strapping, titled bachelor leave during husband-hunting season." He picked up the money without bothering to count it.

Alec rose. "Flattering though the attention might be, I'm in not in the market for a wife."

Jasper chuckled. "You say that now, but have you considered a lady like Miss Anne Devereaux? She has a thousand pounds a year, but she's lonely for a title. Countess would suit her nicely."

"Then I hope she finds a nice, willing earl to give her what she wants," Alec said. "Good night, Kendrick. Enjoy my coin." He eyed the pile of coin in front of his wealthy opponent regretfully and turned away, heading for the door.

A glided cane blocked his path. "Good evening, Glenlorne. I was hoping I might have a private word before you leave." Alec looked at the cane, considered grabbing it and snapping it over his knee. The bearer hadn't even bothered to stand up to stop him. He sat at a table near the door, half in shadow. Alec glared at him, an obscene rebuke on the tip of his tongue. His mouth dried as he looked into the dull face of the Earl of Bray. The earl held his eyes, his expression cold and unreadable.

He indicated a seat across from him. "Join me."

What choice did he have? Alec wondered if the earl knew he'd broken into his home, terrorized his wife, stolen her private letters. He sat down slowly, wondering if he was about to feel the cold steel of a knife under the table as it thrust into his belly.

But Bray merely signaled for the waiter, a jeweled signet ring glinting in the spartan candlelight. "Whisky would be most appropriate, I assume?" he asked Alec. Alec nodded, his jaw too tight to speak. Bray smiled, and Alec recognized ruthlessness masquerading as camaraderie. His skin prickled as the earl's gaze slid over him. Neither Westlake nor his own meager title would protect him if Bray knew. Alec searched Bray's face, but there was no accusation there. Surely if Bray wished to ask about the break-in, he'd simply have waited outside, had a few burly footmen wrestle Alec into a dark coach, or an even darker alley. The man before him was a companion to the Prince Regent, one of the most powerful peers in the kingdom. But if he wasn't here for that, then what in hell did he want?

Bray waited until the waiter had set the drinks before them and taken his leave. He raised his glass, his eyes hard as jet as he stared at Alec over the rim.

"Kendrick is quite right, you know. You'll be very much in demand on the marriage mart now you have a title."

It was on the tip of Alec's tongue to insist the earl call him MacNabb, but he held his tongue, curious now, as well as wary. "You didn't do very well at the tables tonight," Bray stated.

"What's this about, my lord?" Alec asked. Bray let his gaze fall to Alec's untouched glass.

"Tell me, do you make whisky on your estates in Scotland?"

"No." Alec replied shortly, though his father had drunk enough ale to fill the lake below the castle.

"Do you raise sheep, weave wool at Glenlorne?"

Alec was silent.

"Cattle? Oats?"

"Why do you ask?" Alec demanded again.

"Because I'm curious. I wondered what kind of income a Scottish earl might have, so I looked into it."

It was clear enough by the smirk on Bray's face that he knew Glenlorne was penniless. Alec had no intention of playing games with a bored English earl, or listening to another Englishman belittle Scotland—and him—for his own amusement.

He began to rise. "Good night, Lord Bray."

Bray held up an imperious hand. "Do sit down. I have a proposition for you."

"No—" Alec began.

"You have three young sisters, don't you? And all of marriageable age, or very nearly, I understand. How do you provide for them?" Bray interrupted.

That stopped Alec. Bray's cold smile was the kind Alec would normally have taken as a warning, but he was curious now. He wondered if Bray wished to purchase Glenlorne. That would indeed solve many problems. "What do you want, my lord?"

"As I said, I have a proposition for you. A marriage proposal, actually," Bray replied.

Alec resisted the urge to laugh. "You're hardly my type, my lord."

Bray sent him another frost-tipped grin. "Quite. But

I meant my daughter. Sophie made her debut this Season. She's been at every ball and party of consequence. Not the circles you travel in, of course. You probably haven't had the pleasure of an introduction."

New warning bells clattered in Alec's head. "Your daughter, Lady Sophie Ellison?"

"Yes. I want you to marry her."

"*Marry Lady Sophie Ellison?*" Alec repeated stupidly, stunned. Surely there was a mistake. Lady Sophie was the belle of the Season, destined to be the wife of a wealthy duke at the very least. There were rumors of a match with foreign royalty, not a penniless Scottish earl, but Bray nodded.

"I trust you know her then?"

Everyone knew the Earl of Bray's daughter. She was widely considered the loveliest girl in London. Alec had never met her. Alec swallowed. There must be something very wrong with her indeed if Bray wanted *him* to marry the girl. Her father's fortune, his royal connections, would go far in making even a plain girl lovely, and a stupid one fascinating. Pure panic raced through his veins, overriding the hope that somehow Bray's offer meant salvation and solvency and a happy ending.

"I'm afraid I'm not in the market for a wife," Alec said carefully.

"She comes with a dowry of fifty thousand pounds."

Alec stared. "Fifty—" He gulped.

"Yes. Think of that. All the whisky, oats, cattle, and sheep you could want. You could make your manor house—"

"Castle," Alec murmured.

"Castle." Bray waved a dismissive hand as if it mattered

little where his daughter would be housed after her nuptials. "You could make it the most magnificent castle in all Scotland—a romantic little love nest for yourself and Sophie."

Alec stared into his whisky. Romance? He'd never been in love, never even considered the possibility of it. Marriage was a different matter, rarely involving love. Not that he'd considered marriage either. His hand tightened on the glass. Fifty thousand pounds. He could give his sisters dowries, see them marry well—very well indeed. He could rebuild the cottages and farms of Glenlorne, see them rise once more out of poverty, give them back their pride—

He shut his eyes. Those were his grandfather's dreams, not his. He doubted there was anything left at Glenlorne worth rebuilding. It would be a fool's errand, as impossible as trying to bring the dead back to life. It was certainly no place to bring a bride, especially a bride like Lady Sophie Ellison.

"You hesitate," Bray said.

"Why? Why me?" Alec demanded, suddenly angry. His whole life had changed in the past day.

Bray shrugged. "Why not? You're a handsome young man with a title—and a castle," he soothed. "Did I mention that Sophie comes with her mother's jewelry? All of it, more diamonds and rubies and emeralds than any woman could wear in a lifetime."

"She wouldn't have cause to wear them at Glenlorne," Alec muttered.

"No matter. Sophie will grow to love Scotland. I'm sure there'll be no need at all for her to return to London."

Warning bells clanged again. It was clear now that the Earl of Bray wished to be rid of his daughter. He was all but selling the poor girl to a man he hoped would keep her in the farthest reaches of the kingdom, never to be seen again. It obviously didn't matter if Sophie was happy, or if Alec could make her so. He felt pity for the girl, and wondered what she'd done to deserve such a fate. Did she even know this was happening? It struck him like a bolt.

The letters.

If this had something to do with the letter that he'd dropped, the one Westlake said Bray had found, then Sophie's fate was his fault. He felt his stomach rise uneasily.

"Think of the money, Glenlorne," Bray urged.

Alec swallowed. Fifty thousand pounds meant no more lies, no more stealing or spying. Instead, he could live a life of honor, wealth, and privilege. It was tempting. He rose to his feet. "I'll need to consider this more carefully. I'm leaving for Scotland tomorrow. I'll have my man of affairs contact you." Waters, wasn't that the name on Devorguilla's letter?

Bray's hand on his arm stopped him. "Come now, Glenlorne. There are no banns required in Scotland. You could take her with you, marry her once you reach Scotland."

Alec stared down at the blue veins under Bray's knuckles, at the jeweled rings that adorned his hands. No English father wanted his daughter marrying over the anvil. It was unseemly and scandalous, even if the groom was an earl. He thought fleetingly of the red-haired lass he'd helped on her way to just such a fate, felt guilt. If he hadn't dropped that letter, he would never have seen her on the street, and Bray would likely be in a far more elegant gentleman's club, negotiating a far different match for Sophie. He suddenly felt responsible for the unhappiness of both women—and for the misery of his half sisters and Devorguilla too.

"Perhaps a long betrothal, so we can get to know one another," Alec hedged. "When I return, we can arrange it. A year, shall we say?" He wondered where the lass he'd met in the street was now. Married, he hoped, deliriously happy with her faithful, stalwart husband. She was a brave wee thing. Love had made her willing to do anything for a chance at happiness. She'd be the kind of wife who would stand by a man in his hour of need, love him always—if things went as she hoped, of course. What kind of wife would pampered, petted Sophie make?

She'd make him rich.

"A year!" Bray scoffed. "You feel I'm being too hasty, do you? Shall we make it sixty thousand pounds? Here's what I'm willing to do. Since you must leave at once for your estates—and I fully understand you must take up your duties at once—I'll arrange for Sophie to travel to Scotland. You can show her the glories of Glenlorne before the wedding. Would that do?"

"I'm not—" Alec began, but Bray rose to his feet, and held out his hand.

"She'll be there within a fortnight. That will give you time to break the happy news of your impending nuptials to your kin—or is 'clan' the right word?"

"It was once an outlawed word, I believe, especially in England," Alec said. Clans, the Gaelic tongue, the plaid, even bagpipes had been forbidden by the English Crown for decades after Culloden.

Bray chuckled. "His Highness plans to change all that. He adores Highland dress. Sir Walter Scott promised to find him a tailor who could make him a proper suit of Scottish garments, and bring a bagpiper to play for him."

"If he can find one," Alec muttered.

Bray ignored the quip. "I can see you are a patriot, a man of honor. Sophie prides herself on setting new trends, starting new fashions. The prince enjoys things Scottish, but it will take a female, a lady like Sophie to bring it into style. Imagine that if you will. Every Englishman will be tracing his Scottish roots, and Scotland will rise to glory once again—with pipes, plaids, and Gaelic."

Alec swallowed a groan. English interest in Scotland had never, ever, boded well. He stared at Bray's outstretched hand. Whatever reason Sophie was being married off, he was at least partly to blame. And his sisters needed the money. Wasn't that why he'd come here tonight? He imagined arriving at Glenlorne, as penniless and useless as his father, another worthless mouth to feed, even if he was earl. Jasper Kendrick was right. Marrying money was the fastest way to a fortune, perhaps the only way. He had to marry someone, he supposed. Bray had shown him he had no choice.

Reluctantly, he clasped the hand of his future father-in-law.

Chapter Eight

Angus's ghost, transparent as a gauze curtain, stood staring out the window of the old tower, watching over the glen. Georgiana could see the road through his broad back as it wound past this tower on the way to the new castle. Well, it was hardly new. It was older than either of them, and they'd been dead for nearly twenty years, but it was newer than this place their ghosts inhabited.

"What are you watching for?" she asked.

He gave her a steely look from under his white brows. He'd grown from a winsome lad to a fine, handsome man. She would have liked to grow old with him. She felt the familiar bite of regret, and tilted her head to smile at him, imagining what that might have been like.

"Can a man not admire the view?" he asked, crusty at her interruption, obviously wary of her wistful smile.

"Yes, I suppose so," she said mildly, and drifted nearer, letting him feel the weight of her presence. He shrugged, but didn't move away.

"Something's about to happen. I can feel it in my bones

like I used to be able to feel a storm coming down from the hills," he grumbled. "Perhaps it's here already. Devorguilla always was a scheming piece, and young Brodie MacNabb has arrived, all smiles and muscles, even if he hasn't got the wit God gave a bonxie. She's up to something, or he is—something that will change Glenlorne forever." He looked at her like a fierce eagle.

As if he had bones. She suppressed a smile.

"Will it be as bad as Culloden? Glenlorne survived that, Angus." Georgiana let her eyes roam over the width of his shoulders, the strength in the ghostly hands that clutched the windowsill. He turned to look at her, his gaze fierce.

"Aye, Glenlorne survived that, but this is different. My father divided his sons, put a few on each side, half Jacobite, half Royalist, just to be sure the MacNabbs would keep Glenlorne no matter who won."

"And which side did you take?"

His scowl intensified. "How could I have chosen? I was a Scot, but—" He looked away his eyes roaming the glen, his shoulders hunched against the memory.

"But you were in love with an English girl, the daughter of an English lord," she prodded, finishing his sentence.

"I wasn't a coward. I would have fought with my brothers, but they didn't give me the chance." He studied his hands. "The night we planned to run away together, they caught me, packing my things. They knew well enough where I was going. They knocked me senseless, threw me over a horse, and dragged me to the coast. They put me on the first outbound ship they found, not caring where it was headed, just so long as it took me away from you."

"So that's why you didn't come," she said softly, without blame, though she felt regret keenly enough. It was a familiar companion.

"Did you truly believe I'd abandoned you?"

She sighed, and the breeze stirred the stunted trees that had begun to grow up within the tower's ruined walls. "They told me you had done exactly that, later. They said you'd come to your senses and run away rather than face a life with me."

"Bastards!" he hissed. A flock of swallows fled in terror at his malevolence, streaking past Angus's shade and out into the open sky. He flinched, though they could not harm him. "I suppose my brothers paid the price for it. All dead, or captured."

"If you'd stayed, you would have died with them at Culloden Moor, and I would still have lost you," Georgiana said softly. She drifted closer still. "Tell me where the ship took you. I've often imagined—"

But Angus was staring out the window at the road once again. "Dear God! I'm seeing a ghost!"

Georgiana looked down. A cart was trundling by, but the only ghost was the spinning veil of dust chasing the vehicle. The young woman seated beside the driver was staring up at the tower, squinting in the sun, one hand clutching tight to her bonnet. A long red curl fluttered loose in the breeze. "'Tis you, *gràdhach*! What kind of sorcery—"

Georgiana laughed, and he turned to her in surprise. She ignored him for a moment, kept her eyes fixed on the girl in the cart, felt pride and relief swell in her hollow breast. "It's my granddaughter Caroline, here at last," she said. She gave Angus a dazzling smile as the cart rounded a curve of the road and disappeared over the lip of the valley, heading for the new castle.

Angus looked at her, stunned. "How did you manage—" he began, but she gave him a coquettish smile.

"You think she looks like me, do you?"

Angus shook himself and nodded, feeling foolish. "Aye. Same hair, same white skin. Is that the lass you intend for Alec?"

She grinned. "Yes. What do you think?"

He groaned. "Heaven help him. One look into those eyes and he'll be a lost man. That's a feeling I remember all too well!"

"If he ever gets here," Georgiana said, her toes curling at Angus's unwitting compliment.

"Aye," he murmured, staring after the cart. "And he'd better get here soon."

CHAPTER NINE

Caroline sat on the hillside in the shadow of the old tower of Glenlorne with her new charges and watched the clouds hurry across a perfect blue sky like debutantes on a dance floor. The countess had been glad to accept Miss Forrester in Miss Best's place, once she had been assured that Caroline had the same skills and even more talents to teach the girls, and was of good breeding and sound moral character.

"There'll be rain tonight," twelve-year-old Sorcha said gloomily, following Caroline's gaze.

"Then it will make the flowers grow!" Megan said. At eighteen, she was pretty and sophisticated.

"Most especially lavender and wild rose, and mistletoe, Megan," seventeen-year-old Alanna said in a teasing tone.

"And plenty of meadowsweet and damiana," Sorcha added. "Muira said you had to find damiana." She and Alanna nudged each other and grinned like conspirators.

Megan's chin rose, and Caroline watched a blush kiss her cheeks. "And what are the flowers for?" she asked gently.

"'Tis Midsummer's Eve tomorrow night," Sorcha said.

"You celebrate St. John's Eve? Midsummer?" Caroline asked in surprise, more that Devina would allow it than in any disapproval of the old custom on her part.

Alanna giggled. "I suppose they aren't so superstitious in England. We're not supposed to, I know, but lots of Highlanders still honor the old ways. Midsummer's Eve is really just an excuse for a party. There'll be a bonfire and dancing. Nothing to harm our souls."

"I know." Caroline smiled. "We did the same in England where I grew up." They were supposed to be reading a treatise on the housewifely duties of an English lady, but the glorious weather and the excitement of the celebration made it hard to concentrate, even for Caroline. The wind was warm, the wildflowers fragrant, and Glenlorne was undoubtedly the most beautiful place she'd ever been. "How do you celebrate here?"

Alanna shrugged her shoulders. "Cakes and ale by a bonfire, that's all it is."

"No it isn't. Not if you believe in the old ways—then there's magic, and fairies, and love spells to be cast," Sorcha said, grinning at Caroline. "Old Muira's promised to make a love charm for Megan this year, to see if she'll find a true love this coming year."

Caroline watched a blush rise over Megan's cheeks.

"Oh, she's already found her true love!" Alanna said. "She likes Brodie. He's our cousin, and he'll be the next laird if Alec doesn't come home. Mother insists we must marry English lords, but she'll make an exception if Megan marries Brodie. She'll be a countess, won't she, miss?"

"Hush!" Megan got up and stamped her foot to stop the teasing.

"Och, she'll need more than a love charm if she's to win Brodie," Alanna went on, despite her sister's glare. "Every lass for a hundred miles around loves Brodie. He's a braw laddie, even if he isn't very smart, and he's going to be the next laird."

Megan blushed scarlet. "Mother says it will keep Glenlorne in the family, 'tis all."

"If she's lucky, she can jump the fire tomorrow night with Brodie," Sorcha teased. "He's to be the Midsummer king, and he'll have to choose a queen. Megan's sure he'll choose her." She pulled Alanna to her feet and they linked hands and danced in a circle around their sister.

"Maybe he'll dance with you, give you flowers for your hair," Sorcha teased. "And kiss you in the shadows where Mam can't see."

Megan's face flamed, but she raised her chin, clamped her lips shut, and stared up at the old tower as if it was the most fascinating thing in the world.

Caroline followed her gaze. The brittle yellow stone glowed in the sunlight. Trailing streams of ivy seemed to be all that held the old place together now. Caroline wondered how many Midsummers it had seen. The wind sang through the empty windows.

"Do you believe in ghosts, miss?" Megan asked her, ignoring her sisters' teasing. "They say the tower is haunted."

"Only by badgers and rooks!" Sorcha said, but the ivy reached, beckoned, in the wind and a cloud passed over the sun, making the tower's shadow stretch toward them. Sorcha's smile faded. Caroline shivered too. Was it her imagination, or was there a face in the top window? Gooseflesh rose on her arms, and she had the oddest feeling that someone was watching her, waiting for her. The cloud passed and the sensation faded.

"Of course I don't," she said. "Believe in ghosts, I mean."

"It's probably not a ghost at all. They say if you pick fern seed on Midsummer's Eve, you'll gain the power of invisibility," Alanna told her. "Perhaps there's an invisible someone nearby, a lad or lass who picked the seed, and now regrets it, since they must go about unseen by the living, completely unnoticed." She sighed at the romantic notion and the old tower seemed to sigh with her. Caroline thought of William, by now married to her niece Lottie, and remembered how she'd hoped he'd notice her. But he hadn't. She saw the same wistful, bereft expression on Megan's face.

"What goes into old Muira's love charm?" Caroline asked.

"Naught but roses and lavender!" Megan said quickly.

"And St. John's wort, and ivy, and mistletoe," Sorcha added. "We have a list from Muira of what must be gathered."

"We need heather for luck, as well—it protects the cattle from illness," Alanna said. "Or so they say."

"So Brodie says," Megan said. She sat down next to Caroline. "How do English girls learn who will be their true love, Miss Forrester?" she asked.

Sorcha snorted. Her eldest sister sent her a scathing look. "Ladies do not make that noise, Sorcha Maire MacNabb."

Sorcha set her hands on her hips. "I'm not a lady yet! I hope I never grow up if it means mooning over a lad who doesn't love you. Everyone knows he's sweet on Annie from the village, and Kat, and Nan. It's fine for you, but if Mam has her way, it won't matter how many spells Muira casts.

Alanna and me will have to marry proper English lords and leave Scotland forever."

All three girls looked stricken at the possibility, Caroline realized. The wind moaned through the tower in soulful sympathy. "I'm sure that won't be for some time yet. You aren't officially out yet, any of you, and I doubt there's an English lord for miles." She hoped not, anyway. She studied her fingers for a moment. "In England girls look into the fire at Midsummer and hope to see the face of their true love. Perhaps you will see an earl or a duke in the fire tonight, and someday you'll meet him, and you'll fall in love, even if he is English."

Sorcha wrinkled her freckled nose skeptically.

Megan sighed at the romantic notion.

Alanna leaped to her feet. "Look!" she said, pointing down the glen. People were walking up the hill, merry with laughter, bearing baskets. "Everyone has come out to gather flowers for Midsummer. Look, there's Brodie."

Megan sat up, her green eyes widening at the sight of her love.

Sorcha clasped Caroline's hand. "Can we go with them, miss?"

How could Caroline say no? It was summer, and the air was like wine, and there was merriment to be had.

"Your mother expects you back for tea," Caroline said. It was to be yet another lesson on proper English tea, and proper English tea behavior and conversation under the sharply critical gaze of Countess Devina.

"But that's not for hours yet!" Alanna pleaded, looking hopeful. Caroline's heart went out to her.

"Yes, all right. Stay together though." So long as they were part of such a big group, what could happen?

Megan scooped up the hem of her muslin gown and tucked it into the ribbon at her waist, out of her way, like one of the village lasses, exposing her ankles. She took off her shoes and stockings and wiggled her bare toes. Caroline barely had time to be shocked, or to protest, before the other girls did the same. Megan looked like a happy Highland lass, not like a young woman preparing for the rules and strictures of the London marriage mart. She bit her lip as she gazed across the hillside at lovely Brodie, who was surrounded by adoring females, then raced down the hill to meet him.

Caroline gathered the discarded stockings and shoes into a neat pile and watched them race down the hillside, girls again, not ladies. She noted they did not ask her to join them. She was a servant, and they probably imagined she was too old and too English to enjoy activities like flower picking and flirting. Happy laughter floated to her on the breeze, and Caroline shut the book in her lap and lay back in the cool grass.

She looked up at the tower again, yellow as crumbly cheese against the blue sky. The view from the top must have been spectacular once. In fact, it probably still was.

A trill of laughter carried across the hillside, and Caroline leaned on her elbow to watch the girls making their way down the hillside, having forgotten her entirely. She squelched her disappointment. She was a woman grown, and a governess, not a girl seeking posies for a love charm. She doubted if she'd ever find true love now. The tower groaned in the wind.

Caroline looked up at the empty windows. Surely it was just her imagination. No ghost would haunt such a ramshackle place. "Hello?" she called, just to be sure, but the only reply was the chuckle of the wind.

She rose to her feet and shaded her eyes with her hand, scanning the tower. There was a faint sound inside—a soft cry, perhaps. Or a moan. She circled the old stones and found the door open. She hesitated, staring into the shadowy opening, a black mouth against the summer day. The cry came again, louder this time. An animal perhaps—or a child—there were dozens of little ones in the village. What if someone was lost, alone and frightened, or even hurt? She pushed the door wider. "Hello?" The ancient hinges creaked a warning, even as the cry came again. Caroline tucked her skirts up the way the girls had done, and took a deep breath. "I'm coming in," she called, and heard her own voice echo back.

CHAPTER TEN

Glenlorne Castle looked just as it had when he'd left home eight years ago, as if time did indeed stand still in the Highlands. The new castle waited for him at the head of a long valley that overlooked the loch, surrounded by hills and sky, and as the cart he'd hired at the coaching inn carried him nearer, Alec felt a swell of pride, of longing for things to indeed be the way they were once. He remembered standing on the craggy slope above the loch with his grandfather, breathing in the scent of heather and peat fires, and listening to the tales of what it had been like, before Culloden and the English, before the Clan MacNabb had lost everything good, the pride and hope of the clan gone with Angus's seven brothers, all killed at Culloden, or in the brutal reprisals that had followed Prince Charlie's final battle until Angus MacNabb was the only son left. He'd been away at sea, and had come back to find a handful of ragged, broken MacNabbs who expected him to be their laird, to fix everything, to turn back the clock and give them back what they'd lost, as if one man could perform such a feat. Alec remembered the pain in Angus's eyes when he spoke of those days. He'd made Alec promise that someday, when he was earl, Glenlorne would rise again, be a home again, filled with pride and prosperity. Alec clenched his fists and stared at the castle. If his grandfather could see him now, the old man would surely hang his head in disappointment. Alec felt the ache of guilt at the memory of that promise. He wasn't a leader, or a miracle worker. He was a thief, and he'd even failed at that. He wouldn't be surprised if his clansmen ran him out of Glenlorne for good.

He looked at the little burial ground on the edge of the village, the markers sticking up through the grass like rotting teeth. The little kirk stood beside it. His grandfather was buried there, and now his father as well. Would he lie there in his turn? A cloud passed by, leaving the kirk in shadow while letting the sun gleam off the yellow and gray stones of the castle, riming it with light, making it appear to glow.

The cart pulled up at the door. "There you are, Laird," the carter said, jumping down to fetch Alec's boxes from the back. "And may I say it's grand to have ye home again." He grinned as if Alec was indeed the savior, come again. Alec nodded and gave him a coin. He'd sold his meager furnishings and his books and borrowed from Westlake to get enough money to make this trip, to buy a few trinkets for his sisters, so they wouldn't know what he really was when he arrived home.

Home. Was he home? At least for the time being. He wouldn't stay. He couldn't. He renewed his vow to sell, tried looking at the place as a buyer might. He ran his fingertips over the carving by the front door, a wolf's face. Part of the jaw was missing, shot away during the reprisals after Culloden, and the proud creature looked more like a mongrel dog.

"Just one of the sins the English have to answer for," his grandfather had grumbled each and every time he passed the carving. Alec glared into the eyes of the wounded beast. The castle would require a good deal of repairs before he could sell it.

"Alec lad!"

He turned to find old Muira coming around the side of the building, bearing baskets filled with herbs and flowers.

The servant had been old when he was a lad, and she was old now, yet unchanged, as untouched by time as the rest of Glenlorne. He smiled as she hurried toward him, her eyes shining, still blue as the sky. "It is you, isn't it?" She shifted the baskets on her hip and reached out a hand to touch his cheek, as if making certain he wasn't a ghost.

"Aye, it's me, Muira," he said, slipping back into Gaelic.

She stepped back and cackled. "I knew ye'd come! *She's* been saying ye must be dead, but I'd know if you were—I'd feel it in my bones. The castle would feel it. It's been waiting for you, all these years, and here ye are."

Alec watched her eyes fill with sentimental tears. Muira had been at Glenlorne for as long as Alec could recall. She was Glenlorne's cook, housekeeper, healer, and midwife. She knew the clan legends and old stories as well as his grandfather had. She'd also served as Alec's nurse when his mother had died before his father married Devorguilla. Devorguilla made the mistake of trying to send Muira away, saying Muira was a witch. It was her knowledge of herbs and spells that saved her. She'd brought Devorguilla through a hard labor with Megan, saved her life and the child's, and though the two women never spoke of it, an uneasy truce existed between them, and Muira had stayed. Muira refused to speak Devorguilla's name or call her countess, and Devorguilla referred to Muira as "the cook."

Alec opened his arms, but Muira shook her head. "Come away in, lad. 'Tis the Midsummer herbs I have here, and I dare not let them touch the ground."

He'd forgotten the charms and spells and superstitions. "Let me," he said, and tried to take the baskets. Muira hung on with a grip that belied her frail bones.

"Don't be daft. Ye're the laird—ye can't be doing women's work."

She pointed to the front door. "In you go, through the front as is proper. I'll take these round through the kitchen and fetch a dram to welcome ye home."

She scurried away round the corner, and Alec climbed the steps and stared at the massive oak door, scarred by battle and years of use. He touched the deep scuffs left by English rifle butts, and pulled his hand away. This wasn't the time for sentiment. The door needed a coat of paint, perhaps, to make it look less like a medieval fortress and more like a home, so potential buyers weren't frightened off before they even got inside.

He took a deep breath as he opened the door, wondering what he'd find. He stood on the broad step that led down to the castle's great hall. It was cool inside after the heat of the June day. He took note of the familiar room. It was the hall of a laird—a powerful man, in favor with Scotland's king, his confidant and friend. He looked at the dais at the end, which his grandfather said had once held a massive chair for the laird's use. Alec had never seen it. It had been broken apart, used by the English soldiers to fuel the two massive fireplaces designed to heat the vast space on frigid Highland nights. A plain chair sat there now, a placeholder, waiting for glory of the MacNabbs to return.

The walls were barren of decor, save the smashed stone carving of the clan crest above the laird's chair. His grandfather told tales of the days when the hall was hung with tapestries, weapons, and shields, but those were gone, and with the passing of the old folk like Muira, they would soon even be lost to memory. Alec could imagine his grandfather pointing out the place on the wall where each weapon had once hung . . . The targe of Malcolm; a banner blessed by St. Margaret;the dirk and claymore of Alec MacNabb, the first of that name, and the laird who'd built this tower for his bride, a delicate creature who could not abide the icy drafts that whistled through the old tower on the crag. He crossed to the window, and opened the shutters and stared across the valley to the old tower. It was still standing sentinel.

"Here y'are." he heard Muira's voice and turned. She carried in a brimming chalice on a tray covered with a scrap of plaid. "'Tis the laird's cup," Muira said proudly. "Carved from the horn of the great mountain goat that tried to kill the first Alec MacNabb, and trimmed with silver given him by the poorer, weaker clans who came on bended knee to take our name and join the great MacNabbs."

Alec stared into the depths of the whisky that filled the cup to the brim. Whisky, at least, appeared to be in plentiful supply at Glenlorne.

"Drink!" Muira encouraged him. "It comes from the cask

that was hidden deep in a cave by yer great-great-grandsire, for an occasion just such as this."

Alec wondered if it that was true. "Is there a spell on it?" he teased, raising the cup to his lips.

Muira waited until he drank before answering. "Just a wee one, perhaps, and just for good fortune, a bright new future, and strong and healthy heirs, o' course. We hardly need a spell for any of that now ye're here. You'll set things right at last. The Clan MacNabb just needs a leader again, and all will be well."

Sixty thousand pounds would also go a long way toward setting things right, he thought. It was on the tip of his tongue to tell her about Sophie, his bride and the potential mother of those strong and healthy heirs, but he stayed silent. What if he didn't marry Sophie, what if he sold Glenlorne? His sons, if he had any, would never see Glenlorne. He sipped the whisky, savoring the rich, smoky taste of it. Muira was yet another soul he was about to disappoint. He already felt as if his grandfather was frowning at him from the chieftain's chair. He glanced behind him to make sure it was empty.

"Where are the girls?" Alec asked.

Muira grinned. "It's Midsummer! They're out in the hills, o' course, gathering what's needed for the celebration." She pursed her lips, and her skin folded into deep lines and creases. "At least, I hope they are. I'm not their nurse any longer. *She's* hired a new governess, and—"

"Don't you have work to do in the kitchen?" Alec turned to find Devorguilla standing at the foot of the stairs. She hadn't changed. She was still beautiful, and dressed in an elegant

English gown. Her dark eyes traveled over Alec, the cup, and Muira, as she glided into the room. The temperature seemed to drop as she swept in. "Go," she commanded Muira, and reddened when the old woman looked to Alec for confirmation. He nodded, and Muira left the room.

"Hello, Devorguilla," Alec said.

"You didn't tell us you were coming," she said, her eyes offering no welcome.

"I'm not a ghost if that's what you fear," he said, and she tilted her head and smiled.

"No, I can see you're hale and healthy and quite alive, though I expected you'd be as tanned as a peddler from all those years in the sun of the southern climes, and yet you're as pasty as an Englishman. How was your voyage home? How long does it take to sail all that way?" she asked, her tone mocking. Something in her eyes told him she knew he'd been in London all along.

He gave her the most charming smile he could muster. "And you look well. Not a day older than last I was here. Muira knows her potions." He climbed the steps to the laird's chair and sat down, the chalice of whisky still in his hand.

She watched him silently, her eyes in shadow.

"I'll take that as a compliment. Tell me, did you bring gifts? Money, perhaps? We do need money, as you can see." She indicated the room with slim fingers.

Alec's throat tightened. "I have gifts for the girls. As for money, I'll need to see the accounts."

Her eyes sharpened. "There's not much to see. We live simply, as we must."

"Still," he insisted. He was at a loss for words, as unsure as he had been when he was a boy.

"I can assure you everything is in order here."

"I'm home again, alive and well, and I will manage my estates myself. Thank you for doing so for the past months."

Her eyes flared. "Months? I have been managing things for years. Your father wasn't capable—"

"It isn't kind to speak ill of the dead, Devorguilla," he interrupted.

"Devina," she said.

"Yes," Alec said. "I heard that you'd changed your name. I doubt my father would have liked that."

She ignored that, her eyes flashing. "When the girls make their debuts in London, I will change their names as well. Margaret, Alice, and Claire. Have you seen them yet? They're quite pretty, but that isn't nearly enough. I intend to see they find English husbands, titled men with fortunes and land. Of course, a name change isn't enough. They'll need dowries to overcome the taint of the Highlands."

"Oh, and have you a fortune put by for such an eventuality?" Alec asked.

"You're the laird now. It's you who must provide for them. Would you see them wed to crofters and peddlers to live in misery the rest of their days?"

"I'd see them happy. Titles and money don't guarantee that," Alec said. Of course he wanted to see his half sisters marry well, for love as well as fortune. He thought of Lady Sophie Ellison. What happiness could he offer her, here, when she was used to the luxuries of English estates and wealth?

"I see you're as much a fool as you've always been. You used to prattle on about clan glory, how the MacNabbs were proud and fine. But love? Are you a poet now? I'd heard you made your way in London gambling. I would have thought eight years of that would cure you of ridiculous sentiments."

"Everything is a gamble, Devorguilla. You wagered I was dead. You lost."

"Devina!" she insisted. "And I never lose."

He rose from the chair. The whisky buzzed in his veins. He didn't want to have this argument now. No, it would be a fight. He needed time to think, to decide, to find the words. "I think I'll go and find the girls, say hello."

"They're taking a short stroll in the garden with their governess," she said. "They'll be coming in for tea shortly. You can see them then. They aren't children anymore. They're young ladies."

All these years, and she still had the power to make him feel like a clumsy, inept boy, half barbarian, half fool.

"Why wait? It's a lovely day. I'll walk out and meet them," he said. He set the chalice on the table and strode out before the inevitable insults and angry words began to fly. It had always been that way between them, but to his surprise, she simply stood and watched him go.

Stepping out of the castle and into the warm summer air was like coming out of a tomb. Muira said the girls had gone into the hills. He needed time to walk and think. What would he say to them? Surely they'd changed in eight years. He followed the worn tracks in the heather that had been there for centuries, carved by cattle and people, the path he'd taken thousands of times as a boy, heading to the loch to fish, or to the top of the crags to search for eagles, or hunt.

He took off his coat, and slung it over his shoulder, and loosened his cravat. He looked around, watched the sun glint on the loch, and remembered the pleasures of swimming in the icy water at the height of summer.

He felt a hard stab of regret at the idea of selling Glenlorne away, losing it forever. If he sold the land, he might not even need to marry Sophie Ellison. He could give his sisters dowries and go to Ceylon at last. The earldom of Glenlorne was a responsibility he didn't want. He wasn't a laird, or an earl, or a leader. Nor did he wish to be.

He met no one on the path, and before he knew it, he was standing by the old tower, and could hardly say how he'd come to be here, since he'd been deep in thought and not paying attention to where he was walking.

The tower had lost yet another chunk of wall since he'd last been here. The massive block lay in the heather at the base of the tower. The roof was gone almost entirely now. He supposed it should be pulled down for safety's sake. It was like the clan itself—once proud and strong and high, and now a crumbling husk.

A movement in one of the windows caught his eye. A red flag—no, a long lock of red hair—fluttered on the breeze. He saw her face, white against the blue shadows. The wind hummed an eerie tune. A ghost? His throat tightened, and he stared up at her, transfixed. Then she reached up to brush her hair away from her face, her fingers slim and solid, her eyes fixed on the horizon. Anger flared at her trespass, both on his imagination and his tower.

How the devil did she get in? The old oak door was solid and permanently barred—at least it had been the last time he saw it—to keep out anyone foolish enough to try to venture inside.

She was some foolish local girl, no doubt, here on a Midsummer revel, or she'd climbed the rotting tower on a dare. It had once been a favorite trysting place, especially at this time of year. Did she not understand the danger she was in? Panic gripped him. What if his sisters were also in the tower?

He called out a command in Gaelic to come out before the bloody tower fell on her.

She turned to look down at him, her eyes meeting his, her hair a russet tangle around her face, and he felt a shock pass through him.

She was beautiful.

CHAPTER ELEVEN

It was cool inside the tower, and dark. A family of doves cooed among the last few rotting rafters high above, watching Caroline curiously as the she entered. Was that what she'd heard? She shaded her eyes with her hand and looked up at them. Four chicks. Beyond their nest, the roof was open to the sky. There must be other creatures living here as well. The place had a heavy odor of damp and rot, with plenty of dark corners. A massive fireplace took up the entirety of one wall, the dark maw warmed only by a few weak shafts of sunlight now. Save for the fluttering of the doves, and the jaunty whistle of the wind, the tower was silent. There were no children in peril. The thick stone walls blocked out the rest of the world, and Caroline felt oddly safe here. This place had once been a sanctuary, a home, and the echoes of that remained despite years—centuries—of disuse.

She stepped forward, and her skirts rustled over the dry leaves and fallen stones that covered the flagstone floor. Moss fringed everything in green velvet. Light streamed down through broken windows and the missing roof to pool in the center of the floor. She crossed and stood there, felt the ancient place hum around her. Caroline turned in a slow circle, delighted.

A set of crumbling stone steps led upward. At the very top, the light from a narrow window turned the mossy steps to a path of emeralds. The view must be spectacular.

She began to climb. The room dropped below her as she moved higher, and she clung to the cold stone wall and refused to look down. She could hear the cackle of pebbles as they fell from the crumbling steps to the distant floor, but she ignored them, her heart growing lighter the higher she went, the air sweeter. She reached the window at last and paused, breathless, to look out.

The view was indeed wonderful, a sweeping vista down the length of the valley, across the shining loch and up to the very door of the new castle. The valley was green and purple with heather, dotted with yellow and white wildflowers under a brilliantly blue sky. The wind was scented with an intangible perfume that she could almost taste. It made her giddy. She leaned out into the wind, felt it pluck at a loose tendril of hair from the tight knot she'd pinned at the back of her head, stroke it through cool fingers. It felt wonderful. She reached up and took out the pins, and put them in her pocket, and let her hair fly free. How easy it was to believe in magic and true love and old legends here. She was a princess in a fairy tale, and all that was needed was a handsome prince.

An angry male voice yelled something in Gaelic.

Caroline looked down to see a man staring up at her. He had no coat or cravat, and his sleeves were rolled up, revealing muscular forearms. He had his eyes shaded against the sun with one hand, and his dark hair blew in the wind, revealing a wide brow. He yelled again, his voice deep and filled with angry authority. She didn't recognize him as anyone she'd met at Glenlorne.

"I don't speak Gaelic," she called back, and waved him away, not wanting anything or anyone to interrupt this perfect moment.

His jaw dropped. "Good Lord, you're here already? I suppose the chapel is already set for the wedding too," he said in English.

Wedding? Caroline blinked at him. Was this some kind of Midsummer trick, to propose to a stranger? She hid a smile. At least he was more pleasant to look at than Mandeville or Speed. A giggle escaped.

"Come down. The tower isn't safe," he said, his tone still stern, but coaxing too. With his hand held out to her, she could almost believe he had indeed come for her, a prince who would take her away and marry her. She need only reach out, grasp his hand, and let him carry her off.

"I accept," she breathed, leaning out the window, caught in the giddiness of the moment, drunk on the perfume of flowers, the silken caress of the wind on her face. He was handsome, or at least she thought he must be. It was hard to tell from her perch so high above him. She leaned still farther out to get a better look, Juliet to his Romeo. He didn't smile and hold out his arms. His eyes widened in horror.

"Don't lean any further out the window. I'll come up and fetch you down. Don't move!" He was gone then, dashing around the tower out of her sight.

She blinked at the grassy spot where he'd been standing

and felt a moment's disappointment. Perhaps she'd imagined him after all, a fairy king who'd crossed through the veil
between the worlds while it was thin at Midsummer. How
foolish! She'd do better to go and find the girls, take them
back to the castle to dress for tea. If they were late, Countess Devina would scold Caroline, then her daughters, then
Caroline again.

She turned to hurry down, watching her feet on the
narrow steps. If he had been real, he must have gone for help,
thinking she was daft, standing in a rotting tower with her
hair wild around her shoulders.

Suddenly he was there before her, standing on the stair
below her. She gave a whoop as she nearly crashed into him,
and retreated up a few steps. He was indeed handsome—and
tall, and broad-shouldered. His white shirt glowed in the dim
light of the tower. He stared at her for a moment, his brow
furrowed.

"What the devil are you doing?"

Had she heard that voice before? Impossible. He was no
one she knew. A man like this one would be hard to forget.
She raised her chin. "I was just coming down," she said in her
best lady-of-the-manor tone.

He didn't move, or step aside to let her pass. He stood
there staring at her, his deep gray eyes intent on her face,
her hair, sweeping over her body, and pausing. She realized
she'd forgotten her skirt was still tucked up. She loosened it
with nervous fingers and let it fall, covering her ankles. She
straightened her spine, substituting a prim governess look for
the lady-of-the-manor expression, though she could feel hot
blood filling her cheeks.

He grinned at her, the change of expression sudden, transforming his face from handsome to heart-stopping. Her breath caught in her throat. He was the finest-looking man she'd ever seen. It was the kind of smile that stole a woman's breath, a lover's knowing grin. No one had ever looked at her like that—not Sinjon or William, and certainly not Speed or Mandeville. Her heart skipped a beat. Her bodice felt too tight, and it was hard to breathe.

"Are you looking for someone?" she asked, as if he, not she, was the one trespassing.

"I came looking for my sisters. I didn't expect to see you here. Not so soon, at least."

Now what did that mean? She swallowed, wondered if he were dangerous. She backed up one more step. "I'm the only one here, I'm afraid. Perhaps you'll excuse me. I must go." She waited for him to move, but he stood staring at her instead.

"If you please, I—"

Someone pushed her. She felt strong hands on her back, and suddenly she was flying through the air. She cried out and waited to land on the flagstone floor far below.

His arms came around her, caught her against his chest. She felt the sun-warmed heat of his body, the hardness of his muscles, the beat of his heart against her own. She met the surprise in his eyes, her nose was an inch from his for an instant before he turned and pressed her against the wall, keeping her safe, trying to get his own balance. He glanced over the edge, then back at her. She could see her face reflected in his eyes, caught the faint tang of whisky on his breath, and the scent of heather.

"Someone pushed me!" she gasped, and he looked at her

dubiously before stepping back. He kept one hand under her elbow. He didn't even bother to look up to see if there was someone behind her.

"The steps are dangerous. The whole tower is. It should have been pulled down a hundred years ago!" He began to descend the steps, still holding her, one hand on her elbow, one around her waist, assisting her, keeping her safe, as if she were indeed a princess—his princess. His touch turned her to jelly, and the stone wall made her cold on one side, and the heat of his body made her burn on the other.

Caroline stopped walking and looked back up the steps, but there was no one there.

He followed her gaze. "You said yourself you were alone," he said sensibly.

She *was* alone, wasn't she? Except for the handsome Scottish stranger. But he'd been below her. He couldn't have pushed her. She felt her face color again. He probably thought she'd thrown herself at him in response to his impromptu proposal of marriage. She'd probably imagined that too.

He let her go as soon as they were on solid ground, and stepped back to a proper distance. He indicated with a sweeping gesture that she should precede him out the door, back into the heat and light of the real world. She stood numbly mortified as he tugged hard on the heavy wooden door to close it. "How on earth did you manage to shift this?" he said as he picked up a heavy beam of wood, studded with iron. "This door has been barred shut for years."

Caroline frowned. Had the door been closed when she arrived? She didn't remember opening it. She watched him set the heavy oak bar in place, his muscles flexing under the linen of his shirt. She certainly would have remembered moving *that*.

She clasped her hands around her arms and felt a chill pass through her as she recalled Megan asking if she believed in ghosts. Of course she didn't. But as she stared up at the stone walls, at the empty window, it felt again as if someone was watching her. Prickles crawled over her flesh. What an odd place it was.

"I trust I don't have to warn you to stay out of the tower, lass."

Lass? Caroline swallowed. He thought her a local girl, perhaps. She supposed she did not look anything like the daughter of an English earl, or even a governess, for that matter. The wind lifted her hair, and red tendrils reached out to him. She stepped back and caught it in her hands, tidying it, reaching for the pins in her pocket.

A call made him turn. Caroline's stomach dropped to her feet. It was the girls, coming back across the hillside, their arms—and their skirts—laden with flowers. The countess would not approve. Megan's hair was unbound, bedecked with wildflowers, and her feet were bare. Sorcha was skipping hand in hand with another girl her age. Alanna was following with an armload of flowers, her cheeks flushed. Now these were lasses—happy, carefree, and sun-kissed.

She would have to hurry them back to the castle, see that they washed their faces, combed their hair. She would firmly remind them of the rules, tell them they were the daughters of an earl, and— She swallowed. Even in the silence of her own mind, she sounded like Somerson.

And here she stood, disheveled, her skirt stained with

dust and moss, looking like—well, a *lass*. With a *man*. Whatever would the countess say to *her*? She'd dismiss her at once, of course, and rightly so—and then where would she go? Back to London? No.

Her rescuer had turned away from lecturing her, and was watching the girls, his hand shading his eyes, the breeze stirring the dark hair on his forearm where his shirt was rolled up. He was disheveled too, a mossy green stain on his shoulder. She saw a slow smile bloom over his features, transforming him again.

The girls obviously knew him. She could see it in the way they dropped the flowers and ran toward him, yelling like hoydens, with the rest of the lads and lasses following them eagerly.

Propriety. She was a governess now, not a lass. In a moment they'd spot her as well. She could imagine the gossip, the speculation, the comments. The tale was sure to get back to Countess Devina. Caroline edged deeper into the shadow of the old tower, and then fled around the back of it. She scrambled down the path that led through the woods, back to Glenlorne, and sanity.

She needed to change her own gown and wash her face, and remember who she was.

Chapter Twelve

"Alec!"

He turned to watch his eldest half sister racing up the slope of the hill toward him. At least he thought they were his sisters. They were grown women now, not the girls he remembered. Was that truly Megan, the tall lass with the dark hair, and Alanna in the blue gown? Village lads trailed behind them like a pack of dogs on the hunt. Of course, it was Midsummer, and there was sunshine, flowers, and laughter. A dangerous combination, he thought protectively, and realized that he sounded as old as his grandfather, as stiff as Westlake. They'd grown up to be beauties. What lad could resist?

He opened his arm in time to catch the first girl as she hurtled into him. He enfolded her in a hug. "You smell like heather, Alanna!" he said.

"I'm Sorcha," she said, frowning only slightly, regarding him with their grandfather's gray eyes.

"Ah forgive me. Last time I saw you, you were—" He held his hand about three feet off the grass. She'd been barely five when he left, with freckles and missing front teeth and unruly red curls. She grinned at him with a full set of teeth now, but she was still freckled, he noted, happy that hadn't changed. In a few years, little Sorcha would be a beauty. His heart contracted as he thought of the years he'd missed, and would miss in future.

"You look just the same as I remember!" she said, her eyes glowing. "Mama said you were dead, but Muira knew you'd come!"

Another girl arrived. "Alanna?" he asked carefully. She'd grown up to be very pretty, her and her eyes were still as blue as the sky

"Yes!" She smiled shyly.

"And Megan," he said, smiling at the young woman who hung back slightly. She curtsied, and held out her hand.

"Hello, Laird. I'm Megan MacNabb—" She whooped when he pulled her into an embrace, swinging her in a circle before he set her on her feet again.

"You weren't so heavy the last time I did that," he teased, and watched her blush. "Is that lavender water I smell?" he asked.

Sorcha laughed, slipping her hand through his. "It's very English. Mother makes Alanna wear rose scent."

Alec ruffled her hair. "And what about you? What scent do you wear?"

She giggled. "I'm still too young."

"She's just a child, Alec." Megan said.

"I'm almost thirteen!" Sorcha protested. "When I am seventeen like Alanna, I will send to France for the finest perfume—lilies or violets, or even gardenias!"

The village lads and lasses stepped forward, welcoming

him home with shy smiles. "This is Brodie MacNabb," Megan said as the last lad stepped forward. The girls surrounding him sighed at the mention of his name.

"I'm the heir," he said. "Conor MacNabb's lad. D'you remember me?"

Alec had met the boy at his grandfather's funeral, and remembered him as sullen and hungry. He'd spent the day hiding under the table, eating. The heir. *His* heir. If he hadn't come home, this tall boy with blank blue eyes would be laird at this very minute.

"Have you been at Glenlorne long?" he asked. Conor's holding was miles away.

"Devina summoned me when the last laird died—in case you were dead too. I see you aren't."

He didn't sound happy about that, Alec noted. He also noted the way Megan looked at him. He stepped forward and put his arm around his sister. "I'm sure there's plenty of news I need to catch up on," he said, turning away from Brodie.

"What time is it?" Megan asked as a cloud passed over the sun.

Alec took out his watch. "Nearly five. Why? Is the Midsummer fire tonight?"

"Of course not—you have been away too long. It's not until tomorrow night," Alanna said.

"I'm to be the lord of Midsummer at the bonfire," Brodie said.

"Alec is home now, and he's the laird. He'll do it—won't you, Alec?" Alanna insisted.

"We're late for tea!" Megan said. "Mother will be livid!"

"Livid?" Alec asked.

"Fair vexed," Sorcha translated. "She's probably sitting in the drawing room with Miss Forrester, both of them dressed for tea, wondering where we are."

"And who is Miss Forrester? Alec asked.

"Our governess," Megan said distractedly, still gazing at Brodie.

"Did you bring us presents?" Alanna asked, linking her arm with his, grinning at him. She used to have plaits he liked to pull. Her hair was loose now, swirling in the breeze. He twined a lock of it around his finger, and felt the curls cling like vines.

"Of course I did."

"Books?" Alanna asked.

"Silk? Lace?" Megan pleaded.

"Sweets?" Sorcha demanded, and Alec laughed.

"Wait and see," he said, and offered his youngest sister his other arm. Megan walked down the hill with Brodie and a half-dozen other lasses who had the same besotted looks on their rosy faces.

It wasn't until he reached the bottom of the hill he remembered that he'd left poor Lady Sophie alone near the tower. Who else could it have been but Sophie? Englishwomen were hardly common in the Highlands. He scanned the hill around the tower—and the window, just to be sure she hadn't climbed back to her perch—but there was no sign of her.

She'd probably slipped away, gone back to the inn, or wherever she was staying with her father to wait for a proper arrival, a formal introduction. He marveled again that Bray had arrived so quickly. Sophie was a beauty, and he recalled the soft, feminine weight of her in his arms as he'd caught her in the tower. He hadn't wanted to let her go.

Perhaps marriage wouldn't be so bad after all.

Angus and Georgiana watched Alec go down the hillside. Angus wiped away a tear. "He's home at last. I'd say we're off to a good start, wouldn't you?"

"You frightened Caroline witless when you pushed her," Georgiana replied.

"'Twas all for the good. Did you see the look in Alec's eyes when he caught her?" Angus chuckled. "I know what the lad was feeling—the same thing I felt the moment I saw you."

"I remember," Georgiana said. "How could I ever forget?"

CHAPTER THIRTEEN

The countess had assigned Caroline to a room on the top floor of the tower. The room was large, with a bed, large wooden table, a shelf of books, and a window that offered a breathtaking view of the glen. It wasn't a servant's room, but it wasn't near the family's apartments either. In the safety of her quarters, Caroline splashed cool water over her flushed face, but the sun-kissed glow—and the glow of mortification at her own behavior—wouldn't come off. She bound her hair extra tight, and put on the plainest gown she could find, a soft gray muslin with a high neck she had purchased in Edinburgh before arriving here. Now she looked like a governess.

Muira followed her up. "The lasses are back. They found their brother on the hillside, and they all but carried him home." The old woman gave Caroline an almost toothless grin. "It's good to have a laird back at Glenlorne again. He'll set things right now."

Laird? Caroline felt her cheeks flame anew. There could be no mistaking whom she met in the tower, then. Her stomach shrank into her spine. She'd acted like a ninny! She'd have to face him at dinner, since teatime had long since passed. Or line up for inspection with the rest of the servants, the way Charlotte made her staff do whenever she arrived at one or another of the Somerson estates. Impropriety, or even a stain on one's uniform, might result in instant dismissal or a mild rebuke, depending on Charlotte's mood.

"*She* insists there be a formal dinner in the hall tonight to welcome His Lordship home." Muira set her hands on her hips. "His Lordship! He'll always be wee Alec to me, and I know he'd prefer a good hot supper with all the folk, and a dram or two of good whisky to toast his homecoming." She looked around the room. "This was his bedchamber when he was a lad, but he'll be in the laird's quarters now. I was actually sent to say ye'll have to sup with us in the kitchen tonight, miss. The meal is for family only. *She* would like you to help the girls dress, make sure they look like proper ladies."

"Of course." Caroline almost sighed with relief. She wouldn't have to face the new Earl of Glenlorne just yet. She gave Muira a blinding smile. "I would like that very much— dining in the kitchen, I mean."

"Aye?" Muira squinted at her. "Ye're not even curious to get a look at him? He's a braw man. He always was, o' course, but he's filled out now, all fit and fine."

Caroline felt a blush creep over her cheeks. Yes, the man was braw indeed. And strong. She could still feel his hands on her waist, his eyes on her exposed ankles.

"Ye looked flushed, lass. Did ye get too much sun today?" Muira asked.

She turned away from Muira's curious eyes. "I think I'd better go down and help the girls dress."

She took the curved stairs, so like the ones in the old tower, yet broader here. How long could she manage to avoid the new laird? Hopefully, he'd have a great many things to do over the next days, weeks, or even months, and forget her entirely if she kept to the schoolroom. Somerson barely remembered she existed at all—unless there was a problem, such as the need to marry her off so he might forget her permanently. She doubted her half brother had ever bothered himself to even wonder about his daughters' governess. She was a servant herself now, more invisible than she'd ever been before.

Alec looked around the table at the gracious young ladies surrounding him. His half sisters weren't the carefree girls they'd been on the hillside. They sat at their mother's table— his table—with their backs straight, their gloved hands clasped in their laps, and polite debutante smiles pasted on their faces. He could almost believe he was back in London, at the kind of dinner party the Countess of Westlake might give on her husband's behalf for influential people.

The conversation tonight was in English, and the girls were dressed in English finery. Only the excited glow in their eyes gave him hope that they were still the girls he remembered.

Muira substituted for Westlake's proper butler, and two clansmen assisted, lads he'd grown up with, now his servants. Jock MacNabb winked at him as he poured wine into Alec's glass, and Leith Rennie beamed from his post at the sideboard.

"Where did these come from?" Sorcha asked, holding up a crystal wineglass.

"Heirlooms," Muira replied as she served the soup, a rich chicken broth. She refrained from looking at the countess, but Alec knew her next remark was directed at Devorguilla like a poison-tipped arrow shot from a bow. "Many fine things were sold off when old Laird Angus died, but a few of the important ones were preserved."

"Like the tales grandfather used to tell about family treasures hidden after Culloden?" Alanna asked.

Muira's lips tightened. "Best not to speak of that day."

Alec watched Devorguilla's chin rise. "And I suppose these fine things will disappear again after the meal, along with the silver, and the wine?"

Muira smiled archly. "Och, they'll just be put back into safekeeping, so the silver doesn't need polishing all the time. They'll get more use now the laird is home."

"It was necessary to sell some things to feed and clothe ourselves," Devorguilla said, not quite making eye contact with Alec.

"In luxury," Muira murmured in Alec's ear as she served his soup with a flourish.

"Did you expect the girls to wear rags, go about with no shoes on their feet?" Devorguilla demanded. Alec realized that Muira was speaking Gaelic, and Devorguilla was answering in English. "They are the daughters of an earl."

"And the sisters of an earl too," Muira shot back. "He'll see them well cared for." Every eye in the room looked to him for assurance of that. Alec sipped his wine and stared into his soup.

"Oh, no doubt he will—just as his father did." Devorguilla said acidly. "The girls are my responsibility. They must be fit to wed earls and lords according to their station in life."

"How grand that sounds!" Alanna ventured bravely, fording into the rising tide of family enmity. Devorguilla silenced her middle daughter with a lift of her brows, and Alec watched Alanna subside into ladylike silence once again. The soup suddenly became the most fascinating thing in the room.

"Alec, are the tales we've heard about England true?" Sorcha asked cautiously.

"What tales are those?" he asked her.

"The one about English lords having tails they keep tucked in their breeches," Muira interrupted.

Alanna hid a giggle behind her napkin, and earned a sharp look from her mother.

Alec had often wondered if Westlake was the devil, but doubted it could be proven by such an easy method as exposing his forked tail. "Of course not."

"How would they sit down?" Sorcha asked, unperturbed.

"I hear that English gentlemen do nothing but ride roughshod over the countryside, killing babies and eating huge quantities of beef, chicken, and pork for breakfast, lunch, and supper. They drink three gallons of ale with each meal, wash it all down with a cask of brandy, and sleep until noon," Megan added.

Alec couldn't help but laugh. "'Tisn't far from the truth," he said lightly.

"And the ladies," Alanna said. "Is it true they are allowed to do nothing but sit on cushions all day, so they don't dirty their dresses or muss their hair, and spend their time doing needlework?"

"Except gossip and drink tea," Sorcha added. She imitated a lady sipping from her cup with pinkie outstretched. "I hear that gossip is the passion of English ladies. If they haven't heard anything of note, they make things up to cut each other most cruelly."

"Everyone in England has three houses—a country house, a city house, and a hunting lodge—is that correct?" Megan asked.

"That's why London is so crowded that there's no room for anything green to grow. Too many buildings and too many people," Sorcha added. "Is it true there are no flowers in London, and are the houses so tall you can't see the sky? I would be sad indeed if I could not see the sky."

Alec realized his sisters—and Muira—were awaiting his pronouncements on the stories they'd heard.

"Miss Forrester says that Englishmen are gentlemen like any other," Megan said hopefully, and in English too.

"Does she now?" Alec asked. "And what has she to say about the gentlemen's tails?"

"She says the only tails are upon their evening coats," Alanna said.

Alec nodded. "True enough."

"She says men and ladies both sleep until noon if they've been out at a ball or a party. Miss Forrester says they dance until dawn and drink champagne at the best parties. She's been teaching us English dances, though the waltz is still considered scandalous in some places," Megan said. "Still, if we are to take our place in English society as mother believes we must, we must go to London as soon as circumstances allow." She looked to Alec for reassurance that this fate would not be so terrible.

"What's wrong with Scottish lads?" Muira grumbled. "There's plenty of lords with fine, strapping sons here."

"Penniless," Alanna sighed, as if by rote.

"What about love?" Alec asked, sipping the claret. Leith instantly leaped forward to refill his glass. "What if you fall in love with a poor man?"

Megan looked at him as if he'd lost his wits. "I would never be so foolish as that!"

"Miss Forrester believes in love," Sorcha said. "At least I think she does. She likes poetry and stories."

"I certainly hope she is not teaching you any such nonsense," Devorguilla said. "She is here to instruct you about English language and manners and customs, not fill your head with foolish notions."

"What a dreadful thing to say at Midsummer!" Muira said, hovering behind Alec's chair. "'Tis the time when a young lass *should* be thinking of love, reading the omens, watching for a sign of the man she'll marry!"

The three girls looked at her with bright eyes.

"I believe we are quite finished with the soup. You may remove the plates," Devorguilla said.

"I want to marry for love." Alanna sighed, ignoring the brewing argument.

"Then you had better plan to fall in love with a rich English lord, for that is who you will wed," Devorguilla said tartly.

An ancient shield that hadn't been there that afternoon threw itself from the wall and clattered onto the floor. The girls jumped, and Alec instinctively reached for a pistol that wasn't there. This was Glenlorne, not the dark alleys of London.

Jock picked up the shield. "Sorry, Alec. I put this up

myself this afternoon. 'Tis the targe of Malcolm, if you recall.
It's been hidden away for years. Muira insisted we bring it out
now ye're home. I thought I'd done it right."

"Yet more hidden treasures," Devorguilla said sharply, her
gaze clashing with Muira's.

"I canna understand how it fell. That nail has been waiting for that shield to return for nigh on sixty years," Muira
said. "'Tis the spirits of the auld ones, come to welcome ye
home, Laird."

"Or perhaps the nail has rusted at last," Devorguilla said.
"Like the fortunes of the MacNabbs."

Muira ignored her. "There's more, Alec—all the old dirks
and claymores and banners. We'll put them up and make this
auld place look like a home again."

"How wonderful," Sorcha said, her eyes shining. "Do they
have blood on the blades?"

Megan sniffed. "I hear in England children are not allowed to dine with real people until they are at least seventeen," she said in English, and Sorcha stuck her tongue out at
her sister, which earned her a sharp glare from Devorguilla.

Jock pointed to the nail, still fixed firmly in the wall, and
swallowed. Muira cackled. "See? The spirits return at Midsummer, look in on things, express their displeasure when
things aren't right. Perhaps I've mistaken it, and the targe
goes over on that wall. Jock, try it there, will you?"

"You will not. We are in the middle of dinner," Devorguilla snapped. "I will not have superstitious nonsense spoil-
ing the meal."

"'Tis Midsummer," Muira rejoined. "The spirits will have
their way, will ye or no."

Alanna took a deep breath. "Mother, may we attend the bonfire tomorrow evening?"

Devorguilla's lips pursed so tightly Alec wondered if she'd ever get them parted again. "No." She pinched out the single word.

"But Miss Forrester says that in England young ladies are allowed to attend. In fact, earls and countesses make a point of joining their people at the celebrations," Megan said. "We could surely attend with Alec, couldn't we? I mean, it would be a good thing for everyone to see that he's home, and all is well again—"

It was indeed possible for Devorguilla's face to twist itself even tighter. She glared at Alec as if her daughter's request was his fault, and he had made the pronouncement, not the phantom Miss Forrester. He imagined the governess as a lemon-faced spinster, full of advice on subjects she knew nothing about, her yearning for romance thwarted by her lack of looks and fortune.

"I would be pleased to take the girls tomorrow night," Alec told Devorguilla. "Unless you've planned a ball or a soiree?"

Sorcha giggled. "No, but there will be dancing of course."

"All the lasses will all want to stand up with you, Alec." Muira said. "Ye'll be the Midsummer king, as is fitting now ye're home."

"I hope you brought dancing slippers!" Megan added.

"For a reel in the meadow?" Alec feigned a shudder. "Isn't it the custom to go barefoot?"

Megan gasped. "But you're the Earl of Glenlorne. You can't do that!"

"The earls of Glenlorne once painted themselves blue, as I

recall," Alec teased. "Muira, have we any blue paint?" The old lady cackled at the jest.

"Alec!" Megan cried. "You can't!"

"Never fear, lass. I shall see if the lads can play a waltz, and dance you round the bonfire for luck—properly shod, of course."

"I have not given my permission," Devorguilla said, sipping her wine. "It is a barbaric custom. I shall certainly have a word with Miss Forrester for encouraging such nonsense. We shall stay in tomorrow evening and read together—in English."

"But Mother—" Alanna began, her eyes filling with tears, but Devorguilla waved her hand for silence.

"No more arguments." Her eyes met Alec's, hard black and shiny, daring him to contradict her. He kept his mouth shut. He looked around the table. He was not part of the old ways, nor did he wish to be part of the new ways Devorguilla was suggesting. His hand tightened on the stem of the crystal glass. He shouldn't have come back at all. Then he remembered Sophie in the tower, her red hair loose, her face bright with sun, her body warm and soft and feminine in his arms, and sighed. Perhaps there was a way to make this work after all, with her as his wife. It wouldn't matter about the old ways, and together they might find a way to make their own future. He was surprised at how much he wanted that, suddenly.

Was that Sophie, or Midsummer?

"We'll see," Muira whispered over Alec's shoulder, and waved her hand in a magic sign of her own.

CHAPTER FOURTEEN

Muira waited until the household was asleep before she slipped into the stillroom and closed the door behind her. She locked it, then barred the shutters at the window as well, making certain she was alone. She lit a candle and set it on the scrubbed surface of the table that stood in the middle of the room. The bundles and bunches of herbs cast spiny shadows on the walls and floor, adding their dusty tang to the pungent scent of freshly gathered herbs.

The ghosts watched the old servant breathe deeply for a moment before she set to gathering pots and jars, bowls and measuring spoons, setting everything out on the table.

"This isn't part of your plan, is it?" Angus asked Georgiana as Muira passed right through her to get a bowl.

"Don't you believe in magic?" Georgiana asked.

"O' course not. I'm a man of reason," Angus replied, then recalled that he was a ghost, which was hardly reasonable. He folded his arms stubbornly and leaned against the door, out of the way. He watched Muira select a bundle of flowers. "What's that she's got there?"

"Periwinkle. If she chooses seven blossoms or more, then she's making a love charm."

"I count nine. Is that good?" Angus asked.

"Depends," Georgiana said. "Does she know any real magic?"

Angus rubbed his beard. "Probably. Old Muira has birthed babies, healed the sick, and tended the dying for years now. Learned from her mother. No one would cross her, for fear of a curse. You can see how canny Devorguilla is around Muira."

Georgiana smiled. "Then it's good indeed."

"What's this love charm for?" Angus demanded. "I canna see how nine purple flowers can make anyone fall in love, especially a man of sense."

Georgiana smiled. "Muira thinks she's making love charms for the girls, so they'll dream their true loves. She also thinks she's thwarting Devorguilla's plans to marry them to English lords by making them fall in love with local lads."

"Aren't they a wee bit young for such things? They should be playing with dolls, or spinning wool, or tending the sheep."

"They're young women, Angus. I was Megan's age when I was already wed to Somerson. Would you see your granddaughters married away to Englishmen?" Georgiana asked.

Angus's mouth twisted bitterly. "Nay, I would not."

Georgiana smiled. "Nor would Muira, I think, but her plans for now will have to go awry. There are those more in need of immediate help this Midsummer."

"Who?" Angus said like an owl, reading something arch in his true love's eyes.

She grinned like a sailor with a secret. "Alec and Caroline, of course."

He pushed his bonnet back on his forehead and approached the table. "Come now—Alec is a sensible lad. He'll not be fooled by such nonsense! It takes more than a few purple pansies to make a man—"

"Periwinkles," Georgiana corrected.

"It takes more than a few *periwinkles* to make a man desire a lass is what I was about to say. That's why I pushed her into his arms in the tower. Did you see the way he looked at her?"

Georgiana dismissed the idea with a wave of her hand. "He must know her as his true love."

"And yon purple flowers are supposed to bring all that about, as if he had no will, no wit of his own? Perhaps there's another braw lad meant for your Caroline, another lass meant for Alec."

"Don't be ridiculous! Of course they're meant to be together. That's how the curse will end," Georgiana said. "I thought that was clear."

"Clear as mud," Angus muttered. "What's that Muira's got now?"

Georgiana leaned over the table. "Starwort, to attract love, and chicory, to transcend obstacles. For the girls, chicory will help their mother understand their choice, but for Caroline, I think we'd best have an extra dose of that." She nudged Muira's elbow, and the pot in her hands tipped, dropping half the contents into the bowl. Muira simply shrugged, and turned for the next herb, stripping lacy white flowers from a thick stem, filling the room with a cloyingly sweet scent.

"Elderflower, to make wishes come true," Muira whispered, making a sign above the bowl, and Georgiana smiled. "Rose next," she whispered in the servant's ear, and Muira plucked the petals from a wild rose and sprinkled them over the rest of the ingredients.

Muira's ancient hand hovered over the jars on the table. "Figwort, the herb of Venus, I think." She opened the stopper and sniffed deeply. "Good and strong." She cackled.

Angus wrinkled his nose. "He doesn't have to eat this, does he? It looks vile. It's more likely to kill him than make him fall in love."

Georgiana tilted her head fondly. "The girls will wrap it with a lock of their hair in a handkerchief and make a wish. The rest will find its way into the ale to be served at the bonfire. Alec will drink it, but he'll never even notice."

Angus sighed, and the wild roses shivered in their vase. "A man never notices until it's too late. Any herbs for caution, or good sense, or warning?"

Georgiana laughed. "We were never cautious or sensible, Angus. Do you remember?"

"Was it a spell?" Angus demanded. If it was, it was on him still. Georgiana shimmered in the light of the candle, and he felt desire smoke through him. He curled his hands against the inability to touch her, felt the old familiar loss of her.

"Of course not. We never danced around a bonfire at Midsummer, or drank wine together."

"Meadowsweet," Muira murmured, and they turned to watch her.

"There you are—pure magic. Meadowsweet is for casting love spells," Georgiana added. She pointed a sheer white finger at a pair of jars on Muira's left.

Muira turned to look. "Coriander and damiana," she murmured. "Well, why not?"

"What's that for?" Angus demanded.

"Desire," Georgiana sighed.

"For lust," Muira murmured, as if she'd heard the question too. "Lust never hurt anyone. What's love without lust?"

"More of that, then," Angus said, and tipped Muira's hand himself this time. The pot overturned in the bowl, and the three stood and stared at it.

"No matter," Muira said blandly, and retrieved the pot, and left the herbs.

"It won't harm the lasses, will it?" Angus asked.

"Not if they don't drink the ale," Georgiana said.

Muira plucked a leaf from a green plant growing in a pot.

"Smells like the kitchen, that does," Angus said.

"'Tis basil," Georgiana said. "For fidelity."

"His or hers?" Angus demanded.

"For both, forever, undying devotion." Georgiana sighed.

"Undying indeed," Angus muttered bitterly, staring at his invisible hand.

They watched Muira mix the herbs. She took small pinches and made up three tiny muslin bundles, muttering a spell as she tied them closed with red thread. She added the rest of the herbs to a jug of ale, and stared into the depths of the golden liquid as she swirled it, muttering an incantation, watching the herbs absorb the wine, and sink. She set the pitcher on the shelf and turned to fetch another bowl.

"Now what?" Angus asked. He watched Muira take down a jar of poppy.

"'Tis a sleeping draught," Georgiana said.

"Och, I recall nights when I couldn't sleep for thinking

of—" He shut his mouth before admitting that once he lost Georgiana, sleep became his enemy, because his dreams were filled with her. Every time he woke without her made it worse, until he didn't want to sleep at all. He roamed the castle at night, took long cold baths in the loch, and still couldn't forget.

Georgiana obviously understood well enough. She smiled softly at him, her head tilted, and he might have blushed if he'd been able. Suddenly he wished for his grandson all the magic, the passion, the life he himself had missed out on. He rubbed a hand over the ache in his chest.

"I think the sleeping draught is for Devorguilla," Georgiana said. "So the girls can go out tomorrow night. Now all is in readiness, I think."

"Will it work?" Angus asked. "Will it bring Caroline and Alec together?"

Georgiana sighed, and the shutters rattled, making Muira look up, squinting at the shadows. "I hope it will—but Muira has no idea that the potion is for them. She made it for the girls, a love charm, and for the lads and lasses who will dance around the fire tomorrow night."

Angus shook his head. "They're all lost, aren't they? Those fine braw lads who have their freedom, and their whole life ahead of them. They'll wake up in a woman's arms after the bonfire has died and wonder what on earth happened to their good sense. Heaven help a man when women start meddling with his life."

"Love spells don't work on those who have no desire, or need. True love has its own magic and it cannot be created or destroyed where it does not belong. You can't blame love on herbs or the season, Angus."

"Oh, can't I?" he grumbled.

Georgiana's laugh made the candle flicker wildly for a moment until Muira blew it out and left the room in darkness.

CHAPTER FIFTEEN

Caroline looked out the window, across the moonlit hills to the tower. Sleep had eluded her, and she'd wrapped a thick woolen shawl around her nightgown and thrown open the shutters. Pale light from the almost-full moon filled the room. She stared across at the tower, silhouetted on the crag beyond the loch.

She could see his face, standing below her, looking up at her in the tower, calling to her, his hand held out. All she had to do was reach out and take it. She felt her cheeks heat, despite the cool evening wind. She pulled the shawl tighter.

How foolish she'd been to think that he—the Earl of Glenlorne, Laird MacNabb—had proposed to her. She smiled and picked up a comb and drew it through the length of her hair. Still, it made a lovely daydream, a moment of magic.

The comb caught a snag and she winced. Hadn't she once imagined that Sinjon Rutherford, then his brother William, would marry her? How often had she sat in the parlor, waiting for one of them to call upon her, to sink down on bended knee and profess that he would die in agony if she didn't agree to marry him at once—or at least as soon as a license and a suitable wedding gown could be obtained. She'd waited in vain. Sinjon had run away to war rather than marry her. He'd eventually wed Evelyn Renshaw, and they had a new baby daughter. William was probably on his honeymoon with Lottie now. Did he look at Lottie the way the laird had looked at her in the tower when he caught her against his breast?

A shiver rushed through her limbs.

Ridiculous. This was not the time to imagine herself in love—again—only to be disappointed yet again.

She set the brush aside and plaited her hair into a tight braid. She would probably never marry, never have a man look at her that way and mean it, or have a wedding at all, never mind babies or a wedding trip. She felt a frisson of self-pity.

She rose and crossed to the bed, throwing back the dark wool coverlet, revealing the cool white sheets beneath. If she'd been dreamy and romantic before, it was time to be sensible now.

She'd made her choice when she left London, gave up her half brother's protection. She would still rather sleep alone for the rest of her life than marry Speed or Mandeville. They had probably forgotten her by now anyway, gone searching for other rich ladies to wed. Was Somerson looking for her, or was he simply glad she'd gone?

She lit a candle, climbed into bed, and picked up a book of poetry, planning tomorrow's lesson. She was a governess, and she had a job to do. Still, the words disappeared on the page, and in their place was the face of a braw Scottish laird, his dark hair blowing in the wind, staring up at her, offering her his hand. She wondered what the man who rescued her on the street in London would say to that. He'd laugh, tell her again how foolish she was, tell her to go home and live a safe, sensible life.

Was a lifetime of dull security better than that one moment, that heady feeling of looking down from a high tower and seeing desire in a man's eyes?

She shut the book aside and blew out the candle, vowing she would not dream of Alec MacNabb.

Alec paced the vast stone cavern that was the laird's apartment. Muira had insisted he must occupy these chambers now, though he would have preferred his old room in the tower. Apparently, the girls' stodgy governess was housed there. He imagined her up there now, wearing a prim flannel nightgown, down on her bony knees, praying in English to an English God to make the world over—or at the very least Scotland—in the English image of perfection.

He didn't feel comfortable in this room. There were too many ghosts expecting too much of him, perhaps. He could imagine them hovering in the shadows, their eyes bright with hope, ready to load the heavy mantle of responsibility onto his shoulders. He looked around him at the heavy carved furnishings, at the magnificent bed that took up most of one wall under a grand canopy that reached to the ceiling. Generations of MacNabb chieftains had been born in this room, had bred heirs in their turn in this bed, and died in it. It was expected that he'd sire his own heir here, pass on the title in his turn.

He pictured Sophie there, her red hair spread across the

pillow, her hazel eyes wide, her lips half parted the way they'd been when she fell into his arms in the tower. He imagined her in his arms here, in this bed, naked, and felt a sharp pull of lust. She was exquisitely pretty, though daft if she'd climbed that old tower on her own. He turned away from the bed, crossed to stare out the window at the tower, and tried not to think of what might have happened if he hadn't been there to catch her.

But he had caught her, and when he'd looked into her eyes, he'd known she felt it too, the same nascent desire, that shock of fascination.

Perhaps marrying a stranger wouldn't be so bad after all. It might even be a chance for happiness. She had looked very happy indeed when he came upon her, surveying Glenlorne from her dangerous perch. The joy on Sophie's face had reminded him how beautiful Glenlorne was, how he'd loved it as a boy.

With her dowry, he wouldn't have to sell the land. He could rebuild it, make improvements, fix the ramshackle cottages in the village and build new ones. He could restore the Clan MacNabb to everything his grandfather told him it had once been—proud, fine, and prosperous. He imagined a different life—one where he was a Scottish laird with a pretty wife, sturdy bairns, and a fine, happy future. His dreams of a South Seas plantation suddenly seemed less important.

He scanned the dark hills, touched by the magical quality of silver moonlight, and grinned.

With Sophie's huge dowry, he could even afford to rebuild old Glenlorne Tower. He'd give it to her as a wedding present, and enjoy a lifetime of watching her look out over their lands.

Chapter Sixteen

Caroline was reading aloud the poems she had been unable to make sense of the night before. The sun streamed through the windows of the schoolroom, and lit the shining faces of the girls. They weren't out on the hillside today, but sensibly indoors, with hair bound, shoes and stockings on, and skirts that covered everyone's ankles. There was to be no more tempting fate out on the summer hillsides, the countess had decreed.

It hardly mattered where their bodies were—their minds were far beyond the walls of this room. Caroline doubted they'd heard a single word she'd said all morning. Not that she blamed them—the whole castle was abuzz with excitement about the evening's festivities. The oldest inhabitants of Glenlorne village had already been consulted as to the omens for the coming year, and their pronouncements had been all anyone could talk about. The signs were good, especially now Glenlorne had a laird again. Women had been cooking since dawn, and the men had been sent out to gather wood for the bonfire as soon as the sun rose high enough to tell a log from a loaf of bread.

Caroline stopped reading and watched the girls.

"Who did you dream of?" Sorcha asked Megan.

Megan sighed. "A man with fair hair and dark eyes. No one I know."

"Not Brodie, then," Alanna said.

Megan raised her chin. "It might have been an omen of another kind, just a stranger I'll meet, or a friend."

"Or Muira's love charms don't work. I didn't dream of anyone," Alanna admitted.

"'Tis the season, not the love charms, that count. Any girl who is ready for love will see her true love in her dreams at Midsummer!" Megan insisted. She turned to Caroline. "What did you dream of last night, Miss Forrester?"

Caroline felt her skin heat. She'd dreamed of a certain Scottish laird, though he was hardly her true love. She'd once dreamed of William, but nothing had come of that either. So much for Highland magic. Still, just in case, she crossed her fingers and counted herself fortunate that she didn't dream of Viscount Speed. "I dreamed of poetry, of course, recited in perfect English."

All three girls looked horrified. "Truly?" Sorcha asked. "You won't have much fun at the bonfire tonight. Who will you dance with?"

"Didn't your mother say you were not to attend the bonfire?" Caroline asked.

Megan smiled. "Muira promised to talk her round so we could go. What's the harm if Alec is with us? No one would dare to insult the laird's sisters."

Ah, but what might the laird's sisters get up to? Caroline noted three pairs of bright eyes, gleaming with anticipation and mischief.

"Brodie will be there too." Megan sighed. "He'll protect us."

"If he's not busy making eyes at Annie or Maire or May," Sorcha teased.

Megan ignored her. "What will you wear tonight?" she asked Alanna, and Caroline realized that the poetry had been forgotten.

"Oh miss, Alec brought us the most wonderful gifts!" Alanna said, including her in the excitement. "I have a new shawl made of Indian silk, in the most extraordinary design."

"I have a dozen hair ribbons to choose from. I don't know whether to wear the blue one to match my eyes, or the red one," Sorcha said. "Will you help me choose, miss?"

"I have a new sash, green silk, to wear with my muslin gown," Alanna said. "Though of all the presents, I loved the books he brought the best—Walter Scott's novel *Waverley*, and his *Lady of the Lake*. Tomorrow I shall stay indoors all day and read!"

"What if someone kisses you?" Sorcha teased. "A lass in a new green sash is hard to resist!"

Alanna blushed.

"What else did the laird bring?" Caroline asked, changing the subject.

"A dozen dress lengths of beautiful cloth, and pattern books from London!" Megan enthused. "Mama has them— she wanted to be the first to look at those."

"There's sugar candy and spices too. And new bonnets for all of us," Sorcha said. "Even me."

"And there were journals and the softest kid gloves too," Alanna said. "Though we shan't need gloves tonight. In fact, I'm not sure when we'll need such finery."

"We'll hold elegant parties, or get Alec to take us to Edinburgh!" Megan said.

"Or when we go to London to make our debuts," Alanna said a trifle sadly. "As soon as she finds someone to sponsor us."

Caroline saw the mixture of delight and dismay in the girls' eyes at the prospect. "The London Season doesn't start until the spring. You have plenty of time to have the most stylish gowns made, and learn all the newest London dances, make lists of the most eligible suitors, and perfect your manners to win them, but the bonfire is tonight—shouldn't we be worrying about that first?" she asked. "Now bring me your hair ribbons, Sorcha, and we'll choose the perfect one."

The girls rushed to obey, and Caroline smiled. As long as Muira could win the countess's approval, and the laird was there to chaperone his sisters, what could possibly go wrong? In Caroline's opinion, a night of innocent Midsummer revelry would be the perfect counterpoint to the stuffy London balls the girls would soon have to endure.

CHAPTER SEVENTEEN

Alec dressed as the sun rose, and called for a horse. He'd spent a restless night considering the possibility of marriage to Lady Sophie Ellison, unable to get the russet-haired beauty out of his mind. He'd considered the possibility of *not* marrying her, as well. Weighing the pros and cons hadn't been difficult—a lovely wife with a vast fortune on one hand, poverty for himself, his kin, and his clan on the other.

If Sophie was at the tower, she must be staying nearby, probably also weighing the pros and cons of the match herself. It was nearly dawn when it struck him that was quite likely the reason she was in the tower alone in the first place—she was visiting Glenlorne, deciding if she wished to marry him. If she was a biddable daughter, she'd do as her father wanted and wed where she was told to. If she was more willful—and from their brief encounter at the tower he suspected she was at least a wee bit headstrong—she might very well reject his suit in hopes of a better offer, which was sure to come.

If he wanted Sophie as his wife, he had to act now. He would have to ride up to whichever inn Lord Bray was staying at, and greet her formally, escort her to his home in person, and charm her.

He looked in the glass as he tied his cravat, and practiced his most beguiling grin, the one that never failed to make women of all ages lose their wits and leave the thinking to him.

The lovely Lady Sophie was as good as his.

Hours later, Alec was still alone. He'd visited the three inns closest to Glenlorne Castle, and five of the more distant ones. There was no sign of an English earl, or a lovely red-haired lady.

The innkeepers were delighted to have the opportunity to welcome him home and stand him a dram or a tankard of their best ale. It was impossible to refuse a single drop. Every man, woman, and child he met gazed at him with such hope in their eyes, such pride. No one other than his grandfather had ever looked at him that way before. It was damned uncomfortable to be seen as the savior of Clan MacNabb everywhere he went. It also made him all the more determined to continue on until he found Sophie, but by noon he was so drunk he was barely able to keep from falling off his horse, and that only after much difficulty getting back on the beast in the first place. In the end he returned to Glenlorne foxed and frustrated, hoping the horse could see the road more clearly than he could.

By early afternoon, he found himself sitting on the horse and staring blearily up at the tower window where he'd seen her only yesterday, and wondered where the devil she'd disappeared to. He missed her. He whispered her name and swayed in the saddle, and the horse flattened its ears and snorted an insult.

Alec reminded himself that there were a number of estates and castles within a day's ride of Glenlorne. It could well be that she was the guest of another laird, perhaps even an unmarried one. His hands tensed on the reins and the horse sidestepped nervously, and took a step away from the old tower, and a patch of appealing wildflowers.

Alec was about to correct the horse—a rather opinionated gelding kept in the stables for the girls to ride, and which he vowed would be replaced with a much finer and less stubborn stallion, if he could just find and marry Lady Sophie—when he changed his mind. Was that a lock of red hair beckoning him from the tower window, or just a vine glinting in the sun? Would the minx play games with him, expecting him to return to the place he'd met her only yesterday? He grinned, actually found himself giggling, and the horse sent him a look of pure equine disdain. He ignored the beast. Perhaps she liked lovers' games, and wanted to be wooed.

Well, woo her he most certainly would. Wonderfully. Wittily. Wantonly. He grinned again, then laughed out loud. He set his heels to the gelding, who insisted on remaining firmly where it was. When he finally forced the beast to obey, what he had seen turned out to be just a red-leafed vine growing in the empty eye of the window, twisting in the wind, scratching against the stones in the wind, laughing at him.

The door was barred, just as he'd left it yesterday, and there was no sign of a fetching, flame-haired lass. He muttered a curse, and the horse looked at him over its shoulder, as if it had known all along, and felt the same way about Alec as Alec felt about him.

"Good day to ye, Laird," said a voice, and he turned to find a dozen men standing behind him. He hadn't even noticed them there.

"Have ye come to help us make ready for tonight?" Leith Rennie asked.

Alec surveyed them from the back of the horse. Were there a dozen men, or only six? "Actually, I'm looking for a lass."

They grinned and relaxed, elbowing one another, then laughed out loud. Leith produced a skin of ale and passed it to Alec. "Aren't we all?" he said.

"There'll be plenty of bonnie lasses at the bonfire tonight," Jock MacNabb added.

"We're just getting things ready for the festivities—the wheel, the firewood, and such. We're the council, ye see—the ones drafted to do the work," Hamish MacNair added. They all nodded.

Alec nodded back and glanced up at the empty tower again. Perhaps, his drink-addled brain told him, she might she still come if he waited, stayed near to the tower. He looked at the council again. "Could you use more help?"

"Er—you look rather fine for gathering firewood, Laird."

Alec slid off the gelding's back. He took off his coat and tossed it over the saddle. He untied his cravat and tucked that under the coat, and stripped off his waistcoat, for good measure. The horse caught the brocade waistcoat and began to chew on it.

"Whoa now, Blossom," Jock said, catching the creature's

reins, fighting to retrieve the vest from the horse's stubborn jaws.

"Blossom?" Alec muttered. "I'm out wooing—riding—on a male horse named Blossom?" The other men had the grace to look embarrassed for him.

"Wee Sorcha named him," Leith said. Jock let the horse go, and held up the tattered waistcoat. Blossom tossed his head and ambled over to a particularly lush patch of wild-flowers and proceeded to devour them.

"Shouldn't we tie him up?" Alec asked, as the horse moved on to another, more distant patch of flowers.

"Blossom?" Hamish asked. "Nay. Once he's eaten, he'll head home on his own—if that's quite acceptable, Laird."

"Unless he finds the cattle," Leith said. "He's sweet on one particular heifer, and since it's Midsummer—"

Jock rolled his eyes. "He's a *gelding*, you bampot!"

Leith looked hurt. "I didn't mean anything by it. Love comes in many shapes. We're all looking for a lass."

Jock took off his cap and swatted his cousin. "Come on, bampot—we've got wood to fetch, and we'd best get to it as soon as we finish the ale." He passed the skin to Alec. "After you, of course, Laird."

Alec took a long swallow and led the way down the slope toward the woods, then stopped. The men behind him stopped as well, some crashing into one another. Leith, who was at the front of the procession, slid all the way down the grassy hill with a cry. Everyone stood and watched him go. It seemed they were as drunk as Alec was. "I just wish to say I've known all of you since we were lads. Just call me Alec."

CHAPTER EIGHTEEN

"Are you certain the countess won't mind if the girls go to the bonfire?" Caroline asked Muira as the sun set, standing in the kitchen, helping to pack baskets of food and flasks of ale.

"She didna say a word against it when I asked her not half an hour ago," Muira said archly, her eyes wide.

"Perhaps I should check with her," Caroline said, but the old servant cackled. "There's no need—Her Ladyship has taken herself off early to bed, asked not to be disturbed. She has a headache from spending all day starin' at those dress books Alec brought from London. I daresay she won't wake until morning, or possibly even early afternoon. Now don't you worry about her another minute—you'll be wanting to get ready yourself, and there's not much time. The lasses have been watching the sun go down, and as soon as it drops behind old Glenlorne Tower, they'll be off."

Caroline glanced out the window. The red sun hovered just above the ragged roofline of the old tower. She glanced in the mirror and tidied her hair, made sure the top button of her gown was primly fastened under her chin. "There," she said, turning to Muira.

The old servant rolled her eyes. "For the goddess's sake, lass, ye canna mean—"

The door burst open, and the girls entered. They wore plain linen gowns, tucked into tartan sashes at their waists. Their feet were bare, and their hair hung long and loose down their backs. They stopped in the doorway and stared at Caroline.

"Miss Forrester!" Megan squeaked in shocked surprise, as if it were Caroline who was standing with her hair loose and her feet bare for the world to see.

"You can't go out looking like that!" Alanna said.

"We've got to do something, and quickly—look!" Sorcha said. Caroline barely had time to look out the window at the sun, see the sun had dipped lower still, before the girls descended upon her. Sorcha pulled the pins from her hair, and Alanna unbuttoned her prim gown, while Megan went to fetch another gown, a simple shift in Highland style.

"Wait! I'll do it myself!" Caroline said, as they approached, ready to undress her. She ducked into the pantry. The girls examined her when she came out, circling her with their arms folded over their chests. Muira perched on a stool by the fireplace, grinning like a fey crow.

"Well?" she asked.

"'Twon't do," Sorcha said.

"Stockings." Alanna pointed.

They wanted her to go out barefooted? "A lady never—" she began, but the girls took a menacing step toward her. "I'll do it," she said, holding up a hand.

"There are no ladies tonight, lass," Muira said. "Just lads and lasses and the pleasures of dancing and laughter, and no harm ever came o' that." She came forward and tucked a small white flower into Caroline's hair, above her ear. "There now—that looks right."

"She has no plaid sash."

"She can have my red ribbon," Sorcha said, and it was duly tied around Caroline's waist.

"Oh, miss, you look bonnie," Alanna said.

"She does indeed. Now off with you. The sun's going, and I've more to do before I come along myself," Muira said, shooing them out of the kitchen.

Megan and Sorcha grabbed her hands, and Caroline found herself caught in the spirit of the excitement, running with her charges over the cool grass in her bare feet with the soft evening breeze in her hair. They joined the villagers and the castle servants, until there was a long, merry procession of girls heading up the well-worn path to the old tower.

Sorcha stopped, her eyes wide. "Oh look—Alec is wearing his plaid—how wonderful he looks."

Wonderful indeed. Caroline caught sight of the laird among the other men and stopped, her breath catching in her throat. The last rays of the setting sun were upon him, and his brow shone and his saffron shirt glowed, the laces open at the neck showing the tanned skin beneath. He wore the plaid like an ancient warrior, bold and proud, grinning like a pirate. He greeted everyone as they came up the path, truly the lord of this place. He was the handsomest man she'd ever set eyes on.

Breathe, a voice whispered in her ear. *Breathe*.

The air was intoxicating, and she felt pure joy run through

her blood. Above her the moon floated in a deep blue sky, and the stars began to appear, one by one.

Fire flared on the hillside near the tower as the wheel was lit, a symbol the change of the season, the dark half of the year beginning tonight, and the light half giving way. With a whoop, lads rolled the wheel down the slope, racing after it, tumbling in the dewy grass, laughing and cheering. Caroline found herself cheering as well. If the wheel reached the bottom of the hill without going out, it meant a good harvest, and good fortune for Glenlorne.

A cry went up as the wheel began to skip and wobble over the rocky ground, shooting sparks as it flew, red and gold against the blue of twilight, but it reached the bottom of the hill before it toppled in the long grass of the meadow, still ablaze.

A cheer went up and everyone rushed forward to add fuel to the wheel, turning it into a bonfire that would burn for the rest of the night. From across the fire, Caroline watched Alec MacNabb toss a log onto the pile, and the flames leaped, lighting his eyes, his face, the muscles in his neck, and the strong length of his legs. Everyone in turn added fuel, and stepped back to admire the blaze.

Someone in a hood—Muira perhaps—came forward to place a crown of holly leaves on Alec's head, and the crowd cheered again. She handed him a cup carved of horn, decorated with silver, and he drank deeply, the firelight caressing his throat as he swallowed. He raised the cup high, and wiped his mouth with the back of his hand, laughing as his clansmen cheered.

Then Muira placed a second crown in his hands, this one

decked with ivy and wildflowers. "The king is crowned," she announced to the crowd. "Now he must choose the Midsummer queen."

A hopeful female whisper went up. Caroline watched as Alec's fire-bright eyes scanned the crowds, and the lasses giggled and simpered to get his attention. She stayed where she was in the shadows, hoping his gaze would touch her and stop, yet dreading it as well.

His eyes passed over her, moved on, and she felt a shrivel of disappointment. Then he turned, and his eyes locked with hers. She felt a bolt of lightning hit her, saw the recognition in his eyes, the slow curve of his smile, the intent in his gaze, and for a moment her heart stopped. She couldn't look away.

Without taking his eyes from hers, he lifted the crown of flowers high above his head, and petals showered over his dark hair.

"Jump the fire," Muira commanded.

In one athletic motion, Alec leaped through the flames, coming through the sparks and smoke to land by Caroline's side. He gave her an exaggerated bow, his eyes on hers. He held out the crown, and set it on her head. The scent of wild roses filled her. Muira handed him the cup, and he held it to Caroline's lips. The warmth of the sweetened ale flowed down her throat and through her limbs, instantly intoxicating, taking her breath away, lifting her from the ground to float above it. Or was it the laird, his hands on hers, holding the cup, his fingers warm and sure?

"Now we must leap back," he said, and took her hand. "Are you ready?"

Caroline stared into the blaze before her. It was as high

as her hips, the flames licking their lips hungrily. Still, she nodded, and he put his arm around her waist, and together ran forward and flew over the fire, bathed in smoke and sparks, blessing the land for another season. She felt as if she'd been flying forever when she finally landed on the cool grass on the other side of the blaze, breathless. He didn't let her go, but kept his arm around her, and she pressed close to his side, feeling safe and warm there.

Other couples clasped hands and jumped the fire. Lads herded the cattle through the billowing smoke to bless them. The music began to play, drums, flutes, and pipes, and the dancing began, and ale flowed. Lads and lasses paired off, slipping in and out of the shadows, stealing kisses and more. Children chased each other with burning sticks.

Alec MacNabb took her into his arms and began to dance, spinning her from firelight to shadow and back again, until all she could see was the glitter of his eyes, all she could feel was the beat of the drums in her veins, her heartbeat beating in time with his.

Other couples joined the dance, moving faster and faster until they became a blur, and Caroline and Alec were the only people in the world. She threw her head back and laughed as he lifted her off her feet, and spun her in a dizzy circle, then let her body slide down the length of his, until their lips were inches apart. She was breathless, intoxicated by Alec as much as by the ale. He kissed her, and she tasted the sweetness of the brew all over again.

"You taste of honey and flowers, my lady."

"Me? I thought it was you, my lord," she quipped, batting her lashes, flirting with him, moving in close to press against him as the dance went on, then pulling away, until she was half mad with desire for more ale, another kiss. He kept hold of her hand, drew her back to his side when the steps of the dance took her too far from him, laughed down at her.

His eyes were shiny in the firelight, lit from within. She saw desire there, and felt it flow through her limbs as well. He pulled her close against his body and kissed her again, his tongue lapping at the seam of her lips, demanding entry. She opened, tasted the honey on his tongue, the bitterness of the herbs and the ale, and him. She put her arms around his neck and pressed closer, wanting to do nothing but kiss him. The heat of his mouth gave way to the cool of the evening, as he stepped back. He clasped her hand in his and grinned down at her, his teeth white in the firelight.

Alec couldn't take his eyes off the woman in his arms. Her red hair burned as bright as the flames. Her lips were soft from his kisses, her eyes golden-green. Could he truly be so fortunate to have this woman for his bride? He'd marry her tomorrow—this very moment—if he could. The drumbeats filled him, or perhaps it was more than that.

She smiled up at him, bit her lip as she stumbled against him in the dance, the length of her body against his for a moment. She felt right in his arms, familiar, perfect. He'd felt the same surge of desire in the tower when she fell. Arousal stirred, hard, and powerful. She lifted her arms above her head as she danced, her body lithe and sleek. His eyes roved over the firelit silhouette of her breast under the muslin of her gown. Her white feet trod the steps perfectly as she moved away, then came back to him in the rhythm of the dance. He couldn't wait to take her in his arms again, to spin her, to hold her close, to smell the sweet fragrance of her hair under the crown of flowers. He was suddenly glad to be Laird of Glenlorne. Surely there was nothing he couldn't do with this woman by his side, his Midsummer queen, his countess, his wife.

He pulled her close and kissed her again, and she wrapped her arms around his neck, and kissed him back, her tongue tangling with his, her hands in his hair.

"Come with me," he said, grabbing her hand, pulling her up the slope toward the tower.

He let go of her just long enough to lift the bar from the door, and drop it in the grass. He tugged her into the velvet darkness, and the wind blew the door shut behind them, leaving them in deep darkness; the sound of the revelry was distant now, the drums still beating in his ears, his veins, filling him with excitement and need. The roof was open to the stars, and the light of the moon made a soft pool in the center of the room, and he drew her into it, tipped her face up, stared down at her.

Caroline stared up at the moon, breathless, and stepped into the circle of the light. He took her in his arms, held her, looked down at her face, stroked her hair. "You're beautiful," he whispered. She stood on her toes and cupped his face in her hands, her fingers moving over the rough stubble of his beard as she kissed him again. He moaned softly and pulled her closer still, pressing her against the length of his body, breast to chest, belly to belly, thigh to thigh. She opened to his kiss, sparring with his tongue as if she'd done this a thousand times. Could he tell she hadn't? She should stop, but she didn't want to. She was the queen of Midsummer, and he was her king, at least for tonight.

She tilted her head so he could kiss her neck. It felt so good. How was it possible to live as long as she had and never know that such a sensation existed? She could feel his arousal, knew what it meant. He desired her. He groaned as she pressed closer still, shifted her hips, moving against him. She tangled her hands in the rough linen of his shirt, holding him to her, needing more than kisses, yet she couldn't imagine anything more delicious than his kiss. She could not have stopped kissing him if she wanted to. She was bewitched.

He trailed his mouth down her throat while he opened the ties of her gown ahead of his questing tongue and teeth. She slid her hands inside his shirt, felt the heat of his skin under her hands. He pushed her gown off her shoulders, baring her breasts, and drew her nipple into his hungry mouth. The sensation drove the last clear thoughts from her mind. She wanted this, wanted him, and he wanted her. She writhed against him, pleading for more. She pushed back his shirt and the plaid that covered his chest the way he'd done with her gown, baring his shoulders and chest in the moonlight. Hard muscles gleamed in the soft glow, turning him golden and glorious, a mythical Midsummer king indeed. It must be magic. She ran her fingertips over him, exploring the silk of his skin, the fascinating flex of his muscles beneath. His body was marvelous, male perfection. The scent of his skin poured over her, intoxicating her far beyond anything the ale had done.

She pressed her mouth to his chest, kissed him, tasted him, and he groaned. She felt his heart pounding under her lips, felt the breath singing through his body in time to the beat of the drums beyond the walls as his muscles tensed with pleasure at what she was doing to him. Power sang through her own veins. She found his nipple and bit gently, then sucked the hard pebble, and he gasped for breath, his hands tangling in her hair.

"Wait," he murmured. He pulled his shirt over his head, unbuckled his belt, and let the folds of his plaid drop. She drew a breath at the sight of his naked body. He spread the plaid over the ground, a makeshift blanket, a bed padded by the soft moss beneath. He used his shirt to make a pillow. He knelt. "Come here," he said, holding out a hand to her. This time, it wasn't hard to decide what she wanted. She put her hand in his and knelt before him. He tugged her gown over her head, tossed it aside. She held her breath as went still, he looked at her in the moonlight. What was he thinking? No man had ever seen her this way before. Was she beautiful?

"Oh, lass," he murmured, and ran the back of his hand over her cheek, her shoulder, her breasts. "I trust we should go slow," he said. "Or stop. The choice is yours." His voice was thick with desire.

She put her arms around his shoulders, tangled her fingers in his hair, and brought her mouth to his. He groaned and pulled her down onto the soft bed of his plaid. He groaned and tumbled into her embrace, covering her body with his. She reveled at the sensation of hard muscle and hairy legs against her skin, the sound of the murmured endearments he whispered in her ear in Gaelic. He suckled her breast as his hand explored the curves of her body, finding places she hadn't even known existed before he touched them. He set her on fire everywhere his fingers brushed, until she arched upward, restless, desperate.

"Please," she said softly.

"Wait," he whispered against her mouth, and she whimpered as he returned to suckling her nipple, slowly, sweetly. She gripped his shoulders, dug her nails into the hard flesh, begging wordlessly for much more, but he took his time. He blew cool air on her heated flesh, then took the sensitive bud back into his mouth again. She writhed as his palm descended over her belly and hips, moving with infuriating slowness to caress the curls between her thighs. She bucked against his palm, wanting more, wanting—well, whatever it was that made the poets sing, and the ladies swoon. It was within his power to grant it, but he held back. He brought his mouth back to hers and she opened to him, biting and sucking at his tongue and lips, hearing his breath turn into grunts of suppressed desire. His erection pressed into her hip, and she reached down to touch it. She closed her hand on it and he gasped, cried out in Gaelic. His hand still hovered over the delicate lips of her sex, and then his fingers dipped between, found the place she needed him most. She cried out in English, and he began to circle the wild, wet bud with his fingertip, taking her beyond madness to a place of such exquisite pleasure she feared she would die of it. Her hand fluttered over his, half afraid of what was to come, half afraid he'd stop.

The sensation burst over her, like a bonfire roaring to life, shooting flames and sparks, all-consuming, holy. She clung to him, saw the stars above the tower, feeling them descend upon her one by one to sing through her blood, lifting her.

He kissed her, murmured endearments as he shifted, and she felt the blunt tip of him where his fingers had been. She took a deep breath and arched back, her teeth gritted as he drove into her, stifling a cry at the sharp pain. She dug her nails into his shoulder as he waited for her to adjust to him, to being filled for the first time, kissing her neck, stroking her face.

Slowly, he began to move, filled her, withdrew, and filled her again. The pain ebbed and the pleasure returned, and she watched the muscles in his neck cord and tighten, hooked her ankles around his hips, telling him what she wanted. She was breathless with need, and he moved faster, thrust harder, and she clung to his shoulders, wanting this to go on forever. She cried out as the sensation poured over her again, lifting her hips to draw him deeper, and he cried out, tensed against her, buried within her, and she felt him shudder before he collapsed against her, his heart pounding against hers. She folded her arms around him, held him to her.

So this was how it felt to be loved by a man. She hadn't known. She marveled at the joy she felt. It was magic indeed. His heart beat against hers, his breathing slowed to match hers, and he kissed her face, stroked her hair, and murmured to her in Gaelic. Was he professing his love? It didn't matter. He moved off her, and she felt the chill of the night wind against the places he'd warmed. He pulled her against his side, and wrapped them both in his plaid.

Caroline blinked up at the moon, and fell asleep in the warm sanctuary of her lover's arms.

Skylarks held their own raucous celebration as the first fingers of dawn reached over the horizon. They swooped and dove above the tower, wild with joy. Caroline snuggled deeper into the soft bedcovers, unwilling to wake just yet. She'd had the most wonderful dream, all about— The soft exhale of breath beside her made her open her eyes wide. She turned to look at the sleeping profile of Alec MacNabb, lying beside her, sharing the soft blanket.

It hadn't been a dream. Panic gripped her. She looked beneath the covers, and realized she was indeed naked. Another peek told her he was likewise unclothed. She dropped the covers, feeling hot blood filling not just her cheeks but her whole body. It wasn't a dream. She had jumped the fire by his side, danced with him, kissed him, and— She stifled a gasp. She wondered where her clothes were, and saw the linen gown reclining over a chunk of masonry, half covering the carving of a smirking face. The wilted crown of flowers sat askew over carved eyes, a laughing mouth, mocking her. She glanced at Alec again. His face was soft and boyish in his sleep. Long lashes lay against his stubbled cheeks; his mouth was soft, sweet.

Her heart flipped in her chest. He was magnificent. She recalled the pleasure he'd given her quite clearly, the kisses, the caresses . . . It had been the most incredible, unforgettable night of her life.

It had also been the most foolish thing she'd ever done. She was governess to Alec's sisters, a servant in his household. Her cheeks burned at the thought.

The girls. She sat up with a gasp. If she'd ended up here in the tower in a compromising position, where on earth were they? She slipped carefully out from under the warm plaid and scooted around his sleeping figure to snatch up her gown. It was cold as she pulled it over her head and belted it with

Sorcha's ribbon. The dress was wrinkled and stained with telltale green marks of moss, the black of soot, but it couldn't be helped. She glanced up at the sky, pink with promise, and sent up a prayer that it was still early enough that she could make it back to the castle unseen. She cast one last look at him as he lay asleep, as beautiful as an angel, and hurried out into the predawn darkness.

"**D**on't you think we should wake him, send him after her?" Angus asked as Caroline fled down the hillside, her hair trailing behind her in wild, love-tangled curls. He'd loved to coil Georgiana's curls around his finger as she lay in his arms after they'd made love.

Georgiana shook her head. "No, she'll need time to think, to realize . . ."

"What?" Angus prompted when she didn't finish. He grinned. "Let me guess. She'll need time to realize that it was the best night o' her life."

Georgiana rolled her eyes. "She'll need time to realize that she loves him, despite what happened here this night."

"Despite it?" Angus cried. "Because of it, more like."

Georgiana set her hands on her hips and glared at him. "A little rough wooing and you think she can't live without him, that no other man—any other man—could do what he did? How arrogant you are! She was a virgin, and he seduced her in a crumbling tower, on the hard ground."

Angus pushed his cap back on his head, staring at the telltale glitter in her eyes. She floated before him, but her eyes were on Caroline. He felt an almost overwhelming wave of sadness. "I thought this was what you intended to happen between them. It was the same for us, was it not? You were a virgin the night when we—" He stopped to clear his throat. "Are ye saying that ye regret what we did?"

She fixed her eyes on him. "Of course not. I regret that it was the one and only time, and that nothing ever lived up to that moment again. Oh Angus, have we made a mistake? What if we've only caused them more unhappiness, sentenced them to a lifetime of regret and pain?"

He came closer, raised his hand to her cheek, felt nothing but frustration that he could not touch her, even to offer comfort. "Is there a battle tomorrow I don't know of? He's got no brothers to drag him away from the lass, and she's no father to drag her back to England. They're here, together. They aren't going anywhere. Why, later this morning, he'll wake up and return to the castle. He'll seek her out, and drop to one knee and—"

Georgiana whooped as Alec ran right through his grandfather's shade, his plaid belted askew as he tried to pull on his shirt and run down the hill at the same time. They stared after him as he leaped over the last embers of the dying Midsummer fire, dodging the folk still sleeping peacefully in the dew-soaked grass, before pausing, returning to look into their sleeping faces.

"There now, you see?" Angus said smugly, straightening his plaid. "He's looking for her now."

"Sophie?" They turned at the sound of Alec's whisper. "Are you here?"

"Sophie?" Georgiana repeated, her horrified whisper rustling the trees, startling a bird into panicked flight. "He still thinks Caroline is someone named *Sophie*? Even after—"

Angus felt a hard knot of trepidation in his gut. He watched his grandson search among the sleeping lasses for the woman he'd just spent the night with, a woman whose name he didn't even know.

"They couldna introduce themselves?" Angus asked. "Just a potion, ye said, woman. That's all it would take and everything would unfold as it should, and the curse would end."

"It must have been too strong, too much meadowsweet, perhaps," Georgiana fretted.

"It was *only* the potion, don't you see? She isn't the right woman, or he isn't the right man!" Angus said angrily. "It didn't work."

Georgiana's eyes widened. "How can you say that? You saw how they were dancing, the passion in their eyes—"

"'Twas the ale and the firelight, nothing more," Angus grumbled. "He's obviously in love with someone else, someone named Sophie."

Georgiana shook her head, wringing her hands. "No, it's not possible! If he loves this Sophie, then why is he here, dallying with Caroline?"

Angus gave her a level look. "He's a man, *gràdhach*, and she's a lovely lass."

"Oh, what have we done?" Georgiana cried. "I must go to Caroline, though heaven knows what I can do to help her now. Nothing, nothing at all."

Angus watched her fade away against the dawn, and stared at Alec, who was staring up at the tower as if he were daft and bewitched both. Angus recalled exactly that feeling. He'd stood in the same spot on a Midsummer morning long ago, unable to think of anything or anyone but Georgiana, and the sweetness of the night in her arms. Even when his brothers had climbed the hill to take him, he'd stood there, unable to move for pure love, for joy. He'd opened his mouth as they reached him, ready to declare his love for Georgiana, but Niall had drawn back his fist and punched the grin off his face. The next thing he knew he was waking up on a ship, sick as a dog. He'd certainly felt daft and bewildered then too, and for an entirely different reason.

Angus watched as Alec turned to look down at the road. There was a grand coach trundling along the rutted track, followed by several carts, all heavily laden. He frowned at the grand gold crest on the side of the coach, at the six matched white horses that drew the vehicle toward Glenlorne. Angus drifted closer to his grandson's side. "Now who's this coming?" he asked, though he knew Alec could not hear him.

"Sophie," Alec murmured, and took off running down the hillside.

CHAPTER NINETEEN

Caroline slipped through the kitchen door and took the stairs two at a time, heading for the girls' shared bedchamber first of all, dreading what she might find—or not find—there. She almost sagged to the floor in relief when she saw three heads on three pillows, all fast asleep, with nothing more dangerous than a few wilted wildflowers littering the floor. She drew the blanket up around Sorcha's chin, and went to her own room.

She shut the door and leaned on it for a moment. No one had seen her. Relief flooded her, and she crossed to scrub her face in cold water, though it did nothing to cool the burn of her cheeks. She stared into the mirror, regarding her face in the first rays of the sun. Did she look different?

Of course she did. Her hair was a wild tangle, and her lips were pink and swollen from his kisses. The mere thought of his mouth on hers made her knees weaken with desire for more. She watched hot blood fill her face from chin to hairline, and her eyes—oh, how would she ever hide the look in her eyes? They glowed, shone, and there was a soft, bemused look that hadn't been there before. Was it love, or just the satisfaction of a woman who had been well pleasured by a skilled lover? She knew little about such things—well, before last night. She'd heard servants gossiping in hushed tones, of course, their own eyes bright, their cheeks as flushed as hers were now. She held on to the edge of the table, her knees suddenly wobbly, her body sore and sated. She wanted nothing more than to sink into the comfort of her bed and sleep, and dream of Alec MacNabb and what had occurred between them in the tower.

But the sun was coming up and she had duties to attend to. She washed her face again, vainly trying to scrub away the evidence. She chose the primmest gown she could find, dull blue and high-necked. She twisted her hair into a skin-pulling knot until not a curl remained, and fastened it with an army of pins.

Still, when she looked into the mirror, her cheeks were flushed, her mouth still lush. Yes, she understood what the servants had been gossiping about now. She turned away from the mirror. She would simply act as if nothing at all had happened. She'd keep her eyes downcast, and her lips primly pursed. Surely no one would dare to ask questions, to ask where she'd disappeared to last night. If they did, she'd simply tell them—

She reached the door with her chin high and stopped, her hand on the latch. Tell them what? There were no words to explain. And whatever would she say to Alec MacNabb when—if—she saw him? Oh lud!

She stepped back and stared at the latch. She'd say that it had been a mistake—no, not a mistake—an impulse. Not that she was the impulsive sort. Usually. Saying it was the spirit of the evening might sound better—the dancing, the smoke from the fire. It had all made her—well, "giddy" might be one word she could use. She would make it clear that she did make a habit of doing such things, and her behavior of last night would not be repeated. Ever. She put her hand on the latch again. "There, that should explain things."

She drew back again. Oh, but if he smiled at her the way he had looked at her across the fire, or kissed her, she would be lost all over again. She raised shaking fingers to her hot cheek. Perhaps it would be better to find a way to avoid him altogether—at least until he forgot. How long did it take a man to forget a casual conquest in a dark tower? It was certainly something *she'd* never forget, even if she lived to be as old as the tower itself. She took a deep breath and opened the door.

She came out of the tower and nearly collided with a maid coming along the main hall with tea and toast for Devina. The girl simply nodded back and went on her way without saying a word about flushed cheeks or knowing eyes. Caroline let out the breath she was holding. She had passed the first hurdle. She headed for the stairs with a smile.

Chapter Twenty

Alec barely made it back to the castle in time to change his clothes, comb his hair, and wipe the scent of his lover from his skin. She had obviously slipped away when he'd fallen asleep and had gone back to wherever she and her father were lodging, and was now about to make a formal arrival at Glenlorne.

He grinned as he tied his cravat, forgoing Highland dress for English finery. Surely the fact that it was barely past dawn and she was arriving with carts filled with trunks and boxes meant that she had enjoyed last night as much as he had, was eager to marry him and repeat the pleasure, this time in his bed as his wife.

He looked at the grand MacNabb bed, and pictured her there. Beautiful, magnificent, luscious Sophie. He hoped he hadn't been too rough, too overwhelming for her. If her moans of desire and sighs of pleasure were anything to go by, she'd been well satisfied. As was he. He hadn't slept so deeply or so well in a very long time as he had with her in his arms, sated and happy, his mind at peace. He'd been disappointed when he woke alone. She had the damnedest way of disappearing. He'd wondered if she'd been real, but the taste of her in his fingers, the sight of her Midsummer crown was proof enough.

It didn't matter. She was here now. He straightened his cravat, and smoothed a hand over his hair, and left his room.

He paused at the top of the stairs. How should he greet her? He could hardly sweep her into his arms in front of her father and kiss her the way he had last night. Nor could he do what he really wanted and carry her up to his chamber for the rest of the day, though he was aroused just thinking about it.

He straightened his cuffs and headed down the stairs slowly with the proper dignity of an earl. He would play it however she liked. He would pretend they were total strangers if she wished, bow over her hand and call her my lady, even stand by patiently while proper introductions were made. He would offer his arm, and ask her politely how the journey from London was, and if it had tired her. He grinned. She must be tired indeed this morning.

"Alec, the grandest coach just arrived. Who's here?" Sorcha demanded, racing down the hall.

Megan followed her sister. "There's a crest on the side of the carriage!"

"It's the grandest thing I've ever seen—six horses, all perfectly matched. Is it the Prince Regent, perhaps?" Alanna paused briefly as she reached Alec, her eyes shining. "Is this part of our presents?"

Alec felt pride swell his in his breast. "Yes. In fact it's the best present of all," he said.

She was already alighting from the coach when he reached the front steps, her head down, her hand on the sleeve of a footman wearing Bray livery. He couldn't see her face beneath her bonnet. It was more confection than hat, covered with a froth of fluffy feathers, blue and pink and green, with a stuffed yellow bird perched on one side. The poor stuffed fledgling stared up at Alec with bug-eyed surprise. Her dress was pink, her stylish little spencer jacket green. He let his eyes linger over her figure. Odd. He had thought she was taller, not as curvaceous as she appeared now. He tried to imagine her breasts the way he'd seen them in the moonlight, perfect, white, round, and sweetly filling his hands. He found his hand clenching, trying to compare memory with what he saw now. Perhaps it was the dress, or the feminine unmentionables beneath, but she looked far better endowed this morning. He dropped his hand to his side.

He saw her mouth move beneath the brim as she spoke to the footman, her bonnet still hiding the rest of her face.

He felt his gut tense as a gentleman exited the coach, and stepped in front of Sophie, blocking Alec's view of her. The man looked over his shoulder and nodded to him.

"Good morning, Your Lordship. I'm the Reverend Reginald Parfitt," the man said, coming up the steps. "I had the pleasure of escorting Lady Sophie and her maid from London at her father's request." He held out his hand and Alec shook it, trying to see past him.

Sophie had turned to watch the maid descend from the carriage, carrying a hatbox. Alec was aware that Reverend Parfitt was speaking to him, and the girls were pressing in on him, but he kept his eyes on Sophie, desperate now to see her. He wanted to rush down the steps, tear the damned silly bonnet off her head, bend her over his arm, and kiss her senseless; and he didn't give a damn who was watching him do it. He started forward.

And that's when Lady Sophie Ellison looked up at him.

Alec's knees turned to water, and he stopped where he was, and stared. He met a pair of ice blue eyes under a tidal wave of flaxen curls. Hadn't they been hazel last night? And her hair had been red. He couldn't have imagined that, could he?

It wasn't her. This woman was a complete stranger.

Alec felt the smile dripping off his face like melting wax. His body went numb, his outstretched fingers curled back into his side.

It wasn't her.

"May I present Lady Sophie Ellison?" Parfitt said, and Alec dragged his eyes away from her face, and stared at him instead. A long moment of silence followed, until the churchman's brow furrowed. "My lord earl?" he murmured.

Alec blinked. Was it possible he'd been seeing things? Perhaps she'd been in disguise, or looked different without a bird-topped bonnet on her head. He peered at her again.

It wasn't her.

Her wide blue eyes flicked around her like nervous hummingbirds, darting over the castle, his sisters, and himself. There was no hint of recognition. Her gaze moved on again, paused on something behind him. Her smile bloomed.

"Oh!" she cried. "Look, it's Lady Caroline!" She pushed past him, rushing up the steps, and Alec turned.

He had a glimpse of red hair, of white skin and wide hazel eyes for an instant before they were swallowed up in Sophie's embrace and the face of his lover was hidden behind the froth of Lady Sophie's feather bonnet.

CHAPTER TWENTY-ONE

"You must be surprised to see me, and not Lord Bray," Parfitt said. "His Lordship had pressing matters of business to attend. He sent me instead." The clergyman patted his pocket. "Never fear. I come equipped with a marriage license. Is Lord Somerson visiting Glenlorne at present?"

Alec forced his eyes away from the two women at the top of the steps and turned to look at Parfitt. "Somerson? Why would he be here?"

Parfitt regarded him as if he were daft for an instant before he smiled uncertainly. "Why? Because his sister is here, of course! Until very recently Lady Caroline was on the marriage market in London. There has been some speculation as to the reason she left Town unexpectedly." He was obviously waiting for an explanation, but Alec didn't have one.

Lady Caroline. That was her name. Alec turned to look at her, to confirm that it was she whom he had— His stomach turned to liquid. Good God—he'd seduced the sister of the Earl of Somerson.

She was facing Sophie, her back to him. He looked at the

familiar curve of her back. He surely knew every vertebra of her spine intimately, knew exactly what it would feel like to put his hand on her waist, to caress the curve of her breast. Her hair was bound and gagged this morning, held captive in a cage of lethal-looking pins, but it was the same hair that had cascaded around her face as he made love to her by moonlight. If he were to pluck out the pins and free a lock, it would smell like wildflowers and honey, and it would curl around his fingers.

"Lottie absolutely refused to marry if you weren't by her side!" Sophie was saying loudly, clasping Caroline's hands—hands that had caressed him only hours earlier. "She's been frantic, and here you are healthy at last in Scotland! I must say, the air here seems to agree with you. You look radiant!"

He watched Caroline bite her lip. He waited for her eyes to fall on him, the real reason she was radiant, but she refused to look at him. She was aware of him, he knew, because her cheeks were red as summer plums.

"Why are you here, Sophie?" she asked breathlessly, and he heard the soft sound of that same voice pleading for more, uttering soft cries of passion.

Sophie turned to look at him, batting her lashes, offering his a shy smile. "Why, I'm to marry the Earl of Glenlorne."

The plums in Caroline's cheeks faded, as if a sudden frost had invaded paradise. His sisters, standing quietly until now, exclaimed and came to hug him, to tug on his arms, to kiss his cheeks. He felt nothing. He could not tear his eyes away from Caroline.

"Oh, Miss Forrester, isn't it wonderful?" Alanna asked.

"Miss Forrester," he murmured. He never even considered

she might be related to Somerson. The earl's family name was Forrester, and while he'd never met the man, he'd seen him a number of occasions. His wife was famous for her incautious tongue, and an indiscreet remark she'd once made about His Highness at a ball.

Alec felt a sudden flush of anger. It had been simple in London, digging into the private foibles and mistakes of others—he'd had to come all the way to Scotland to find a scandal of his own. He looked longingly over his shoulder at the hills, avoiding even a glance at the tower. He wondered what would happen if he simply started walking, escaped. He looked at Caroline again, and despite everything that had transpired in the past quarter of an hour, felt another tug of desire. He groaned aloud.

"Are you well, my lord?" Mr. Parfitt asked.

"It was Midsummer's Eve last night. It's just the aftereffects of the celebrations," Alec said, and the prim Mr. Parfitt pursed his lips, no doubt considering the potential for sin and blasphemy such a celebration would provide an unruly flock. Alec gave him a bland smile. If only he knew.

He climbed the steps, forcing himself to ignore Caroline. He bowed to Sophie, and kissed her hand. "Welcome to Glenlorne, my lady. Please come inside," he said, surprised at the gruffness of his tone. He took Sophie's arm and led her inside, brushing past Caroline Forrester without a single glance. The faint echo of perfume was almost his undoing. She smelled as he remembered, like summer flowers and something indefinable that made desire course through his veins again.

"Alec, why didn't you say?" Megan demanded, catching

his other arm. "I'm Megan," she said in careful English. "Alec's sister. Well, half sister. And this is Alanna, and Sorcha." His younger sisters dipped perfect curtsies.

"Your bonnet is divine, my lady!" Sorcha gushed, and Sophie smiled sweetly and began to chatter about hats and feathers and the latest London fashions. Alec could feel Caroline Forrester's presence behind him. She'd lain naked in his arms, made love to him, fallen asleep with him.

"Go and fetch Devorguilla," he whispered to Megan, and she shook her head.

"She's *Devina* in company, Alec," his sister said soberly. "Especially English company. She's probably not even awake at this early hour. I'll send Alanna up to tell her we have guests."

"And what should I call Muira?" he asked.

"Just Muira," Megan replied. "I suppose we'll want"—she looked around—"tea, or whisky, perhaps? You do look a little green this morning, Alec."

"Tea," Alec said firmly. "And you'd best have her prepare rooms for Sophie and Mr. Parfitt."

"I'll do it," Caroline said, her smoky voice vibrating over his tightly strung nerves. She hurried away, and he watched her go, resisting the urge to follow her and demand an explanation. Was there an explanation beyond the fact it was Midsummer, and he'd been a fool? He'd been so sure, so stupid, that he hadn't once asked for her name. He'd just assumed she was Sophie. And what now? A bead of sweat rolled down his back.

"What a charming room!" Sophie said as she entered the hall. "With some chintz drapes—yellow ones, perhaps, and a little plaster and paint, well, perhaps quite a lot of plaster and paint—and some new furniture in the style of Carlton House, it could be quite a pleasant space indeed."

Alec held his tongue, but he and everyone else looked around, and he saw the flaws of his family home for the first time. The stone walls were hung with threadbare tapestries and more of the rusty weapons that had been kept hidden away for nigh on seventy years, which Muira had now seen fit to bring out and display. The furniture was spartan and faded. Sophie took off her hat and set it on a table, and the yellow bird stared at the cold stone walls in open-beaked horror.

Sophie was wrinkling her dainty nose at a pillow that Megan had embroidered when she was just nine, and his sister's cheeks flamed. Sophie Ellison was even more of a stranger than he had feared. He'd felt an instant attraction when he'd seen Caroline in the tower. He looked at Sophie again, and felt nothing. Yet she would bring sixty thousand pounds to Glenlorne.

Even so, marriage once again seemed a sad prospect, even though he'd been willing, even eager to marry her when he thought she was Caroline, or that Caroline was Sophie. He rubbed his forehead, confounded. Would he still marry her? He must. Was there any choice? And Glenlorne would be painted and papered and his sisters would all learn to speak perfect English and sport egregious bonnets with dead wildlife mounted on them—a fox for Megan, a squirrel for Sorcha, and a dove, perhaps, for Alanna.

"Perhaps we could have a word about arrangements, my lord?" Mr. Parfitt suggested. "Lord Bray was most anxious to see everything settled."

"Could it wait until after breakfast," Sophie insisted. "I'm starving. Is there any English food in the place? No matter. I insisted we bring suitable provisions just in case. And a cook."

"We have a cook," Alanna said carefully, her smile fading a trifle.

Sophie laughed, the sound like sweet water flowing into a crystal goblet on a hot day. "Not an English one, I'll warrant."

"Warrant?" Alanna repeated, running her tongue over the unfamiliar English word.

Sophie babbled on like a stream on a flood tide, carrying the entire conversation by herself, comparing the virtues of French paper to English plasterwork, using more words the girls didn't recognize, if the looks of bafflement that passed between them were any indication. His sisters cast a few questioning looks at Alec as well, as if wondering just how and where he'd found Lady Sophie Ellison, and if it was too late to send her back. It was. Alec stared at the door, hoping Lady Caroline would walk through it. If she did, he would rise from his seat and cross the room. Then he'd take her in his arms—and strangle her.

Devorguilla—Devina—came downstairs dressed like an English lady in a stylish morning gown. Her clothing, her hair, even her shoes would have fit right in with the expensive English decor Sophie was suggesting.

The countess greeted her unexpected guests as if she hosted English nobles in her home all the time. She waved a gracious hand to indicate that Muira could pour the tea. Muira rolled her eyes.

"Mama, this is Lady Sophie. Alec is going to marry her," Megan said.

Muira would have dropped the delicate English teacup in her hand if Alec hadn't reached out and caught it. "Truly?" she whispered in Gaelic, looking at him. "A Sassenach countess?" She made a subtle sign of protection against evil.

Devina's eyes bulged, and she looked more carefully at Sophie, sliding her eyes over the lady's gown and jewelry, assessing her value. Sophie shifted under her hot stare.

"Will Caroline be joining us for tea?" Sophie asked.

"Caroline?" Devina warbled, only half recovered from her surprise. "Who is Caroline?"

"Why, Lady Caroline Forrester. It was such a pleasure to find her here. I am a dear friend of her niece Lottie. We have so much to talk about!"

Devina's brow furrowed.

"Your Miss Forrester, I believe," Alec said.

Devina's eyes bugged out again. "*My* Miss Forrester? The girls' governess?"

"Yes—she's the Earl of Somerson's sister." Alec pinned her with a look, and watched Devina's throat bob.

"Well, his half sister actually," Sophie said. "His father married a second wife less than half his age, and Caroline was born. It was a dreadful scandal some twenty years ago. Lottie told me about it."

"*Somerson?* The one with all the money?" Devina squeaked.

Sophie tilted her head, her eyes wide. "Yes, that's him—though my father is richer still."

Devina made another sound of strangled surprise.

Megan looked at her mother in concern. "Do you want the hartshorn, Mama?" But Devina was staring at Alec.

"You're going to marry—" She pointed discreetly at Sophie.

"Yes indeed. I'm here to perform the ceremony," Mr. Parfitt said firmly.

"If Lord Glenlorne formally proposes, of course," Sophie said, and gave him a shy smile.

Alec watched Devorguilla—Devina—assess Sophie's value again, taking in the diamond pin at her collar, the stylish hat, the cut of her clothes, the exquisite pearl and emerald earrings. Her smile stretched, until it nearly reached her ears on both sides.

"Tell me, Lady Sophie, do you have any unmarried brothers by chance?"

Sophie giggled. "Oh no. I'm an only child. My father's title will be inherited by a cousin."

Devina batted her lashes. "A single cousin?"

Sophie laughed aloud, and clamped a hand over her mouth. "Dear old Cousin Kenneth is near to fifty, and on his third wife. His only son is but three years old. Are you looking to marry, Countess?"

Devina considered. "I did mean my daughters, but perhaps . . ."

"Well, when Glenlorne and I marry—if we marry—I shall personally see that your lovely girls are offered the best introduction into society, Countess, and ensure that they travel in the very highest social circles."

Devina's eyes glowed.

Alec felt all eyes on the room come to rest on him. Did they expect him to drop to one knee now, here in the middle of the hall? He couldn't. He kept his expression bland. "I'm sure Lady Sophie would love a chance to see her room once breakfast is over, and perhaps a tour of the castle is in order. Megan, would you do the honors?" He rose from his seat, and bowed to the stranger he was supposed to marry. "If you'll excuse me, I have things to see to that cannot wait." He left Sophie and the Reverend Mr. Parfitt in Devorguilla's capable, covetous hands.

"So that's Sophie," Angus said, stepping aside to let his grandson pass. He needn't have bothered, of course, but he was tired of people walking straight through him. "She's a bonnie enough lass. Did you hear the part about her father being rich?"

Georgiana sniffed. "She's not as pretty as Caroline. She's only bonnie because her clothes and jewels are expensive. Her eyes protrude, and her teeth are too big."

"Still, what more does a man need?" Angus argued, his eyes on Sophie as she sipped her tea delicately. "She's obviously got money—did ye see the coach and the beasts pulling it?"

"Did you see that hat?" Georgiana snapped.

Angus glanced at it and winced, touched a hand to his own feathered bonnet. "Ach, what does a hat matter? She's rich. Alec can build new cottages, mayhap a school."

Georgiana set her hands on her hips. "Doesn't it bother you that she wants to turn Glenlorne into a proper English castle, in the very image of her father's home—or Somerson's?"

That got Angus's attention. "What? She wouldn't!"

"What do you think chintz is, my love?" Georgiana asked.

He had no idea but was loath to admit his ignorance. "Alec wouldn't allow chintz."

"With Devorguilla on her side?" Georgiana smirked. "Look at her. If Lady Sophie Ellison wished to tear the whole castle down and rebuild it as a fine Palladian mansion, Alec and an army of clansmen would be powerless to stop it happening."

"You're daft, woman!"

"Daft, am I? Look!" She pointed to Devorguilla, who was now in deep conversation with the Reverend Mr. Parfitt.

"What are they talking about?" Angus asked. He didn't like the look in Devorguilla's eyes. She was a scheming baggage, and he knew trouble when he saw it.

"Sixty thousand!" Devorguilla's cry rang to the rafters.

"Change, Angus. They're talking about change."

CHAPTER TWENTY-TWO

Caroline paced her bedchamber. Her hands were shaking. She paused and made a sound of rage. "His fiancée!" Alec MacNabb *knew* he was betrothed—and to Lady Sophie Ellison of all the women on earth, and he dared to dally with another woman? Not just another woman—her!

She'd been a fool, but what did she expect, that he'd marry her after a hasty tumble in the dark? No, she'd never expected that, not for a moment. Her face heated at the lie. She'd spent her life dreaming of true love. She was thoroughly convinced now, if she hadn't had proof enough before, that there was no such thing—and she was still a fool.

What now? Sophie Ellison was one of Lottie's closest friends, and she was a dreadful gossip. Surely the first thing Sophie would do, once she had rearranged the furniture in her assigned chamber, changed her dress, and had her hair redone by one of the three maids she'd brought with her, would be to sit down and write to Lottie. Lottie would write to her mother, who would wake up screaming after fainting in horror at the news that Caroline was a governess in Scotland, and then she would inform Somerson.

And then? Her brother would come and drag her to the nearest anvil, since nunneries were scarce, and she shuddered to think who might be waiting there to take her hand in marriage this time. She wrapped her arms around her body to still the shudder of distaste. She'd do better to go out right now, climb the bloody tower, and jump off the top. She groaned, her cheeks flaming.

Damn Alec MacNabb! He'd stood at the door of his castle this morning, calmly waiting to greet his bride, his expression closed, unreadable, as if he hadn't—they hadn't—well!

He'd bowed low to Sophie, had taken her arm and led her indoors, a gentleman, a *fiancé*.

And yet hours earlier, he'd carried her off to his tower like a pirate, and—no, she couldn't accuse him of anything beyond accepting what was freely offered. Oh, how would she ever be able to face him again? Or Sophie, or anyone else she knew for that matter? How foolish he must think her, how horrified he must be to think that such a wanton creature was governess to his innocent young sisters!

She crossed to the window and stared at the dusty road that wound past the old tower. She would be dismissed, of course. She couldn't expect a reference from the countess. What then? She could go to Edinburgh or Glasgow, perhaps. Or she could go home, beg her brother's forgiveness, and do as she should have done in the first place. She'd been raised to be demure, ladylike, obedient. What on earth had happened to her good sense? Alec MacNabb, that's what had happened. She sighed. No one but her mother had ever told her she was beautiful.

It seemed as if the curse that lay upon her had taken an even darker turn. It was far worse this way, having tasted passion, to wake up to see that she was destined to live a dry, loveless life.

She spun as the door burst open.

Alec MacNabb stood there, glowering at her. Her heart flipped over in her chest, and kicked to a gallop. He was utterly terrifying, infuriating and gorgeous. Her lips tingled. Everything tingled.

"Hiding, my lady?"

At his sarcastic use of her title stirred her to anger. "Do you not knock before you enter a lady's chamber?" she demanded in icy tones.

He threw back his head and laughed, then kicked the door shut and strode further into the room. "I think we know each other well enough to dispense with polite formalities like knocking, don't you?" He pulled down the edge of his cravat to reveal a small red bite mark on his throat. "I discovered it this morning."

Caroline felt her face heat. "I didn't mean to injure you, my lord."

"It didn't hurt in the least."

"I don't usually—I mean I've never—" she spluttered. "You—you *knew* you were betrothed, and you still—oh, how despicable!"

He raised his chin. "In my defense, I thought you were Sophie."

She folded her arms across her chest. "It wasn't that dark!"

He colored. "I'd never met her! I only knew she was coming to Scotland, so we could discuss the possibility of marrying." He ran his hand through his hair. "Look, you were in the tower, and you were English. How many English ladies could possibly be here in the Highlands—my Highlands—at the same time? It was a natural assumption to make."

She felt the blood drain from her limbs. "That's why you proposed, I suppose."

"Proposed? I did no such thing. I may have said a great many things in the heat of passion last night, but I am damned sure I did not propose to you!"

She shook her head. "No, at the tower, the day you arrived. You said the chapel was all ready for the wedding ceremony." She held up a hand when he began to object. "There's no need to worry—I thought it was some kind of Highland Midsummer prank, to propose to the first lass you see, or something of the sort. The girls and I had been talking about the Midsummer celebrations, you see."

"I thought you were Sophie. I thought I had . . ." His voice trailed off.

"Thought what?" she demanded.

"That I had the right to . . . I decided to marry you—her—for the sake of Glenlorne. I wasn't even certain I would marry her until I met you."

"Her," Caroline corrected.

"You," he said. "Sophie has money and position, and I need both—for my people, this damned pile of crumbling rocks, and my sisters. They deserve a future. What I don't need is complications, or problems. What exactly do you intend to do?"

Caroline stared at him. "I? Did you really imagine that I would force you to marry me?"

She began to laugh. She couldn't help it. If only he knew

the truth—she'd come here to the ends of the earth to *avoid* marriage. "I am your sisters' governess!" she said at last.

He leaned against the table, and folded his arms over his chest, his long legs stretched out before him. "That's another thing. Do you truly expect me to believe that the Earl of Somerson allowed you to take a post as a governess?" he asked. "If not for marriage, is this some kind of adventure, a family scandal I've somehow stumbled into the middle of?"

She lowered her eyes, all mirth fading.

He uttered a sharp oath and took a step toward her. She moved to the other side of the bed to avoid him, and he stood staring at her across the narrow width of it. The scent of her perfume rose around him. "Don't tell me—he doesn't even know you're here, does he?"

She raised her chin. "I am an independent woman."

He narrowed his eyes in disbelief. "Ah, but would Somerson agree?"

Her cheeks filled with blood. "Of course. I am twenty-three years old." It was a lie. She lacked three weeks until her twenty-third birthday, and Somerson was her guardian in all respects.

He came around the bed, and she backed up again, right into the bedpost. He stood before her, and put his finger under her chin.

"You ran away," he said.

She turned her head. His nearness made her mouth water to kiss him, her hands itch to touch him. "I chose to leave."

He lowered his eyes to stare at her mouth, and for a moment she thought he *would* kiss her, but he stepped back, began to pace the room. "I am going to marry Sophie Ellison," he said fiercely, and she stared at him. "Do you understand?"

She curled her fingers into the folds of her skirt and nodded. He stopped and looked at her, his eyes glowing with fury. "Do you happen to have sixty thousand pounds?" he asked.

Her jaw dropped. "Sixty thousand pounds?" she parroted. She had a respectable dowry, but did not come to nearly that much. She assumed Somerson could simply refuse to pay it if she did not marry, or married where he did not wish. "No," she said simply.

He began to pace the room. "Have you been to the village? Glenlorne needs money. Every single cottage needs repair. Hell, they should have been torn down years ago, new ones built. Some of them are older than that damned tower!" He pointed out the window and they both looked in the direction of their trysting place. She felt blood fill her cheeks. Was this an apology?

"Look, I'm not the kind of man the Earl of Somerson would even *consider* for his sister. Despite—what occurred between us—he'd never see me a fit husband for you. D'you see that?"

She didn't. If he knew the kind of man Somerson wanted her to wed . . . and if the Earl of Bray found Alec worthy enough to marry his only daughter, then . . . Still she nodded. He didn't want her, was seeking an excuse. Her cheeks burned. She would not force him to do the gentlemanly thing, especially since it was so plain that he didn't wish to marry her.

He was staring at her again, his eyes roaming over her. She felt heat rise under her prim gown. It was hard to breathe, hard to think.

"This is impossible," he muttered.

"Are you dismissing me?"

"No!" he said, then considered. "Yes. Perhaps it would be for the best." She felt her stomach cleave to her spine. "You should go home, back where you belong."

"I—" she began, but there was a knock at the door. He froze, looked panicked. If he were caught here in her bedroom, alone, their fate would be as good as sealed; she knew that. How fortunate he wasn't caught in her arms, both of them stark naked, the night before. He must be very relieved indeed. She pointed to the screen in the corner, and watched as he dove behind it.

She opened the door to Muira. "Is the laird here?" she asked, her bright bird's eyes poking into every visible corner.

"Of course not!" Caroline said, feeling her skin heat. "Why would you think he would be?"

Muira smiled a knowing smile, but waved her hand. "Och, just an old woman's Midsummer madness. Two more guests have just arrived at the door—more Sassen— er, English folk—gentlemen this time, insisting they've come to rescue Lady Sophie. Now I thought perhaps it was my poor command of the language, and ye might be able to help, since I canna find Alec. The young lady is in the blue room, unpacking, or at least watching her maids do it for her. She's got a dozen trunks, one full of carpets and hangings and new bed curtains, as if ours aren't good enough."

"Did these English gentlemen give you their names?" Caroline asked, crossing to tidy her hair in the mirror. Alec stood behind the screen to her left, but she avoiding looking there while Muira was watching. She could feel the heat of his eyes on her.

"I believe one said his name is Mamble. The other is a viscount called Speed."

Caroline dropped the comb, her fingers suddenly numb. "Mandeville and Speed? One with red hair, the other wide as a barrel?"

Muira grinned. "Aye—the very ones! Do you know them?"

Caroline felt her chest cave in. She hurried toward the door. "Unfortunately, yes, and they aren't here for Sophie." She slipped around Muira and hurried down the hall. How on earth had her suitors found her here in Scotland? Somerson had long arms, it seemed, and a sharp sense of smell. No doubt he'd set them on her trail, armed with warrants, letters, and marriage licenses. She'd be wedded and bedded and gone before anyone at Glenlorne was the wiser. She paused at the top of the staircase. She could hear them in the hall below, talking loudly about disemboweling cutlasses, pistols, and rapiers. Apparently, they were armed to the teeth.

She shut her eyes. She had to send them away.

And if they wouldn't go?

She glanced at the display of ancient weapons that now adorned the wall. She could hardly walk into the room carrying a pike, and she doubted she could even lift one of the claymores. A pair of dirks flanked a battered shield—long thin knives, their hilts once jeweled, if the empty holes were any indication, but the stones long gone now. She took one down, and weighed it in her hand. Could she really— She considered the alternative, and tucked the dirk into her sleeve. She took a deep breath and went to greet her suitors.

CHAPTER TWENTY-THREE

The first thing she saw was their dress swords, laying naked on the table next to their booted feet, as if they were ready to fight—if they ever finished the tankards of whisky. She clutched the dirk a little tighter and took a breath.

"Good morning, my lords," she said when they did not notice her entrance into the room. She stayed a safe distance back as they leaped to their feet, reaching for their weapons.

They didn't rush toward her. They gaped at her from a distance as if they were seeing a ghost.

"Lady *Caroline*!" Viscount Speed cried. Mandeville's heavy jowls flapped as he strove to speak and failed. He wheezed, turned red, and fumbled for his handkerchief. He held the lace-edged square to his nose, staring at her over the top of it, his eyes bulging with horror, not passion or even triumph.

"May I ask if you're quite recovered, my lady?" he asked, the question blurred behind the linen. Speed peered out from behind the protective bulk of his companion.

"Recovered?" she asked.

"Countess Charlotte informed us some weeks past that

you had fallen ill, and had retired to the country to recover your health," Speed replied.

"We thought she meant Somerson's country estate, not another country entirely!" Mandeville added.

"There was some speculation as to the nature of your illness," Speed said. "We were given cause to believe it was the plague. Is it plague, my lady?"

Somerson had explained her disappearance by telling them she had the plague? She almost laughed, but Speed looked mournful. "It has been some weeks since we've had any news of your condition. We assumed you were—" Mandeville elbowed him hard enough to knock him back into the chair he'd so recently risen from.

"We *feared* you were lost to us forever, shall we say?" Mandeville said, lowering his handkerchief an inch.

"Yes, we *feared* you were dead, especially when Lady Lottie canceled her wedding so suddenly," Speed said, getting back on his feet.

"As you can see I am far from dead, gentlemen," Caroline said.

"Indeed—we are indeed joyful that the Scottish air, damp and unwholesome though it is, has been kind to you," Mandeville finished, but he didn't venture any closer to her, or put away his handkerchief.

She took a step toward them, and they retreated. "Still, I am afraid your journey has been in vain—"

Speed put a hand to his heart. "The wedding has already taken place? We are but a day behind!"

"I assure you I have not—" Caroline began, but Mandeville reached for his sword.

"Where is the blackguard Glenlorne? I swear I shall make Lady Sophie a widow, and wed her then."

"Sophie?" Caroline cried. "You've come to marry *Sophie*?"

"I know she must be here," Speed said. "We saw Lord Bray's coach come this way. I'd know his matched cattle anywhere! Finest in London!"

"Scotland," Mandeville reminded him.

"Anywhere!" Speed replied, raising his finger in the air for emphasis. The loose skin under his chin wobbled like a rooster's wattle.

"Where is the fair Lady Sophie? I swear I can smell her perfume in this very room—that is, I'm certain I would be able smell it if I *knew* her perfume!"

"You're here to marry Sophie?" Caroline asked again, baffled. "Lady Sophie Ellison?"

Speed drew himself up. "Forgive me, my lady. I do understand your dismay, but we must withdraw our offer for your hand. I am the last of my line—I cannot take a chance on a bride who has had the plague so very recently, even if you appear recovered. You may turn out to be a poor breeder." He sighed, and put a bony hand over his heart. "Lady Sophie was in the bloom of health last I saw her."

Mandeville looked at his friend fiercely. "I will marry Lady Sophie if it is the last thing I do!" Speed glared back.

"Then I am not . . ." Caroline paused. She smiled. "You are not here to—?"

"Good afternoon, gentlemen." Alec descended the stairs behind her.

"Why it's Alec MacNabb!" Mandeville said, grinning. "How odd to find you here as well. I had no idea you'd left

London. Tell me you are not in pursuit of the Lady Sophie as well—we fear that the black lord of this castle has married her already!"

Alec raised one eyebrow and looked at Caroline, but she was as baffled as he was.

Speed picked up his sword and brandished it. "I swear I shall run this impudent Scottish earl through and claim the lady back for England!" the viscount said. "Where is Glenlorne? Simply point out his direction!" Mandeville picked up his sword as well.

Alec opened his mouth, but Caroline pointed away from Alec, out the window, over the hills. "That way. At the, um, Glenlyon Inn. It's only a dozen miles away."

"The Glenlyon?" Speed said, swinging his gaze to the horizon.

Alec was silent, watching her with amusement.

Mandeville brandished his sword in the direction of Caroline's point. "Then we shall go forth to the Glenlyon Inn, and we will drag the fair Lady Sophie from his bed if we must, and run him through if the match has already been—"

"Gentlemen, there is a lady present," Alec said.

They both bowed, looking contrite, tucking their swords behind their backs. "Of course—your pardon, Lady Caroline," Speed said. "I cannot stop thinking of you as—deceased."

Mandeville bowed as well, and strode toward the door. "Please excuse us, we must go forth and woo our bride," Mandeville said, sidling carefully past Caroline to the door. "It has been most pleasant to see you looking so well, my lady. MacNabb, keep a watch for that blackguard Glenlorne."

Alec watched them go and turned to her. "I can explain—" Caroline began, but he looked dubious.

"How two gentlemen—three, actually— can possibly marry the same woman?"

"Well, no, I can't explain that," she said. "They were supposed to marry me," Caroline murmured, and took the dirk out of her sleeve. She laid it on the table. Alec stared at the weapon.

"Both of them?"

"Whichever one I chose," she said. She almost laughed. "But it doesn't matter now."

"I see." He crossed to her side and picked up the dirk, examining the places where the gems had been pried out. His mouth tightened. "I trust the possibility of marrying either one is why you ran all the way to Scotland and took the lowly post of governess?"

He was so close that Caroline could smell his skin, feel the heat of his body beside hers. She lowered her eyes.

"Which one would you have chosen?" he asked softly, and she shuddered, imagining Speed's bony fingers on her flesh, or Mandeville's weight upon her in bed. She tried to stifle her revulsion, but he laughed softly.

"So now we have the truth, I suppose. You ran away. Apparently you've been forgotten, and Sophie is the new prize."

Caroline felt a flare of anger. Did he think she wasn't even good enough for Speed or Mandeville? Or him?

"It appears you're not the only one who wishes to wed a fortune, my lord," she said sharply. "Does it matter what Sophie wants, or if she is happy? Do you have any more regard for her than Speed or Mandeville do, or is it just her huge dowry you fancy? I suppose a fortune as vast as Lord Bray's goes a long way to making a lady lovable."

His cheeks colored at the insult, but his eyes hardened. "Jealous?"

She looked down at her fingertips. She shut her eyes, stemming the sharp, sudden bite of tears as she imagined Alec in Sophie's arms, doing to her what he'd done to Caroline in the tower, making *her* feel loved and lovely for the first time. It was almost unbearable.

"Of course not."

"You are not a governess, Caroline," he said.

She stiffened. Then what was she? Nothing to anyone. "I beg to differ," she said.

"You could have married one of those gentlemen, yet you ran away. Do you love someone else?" he asked.

She bristled. "Do you imagine that one night with you, and I am—" She clamped her lips shut on the admission.

He put a hand under her chin, raised her eyes to his, mere inches away. "You are what?" His voice was husky, soft, whisky-potent.

She pulled away. "Infatuated! I am not, I assure you. I was given a choice of suitors, and I made my own decision in the matter. I am, my lord, indeed a governess—that was my choice."

He groaned. "What of my choice?" he said, and she wondered what he meant. "You can't stay here, Caroline."

Caroline folded her arms over her chest. "Why not? Am I not performing my duties satisfactorily?"

"It's not that, it's—" His eyes moved over her like a touch, and she read desire in his eyes, frustration. "Go home, Caroline, back to Somerson. Find a man you can marry."

The weight of her plight fell over her like a pall. It was too late for that. She considered her options, and saw none. "If you'll excuse me, I have lessons to see to." Before the tears of frustration could fall, she fled.

Alec watched her go, and slammed his fist into the solid oak table. Another mistake—this one worse than dropping a damned letter. This time, it was personal. He'd involved Caroline, an innocent—or at least she had been until he got hold of her. He doubted even Mandeville or Speed would have her now. Or Somerson. He should do the right thing and marry her himself, but that would be another mistake. He'd consign her to a life of poverty by his side, destroy his clan, his sisters. She'd grow to hate him.

He shut his eyes. He'd almost believed he could be Laird of Glenlorne, be able to lead his people the way his grandfather had, bring them from misery and poverty back to prosperity if he had Sophie—Caroline—by his side. But he wasn't a hero, or a leader. He was a fool.

Caroline had to go, for both their sakes. If she stayed, he could imagine the temptation to touch her again, to make love to her. He was hard as a pole just thinking about it.

And Sophie? He'd do his duty, do his best to be a good husband and spend her money wisely, but she didn't fire his blood like Caroline Forrester did. Was there even a chance he could make his marriage work if Caroline stayed at Glen-lorne?

He imagined speaking his vows to Sophie, knowing Caroline was standing in the chapel, remembering the night in the tower. And what of his wedding night, blowing out the candle and climbing into the laird's bed, thinking of Caroline, not Sophie? How long would it take desire to die?

He headed for the study, seeing it now through Sophie's eyes, a shabby, threadbare little room, and crossed to the desk. He took out a sheet of paper and sat down to compose a letter.

Caroline Forrester had to go.

CHAPTER TWENTY-FOUR

Devorguilla watched Brodie MacNabb over the tea table in her private sitting room. He hunched awkwardly on a dainty side chair, his big frame overfilling it, making it creak under his muscles. The delicate teacup in his meaty hand looked equally out of place, and he slurped when he sipped, regarding her with bright, witless blue eyes over the rim, and she smiled. He was perfect. Not as a man. As a pawn.

"She's the prettiest lass I've ever seen," he said through a mouthful of cake.

"Megan?" she asked, though she knew he meant someone else.

"Lady Sophie," Brodie said, spraying crumbs.

"She's to marry Alec. She'll be the new Countess of Glenlorne," Devorguilla said blandly. She watched the color rise over Brodie's ruddy complexion, saw jealousy narrow his eyes. He looked like an ox, brainless and dull, but ready to charge. She had thought to wed him to Megan, to sacrifice her daughter to get what she herself wanted. Brodie hadn't the sense to run an estate. He'd allow Devorguilla to do it, put his rights in her name, just the way she'd tricked Alec's father into doing. All her life Devorguilla had controlled men using her beauty, the lure of her body, but she was too old now to tempt Brodie. She still had ambition, wits, and an all-consuming desire to be wealthy. She'd lived in poverty long enough. All over the Highlands, lords—and ladies too—were using their land to make them rich. All it took was boldness. She'd hoped Alec was dead, that her chance had come. Even so, she hadn't been surprised when he returned. Disappointed, yes, but not surprised. It simply meant her plans had to change. She had no idea how he'd managed to catch an heiress like Bray's daughter, but she knew she'd not see a cent of the chit's dowry. He'd turn her out as soon as the vows were spoken, and waste the funds on building cottages for the hordes of useless and hungry mouths that inhabited MacNabb territory. To her, it was simple—why buy bread for peasants when you could buy a woolen mill, and make room for it by setting a torch to the miserable hovels people inhabited, living four or five to a bed, with more constantly being born the minute one wed, and moved into the cottage next door to breed yet more starving bairns?

It would be a kindness to expel them, make them go elsewhere, to beg someone else for their sustenance. She'd keep a few folk to work the new mill, tend the new flocks. She wasn't heartless. They could sleep under the machines, or in the barns. And she could live the life she deserved, buy a grand house in Edinburgh, or even England, and have servants to tend her every whim. Sophie Ellison's dowry would go a long way toward making that happen, but only if it wasn't wasted on the futile task of restoring the clan. The clan was all but finished, dead.

She was a smart woman—smarter by far than most men she knew. She had managed her husband for years, and had gotten rid of him when he ceased to cooperate, refusing to sign any more of the papers she put in front of him while he was drunk.

If Alec were as dead as his father, and Brodie was laird, she could control everything once again. A simple accident was all it would take, and the clan would be calling Brodie laird. It made her teeth ache to hear Alec called by the title. He'd been the one to warn his father about her. At first Dougal hadn't believed him. She'd told him Alec was lying, and convinced him to send his son away. It took some time, but Dougal finally understood what he'd done. He was too stubborn to bring his son home, but he never trusted Devorguilla again. She'd suffered for her mistake, but now she would see to it that she got rid of Alec for good, and never suffered again.

"Have another slice of cake," she said to Brodie. He held out his plate eagerly. "Now, how would you like to be Earl of Glenlorne?" she asked.

His brow furrowed. "But Alec is the earl," he said.

"But you're still his heir, until he gets a son on Lady Sophie."

She watched Brodie imagine the getting of that son, saw him shift, his eyes hardening, his fist tightening on the delicate teacup. She took it from his hand before it shattered. "Of course, if you were earl, you could marry her."

His eyes brightened, but faded again as he shook his head.

"My father sent me so Alec could teach me some sense, or so he said. I don't know how to rule over a place like Glenlorne."

Devorguilla smiled. "I do, Brodie. I do. I can help you, and if you were earl, you could marry Sophie too."

"Aye?" His eyes widened like a child's. Perfect. She patted his knee.

"Aye."

CHAPTER TWENTY-FIVE

"Lady Sophie, may we speak privately?"

Alec had found her standing on the terrace that ran the length of the back of the castle, staring down across the loch. She turned and smiled at him, her long teeth glinting in the sun. Her blond hair shone as well, Alec thought, choosing to notice that instead. Her fashionable walking gown seemed out of place here, especially with a fur muff, cashmere shawl, and fur-lined gloves in the height of summer. She looked cold, yet to him, the day was warm.

"Of course, Lord Glenlorne," she said. "I was just looking over the estate. This lake is a touch big, don't you think? If that half of it were filled in, then there would be space for a rose garden, or even a maze. We might consider putting a folly on the island just there. It would make the view so much more interesting."

Fill in the lake? Alec blinked. He'd followed Sophie outside to formally propose to her. He'd grown tired of Mr. Parfitt chasing him through the castle with a pen in one hand and a formal betrothal contract in the other. He'd promised the man he'd propose today, and had signed where Mr. Parfitt indicated.

Once he'd proposed, he could forget Caroline, concentrate on planning a future with Sophie. He felt a twinge of guilt. If he met Sophie in London, at a ball, he probably would not even ask her to dance, never mind consider marrying her, her fortune notwithstanding. But this wasn't London, it was Glenlorne, and without her money . . . He let his eyes roam over the hills, the loch, the village.

He remembered the hope and joy on the faces of the clansmen who'd welcomed him home. They thought he could make everything right again, work a miracle.

He looked at Sophie again, at her bland face, her slightly protruding blue eyes, and hoped they were right. This time, he wouldn't fail, he vowed, and turned back to Sophie with determination, since he felt nothing else. Perhaps in time they would grow to love—or at least like—each other.

"And the folly there, on the hill—it's rather gloomy, isn't it?" Sophie simply carried on discussing the landscape, hardly noticing he hadn't said a word, or even nodded. He realized she was pointing to the old tower. "It really should have been built in a more pleasant spot, where ladies can stroll, and gentlemen might propo—" She folded her hands in her lap demurely. "I'm sure Glenlorne offers many pleasant vistas to be enjoyed. Will you show me one of them?"

Alec looked around at the hills, dotted with purple heather and white sheep, at the cloud-cast shadows that moved over the long grass, chasing the wind as it swept down the long slopes, at the way the loch shone in the sun, deep and black with ancient secrets. He took a deep breath of fresh Highland air, and his heart sang, and he wondered what better view there could possibly be.

Still, he offered his arm, and Sophie laid her gloved hand on his sleeve, and he set off toward the loch. Perhaps looking back up the hill at Glenlorne Castle, set against the majesty of the mountain peaks, would please her.

"What a steep slope this is!" she said after a moment, and Alec glanced back at the gentle hill they'd descended. They hadn't gone more than twenty paces from the terrace. "It needs steps, something in a Palladian style, with a Greek temple halfway down so one might rest and contemplate the improvements one could make," she continued.

"Do you wish to sit here? It is not a Greek temple, but I have often found it a good place for contemplation." He indicated the long, soft grass of the hillside.

Her blue eyes widened as she looked around, then she laughed. "How silly you are, my lord! There isn't a bench!"

"I meant to sit on the grass," he said with one of his most charming grins, and realized it was a mistake at once. Sophie looked horrified.

"On the lawn? Like a dairymaid?"

"I thought dairymaids sat on stools, in dairies," he quipped, but she looked at him blankly. He took off his coat and gallantly spread it on the grass for her. "Will this do?"

Her lips rippled over her long teeth, but she gingerly took her seat. "Lady Sophie, I—" he began, but a gust of wind snatched the words from his lips. She cried out as it tugged savagely at her bonnet. He stood between her and the gust, forming a windbreak with his body. Sophie blinked up at him, looking chilly.

"Do you like it here at Glenlorne, Lady Sophie?" he asked.

"It is rather wild, is it not? Are there wolves in the hills?" Her china blue eyes flicked across the landscape, and he had a sharp feeling that she did not belong here, like a needle in the gut. He forced himself to smile reassuringly.

"Wolves? I suppose so—a few, perhaps, but very far off. There are deer as well, and foxes and—"

"Foxes?" Lady Sophie brightened. "Do you ride to a hunt here? I do enjoy a hunt ball!"

"Er, no. We mainly hunt grouse and deer here at Glenlorne," he said.

"Oh." The sigh was filled with disappointment.

"There are some glorious walks in the hills," he offered.

She pursed her lips and examined an invisible mark on her glove, but did not reply.

His proposal of marriage stuck in his throat. He looked across at the village. Every cottage he could see needed a new roof. Plenty looked crooked, ready to crumble into the loch. That would certainly fill it in.

He took a breath and pressed on. "My lady, I assume you know why your father asked you to come here."

Sophie's gaze was sober. "Yes, of course—to see if we'd suit. Papa seemed quite sure we would."

Alec waited for her to give her own opinion of the matter, but she simply blinked against the wind and waited for him to continue. He wondered if he should get down on one knee, but it seemed silly to do so on a hill. He'd be kneeling uphill, and if he went around her, then downhill. He kept to his feet instead, and clasped his hands behind his back. Then he unclasped them, and set one on his hip, and hooked the other thumb in his watch pocket, the way he'd seen English gentlemen do when they wished to look important, yet still at ease.

"My lady—" he began, but the wind reappeared and snatched the muff out of her hands. It tumbled down the hillside like a runaway lapdog. Sophie cried out in dismay, and Alec ran after it, trapping it under his boot before it could reach the loch. He held it up like a hunting trophy and grinned at her. She frowned at the boot print.

He climbed the hill against the stiff breeze, only to find the wind was battering the feathers adorning her fashionable straw bonnet, threatening to steal them too, and fling them into the sky where rescue would be impossible. In Alec's opinion, the hat would be much more attractive without the outlandishly colorful embellishments, anyway.

"You were saying, my lord?" she asked, half shouting against the wind. How odd. It hadn't been windy in the least when they came outside.

"I was about to ask—" he yelled, but her shawl caught the breeze like a sail and tangled around her face, pasting itself to her features, outlining her nose and eyes and wide open mouth like a paisley mask, knotting the long fringe in the ribbons of her bonnet as she scrabbled at it, her shrieks muffled. Alec wrestled with it, trying to tear it free from the wind's grip. He yanked the shawl loose and stuffed it into his pocket, where it snapped against his leg like the tail of an angry cat, cornered but far from vanquished.

"Thank you, my lord. I am very afraid of the dark," Sophie explained, breathing hard.

"You are?" Alec asked. It got very dark in the Highlands. You could see the stars here, count them, almost touch them.

He'd missed that in London. He loved the dark, peaceful nights here. He shook himself, remembering why he'd brought her outside. It appeared the wind was getting more violent by the minute. "I mean . . . Lady Sophie, would you do me the honor of—"

Something tugged hard on his legs, hooking itself around his knees, and he lost his balance on the slippery grass. The wind tore the oath from his lips as he tumbled down the hill, head over heels. He landed hard on his tailbone, a large jagged rock between his outspread legs, and he realized in horror that if he hadn't stopped when he did, then he certainly would have proven to be a disappointment to Lady Sophie on their wedding night.

He lay in the heather for a moment to catch his breath. Odd, it almost felt as if someone had tripped him, yet there was no one here but himself and Sophie. He got to his feet and climbed the hill yet again to her side. Sophie's eyes widened at the sight of him. He glanced down. There was a green streak down one sleeve of his shirt, and a smear of dirt. His face stung, and his fingers came away bloody when he touched the scratches on his cheek. He must look like a wild Scot after a battle. He imagined his ancestors climbing this hill after a hard fight, clutching their swords in their blood-stained hands, looking forward to seeing their womenfolk— He looked at Sophie, sitting miserably in the wind with loose tendrils of blond hair snapping around her face like the riggings of a ship in a gale. Her nose was red, her lips white.

He remembered the first time he'd seen Caroline in the window of the tower. The wind had made her cheeks pink, and her eyes glowed. Her glorious hair had floated around her like a battle flag. He could imagine the joy a warrior would feel coming home to such a sight. He looked across to the tower, but the window was empty. He clutched his fist around the imaginary sword in his hand and looked back at Sophie's pinched face. He almost turned and fled back down the hill, but he forced himself to stop. It had to be done.

"Lady Sophie, will you do me the honor of becoming my—" he demanded more gruffly than he'd intended, but the wind spun around him, stealing his words away.

"What?" she screamed. "I can't hear you!"

"Will you marry me?" he bellowed.

She looked relieved, if not pleased. "Yes. Can we go inside now?"

"I think that's a good idea," he murmured, though he knew she couldn't hear him over the blast. He helped her to her feet and retrieved his coat. Should he thank her, say something about her beauty, or how happy he was? But she was already three paces ahead of him, running for the safety of the castle.

By the time they'd reached the terrace, and Sophie had run across the flagstones with tiny, clipped steps and ducked inside. The minute the door closed behind her, the wind died to a disconsolate sigh.

He saw Megan in the hall, and she paused to stare at him. "You're all bloody and scratched!" she exclaimed. "What have you been doing?"

"Proposing," he muttered darkly.

Angus paced across the width of Caroline's room, and back again. She was quietly reading by the window, and couldn't hear him. "They mean to wed him, bed him, and kill him. Then, Brodie will do whatever Devorguilla bids him to do."

He paused in front of her, though she didn't notice. "You know this means the end of Clan MacNabb, don't you, lass? It's a disaster. 'Twould be better if he wed you, penniless though you are!"

Caroline turned the page, and he smiled softly. "Ach, you look like your grandmother did, the summer I fell in love with her," he said, and put out a hand to touch her cheek. She looked up, her gaze passing through him. He felt a jolt of surprise. "Did you feel that?" he whispered. He put his hand on hers, clasped it as hard as he could, and her fingers curled for a moment. He felt a flare of warmth.

He squeezed harder, but felt nothing more. "Lass, I need your help. *Alec* needs your help," he pleaded, and she blinked, and looked around her in surprise.

Georgiana appeared. "She can hear me!" Angus said, pointing at Caroline. "She knows I'm here!"

Georgiana looked at Caroline in surprise, but her grand-daughter sat calmly reading a book, unaware of Angus, or Georgiana. Georgiana put her hands on her hips. "There's no fool like an old fool! What the devil are you doing? I needed your help!"

Angus waved his hand between Caroline's eyes and the book, but she didn't even blink. Hope fizzled. He floated over the Georgiana. Caroline had her eyes, her straight, slim, elegant bearing. Even the way she pursed her lips while she read was like Georgiana. There was a pain in Angus's chest where his heart had once been, beating just for her.

"Well, what is it?" he demanded.

Georgiana looked wistfully at Caroline. "I tried to stop him, but Alec proposed to Sophie."

"When?" he demanded.

"Not a half hour ago."

"Did she accept?"

Georgiana sighed, and Caroline looked up. "Of course she did," Georgiana said.

CHAPTER TWENTY-SIX

Viscount Speed paced the floor of the comfortably appointed dining room he had hired—along with the innkeeper's two best bedrooms—at the Great Glen Inn. As inns went—or glens, for that matter—he could find nothing great about this place at all. "By God, I shall make sausage from his entrails!"

Mandeville, who was gnawing on a sausage skewered on a fork, set it down. "We did not specifically ask him if he was Glenlorne, though he was in the man's castle. Perhaps we should have guessed that MacNabb and Glenlorne were one and the same?"

"How could we have ascertained that?" Speed griped, as he made another turn around the threadbare rug. "He looked no different than he ever did in London."

"Course he did." Mandeville took another bite of sausage. "He was standing in a castle, and now that I think on it, two of England's wealthiest heiresses were in that castle right along with him."

"He can't marry them both!"

Mandeville shrugged, chewing thoughtfully. "This is Scotland. Perhaps the laws here allow such things."

Speed frowned. "The laws of chivalry make no such allowance! It should be one heiress per lord in all places. 'Tisn't fair otherwise." He crossed to the fly-blown mirror above the sideboard. "How does he do it, I wonder? I have always cut a certain dash with the ladies. My face is surely just as handsome."

Mandeville looked at his companion dubiously. "'Tis derring-do, old man."

"What is that, some kind of Highland beverage, a dish made with sheep's entrails, perhaps?"

"It's sheer gall for the most part, though ladies like to think of it as the essence of heroism. They want derring-do in a man the way we want—" He rolled his hands out in front of his waistcoat, and nipped them in at his waist.

Speed looked into the mirror again, seeing something entirely different from his long, crooked nose, his small eyes, his thin, lopsided lips. "Surely we have plenty of that," he said, and ran a hand through his greasy hair, practicing his most seductive smile, though he was missing two teeth.

"Indeed, but I fear MacNabb has more."

"Then what are we to do? In London, we would simply start a rumor that he's penniless, or call him out for cheating at cards and shoot him. How the devil do gentlemen deal with these matters in the Highlands?" Speed demanded, turning away from the mirror to pace again. "Not that it likely comes up often. There are few heiresses here of Lady Sophie's caliber, and damned few gentlemen from what I've seen."

Mandeville pushed his empty plate away and sat back.

"Then I think we are free to make our own rules, wouldn't you say? Think of the old Scottish custom of reiving, taking what you want."

Speed stroked a pimple on his chin thoughtfully. "I thought that only applied to cows?"

Mandeville grinned. "Not at all. In days of old, a bold man simply took what he wanted, wedded it, bedded it, and the matter was settled to everyone's satisfaction."

Speed frowned. "Are we still talking about *cows?*"

Mandeville poured himself a glass of the innkeeper's finest port and held it up to the light. He paused for a moment to stare into the ruby depths before turning back to his friend. "Not cows, no. But a fine woman is worth every bit of the same effort it takes to capture a fine heifer, I believe." He set the glass down, and leaned toward Speed. "What if Glenlorne was accidentally injured—or worse? Dearest Sophie would be ours for the taking."

Speed's eyes lit. "Ah, derring-do!"

Mandeville nodded. "Precisely." Mandeville picked up the glass and drained it.

Speed sat down at the table across from his friend. "But how will we do it? We could bash his head in on a dark night, or strangle him in his bed."

Mandeville's smile rolled up the flesh of his red cheeks like a sail. "It's a fine land for hunting, don't you think? I hear there's plenty of game in these hills. Surely Glenlorne could be convinced to invite us out for a day's shooting," Mandeville explained. "'Tis the gentlemanly thing."

Speed's eyes glowed like the furnaces of hell. "I see. An accident, then—a shot through the heart."

"Almost like a duel, a way to settle the manner honorably," Mandeville agreed. "What could be fairer than that?"

"But how will we determine which of us will marry Lady Sophie in Glenlorne's place?" Speed asked.

Mandeville folded his arms over his massive belly, giving his friend a friendly smile. "Whoever bags the earl shall win the lady."

"And the loser?" Speed asked. "Seems a shame to go home empty-handed."

"There's still Lady Caroline."

There was a discreet knock, and the innkeeper entered. "More wine, gentlemen, or ale, or another haggis?" he asked politely.

"Haggis?" Mandeville said, holding out his glass to be filled.

"I believe you referred to them as sausages when I brought the first one in, sir. I have never seen anyone eat nine of them in all my days."

"The chill in the air gives one an appetite," Mandeville said. "No, I am replete. Bring me some writing paper, if you have it, and find a lad to take a note to Glenlorne, sirrah."

The innkeeper nodded and left. "You don't mean to commit our arrangement to paper, do you?" Speed asked.

"Of course not," Mandeville replied. He extended his hand across the table. "A handshake will do. I mean to write to Glenlorne, give him our congratulations, and get him to host us for a day's shooting in the hills."

Speed grinned gleefully. "Get him to ask us for dinner as well. I am not as fond of haggis as you are."

CHAPTER TWENTY-SEVEN

The great hall was filled with people. Every MacNabb for miles around had come to the ceilidh to welcome the new laird home. They wore their plaids proudly, and the pipes to played him to his seat at the head of the table, and everyone declared that such a grand celebration had not been seen since before the Battle of Culloden, or after, when the wearing of tartan and the playing of pipes and even the speaking of Gaelic was prohibited by the English victors. Alec was the first new laird since that law had been repealed. If the English hoped the old ways would die out in the years between, they would be sadly disappointed to see that the spirit of the Highland clans was alive and well in Glenlorne tonight.

Lady Sophie, newly betrothed to the laird, sat by his side, and received the felicitations of the clan on her upcoming nuptials. Since she understood little of what the Scots said, even in English, Alec had to act as her translator. "We shall start a school and teach them to speak properly, in English," she said loudly, which drew many frowns and grumbled comments in Gaelic.

Caroline sat among the servants, ignoring Sophie's plea that she take a place at the head table. Caroline pasted a bright smile on her face and held it there, despite the fact that her stomach was tight and her heart dead in her breast. She'd been through this all before, and one would think she'd be an old hand at it by now—watching a man she admired celebrate his betrothal to someone else. It was hard enough to sit at the back of the room and smile without having to watch the happy couple bill and coo up close. She ate little, and drank less, remembering all too well what had happened the last time she drank ale at a celebration. She tried not to watch the happy couple, but couldn't help herself. Alec regarded Sophie politely, smiled at her comments, whispered in his ear, held her hand. Sophie was as nervous as a bird, breathless, fluttering and twittering. She wore a king's ransom in jewels, and an evening gown that would be better suited to a grand Carlton House ball than a Highland ceilidh.

"Damned fool. He's making a grave mistake, if you ask me," someone said beside her muttered. "She's the wrong wife for him. He'll spend eternity regretting this."

Caroline turned to regard the elderly gentleman beside her, his eyes intent on Alec. He wore the MacNabb plaid from head to foot, and a deep scowl of disapproval.

"Sophie's a lovely person," she said. "She'll make a wonderful countess, and I'm sure they will be very happy together."

He looked startled, as if he hadn't known she was there. "Can ye see me, lass?" She raised her eyebrows when he waved his hand before her eyes, following it. Was he drunk? There wasn't a cup before him, full or empty.

"Don't you want to raise a toast to wish them happy?" she asked, looking around for a tray of ale.

"Happy? 'Tis a mistake! She'll be the death of him, or Devorguilla will, and there's not a thing I can do but watch it all happen. Ach, it's my own fault."

The old gentleman kept his eyes on the happy couple, and his fist clenched on the tabletop. She wondered who he might be. There were plenty of clansmen here from other MacNabb holdings, distant parts of MacNabb lands. "Are you one of the earl's kinsmen?" she asked. "Have you had a long journey?"

"A long journey?" he chuckled. "Aye, I suppose you could say so." He was staring at her, and she felt her face heat. "Forgive me. You are very much like your grandmother."

Caroline tilted her head. "My grandmother was the Countess of Somerson, sir, in England."

He frowned. "Aye, but she wasn't always. She lived here in the Highlands once, at Lullach Grange, with her aunt and uncle. He was a soldier at Fort William."

"I think you must be mistaken, sir," Caroline said.

"Did ye not know, lass? Did she never speak of Scotland, or of me?"

"She died when I was only seven. I do recall her saying she had visited Scotland once, in the summer."

He looked pointedly at the corner of the room. "You never told her?" he murmured. "Did I mean so little to you, *gràdhach*?" Caroline followed his gaze, but saw only shadows. Her companion looked so profoundly unhappy that her heart went out to him.

"You should eat something. Can I get you some food? Muira has made so much."

He looked around at the folk nearby, watched them happily eating, drinking, and chattering, their cheeks flushed with drink and the pleasure of the evening. He smiled. The smile looked familiar. "'Tis a joy just to see the clan happy again. They've known little enough joy for a very long time. In my father's day, there were gatherings and ceilidhs regularly. The se-annachie would tell stories of our ancestors, of Scottish history. There wasn't a man, woman, or child who didn't know where they came from, and took pride in it. But not after Culloden. It all ended with Culloden. And now . . ." He shook his head sadly. "'Tis a broken clan. I had such hope that Alec might—"

He looked at the corner again, and tilted his head as if he were listening. Caroline studied his profile. He looked like Alec—the same strong chin, gray eyes, and broad shoulders. She could imagine that in years to come, Alec would resemble this kinsman, and be handsome well into his old age. She felt a pang of regret and cast a glance at the head table. Sophie had gone to speak to the girls. By the way her delicate hand was cupped to her mouth, she was no doubt gossiping.

Alec sat alone, his expression set. She drew a sharp breath as she realized he was staring at her, his eyes in shadow in the candlelit hall, the laird's cup in his hand. His jaw softened when he met her eyes, and he smiled faintly, and nodded. She couldn't look away, couldn't unlock her gaze from his. She felt a wave of desire, and loss, and a sense of drowning in the depths of his eyes, as if she'd plunged into the icy depths of the loch. She watched as he swallowed, saw the light playing on the muscles of his throat, his high cheekbones, glinting in his eyes.

"Are ye all right?" Muira asked her, leaning over her shoulder. "Ye're sitting here all alone."

"Alone? I was just speaking to—" She looked beside her at the old gentleman, but the bench was empty.

When she looked back at Alec, his eyes were on Sophie.

CHAPTER TWENTY-EIGHT

"I want Caroline Forrester dismissed."

Devorguilla looked at her stepson in surprise. "Has she done something wrong?"

"She's the Earl of Somerson's half sister, a lady, not a servant."

Devorguilla studied her nails. Now what did he have against her choice of governess for her daughters? She hadn't known Caroline was a lady when she arrived to claim the post. Not that it mattered—in fact, it was even better this way, even if Alec did not approve. The household and the girls were her responsibility, surely. She was not about to allow him to interfere. Besides, Lady Caroline's connections to the Earl of Somerson would be just the thing to launch her daughters into English society. She just had to keep Caroline here until the next London Season.

Of course, Alec would be dead by then. The thought made her smile.

"All the better for the girls to keep her, don't you think? The more high connections they make, the better their chances of success on the marriage mart. Lady Caroline came here of her own free will, and she has not tendered her notice. I will invite her to stay as a guest, if that's more appropriate, and ask her to help me prepare the girls for the Season out of kindness. Will that do? Besides, what if Lord Somerson took exception to our dismissing his sister without cause?"

"I doubt he even knows she's here. She doesn't belong at Glenlorne. She should be in London, making her own connections on the marriage mart."

"Megan will make her come-out next spring. Lady Caroline is helping her learn what she needs to know. Would you have her stop now? Megan will need to know how to speak proper English, how to dance and flirt and behave if she's to have any chance of success. Caroline has agreed to teach them some French as well, in fact—an added skill." She got to her feet.

"Sophie can help them," he said.

"Sophie doesn't speak French, and she cannot play the piano like Caroline can."

She read the frustration in Alec's eyes and wondered at it. Why should he care whether Caroline Forrester stayed or went? It was, she decided, an attempt to usurp the small amount of power she had, and she wouldn't stand for it.

In the few short weeks he'd been at Glenlorne, he'd lit a spark in the people. She'd never seen such hope, such joy. She'd woken this morning to the sound of pipes somewhere in the hills. *Pipes!* It was as if he were William Wallace come again. Clansmen she hadn't seen for years had come to pay their respects, to bend their knees to him and pledge their loyalty to Alec MacNabb. Brodie would never inspire such awe, such hope. Brodie was an ordinary man. She understood ordinary men, the kind driven by lust and greed. She had no idea what drove Alec. He was like his grandfather, honorable. She recalled the old man's bluster over honor and the pride of the MacNabbs. While Alec would try to save the world, Brodie wouldn't quibble about governesses or land sales or sheep. He'd leave all that to her.

She took a last stitch in her needlework and tucked the needle into the linen, and got to her feet. "Lady Caroline is useful to me—more so now I know of her family connections— and to the girls. She stays."

Without a backward glance, as if her stepson were already dead, she swept out of the room.

CHAPTER TWENTY-NINE

The hills were beautiful in the rain, Caroline thought, walking through the glen, skirting the loch, climbing the path until she stood overlooking the whole valley, which spread out before her, half shrouded in the mist, mysterious and soft. The chimneys in the village smoked, and the tower's yellow stone glowed against a pewter sky. The loch was moody and gray, the same color as Alec's eyes. She turned away and kept walking. It was threatening to rain any minute, which was probably why she hadn't met anyone else on the path.

The girls were looking over pattern books with Sophie, and Caroline had excused herself as Sophie offered a lesson on the subtle differences between Belgian lace and French lace, stunned the girls didn't know already. Mostly, Caroline left because she knew they needed time to get to know their new sister-in-law.

After the ceilidh, she had decided it would be for the best if she left Glenlorne before the wedding. She would go to Edinburgh and look for employment with another family that wished their children to learn English. She had come out today to say farewell to Glenlorne.

She stopped at the top of the craggy hill on the opposite side of the loch from the castle, and stared at the gray stone, memorizing every detail. The castle had come to feel like home in the short months she'd been here, though she knew it was not. It was Sophie's home, or it would be in a week, when the wedding took place in the old chapel. She avoiding looking at the chapel, and turned away to take the path over the hill and down through the woods. She came upon a house in a clearing. The old place hunched among the trees, a dowager with good bones fallen on hard times, drawing a ragged shawl of ivy around her. The driveway was badly overgrown, the roof sagged, and the shutters were crumbling for want of paint. It must have been beautiful once, here among the pines. Caroline drew closer, leaned on the stone wall that surrounded the garden, and peered at the front door, which was barred firmly against intruders. She felt a moment's sadness that the old place had been abandoned and forgotten. A flagstone path led the way into a tangled garden. There were roses struggling through the wildflowers—English roses. Caroline smiled at the heavy pink heads, gaudy among the white and yellow weeds. They were like the ones in her mother's garden, and she'd often gone out to cut them to bring the heady scent indoors on a summer afternoon. Caroline slipped past the broken gate, and bent to sniff one of the roses. She shut her eyes at the familiar fragrance.

"Ye can't mean to leave, lass," a voice said, and she jumped. A thorn bit through her glove and into her finger. She pulled her hand away. The old gentleman from the ceilidh stood watching her.

"You startled me," she said, and tried to move past him toward the gate. "Forgive me. I fear I'm trespassing."

"No ye're not. If anyone has a right to be here, you do. D'you know what this place is?" he asked. She turned to look at him. "It's Lullach Grange, lass. Your grandmother lived here once, long ago."

"It seems so sad," Caroline said.

"Aye. No one has lived here for a very long time. I thought she belonged here, in Scotland, at Glenlorne, but others didn't agree." His thick white brows drew together. "And now you mean to leave as well." He looked as sad as the house, and she felt the sting of the thorn, and looked down at the spot of blood on her glove. "I thought maybe you were meant to make your home here, to stay for good."

Caroline felt the prickle of tears behind her eyes, as sharp as the thorn. "Will you excuse me? I must get back to the castle," she murmured.

"Do you love him?" he demanded as she reached the gate.

"Who?" Her voice shook as his face filled her mind's eye.

"Och, ye know who I mean. Alec, of course."

Her response hovered on the tip of her tongue. Of course not. But she did. She found she could not speak the lie without crying. Instead she shook her head, and watched his face crumple into sorrow. The breeze shook the petals from the rose, and they fell at his feet, pink and white against the black stone, and it began to rain.

Caroline pulled her hood close and hurried up the path between the trees. When she turned to look back, the garden was empty.

CHAPTER THIRTY

A lec looked at the records in frustration. Glenlorne hadn't had a good harvest in twenty years. The books showed the people who'd died and been born, and the expenditures during his father's time as earl. Dougal had sold nearly a third of the land the MacNabbs had once owned, using the funds to benefit the folk in the castle. Devorguilla's expenditures on clothes were astronomical.

There were notices and letters from his father's man of affairs in Inverness, years old, warning his father of mounting debts. There were also petitions from the clan chiefs to their laird, and from ordinary clansmen, asking for an extension on their rents, or a bit of food to help them through a harsh winter. Conditions had grown steadily worse after his grandfather's death, nearly twenty years ago. And still Devorguilla's spending had gone on. Six casks of wine, smuggled from France at exorbitant cost, a piano, a down mattress made in England, four dozen yards of costly silk. How could she, with so many mouths to feed, so much to take care of? He had a lot to put right. He ran his hand through his hair and wondered where to begin. His father's gambling debts alone ran to thousands of pounds. It wouldn't be long until creditors began beating a path to his door, demanding payment that was long overdue. Sophie's dowry would be sucked up in no time, he realized. Even that astronomical amount would not be enough.

Muira rushed in. "There's an army of coaches comin' up the glen. Are we being invaded again? Surely they're English. Local folk come on foot, or by pony or cart. Should we bar the doors?"

Alec crossed to the window, and looked at the dark stream of vehicles pouring over the lip of the valley, parting the heavy veil of rain, heading for the castle, and felt a moment's surprise. "What now?" he muttered, and turned back to Muira.

"Best prepare tea for now, I think, boiling oil later. It's probably nothing more sinister than a parade of English modistes and mantua makers summoned by Lady Sophie to outfit her for the wedding." The word "wedding" stuck in his throat.

Muira sniffed. "Wedding! Did ye know she wants to plaster the walls in the great hall, paint it *yellow*, put up Chinese curtains? There's to be no more swords or shields on the walls, and positively no tartan, especially at the wedding."

Alec winced inside, but he forced himself to smile. "It will be her home, Muira. She'll want to put her stamp on it, like any bride. A lick of paint won't be so terrible, will it? Go on now and boil the kettle for tea."

Muira tossed her head. "It's my home too, and yours, and every MacNabb's."

Alec watched her go and wondered how much refurbishing Glenlorne to Sophie's tastes was going to cost.

He hurried upstairs and put on English clothes, since

Sophie had let him know she didn't like kilts. He'd not dared to tell Muira that. He straightened his cravat, checked his watch, and pulled on a dark blue coat, resisting the urge to add a sword and pistol under his coat just in case.

He heard them coming before he'd even reached the castle steps. Someone was yelling, a high-pitched female outpouring of rage.

"This weather will not do! We shall end our days in this dreadful place with lung fever and the pox from all this rain! Gout too—mark my words. What the devil was she thinking, coming here, of all places? Could she not have fled to Brighton or Bath? My only comfort is that she is probably as bruised as I am by the dreadful rough roads. And the mud—I shall need new gowns, I say, and new shoes, and I am not happy at the necessity of waiting until I return to London to get them! Every single garment I own is ruined! Even so, I shall not stoop to wearing anything plaid!"

Not a flock of modistes then. Alec pursed his lips and waited for the footman to descend from his perch and open the door. His livery was indeed muddy, and the rain poured over him.

"There had better be something decent to eat, or I shall order this coach back to civilization at once. At once, d'you hear? They probably don't even drink tea, and if they do, it's likely made of boiled nettles!"

The door of the coach opened, and a gentleman got out with a frown. He looked at the façade of the castle for a moment, then stalked up the steps. He did nothing to assist the virago inside the coach, who continued unabated with her litany of complaints and threats.

"Good afternoon," Alec said, stepping forward.

"Somerson," the man introduced himself gruffly, not bothering to extend his hand. "You have my half sister here I believe?"

Alec let his glance flick over the powerful English earl. He was red-faced and sweating, with the stance of a bully. He stood before Alec with his chin high, his fists clenched, his stance challenging. Alec couldn't detect the slightest family resemblance between the earl and Caroline.

The footman assisted the lady out of the coach. She slipped on the slick step down, and whooped as she fell on the footman. He valiantly struggled to hold up her great weight. Another footman rushed to assist as the lady bellowed at them. They finally succeeded at setting the lady safely on her feet with her bonnet askew.

She pinned Alec with one sharp eye, like a bird of prey spotting a hare, and marched up the steps toward him. "Where is she? I swear she'll be horsewhipped for this foolishness!"

"My wife, the Countess of Somerson," the earl said, without a hint of apology, and without even glancing at her. The lady weighed at least twenty-five stone, and was clad in a vivid pink velvet traveling gown, trimmed with frills, with a matching bonnet. Alec bowed, resisting the urge to blink. She reminded him of a prize sow at a country fair, he thought unkindly, and forced himself to smile at her as he bowed over her hand.

Another gentleman got out of the coach, looking pale. He straightened his cravat, and blinked like a sheep lost in the woods. "My future son-in-law, Viscount Mears," Somerson said.

The last one to alight was a young woman who was pretty, despite her family resemblance to Somerson. Her nose and eyes were swollen from crying, and began streaming anew as she set her red-rimmed eyes on Alec. "Please, where is my aunt, sir? Do not say she isn't here, or I shall faint here on the very steps!"

"My daughter, Lady Charlotte," Somerson said.

"Don't be so dramatic, Lottie!" the countess commanded. "We'll tear this place apart stone by stone if we have to find her, and then—" She raised thick talons, as if she already had Caroline's delicate neck in her claws.

"Lottie!" Alec stepped aside just in time as Sophie barreled past him and hurled herself into Lottie's arms.

"Have you heard the news? Is that why you're here?" Sophie babbled. She reminded Alec of an overenthusiastic puppy. "I'm to be married! Oh, how pleasant to see you, and what a lovely bonnet!"

"Lady Sophie?" the Countess of Somerson cried, her eyes bulging in alarm. "Whatever are you here for?" She glared at Alec. "I'm beginning to suspect foul play, when two—now three—of England's premier heiresses have ended up all together in one damnably remote castle. Where is this Glenlorne fellow? I shall give him a piece of my mind!"

"I believe this is he, standing before you, Charlotte," Somerson said dryly. "Have I the right of that, sir?"

Alec bowed. "Indeed you do. Welcome to Glenlorne Castle. Please come inside before the rain starts in earnest."

"In earnest? It began raining the moment we crossed the border, and it hasn't ceased for a minute since," the countess grumbled. Alec offered her his arm, since Sophie was linked with Lottie, patting her back, offering her a fresh handkerchief to stem the deluge of tears. Somerson strode up the steps on his own, his expression suggesting he held no real hope of comfort within.

"Have your grooms see to the horses. Our servants and luggage should be arriving within the hour. These three coaches contain just the essentials, my valet, the countess's chef, Lottie's maids."

Three coaches, and still more to follow? Alec clenched his teeth and nodded. Where the devil would they put everyone? And just how long were his unexpected guests intending to stay?

"We shall trouble you only long enough to collect Caroline," Viscount Mears said as he climbed the steps. "The ladies are eager to return to London."

"Good afternoon, Glenlorne. There's quite a crush here." He turned to find Lords Speed and Mandeville picking their way through the mud. "Is there a party?" Speed asked, eyeing the army of servants bearing boxes and bags and trunks up the steps.

"We've come to invite you to go hunting," Mandeville said with a broad grin.

The rain began again, a sudden downpour that threatened to drench everything within seconds, and Alec stepped aside. "I think we'd best discuss it inside, my lords. I assume you know the Earl and Countess of Somerson?" But the keen hunters had already scampered up the steps, whimpering about cold water falling down their backs, leaving Alec talking to the rain.

"'Tis an invasion after all," Muira said, watching the mayhem.

Alec gritted his teeth. "Get Lady Caroline at once."

Chapter Thirty-One

The sky was as dark and grim as if it had been twilight by the time Caroline returned to the castle, though it was barely teatime. The mist had turned into a strident downpour, needle-sharp and chilling.

She entered through the kitchen, and Muira was stirring a pot over the fire, which smelled delicious. A joint of venison was cooking in the vast fireplace, along with three plump hens. A pair of fat salmon lay on the table, staring up at Caroline in dull surprise, waiting for their turn.

"It smells like Christmas in here!" Caroline said, taking off her sodden bonnet and cloak.

Muira turned on her, a wooden ladle at the ready. "Out!" she shrieked. "Ye'll not invade this patch o' Scotland, you Sassenach dogs!" She lowered her weapon when she saw it was Caroline. "Och, I didn't mean you—I thought it was the other one, back again—that English cook the company brought with them. She insists she must prepare a proper meal. I insisted she leave before I got out the cleaver." Her face softened as she looked at Caroline. Caroline assumed she meant Sophie's cook, who was terrified to set foot in Muira's domain.

"Ye looked like a drowned kitten, lass! Where've ye been? 'Tis no day to be outdoors—though it's just as stormy within. The laird's been looking for you all afternoon."

Caroline's chest tightened. "Oh? Well, he'll have to wait for a while longer. I need a bath and a dry gown at the very least." One of the very reasons she'd gone out was to avoid Alec.

Muira took her cloak and hung it by the fire. "And ye'll need a dram of warmed whisky along with it to ward off the chill. It won't take a moment to fix. Sit ye down, lass."

"I'm quite all right, Muira. I walked over to Lullach Grange and got caught in the rain. There's no harm done." Caroline sat on the bench by the fire to remove her sodden half boots. Even her stockings were wet, but removing them would have to wait until she was in the privacy of her own room, the same as her gown and petticoats.

"The Grange?" Muira said. "Now why would a body want to go there, even in fine weather?"

"I had company. The old gentleman from the ceilidh was there."

"What old gentleman would that be?" Muira asked, giving the soup a stir, and pushing a poker into the heart of the fire to heat.

"I didn't even think to ask his name."

"Well, we'd best tell Alec there's someone in the old place that shouldn't be there. The Grange has been locked tight since Laird Angus died, some twenty years past, and even before that. There was an English major who lived there once.

He was killed at Culloden, and the place was left to itself. Some folk think it's haunted." Her eyes widened. "Och, did ye see a shade?"

Caroline smiled. "No, of course not. This was no English major—he was a Scot."

"Oh? And how could ye tell?" Muira poured a tankard half full of whisky, golden in the firelight. She pulled out the poker and thrust it into the cup, and it sizzled as it heated the whisky. Muira's lined face was radiant in the fire's glow, her eyes sharp as a bird's.

"He was wearing MacNabb plaid from top to toe, for one thing. He said he knew my—"

The kitchen door burst open. Muira's ladle came up yet again. Jock MacNabb reached for his dirk, then dropped his hand. "For pity's sweet sake, Muira, ye scared the life half out of me!"

"We've just been talking about ghosts," Muira said, dropping the ladle and crossing to baste the chickens.

"Och, there ye are, Lady Caroline. Alec's fair anxious to see you. He told me to go out and look for ye. I'm glad that won't be necessary now." He rubbed at his elbow.

"The ache again?" Muira said, noticing the gesture. "Ye'll need liniment for it. I'll make some up once the bread comes out of the oven. "You'd best go and tell Alec that Lady Caroline needs a hot bath before she sees him. She's soaked to the skin."

Jock stole a sweet roll off the cooling rack when Muira turned away. "Aye, I will—but he won't like it."

She swallowed, wondering what he wanted. She wasn't ready to face him yet, not knowing she loved him, not until she got her emotions under control, was certain she could hide her feelings.

"Please tell His Lordship that I'll speak to him before supper, as soon as I'm dry." Caroline said. Her wet stockings left dark footprints on the flagstones as she crossed to the back stairs.

"I'll send up with some hot water," Muira called after her.

Chapter Thirty-Two

Georgiana leaned on the railing of the gallery to survey the guests in the hall below.

"Is that your grandson? The blustery fellow with the bulgy eyes?" Angus asked.

"Yes." Georgiana sighed. "That's Somerson." She took no pleasure in seeing him here. He'd come for Caroline, and she hoped her granddaughter would be strong enough to resist him. She could feel the anger emanating from Somerson, saw him looking for Caroline, checking his watch. The longer she made him wait, the worse it would go for her.

"I see he takes after your husband's side of the family," Angus said acidly.

"What's that supposed to mean?" Georgiana demanded waspishly.

"He's not an attractive lad, now is he?" Angus mused, stroking his chin. "Not like you and Caroline."

"Neville is hardly a lad, and he's one of the most powerful peers in England." Georgiana sniffed.

"Neville?" Angus snickered. "Powerful, and one of the nicest chaps too, by the looks of him."

"He's the very image of his grandfather," Georgiana said, recalling her husband. "The apple has not fallen far from the tree."

"Looks like it's got a worm in it, if you ask me. Tell me, do you ever see *him*? Or his shade at least, the way you see me?"

Georgiana shuddered. "My husband? Of course not. Nor would I wish to. The long years of our wedded life were enough time together for both of us. More than enough."

"Lucky man," Angus muttered.

"Do you miss your grave so much?" Georgiana demanded, anger flaring.

"I meant I resent every single minute he spent with you that I was denied," Angus snapped back. "I meant it as a compliment. Did you not recognize it as such?"

Georgiana looked at her hands, remembered where her lavish wedding ring had weighed on her finger, and looked at the finger of her other hand, where she'd worn Angus's modest promise ring until she died. She had treasured the tiny ruby far more than the massive sapphire and pearl ring. Both were gone now, of course. The sapphires graced Charlotte's fat finger.

"Forgive me. Somerson was not a one for giving compliments—at least not any that were directed my way. I quite got out of the habit of being complimented."

"Then he was a fool, as well as uggsome. I would have told you every day how beautiful you are."

"Uggsome?"

"The opposite of beautiful," Angus said, staring down at Neville Forrester.

Georgiana felt tears come to her eyes. "We can't change what's past. Our time has come and gone. We can only help Caroline and Alec see how important it is to love and be loved. Do you understand that now?"

"O' course I do. And I'm certain that's why your Caroline can see me."

"Because she's in love with Alec?" Georgiana asked hopefully.

"She says she isn't. I asked her directly. I would have sworn . . . Och, I've seen the looks that pass between them. They scorch the air." He pushed his bonnet back. "I thought it was working, our plan. I thought the lass could see me because she *belongs* here, that she's meant to be at Glenlorne. O' course, I believed that of you too. We failed in our own time, *gràdhach*, and there's more at stake now." He turned to her, and she saw tears in his eyes. "Can we fix this—make them see—or will yon fool of an Englishman destroy everything?"

Georgiana looked down at her grandson's hard, unfeeling face. "It's up to Caroline now, and Alec. They must face the past and find a way. We can only do so much."

Angus's mouth twisted bitterly. "Then sixty years hence, it will be Alec and Caroline standing here, mourning the past," Angus said, "and I'd not wish anyone that kind of torment."

"Where is she, Glenlorne? Your letter said she was here." The Earl of Somerson looked around Glenlorne's great hall as if he was in the darkest slums of London, and his half sister had taken up a life in the demimonde. It made Alec look around his home himself, but instead of shame, or guilt, he felt pride. The walls were strong, the clan proud. They cared for each other, unlike this fool, and Bray too, who had everything money could buy, but lacked any human kindness.

"I assure you she's here, my lord," Mandeville said, quaffing another mug of ale and reaching for the pitcher. "We saw her only yesterday."

Alec ignored him. "I understand that Lady Caroline has simply gone for a walk. She will likely be back shortly."

"In this weather?" Countess Charlotte cried. "She'll catch her death!"

Indeed. Alec glanced out the window at the steady downpour. Where the devil was she? He had images of flash floods, slippery crags, deep crevasses, and Caroline lying broken and bloody in the heather. He looked at his watch. He'd sent Jock and Hamish out to look for her an hour ago. If they hadn't returned in ten minutes' time, he'd go himself, abandon his guests, or let Sophie and the girls amuse them. Sophie had taken Lottie up to put her to bed. Devorguilla and the girls were managing the herculean task of finding quarters for everyone from the earl to his lowest footman. Was there anyone left in England?

"Fear not, dear countess. Lady Caroline looked very much recovered yesterday, and hardly on the verge of death now," Speed said. "You were quite right to send her here to the Highlands. It appears to have done her a world of good and put the bloom back in her cheeks, so to speak—providing she doesn't drown in the deluge, that is."

"Drown?" Charlotte said. Alec noted she looked more hopeful than sorrowful at the prospect. "Is that a possibility?"

"No," Alec said quickly. Unless the ground became slippery, or she lost her footing and fell against a rock . . . "No," he said again. "She has probably taken shelter in the village. The local folk are very kind to—" He stopped himself from saying "strangers." Caroline was hardly a stranger now. She knew most of the villagers by name, knew their children, took baskets of food and Muira's medicines to the sick and elderly, stopping to listen to their stories. Caroline would be welcomed warmly at any hearth to wait out the weather. He felt a moment's pride fill him.

"She's with peasants?" Charlotte's face creased with disgust. "She'll get fleas—or worse. She's already on the very verge of ruin, and fleas will certainly tip her over the edge."

"I would go myself and look for her," Viscount Mears said boldly, then subsided instantly. "If I knew the way."

"And risk your own health?" Charlotte demanded. "I should say not."

"I have no doubt that she'll be back as soon as the rain stops," Alec said again.

"Will that be anytime today?" Somerson said impatiently. "I understand it rains nearly constantly in the Highlands."

"His grandfather said as much—he told terrible stories of the weather. He fought with the king's army in the '45," Charlotte said.

"Well done, my lord!" Mandeville said, raising his glass, then met Alec's sharp look and colored. "Er, we could mount a proper search for Lady Caroline."

"Once the rain stops," Speed added.

Alec looked at the gentlemen in the room. Mears looked worried, but meek. Mandeville was helping himself to more ale. Speed was examining the maker's mark on the bottom of the pewter mug, assessing its value. Somerson looked annoyed by the delay, and Charlotte was hopeful that Caroline might never return at all. Not one person cared if Caroline was safe or not.

He'd made a dreadful mistake, sending for Somerson.

He looked out the window at the old tower, standing lonely and forlorn in the wet, and wondered if she was there. He imagined finding her there, kissing the rain from her lips, holding her body against his to warm her wet skin . . .

Jock came to Alec's side and whispered in his ear. "She's upstairs, safe. Came home an hour past, looking like a drowned stoat."

Relief and anger flooded through Alec's breast. She was safe.

No, she was hiding. He looked around the room. He'd be tempted to hide from these people himself, if they were his kin. Still, she could not avoid them forever. He frowned at her cowardice.

He got to his feet. "Will you excuse me?" He didn't wait for a reply. He turned on his heel and left the room. He took the stone steps two at a time and didn't stop until he reached Caroline's room in the tower.

Chapter Thirty-Three

The tower room Caroline now occupied had once been his bedchamber. He knew every nick on the steep stone stairs that led to it, every stone in the wall. It had been a sanctuary, a place to keep boyhood collections of smooth pebbles and bird's eggs, slingshots, wooden swords, and the few well-loved books he owned.

He knocked, and waited. "Come in, Muira," she said. He threw open the door, furious that she'd put herself at risk, that she'd left him with her family, that she'd left London at all.

Caroline was indeed dripping wet, but in no way did she resemble a drowned stoat.

She sat in a tub of hot water, the steam curling around her. Her eyes widened above pink cheeks at the sight of him in the doorway before she grabbed the nearest covering at hand and dragged it into the tub with her. The thin muslin shift soaked through and molded itself to her figure. He could see the dark outline of her nipples, the long length of her legs. An image of those legs, those breasts in the moonlight dried his mouth.

He should turn away, leave, but he couldn't move. Hell, he couldn't even breathe.

"What are you doing here?" she demanded, wrestling with the muslin.

"You told me to come in," he said.

"Only because I thought you were Muira with more hot water!" She was getting water all over the floor as she tried to sink deeper into the bath, and control the flimsy muslin at the same time. "Go away!"

He *should* go. It was the gentlemanly thing to do, the smart thing, but she was naked, wet, and lovely, and the room smelled of wildflowers—the soap, he assumed, or perhaps it was just Caroline. This room had never smelled of wildflowers when he lived here. It should have felt strange, but the chamber still felt like home, sanctuary, even with her things strewn about—her books, her hairbrush, her wet undergarments hanging over chairs and hooks. He couldn't make his feet move, couldn't take his eyes off the wide golden pools of her eyes, her sweet pink lips, the wet slope of her breasts, the long white length of her legs. He'd caressed those breasts, suckled them, and those legs had been wrapped around his hips as he—

"If you're not going to leave, at least turn around, or hand me a towel, or a blanket, or anything!"

He handed her a towel, and turned away. He heard her rise from the water, resisted the urge to peek, heard the rustle of fabric as she wrapped herself up. "Where have you been all day? Somerson is assuming you've been drowned in the storm," he said.

The rustle of linen stopped. "Somerson? Here? How did he—I suppose Sophie wrote to Lottie."

He turned to face her, the admission that he'd written the letter on the tip of his tongue, but his tongue got caught between his teeth when he saw her. She stood beside the wooden tub like a Greek goddess. The wet linen outlined her slim figure from breast to thigh, her shoulders white and wet and perfect. Desire stirred, driving out any chance of intelligent thought, and he was instantly hard, as ready as he'd been in the tower. He looked away, but his eyes fell on the bed, which made it worse still. "He's—downstairs. Somerson, I mean. He arrived a few hours ago," he said thickly.

"Is he alone?"

"Alone? No. He brought the whole family."

She gasped and the towel slipped, sliding down the slopes of her breasts. She spun, walking toward the screen, but the linen outlined her perfect bottom. He swallowed a groan. "Lady Somerson is here too, Lady Charlotte, his future son-in-law, and Mandeville, and Speed, all downstairs, waiting for you." He concentrated on counting them on his fingers, but it did no good. His erection refused to give up. The wet towel was ejected from behind the screen, and it landed on the floor next to the tub, mocking him. He didn't have to see her. He knew every curve of her body, how silky her skin was, how sweet her mouth tasted, the sweet sounds she made when he loved her. It was all he could do to stay where he was.

"What's Starbury?" he asked her, trying to ignore the rustle of fabric as she dressed.

"Starbury? It's one of Somerson's estates, a very small one in Shropshire, on the border with Wales. Why?" she asked.

"Because Somerson mentioned Starbury to Mears as their next destination on the way back to London."

She was silent.

"Is it a pleasant place?" he asked.

"It's—remote and rather desolate. My mother hated the place. She called it more a prison than a house, the kind of place someone ill goes to die alone."

Alec shut his eyes. Of course it sounded like a prison. It was meant to be a prison—for Caroline. Somerson meant to take her there and leave her.

She came out from behind the screen, wearing a prim gown. Still, his breath caught in his throat, and he wanted nothing more than to undo the tiny buttons that fastened the garment up to her chin, lay her bare again, and carry her to the narrow little bed. She stayed out of his reach, and he noticed her feet were bare under the hem of the gown, the way they'd been at Midsummer. Her hair was loose as well, curling damply around her face. She pointed to her stockings, hanging on the back of a chair. "I will come downstairs as soon as I finish dressing." He couldn't look away. She met his eyes, must have seen the heat there. The spots of color on her cheeks expanded, and her eyes darkened, before she looked away. "Please go," she begged.

"What do you want me to do, Caroline?" he asked instead.

A dozen emotions cascaded through her eyes—hope, fear, anger, and resignation—before her lashes swept down to hide what she was thinking. She stood with her head bowed, but her spine was stiff. "I want—I need you to go, before I do something I will regret," she whispered.

He walked toward her instead, his boots crackling on the woven straw mat. He cupped her cheek, and she pressed into his palm like a cat, sighing at the touch.

"I can't," he murmured. "I should walk out that door, but I cannot make myself do so," he murmured, his other hand finding her waist, drawing her close. He leaned forward, his forehead resting on hers, breathing her in, feeling the warmth of body. He wanted to kiss her. He lifted her chin, but she turned her face away with a murmured objection.

He kissed her cheek instead, her ear, the side of her mouth until she moaned, and kissed him back, her lips meeting his, clinging. She slid her hands up the front of his coat to his lapels, then around his neck, tangling her fingers in his hair as he deepened the kiss.

It hadn't been the Midsummer ale. It hadn't been the drums or the firelight. It had been Caroline. He wanted her as he'd never wanted any woman, and not just physically. He wanted to look into her eyes, know how she felt, talk to her, walk over the hills with her by his side, hand in hand, fall asleep and wake up next to her. He tasted the salt of her tears, and he pulled away.

Her eyes were bright with tears, dark with desire. He could have her if he wanted. He could carry her to the bed, lay her down, and make love to her—and she would never forgive him. He felt a flare of anger, at her, at himself. What the hell was he doing?

"I have responsibilities," he said aloud. "I am betrothed to Sophie. Your brother is here—downstairs." He looked again at her lips, half parted and luscious, red from his kisses, and his mouth watered. He shut his eyes. "You know what would happen if you stayed. You deserve better. Sophie deserves better."

"Do you think I would consent to stay here and be your

mistress, live under the same roof with your wife, compete with her for the crumbs of your attention? How would you do it, Alec? Would you set me up in a cottage in the village, slip down to visit me on moonless nights?" She was angry, and she had every right to be.

He ran his hand through his hair, wanted to tear it out by the roots. "It was a mistake," he said. "That night in the tower. It was wrong, but if I make it right now, I will make so many other things wrong, don't you see?"

She raised her chin. "I have not asked you to make it right! It was my mistake as well, my lord. I have asked you for nothing, and I will not ask, if that's what you fear."

"Then where will you go?" he asked again.

"Do you care, so long as I am gone?"

Alec didn't answer. She took her stockings and went back behind the screen. He stood and waited, not knowing what to say, or how to fix this. She came out from behind the screen and crossed to the dressing table. She wound her hair into a tight bun with fierce efficiency. When she was done, she looked every inch the prim, untouchable governess—except for the vulnerability in her eyes, the set of her shoulders when she met his gaze in the mirror.

"You could still marry," he said slowly.

She shook her head, and said nothing.

"Look, you could still wed Speed or Mandeville. He might not care that you aren't a maid. He might not even know," he said, and she looked up at him in astonishment. To his surprise, she laughed, a mirthless, bitter sound.

"Have I said something amusing?" he said, suddenly annoyed.

"Not at all, my lord," she said sarcastically. "If you see my brother, you may tell him I will see him at dinner." She swept to the door and opened it, leaving him in the room alone. He listened to her footsteps hurrying down the steep stone steps as if she could not get away from him fast enough.

CHAPTER THIRTY-FOUR

Caroline took Lottie a cup of her favorite peppermint tea when Muira told her the young woman was feeling poorly after her journey.

As expected, she found her niece sitting with Sophie, and also as expected, Lottie was filling her in on the latest gossip from London about friends, acquaintances, and enemies.

"I came to borrow a dress to wear to dinner," Caroline said as Lottie launched herself into her aunt's arms.

"Of course, you poor thing. My mother said you'd left without anything at all. I was so worried!"

"You ran away? Yet everyone believes you retired to the country with a serious illness." Sophie said, blinking. "I believed every word!"

"Mama put that story about, at least to anyone who cared to ask, since we truly had no idea what had become of her!" Lottie replied. "I suspected she'd been kidnapped by pirates, and sold into a pasha's harem," Lottie told her friend. "I swore off wearing cashmere shawls forever for Caroline's sake, and then Papa received Lord Glenlorne's letter."

"*Glenlorne's* letter?" Caroline murmured. "Glenlorne wrote to Somerson?" She felt heat rising under her collar. She assumed Sophie had written. How desperately he must want her gone. Her heart dropped into the pit of her stomach.

"When Papa showed Glenlorne's letter to Mama, she screamed so loudly the neighbors sent three strong footmen to see if anything was amiss. She screamed so long that she fainted, and the doctor had to be summoned to attend her."

"I didn't mean to cause such a fuss," Caroline said, though she wasn't surprised the household had been turned upside down, both by her departure and by the news that she was safe in Scotland. "I simply didn't wish to—"

"Oh, I understand completely!"

"You do?" Caroline asked.

"Of course! How sweet you are, Caroline. You didn't want your wedding to take attention away from mine. You needn't have worried—I would have welcomed a double ceremony. Now I am hoping we can both marry here, with Sophie, a triple ceremony. I'm sure Papa would not object. He and Mama are most anxious to see you married at last."

"Oh, Lottie, how marvelous!" Sophie cooed. "We shall put our heads together and make plans at once! You and William, Glenlorne and I, and Caroline and—"

"It doesn't matter who you've chosen. You can announce it at dinner. I'm sure Papa will insist you do, in fact," Lottie interrupted.

Did Somerson still believe she would choose? Did he not understand why she had fled into the night, or perhaps it was simply that he didn't care. He couldn't force her to wed, of course, but as her guardian, he could make her miserable until she did as she was told.

"But—" Caroline began, but Sophie crossed to throw open the door of the wardrobe, and began pulling dresses out. "I think we should all dress alike tonight—perhaps all in the same color. Or should we all wear white, but with the different sashes?"

Caroline allowed them to choose a dress for her—white with a red sash—not caring what she wore. She had escaped from London simply to be forced to make the same choice here, and this time, there was nowhere to run. And it was Alec who had ensured her fate. Her chest ached at the idea that he had betrayed her. She let Lottie's second maid help her into the gown and looked at herself in the mirror. She was as pale as the muslin. She took a deep breath, and the maid fastened the necklace Sophie had insisted she wear—a violet pendant, made of amethysts and sapphires. Violets grew in the shadow of the old tower. She decided she hated violets. Lottie wore a heart made of rubies on her breast, and Sophie wore a diamond tiara.

The reflection in the mirror told Caroline she was the same woman who'd fled London, and yet she was not. The old Caroline was a lady born and bred to wed a lord, to bear heirs and run a household, and that was to be the extent and purpose of her life. But things had changed. There was a new light in her eyes, a determined—Somerson would say stubborn, and Charlotte would say willful—set to her chin. She managed a smile when Lottie's happy face appeared in the glass next to her own.

She would not let Somerson decide her fate. She would not be forced into making a decision she would regret all her life, even as she dreamed of Alec MacNabb's arms around her, his mouth on hers, his joined with hers. She watched a blush bloom over her cheeks, growing brighter still when Sophie looked over her opposite shoulder, the picture of bridal joy.

She was alone in the world, but she'd made it to Glenlorne, found honorable employment. She could do so again. She felt a new sense of purpose and she raised her chin.

"Please excuse me, I must check on the girls before we go downstairs," she said.

Chapter Thirty-Five

"Let me see," Caroline said. Alanna spun in place, showing off her pink and white muslin gown, trimmed with lace at the sleeves and hem.

Megan was still primping at the mirror, fussing with her hair.

"You look so pretty!" Sorcha chirped, watching her sisters, and pretending she didn't care that she was too young to be allowed down to dinner in such esteemed company. "Sophie says you're an earl's daughter the same as we are, Miss Forrester. Should we curtsy when we see you?"

"Mama said we're to call you Lady Caroline instead of Miss Forrester," Alanna said.

"I'm still the same person," Caroline said. She crossed to Megan, and took the comb to add a curl or two to her hair.

Megan's reflection looked up at hers. "Mama has invited Brodie to supper. I think she might be able to see at last how very much I—" She swallowed, blushing. "Oh, I wish I had something truly stylish to wear, like Sophie and Lady Lottie."

Caroline unfastened the necklace Sophie had insisted she

wear. She put it around Megan's neck instead. "There. That looks lovely."

Sorcha leaned in to examine the jeweled violet, and pouted. "I still think it's quite unfair that I'm not allowed to come down to dinner. I dine with the family every other night."

"Mama says we must strictly observe English rules tonight," Alanna said. "And in England you'd be a child, still dining in the nursery."

Sorcha stuck her tongue out at her sister. "I'll still be there, watching from the gallery above the hall."

"I'll tell Muira to fetch you down and send you to bed," Alanna retorted, her hands on her hips.

"Muira's probably more likely to be up there beside her, watching too, muttering about 'bloody Sassenachs,'" Megan said, then raised her hand to her lips and looked apologetically at Caroline. "Oh, I'm sorry, Miss—Lady—um . . ."

"It's time to go downstairs, or we'll risk being late," Caroline said primly, and herded her charges toward the door. She took a deep breath, and wished for a moment that she could stay with Sorcha. Alanna slipped her hand into Caroline's as they descended the stairs, and Caroline was glad of the comfort, though she supposed Alanna thought Caroline was comforting her. She steeled herself to face her half brother's anger and the sting of Charlotte's scorn.

The gentlemen rose as the ladies entered the room. "There you are, Lady Caroline. We were just speaking of mounting a search since the rain has stopped at last, but you would know that since are quite dry," Viscount Speed said.

"How well you look, Caro," William said, coming to

clasp her hand and kiss her cheek. He was almost a stranger, though they'd grown up together, had been friends once. She'd dreamed of being his wife, though she couldn't imagine marrying him now. Or anyone. She avoided looking at Alec, and gave William a brilliant smile.

Her brother stood waiting for her to come to him, his hands clenched into fists, his color high. She curtsied, feeling his blistering gaze boring into her. "Well, well, here you are at last, and looking very well indeed." He said it as if the fact of her good health annoyed him. "We have a great deal to discuss, and even if your foolish little adventure has lowered your value as a wife, I have other plans for your future. We will speak immediately after dinner is finished." He made it a command. Caroline felt a wave of anger. Did he truly expect things would simply go back their last conversation, as if nothing had happened?

She raised her chin. "I'm afraid I will be putting Lady Sorcha to bed after dinner. Perhaps tomorrow, after the girls lessons conclude at eleven o'clock."

She watched Somerson's face change from red to purple with rage. His fist clenched, and for a moment she feared he intended to strike her. She felt Lottie's eyes on her, and Alec's, but she kept her eyes fixed on her half brother. He lowered his hand.

"Of all the nerve—" Charlotte began, but Lottie put a hand on her mother's arm.

"Perhaps we should take our places at the table," Lottie said. "Perhaps it's the Highland air, but I for one am quite famished."

"Lottie!" Charlotte turned her ire—and the vast bulk of

her person—upon her daughter. "A lady never describes herself as famished!"

"Och, there's a laugh—I saw Her Ladyship at tea, devouring all the tea cakes," Angus said to Georgiana from their perch in the gallery, right behind young Sorcha, who pressed her face eagerly through the railing. "I've known warriors who could not eat as much as she—but they weren't as big, of course." He laughed at his own joke.

Georgiana was gazing at her granddaughter, pride clear in her eyes. "Caroline does look fetching tonight, doesn't she? I don't think Alec has even glanced at anyone else in the room since she arrived. And I rather liked the way she stood up to Somerson. That took courage."

Alec felt himself bristle when Somerson had threatened Caroline. He would not allow him to harm her, guardian or not. She had faced him down, and as with most bullies, his bluster had collapsed at her show of strength.

He watched Caroline turn away, fix Mears with a doting look. She hadn't even glanced at Alec.

Muira announced the meal and Alec took Sophie's arm and led his fiancée to a place on his left, but Devorguilla patted the seat beside herself, farther down the table. "Come and sit here, my dear girl, between myself and Brodie, so we can all get better acquainted." He watched as Sophie took that seat instead, and offered Brodie a soft smile. Brodie giggled. Everyone in the room looked askance at the hulking young man, who was staring at Sophie and blushing like a lass.

Megan eagerly moved to sit beside Brodie, but her mother shook her head. "You must sit further down the table. Next to Viscount Speed, perhaps? Alanna, you sit next to Lord Mandeville." Angus noted that Megan looked devastated. Lord and Lady Somerson took their places, and the reverend Mr. Parfitt sat next to Viscount Mears and beckoned to Caroline, who took her place to the left of Alec's seat at the head of the table. He could smell her perfume, see the agitated pulse in her throat, hear the rustle of the taffeta gown as her breath caught in her throat. Her color was high, and in the candlelight, she was lovelier than any other lady in the room. Mr. Parfitt cleared his throat and intoned the grace, and Caroline kept her eyes downcast, as if the pattern on her plate was intensely fascinating.

Caroline refused to even look at Alec, since it was his fault that Somerson was here. When he moved his knee to nudge hers, she shifted her skirt out of reach, and ignored him. On her other side, William grinned as she bumped him. She moved her knees back toward Alec again.

Alec turned as Viscount Speed leaned forward. "I think tomorrow would be a grand day for hunting, Glenlorne. Mears, Somerson, are you 'game' to come shooting?" He chortled at his own poor joke. Alec forced a smile. He tried to imagine Caroline married to Speed, and could not.

"I have a taste for boar," Charlotte enthused. "Do you have boar here?"

"Alas, no, my lady. They've been extinct for several centuries, I believe," Alec replied. "I can offer grouse, or venison, perhaps, if the shooting is good. The loch is filled with fish, and the river teems with salmon."

"I adore the way Muira makes grouse in whisky sauce," Alanna chirped, and Mandeville sat up.

"Whisky sauce? What an ingenious use of the spirit," he said.

"Indeed I think we simply must have that for dinner tomorrow, after the hunt," Charlotte said eagerly.

"I think I will join the hunt as well," Sophie said. "For the fresh air."

"I'll go too," Brodie added at once, his eyes on Sophie.

"What time are we leaving?" Megan asked, her eyes hard on her straying beau.

"I will go if Caroline is going," William said, giving her a soft smile, and Caroline smiled back. To Alec's eyes, Mears looked near as besotted as Brodie, and Caroline had eyes for no one else. He felt a hard nudge of jealousy.

"If the girls are going," she said. "And Lottie, of course."

"Oh. Of course," Mears said, blinking at his fiancée as if he'd forgotten her entirely.

Alec frowned. Was there something between William Mears and Caroline? The viscount began to chatter about his mother, and someone named Sinjon, and Caroline's eyes sparkled as she hung on every word, ignoring Alec entirely. He nudged her knee again under the table, saw a tide of color flood her face, watched her fingers tighten on the stem of her wineglass. She was aware of him, then, even if she pretended not to be. It brought out the devil in him.

As Muira cleared away the cock-a-leekie soup and served

the second course, salmon, he took off his shoe. As Hamish came to refill the wineglasses, he found the hem of her skirt and worked his foot through the froth of her petticoats to touch her ankle. Her eyes widened, and her lips parted in surprise, but she kept her gaze fixed on William, laughing at his jokes, pretending Alec wasn't there. He wouldn't stand for that.

Unless she was very much mistaken, Alec's stocking foot was caressing her ankle. What was he playing at? It tickled, and Caroline tried to move her foot away, but she bumped into William and his brows shot upward, and he gave her a wicked smile. He thought she was flirting with him? She moved her legs back again. Alec's foot returned.

"And your mother, is she well?" Caroline asked William, trying to ignore the fact that Alec's foot was climbing her calf, rubbing, teasing.

William's knee pressed against hers on the other side, and she shifted, but that brought her closer to Alec. She shot him a sharp look, but he merely smiled at her and sipped his wine.

"We've just established that she is very well indeed," William said.

Alec's questing toes reached her knee, tickled. She swallowed a giggle, hiding it by taking a forkful of salmon.

"And Sinjon and Evelyn?" she asked after William's brother and his wife.

"Healthy, as far as I am given to understand." William leaned forward and smiled at her, just as Alec's toes slipped behind her knee, moving against the sensitive flesh there. She gasped, and William grinned at her. "May I say you are looking particularly lovely tonight?" William said, his eyes scanning her face. Once she would have given anything to see that besotted look on his face. Now she was horrified.

"Thank you," she murmured. Alec's foot was insistently working at her knees, trying to force them apart. She stubbornly kept them closed. What on earth was he doing?

"And how is your father?" she asked William, only to recall they'd already discussed him too.

Alec's foot edged higher, his toes flexing insistently where her stocking ended, and her naked flesh began. She shot him a sharp look, and he raised one eyebrow, and wiggled his toes. Her garter snapped, and she jumped.

"Are you quite all right, Caro?" William asked, patting her on the back, his touch warm between her shoulder blades, lingering just a little too long.

"Isn't the tower lovely in the moonlight?" Alec asked. "It's been a trysting place for centuries, especially at Midsummer." Everyone else glanced out at the picturesque scene beyond the window, and Caroline shot Alec a sharp look. He smiled at her, a slow, lopsided grin of pure seduction. Her heart did a slow somersault. He took advantage of her shock to slip his foot between her knees. She took a sip of wine to hide her gasp.

"I believe I will remain safely indoors tomorrow," Somerson was saying. "I dislike hunting at the best of times. The wet weather here does not agree with me."

"Sometimes it's quite windy," Sophie added.

He was caressing the inside of her thigh. Caroline felt a shiver of desire pass through her.

He was sitting beside her, calmly eating his dinner, presiding over the table filled with guests as if he'd had his shoes on, his feet on the floor where they belonged, and was not driving

her wild. She tried to shift away, but other than unbelievable rudeness of shooting to her feet in the middle of the meal, she was trapped. Had he no mercy? She sent him a pleading look, but he merely raised one arched brow and grinned. His foot remained.

"Shall we set out at dawn?" Speed asked eagerly.

She reached down and dug her nails into Alec's foot, and he shot her a wicked look that told her he did not intend to stop. She gasped as his foot slid farther still, coming to rest against a very sensitive spot indeed at the apex of her thighs. A soft cry of surprise escaped her lips. She couldn't help it.

"I quite agree with Caroline," Sophie said. "I should say that ten o'clock is plenty early enough. Perhaps even eleven."

Alec's toes wiggled, stirred, and Caroline shot him a look of pure anguish, begging him to stop. "More wine, Lady Caroline?" he asked politely. "You look flushed."

Flushed? She was on fire. He was the devil himself, she decided. She bit back a sob when he shifted his foot again, pressing gently.

"Or we could plan to set out at noon, and take luncheon outdoors if the weather is fine." Lottie suggested hopefully.

"You could be back in time for tea." Charlotte said.

Caroline was melting. Sophie and Lottie were now talking about what they would wear, if riding habits or walking gowns would be more suitable. Alec's toes were as persuasive as his fingers, teasing her, demanding a response. It was almost impossible to breathe. She licked her lips. Whenever she turned her attention to William, began a conversation, Alec would wiggle his toes. Who knew a man could do such a thing with his feet? She did her best to listen to what William was saying, to respond to the remarks others made to her, but she was in truth aware of no one but Alec, and what he was doing to her. It was the longest meal of her life.

In the gallery Angus watched as Devorguilla leaned forward to whisper to Brodie. She pressed something into his hand. He excused himself, and left the room. "What's he up to?" Angus said. "Something's not right." He watched Devorguilla turn and give Alec a smug, slit-eyed look of pure hatred, but Alec was too busy watching Caroline to notice. The lass was uncommonly flushed, and Alec's eyes were heavy-lidded. Angus turned to watch for Brodie's return.

Caroline could barely think, let alone carry on a conversation. Alec kept up the slow, gentle torment throughout the meal. Despite her dismay, sweet, hot desire flowed through her veins. She nipples hardened, rubbed against the linen of her shift. She twisted her napkin in her lap, strangling it tighter with every little movement of his toes against her sex. Her cheeks burned. Her whole body burned. She couldn't look at him, didn't dare, knowing that if she did, she'd explode. She twisted the linen napkin harder to keep from sobbing.

Finally the last plates were removed, and she gave thanks

that the meal—and surely the slow, sensual torment—was over. Surely they would now rise from the table and retire, and she would be out of his wicked reach at last. She was exhausted, her nerves frayed as taut as a bowstring.

Hamish carried in a tray of glasses and a decanter of golden whisky and set it on the sideboard. Muira snuffed half the candles out.

"What's this?" Sophie asked.

Devorguilla smiled. "A special treat. Wait and see."

Hamish and Leith opened the kitchen doors and took their places on either side of the portal, dressed in their plaids.

"Do you like a man in Scottish dress, Caroline?" William asked her. "I can't decide if I do or not. It's very different from what English gentlemen wear. I cannot help but feel a little frightened by it. Living in the north of England, I grew up on terrible tales of the '45 rebellion. My nurse used to tell me that if I didn't go to sleep, Bonnie Prince Charlie himself would come down from the hills and drag me across the border and eat me. For the longest time, I imagined a nation of baby-eating men in skirts lurking right next door to Halliwell Hall."

Alec's foot tensed indignantly, pausing at last. He would surely withdraw it now the conversation had taken a serious turn, she thought, and she would be free.

But he didn't. Instead, his toes curled and flexed and played, and she swallowed a sob of misery.

She heard the low moan of bagpipes as they drew breath to sing, rising to the heart-stopping skirl of bright sound that filled the room as the pipers came out of the kitchen.

Megan, Lottie, and Alanna cried out in delight as the pipers appeared, and slowly marched down the length of the table, playing a merry tune. Sophie flinched at every note.

Caroline drew a sharp breath—not because of the magnificence of the ancient music that filled the hall, but because Alec's toes were on the move again. She could not bear it. Surely she would die of the torment. She let her eyes drift shut, and her breath came in short gasps she couldn't control. She gripped the edge of the table. How dare he make her feel this, bring her to the edge, threaten to push her over. Heat rose from the tender, inflamed bud his toes teased, and she felt it rise over her belly and breasts, until she was sure she'd burst into flames.

Behind the pipers came Muira, carrying a pudding on a huge platter, decorated with the clan symbols of heath, pine, and crowberry.

And behind her, Brodie carried in the laird's cup.

Alec's foot caught the rhythm of the music, throbbing, thrusting, toying, rubbing faster and faster, dancing a mad reel.

Muira touched a lighted taper to the pudding and it burst into flames. Everyone at the table cried out, Caroline loudest of all, as the sensation carried her over the edge. Alec gripped her hand under the table, squeezed it.

She stared at him in horror, mortified. Fortunately, all eyes were on the pudding, and not on her.

He had the audacity to smile, giving her a grin of pure male pride.

Caroline slipped her fork under the tablecloth and stabbed

him in the leg, her smile rising as his faded. This time, it was his cry the skirl of the pipes hid.

"Why would Brodie be carrying the cup?" Angus asked. "It goes against tradition."

"What?" Georgiana was watching the blue flames flicker over the pudding.

"It should be Jock, Alec's seneschal." Angus stared at Brodie, saw him flick a glance at Devorguilla, who smiled like the vixen she was. There was no pride or joy in her smile, just pure malice. It rose from her like grave rot. She nodded, and Brodie moved forward, carrying the cup down the length of the table toward Alec. Angus looked into the cup as it passed under his perch, felt the prickle of warning and fear.

"No," he hissed. "She wouldna!"

"Whatever is the matter?" Georgiana asked. "Look at Caroline—she's positively radiant tonight."

"*Gràdhach*, she's going to poison him."

Georgiana's brow furrowed. "Why would Caroline poison Brodie?"

"Not Caroline, Devorguilla, and not Brodie—she's going to poison Alec!"

Angus looked at the assembled company desperately. Megan's eyes were shining with pride as Brodie passed her. Sophie was regarding the pipers as if she wished them to the depths of Hades. Somerson looked bored. Alec, the fool, had eyes only for Caroline. So, apparently did the young viscount seated beside her. "Alec!" Angus cried out. "Alec, don't drink it, lad!" But he couldn't hear.

Angus leaned over the railing, floated down, tried to stop Brodie, to push him, or knock the cup from his hand, but Brodie passed straight through him. Angus clawed uselessly at the cup.

It was then that Caroline turned and saw him over her shoulder. She smiled a welcome. She imagined he was part of the damned fool ceremony. He shook his head, desperate now. Brodie had arrived at Alec's side, bowed, and was holding out the laird's cup with a sickly grin on his florid face. Alec nodded to his cousin, reached out to take the cup. Angus looked at Caroline desperately. "Lass, do something!" he cried. He saw Caroline's smile fade, watched her high color turn to ashes. She began rising to her feet, her eyes still on him, a frown drawing her brows together as she opened her mouth to speak. Angus watched as her shoulder hit the cup, sending it spinning out of Brodie's hands.

Everyone in the room watched the chalice arc through the air, the candlelight glinting off the cup's silver embellishments as the ruby wine splashed, sparkled, and dropped to the floor. The chalice rang on the stone, echoing through the ancient hall to the very rafters, like a bell warning of treachery and murder.

Devorguilla shot to her feet, her chair tipping backward. It landed in spreading pool of wine with a crash. She stared down at the rivulet flowing toward her in dull surprise, evil seeking its source, Angus thought as she lifted her skirts out of the way.

Angus looked back at Caroline, who hadn't taken her eyes

from him. She stood staring at him, her eyes hollows of surprise as if she'd seen a ghost.

He smiled. What else could he do? She knew what he was now. No one else had seen him. He smiled at her and touched a hand to his bonnet, and slipped back into the shadows.

Muira hurried forward to wipe up the spill, the white rag soon blood red. A faint and familiar smell reached her, and she frowned. Muira dipped a finger into the dregs in the cup and tasted it. In horror she stared at Devorguilla, who was sitting quietly again, her face tight. Devorguilla caught her look and returned one of pure malice. Muira made a sign against evil.

CHAPTER THIRTY-SIX

Somerson threw down his napkin and rose. "If the evening's festivities are finished, I need a quiet place where I can speak with Caroline alone."

Alec felt her tense, but she nodded. "Of course," he said. "My study is at your disposal." He still wasn't certain what had just happened. Brodie had raced for the kitchen, and Muira and Devorguilla were glaring at each other like two cats about to fight. Caroline's hazel eyes were as big as saucers as they darted into the dark corners of the hall. Perhaps he'd gone too far teasing her, pleasuring her at dinner with her half brother right across the table. He looked again at William Mears, who was staring at Caroline as if he'd been the one to have the pleasure. He wondered again how well she'd known him as a girl—a few stolen kisses perhaps, or even a deep friendship. Did he feel what Alec felt for her? Hardly. Alec watched Caroline depart with Somerson, saw the sway of her hips, the elegant set of her head. Moments ago, he'd been teasing her, but he was the one left wanting, burning with desire that was even worse now. He'd made another grave mistake. How would he keep himself from climbing the stairs to the tower now?

He needed a cold bath, or a long swim in the icy loch. As the company dispersed, he went upstairs, changed into the ease and comfort of his plaid, and slipped out into the dark night. The air was sweet and cool from the rain, fragrant with pine and heather.

He heard the sound of his sister's sobs before he saw her huddled on a stone bench by the wall, her knees curled under her white dress. Megan looked like a heartbroken ghost.

Alec sat down beside her and pulled her against his shoulder and let her sob until her sorrow turned to hiccups.

"What's this about?" he asked.

"I thought Brodie loved me."

"Perhaps he does," Alec said.

"Then why was he staring at Sophie all night? Why wasn't he looking at me? He has hardly said two words to me since she arrived."

How could Alec not understand? All Mears had to do was glance at Caroline and he was consumed with jealousy, but if Brodie had pulled Sophie into his arms and laid her on the table to have his way with her during the meal, he would have felt nothing but mild surprise at the lad's lack of timing—not that he'd allow any such impropriety after they were wed, of course. He recognized his sister's feelings in his own regarding Caroline.

"Brodie's very young, as are you, lass. He's never been any farther from home than Glenlorne," Alec said. "And Ben Ardle is barely ten miles away, and not nearly as grand as Glenlorne. Did you see the tiara Sophie had on tonight? Perhaps he was staring at that. It would impress anyone."

"I have jewels as well." Megan sniffed. She showed him the pretty flower at her throat. The purple and blue stones glittered in the candlelight that poured through the window.

"Where did you get that?" Alec asked.

"Lady Caroline lent it to me. I believe it's Lady Lottie's. She was going to wear it herself, but she could see I wanted to look especially pretty tonight for Brodie. Isn't that kind of her, Alec? She's a lovely person. I overheard Countess Charlotte say they mean to keep her locked up for the rest of her life, or marry her off to a tinker for tuppence."

Alec shifted uncomfortably at the change in topic. His sister put her hand on his sleeve. "You wouldn't let them do that, would you? People have to listen to you, because you're laird, don't they? She could stay here, bide with us."

Alec shut his eyes for a moment. "Lord Somerson is her brother, and her guardian. He only wants what's best for her," he said, but even he could hear the doubt in his tone. He felt another pang of guilt. He should never have written to Somerson.

"I know you don't like him, or Countess Charlotte. I won't let on for Lady Caroline's sake, but isn't there anything you can do? If you weren't already betrothed to Sophie, you could marry Caroline, couldn't you? I wish Sophie had never come. She wants to change everything."

"I thought we were speaking of Brodie?" Alec tried for a light tone.

"I suppose we were, weren't we? Could you command him to marry me?"

Alec stroked his chin. "I could, I suppose. And if he refuses, I could have him executed," he joked, but she didn't smile. "Would you want that, sweeting, a man who had to be ordered to take you? You're young yet. Go to London for the Season, see the city, meet people, and then—"

Megan gasped. "Don't tell me you want me to marry an Englishman as well!"

He shook his head, tapped the tip of her nose, and wondered again where her freckles had gone. "I want you to marry a man you love and who loves you."

She thought for a moment, then leaned in to kiss his cheek. "I had no idea you were so sentimental, Alec."

"Wait a while. Men are slower to grow up than young ladies. Let Brodie be for a year or two, see if he still has your heart then."

"Thank you, Alec. You're very wise. It's a good thing you're Laird of Glenlorne. Things will be well again now, won't they? You'll make them right." She got to her feet. "I'm going inside to speak to Lottie. She said she knows everyone in England who's worth knowing, and she'd be happy to sponsor me. She'll be a married lady herself by then, of course."

He stayed where he was and watched her go. If only all problems of the heart were so easy to fix, he thought.

He stared out at the hills, at the old tower, its crumbling walls so full of holes that the stars shone right through it. Was it a symbol of the clan's permanence here on this land, or the emblem of a people as tumble-down and desperate as the tower?

It had stood for four hundred years against wind, rain, snow, and even war. It had been there throughout his life, yet he'd scarcely paid it any notice until the day he saw Caroline standing in the window. The memory of finding her there, of making love to her under the open roof on Midsummer's Eve had him instantly, uncomfortably hard again. How long would it take to forget her once she left Glenlorne? What if she were to stay, as Megan suggested?

He couldn't imagine Glenlorne without her. He looked forward to the sight of her every morning, to catching a glimpse of her walking to the village, or climbing the hills just to see the view. The clan just accepted her as a fixture here—even Muira—a rare honor for a Sassenach. Between Alec and the tower, the loch glittered and the wind was busy blowing the last of the rain clouds out of the sky. He took a deep breath, and realized how much he loved Glenlorne, the way he had as a child, when his grandfather still lived.

Alec felt alive here, not the creature of shame and shadow he'd been in London. Angus MacNabb had been dour and taciturn during his lifetime, but he made his clan feel safe and cared for. Alec wondered if he could do that too. He pictured himself with a family, a happy home, the village rebuilt, a school, the hillsides dotted with fat sheep and sturdy Highland cattle. And a loving wife, of course. Sophie.

Yet Sophie was the only part of the picture that rang false. And she was the one person he needed—along with her fortune—to make it all happen.

"What the devil were you thinking?" Somerson's harsh voice demanded, drifting through the window above Alec. "Did you consider my position for even a moment before you ran off, the embarrassment you might have caused?"

"You told people I had retired to the country, ill. How long before you simply told them I was dead?" Caroline replied. "It seems to me as if you found a most convenient solution."

"Don't be impudent!" he bellowed. Alec heard Somerson's heavy footfalls cross the floor.

Alec was on his feet in an instant. He flattened himself against the wall and peered in the open window from the shadows, ready to stop Somerson from harming Caroline. She was standing before him, her chin high.

Alec stepped back into the shadows to watch and listen. Eavesdropping was a useful skill he'd learned in Westlake's service.

"You won't strike me, Neville. People would see the marks. I didn't mean to cause you any inconvenience. I simply felt I had no choice."

"You had plenty of choice. Two fine suitors—"

"I don't love either of them. I could never love them," Caroline said breathlessly.

"Love? You sound like your mother. She told me she loved my father, but she was nothing but a fortune hunter. Love has nothing to do with marriage for our class. Noble matches are made for financial reasons, for political gain, for land and pedigree. I chose suitors for you who answered all those requirements. Love had nothing to do with it. You are most fortunate to receive proposals at all. You've never had a Season, never been introduced at court. I spoke to Speed and Mandeville both. They are still willing to entertain marrying you, ruined though you are. If you had done this in England, no one would marry you. As it is, you are damned fortunate I can still conceal this—this—fool's errand."

"I don't feel fortunate," Caroline replied evenly. "Nor am I willing to marry either gentleman."

"Then you will not marry at all," he threatened. "I am your

guardian, and if you will not obey me, then I will take you to Starbury Manor. You will stay there permanently, and wish you were dead indeed. You have no choice."

"There is one other choice, Neville," she said softly.

Caroline was standing on the rug in front of his desk, her hands clasped, but she did not look submissive in the least. The candlelight flamed over two spots of color on her pale cheeks, and she held her head high. Alec felt a surge of pride.

"Then you'll do as I say and marry where I tell you?"

"No." Her voice was quiet, but firm.

"No?" Alec heard anger in Somerson's tone.

"I will sign a paper, give everything I own to you—you may have my dowry."

Somerson stared down at her, his eyes narrowing in disbelief. "What? You would be penniless!".

"I am aware of the consequences. I understand my dowry is quite large. Let me go, Neville, and you may keep the money. It is a better arrangement, is it not? You wished to marry me off to whoever would take me. You would still have had to pay my husband my dowry. This way, you can keep it, and still be rid of me."

Somerson considered the matter in silence.

Alec stared at her. Lady Caroline Forrester, half sister to one of England's most powerful peers, was throwing everything away just to be free. Wasn't that what he'd done when he left home, swearing to go to Ceylon, to make his own way in the world and never return? It hadn't worked out for him. He'd been beaten and robbed the very day he reached London. If not for Westlake picking him out of the gutter, he'd likely be dead by now. Caroline had no such protector, no such hope, yet she stood with her shoulders square, her chin high, her eyes clear, sure of what she was doing.

"Very well. If that's what you want. I shall write something out tonight."

She shook her head. "I want Father's man of affairs in York to do it. He dealt with my mother's will as well. I want it done legally, so neither you nor I can ever come back and say we were cheated."

"I am the Earl of Somerson! He'll write what I tell him to."

"Perhaps so, but he knows me, knew my mother. I insist upon that condition."

"You are in no position to insist upon anything!" Somerson reminded her.

"If you keep me, it will cost you money, whether I marry or live out my life in isolation at Starbury. You have everything to gain, and only one unwanted half sister to lose."

Alec watched her move toward the door. "Where are you going? I didn't give you leave to go," Somerson spluttered.

Caroline turned to face her half brother. "I have said what I wished to say. What more is there to stay for? Please excuse me. I am still employed here, and I must check on the girls."

"Why you—" Somerson began, but stopped when he realized she'd slipped out of the room, and he was talking to empty air.

Alec slumped down onto the bench to consider what he'd heard. She was brave, and smart—she'd known exactly how to defeat Somerson, even if it had cost her everything. She understood what she was doing, it was clear in her eyes. Her freedom, her honor, her independence, her very life was worth more to her than money. He leaned his head back and laughed silently.

She'd been beautiful, bold, a tigress facing down a dragon.

He was more tempted than ever to go and find her, to pull her into his arms and— He groaned and got to his feet, and took the path that led down to the loch. He needed a long, cold swim.

"Did you see that?" Angus asked Georgiana as Caroline left the room. "First she saved Alec's life, and then she put the uggsome bastard Somerson in his place! She's magnificent."

Georgiana sighed. "She'll still leave, Angus. She can't stay."

"Why not? Alec will see her safe," Angus said. "He's a man of honor. He'll do right by her."

Georgiana folded her arms over her chest. "I'd say she's more than proven she can take care of herself. Alec is betrothed to Sophie. If Caroline stays here, she'll still be doomed to live a life of heartache and sorrow, don't you see? She has pride and honor of her own. She would never consent to live as your grandson's mistress."

Angus glared at her. "What of the girls? They've come to love her. So have the villagers. I doubt they'll love Sophie. Caroline belongs at Glenlorne, but Sophie will forever be an outsider." He looked at his beloved, realizing that she would have been an outsider at Glenlorne too, if she stayed, hated by the clan just for being a daughter of the enemy. "You could never have stayed with me, could you, all those years ago?"

She smiled sadly. "Do you think I haven't got Caroline's

courage? It would have been nigh impossible—but I would have tried, Angus. I would have endured anything to be with you, to spend my life here. How can you even ask that?"

"How can I not?" he demanded. "It is impossible, even now."

"If you believe that, then this curse will never end," Georgiana said sadly, and faded into the darkness.

Angus sat on the bank of the loch, watching Alec swim in the icy waters in the dark. He'd been in there long enough to shrivel his flesh to ice, yet he swam back and forth, back and forth, his muscular body cleaving the black surface like a man trying to escape a shipwreck.

Angus was still waiting when Alec came out at last and flopped down on the bank beside his plaid. Angus knew well enough why Alec was here. It was Caroline. He'd spent plenty of nights in the icy water himself, trying to forget Georgiana, his body as stubborn as his broken heart about letting her go. He stared out at the cold water and knew Alec was facing a lifetime of nights here.

"Lad, you're going to have to fix this," he murmured, though he knew Alec couldn't hear him.

"How the devil am I supposed to fix this?" Alec murmured to the loch.

"It's a puzzle. I know ye need the money."

"Sophie," Alec mused.

"Aye. She has plenty, but there's more to this than just money. I lived my whole life without love, swimming in this bloody loch because I couldn't forget her."

"Caroline." Alec sighed.

"Georgiana." Angus sighed. "Not that I could have married her, ye understand." He took off his bonnet and tossed it on the ground in frustration. "I didn't have a choice, and you do. I understand, lad, truly I do. You have to choose between your heart's desire, and your duty as laird."

Alec stared across the loch at the tower, not hearing a word, and Angus followed his gaze. "Aye, I have my own history with that tower, lad. I know well enough that it can drive a man daft, remembering, wishing things had been different." Alec didn't move. "Och, didn't I teach you anything? Responsibility, duty, I remember teaching ye that. Probably sitting right about here too. The clan comes first, I recall telling ye. I believed it then. I should have taught you about love. When I lost Georgiana, I married for money. I had to, after Culloden. Yer grandmother's family was loyal to the Crown. They kept their land, their fortune, and they helped hunt down the poor fools who fought for Charlie, but marrying her meant I could keep Glenlorne, and I thought that was all that mattered. I couldn't have gone after Georgiana, ye understand—she was already married to Somerson, lad. It was too late for us. But you, Alec, you have a choice to make, and I hope ye'll make it before it's too late."

Alec rubbed his wet hair with a fold of his plaid, oblivious. "I know what you're thinking. I spent many nights swimming here myself, trying not to remember," Angus said. He smiled out at the water. "Och, she was a sweet thing, just like Caroline is—"

Alec got up and wrapped his plaid around his hips, belting it in place. He didn't bother to put on his shirt. He slung it over his shoulder and headed back toward Glenlorne.

Angus watched him go, and felt the agony of loss all over again.

Chapter Thirty-Seven

It was done. Caroline paced the floor of her room. She was free. Or was she?

Freedom came at a price. A terrible price. She would most likely spend her life taking care of other people's children as a governess, or a teacher. Yet she would not have it otherwise.

She would probably never marry at all, and had no desire to. Her heart belonged yet again to a man she could not have. Unfortunately, this time she wasn't merely fondly hoping that a certain gentleman would propose, and doing her very best to convince herself she was in love with him.

She knew now that those pallid feelings hadn't been love at all, just a desire to belong somewhere, to someone, because she'd been raised to expect to marry within her class, breed heirs for him, and run his estates. There would have been no adventures, no surprises, no Alec.

As much as it hurt in this moment, she would not have missed the past weeks for the world.

It was a relief to be free of Somerson, to be independent, though she had been pampered and cared for all her life, had

money and luxuries. She could live without those. Losing
Alec was harder. Now her choice was made, she knew now
she couldn't remain at Glenlorne and watch as he married
Sophie.

She crossed to the window and sat on the window seat,
looking out at the old tower, standing sentinel over the glen.
"Keep him safe, make him happy," she whispered.

The crunch of gravel caught her by surprise. Who was out
at this late hour? Alec came up the drive. Her eyes widened,
and she stared at him from the anonymity of her window,
high above him. He was wearing his kilt, but his chest was
bare, his shirt over his shoulder. His hair was wet, sleek
against his head. The light of the torches that lit the outside
of the castle flared over his broad shoulders and naked chest,
turning his flesh to gold.

Caroline's mouth watered, and she remembered exactly
how warm his skin was, how hard the muscle beneath, and
how she had dug her nails into his shoulders as he loved her.
Her first time. And the last, if one didn't count the wicked
game he'd played with her at dinner. Her body flushed and
tingled. She wanted more.

She bit her lip and shut her eyes, trying to still the longing.

When she opened her eyes again, Alec had stopped walking. He stood below her window looking up at her, just the
way he had the day she first saw him. She held her breath and
tightened her hand on the stone sill, and felt his gaze like a
gentle finger moving over her skin, quickening her heartbeat,
raising goose bumps, making desire rush through her veins.
She stared back, unable to move, even to break the spell.

He groaned, and the soft sound echoed off the stones.

She watched as he turned back the way he'd come and disappeared down the path that led to the loch.

For a long moment Caroline hovered in the window, watching the dark path, wishing he'd come back, climb the stairs, throw open the door to her room as he did before. He didn't come. She should go to bed, be sensible, but what point was there in lying down? She wouldn't sleep, not with so much in her head to prevent it. She needed— She shut her eyes. She shouldn't.

She grabbed a shawl and hurried down the stairs.

Chapter Thirty-Eight

She heard the splash of water as she neared the loch. She paused in the shadows and looked out across the dark, silken surface. She saw his head appear, like a seal or an otter, and she slipped deeper into the darkness under the trees, and almost tripped on his discarded clothes. She should go, she thought, walk away before he saw her, demanded an explanation. She didn't have one. She was on a fool's errand. She turned away.

"Don't go," he called. "Or at least don't go if you were looking for me."

Caroline clasped her hands together tightly as she stepped into view. "I wasn't," she said. "Not really. I couldn't sleep. I was just walking." That sounded like a thin excuse indeed—what kind of a ninny went walking all alone at night? Mind you, what kind of ninny went swimming at midnight? "Is the water cold?" she asked, striving for a conversational tone.

"Not nearly cold enough," he replied.

Caroline frowned. "What does that mean?"

"Care to join me and find out?"

She blinked. Was he suggesting she remove her clothing, lay it beside his on the bank, and swim? She'd never done such a thing, not even as a child. Still she was tempted. She'd seen the local children swimming in the loch by day. It was just one more of Glenlorne's pleasures. A bolt of dismay pierced her. "I'm leaving," she said.

"Suit yourself," he called back.

"I mean I'm leaving Glenlorne."

He was still in the water for a moment. She stared down at her fingers, white as bone in the moonlight. "I will stay for the wedding—Lottie's wedding—then I will go." She made the decision as she spoke. She could not stay for his wedding, watch Sophie simper and blush while Alec smiled down at her, kissed her, cherished her.

Too late she realized he was coming out. She watched his silhouette rise from the loch, broad shoulders, narrow hips, long legs, the water cascading off his skin as he strode toward her. She couldn't take her eyes off him. Her heart clenched and her mouth dried to ashes.

He stopped a few feet from her. "And where will you go?" He set his hands on his hips, as if he was completely oblivious to his nakedness. He looked like a Greek statue—minus the fig leaf—sculpted and perfect. A shiver of desire coursed through her. She bent to pick up his shirt, handing it to him with her eyes properly averted.

He tossed it aside and stepped toward her. He put a finger under her chin and forced her to look at him. "And go where?" he demanded again. "I think I deserve an answer."

Anger flared, and she pushed his hand away. "How can I stay? After dinner tonight, after—" She stopped.

"What's William Mears to you, Caroline?" he asked. "You lit up the moment he smiled at you."

"William?" she squeaked. "You did—that—because I *smiled* at Will?"

He put his hands on his hips, and she tried her best not to look down the length of his body.

"Will, is it?"

"We grew up together. Everyone thought we might marry someday, but he's betrothed to Lottie. You can't possibly be jealous of Will. I don't love—" She stopped before she admitted something best kept hidden.

"He certainly seemed enamored of you. I know lust when I see it."

So did she, and the evidence of his desire was obvious. She folded her hands over her chest. "Will is like a brother."

"He wasn't looking at you like a brother."

"Still that gave you no right to do what you did."

"You enjoyed it."

"I was mortified."

They were standing nose to nose. He reached up and caressed her cheek, his finger icy. "Do you know how beautiful you are when you are properly pleasured?"

"That was hardly proper! Why do you think I stabbed you with a fork?" She made the mistake of looking down at his leg, searching for the puncture wounds. Her breath caught at the sight of his erection.

"Don't go," he whispered.

"Do you mean now, this moment?" she asked, surprised at the huskiness of her voice, the weakness in her legs. "It's all there is, Alec. I can't stay."

"The girls need you."

"It's not about that," she murmured, intoxicated by the nearness of his body.

"I need you too," he said.

Caroline saw the movement of his throat as he swallowed. She shook her head.

"Only because I am your servant. Because I was— convenient. You have Sophie. There's no need to apologize for—for what happened in the tower. It was the fire, the drink, the—"

His fingers on her cheek stopped her. His hand was soft, cool, gentle as it stroked her face, cupped her cheek.

"It was more than that. Don't sell yourself short. I wanted you."

She stared into the dark hollows of his eyes. "You thought I was Sophie."

"I thought you were perfect."

She felt the nearness of his body, the warmth of his skin, despite the fact that he'd been swimming in near ice water moments before. She pressed her cheek into his palm, and shut her eyes for a moment, wished just this once, it was all true, and real, and she wasn't cursed—

He groaned. "Damn it, Caroline, either kiss me or send me back into the bloody loch! I can't bear this any longer, being close to you, not touching you."

With a cry of need, she kissed him, slamming her lips into his, pressing herself against the wet length of his naked body.

Alec caught her lips against his. Her body was warm against his loch-chilled skin, and he molded the length of her body to his, devouring her, thrusting his tongue into her mouth, reveling in the taste of her. She was everything he remembered she was, everything he'd dreamed of for weeks. More. He broke the kiss, pressing gently on her shoulders.

"God, Caroline. This time I'll give you the chance to say no, to refuse me. Go—run—back to the castle and lock your door," he muttered against her ear, kissing the shell of it.

"No," she said.

"I can't ask you to stay . . ." His hand dipped into the low bodice of her gown to cup her breast, the soft weight filling his palm, the nipple peaking at his touch.

"I'm leaving," she murmured, kissing his cheek, his chin, his mouth.

"This is the last time," he said against her lips.

"The very last time," she agreed, her voice husky.

He couldn't think anymore, didn't want to consider what the morning would bring, or what it would be like at Glenlorne without her. She nipped at his earlobe and he groaned.

He pressed his back against a tree, spread his legs, drew her between them, and she arched her hips against him, rubbing, soft little gasps of need escaping from her. There was no need to tell her what he wanted. She already knew. She reached down and grasped his cock and he groaned.

His hands fumbled at the buttons on the back of her gown, lust making him clumsy. Her gentle exploration of his body was driving him wild, making it difficult to concentrate. He abandoned the buttons and slid his fingers down the warm slopes of her breast to scoop them out of the low bodice. Her nipples peaked instantly under his thumbs, and she gasped and threw her head back, thrusting herself into his hands, wordlessly demanding more.

He grasped her hand, took her the few steps to where his discarded plaid lay, and fell back, drawing her down on top of him. Long locks of hair fell over him, tickling his face and his chest. He could feel the heat of her as she straddled his hips, and he fumbled to raise her skirts, sliding his hand up over the silken thighs, dipping between her legs until he brushed the curls at her center. He inserted a finger into her, felt her tremble and sigh. She was wet, ready for him, and he stroked the soft petals of her flesh, making her wetter still. He caught her cry, kissing her hard, using his tongue in his mouth as he used his fingers below, driving her release higher.

"Now," he commanded, grasping her hips, positioning her. She plunged down onto him, and shivered in renewed climax almost at once. He thrust into her, hard and fast, overcome with need, holding her buttocks in his palms, feeling the flex of the warm globes of feminine flesh as she moved with him, strove for pleasure in time with him. In the dappled darkness, he could see her exposed breasts above him, the nipples round and dark, saw her lip caught in white teeth.

"Again, love," he murmured, holding back his own release, It was like trying to hold back a team of runaway horses. He was on the edge, buried deep in the tight paradise of her body. She gave a soft cry, swiveling her hips, trying to drive him deeper still. He stopped thinking about anything but how good she felt, how right. He gritted his teeth and thrust into her until she cried out, and he pressed into her as far as he could go, and let the molten waves of release claim him.

He clasped her to his chest. Still inside her, caressing the smooth planes of her back, listening to her breath singing through her body. He kissed her neck, and she raised her head to kiss his lips again. He stroked her back, memorized the curves of her figure, the softness of her thighs and buttocks, the smell of her skin.

"When will you go?" he asked.

"A few days. Once arrangements are made," she said, and rose, slipping off his body. He felt the chill night air rush in. She tucked a strand of hair behind her ear and turned away, rising to straighten her gown shyly. He leaned on his elbow.

"Come and sleep for a while," he said, holding out his hand. "My plaid will cover us both."

She stayed where she was. "I know. But it's almost dawn. Someone might see, and we have to get up in a few hours for the hunt."

He'd forgotten that. "Of course," he said, rising. "I'll walk back with you, at least as far as the bottom of the hill." He pulled his shirt over his head, and shook out his plaid, folded it, wrapped it around his hips, and fastened his belt. She walked ahead of him along the narrow path, ferns and flowers brushing against her skirt.

They reached the spot where the woods ended and the lawn began, and she stopped, turning to him in the shadows. He touched her face.

"I wish—" he began, but she lowered her head, pulled back.

"You are betrothed to Sophie."

"Yes. It would it be dishonorable to break the betrothal, it would—" He groaned. "I've never done the honorable thing in my life, so why does it matter so much now?"

She smiled in the half light. "Because you are the Laird of Glenlorne. Your clan needs a leader, Alec," she said softly. "This is what matters."

"I've hardly been honorable toward you."

"I don't blame you for any of this. Nor do I regret it."

"You are a remarkable woman, Caroline. Where will you go when you leave?"

She shook her head, remained mute.

"At least let me help you find a place," he offered.

"No, Alec. I don't want that."

"Why?" he asked, though he already knew the answer.

"Because you'll know where to find me. It's better if we part without any attachments." She turned and began to walk toward the castle. He caught her arm, drew her back.

"You'll know where to find me, though. You'll come back to me if you need help, won't you?" He wanted her again, wanted to drag her down, lay her in the ferns, and let them find her in his arms, but he could not.

He had responsibilities. How he hated the word.

He turned away, frustrated, angry, and headed back into the woods.

"Aren't you coming back to the castle?" she called after him.

He stopped. "I think I'll take another swim," he said. He came back and kissed her forehead. "Good night, Caroline," he said softly.

She met his eyes. "Good night, Alec."

He knew she stood and watched him walk away, but he didn't look back.

CHAPTER THIRTY-NINE

The hunting party waited for the mist to clear before setting off into the hills to hunt. Leith glanced at the straggling trail of folk behind him and pushed his tam back to look at his companion. "What exactly are we looking for, Jock?"

Jock scanned the heather, the woods by the loch, and the slopes that led up toward the old tower. "Anything the Sassenachs can shoot at."

Leith puffed his cheeks and blew air out. "Grouse season doesn't start for nigh on a fortnight."

Jock spit into the heather. "Aye, I ken it. The Sassenachs ken it as well. Let's hope the grouse don't ken it."

"There are hares about. Will they do?"

Jock sighed. "So long as they don't shoot the sheep, it's fine with me."

He ducked as a shot rang out, and Leith dove into the heather. A bird on the wing flapped away, squawking its displeasure, but unharmed. "That's a bonxie!" Leith pointed. "Ye can't eat those!" He picked up his tam and gaped at the bullet hole.

The gull wheeled and came to dive at its would-be murderer. Several ladies in the party screeched, sounding like gulls themselves, and the men ducked and tried to reload at the same time. Only the laird and his sisters waved their arms to drive the bird off. Leith brushed dirt off his trews and Jock elbowed him.

"Come on, lad. Start looking for something they can shoot. Point it out and run like hell the other way."

Lottie watched as Sophie pulled her elegant cashmere shawl more tightly over the heavy coat that was buttoned to her chin. Her nose was red with chill. In Lottie's opinion, the weather was quite pleasant, though a silver mist lay over the hillsides.

"Perhaps Lord Somerson, Charlotte, and Countess Devorguilla were sensible to stay behind. I do hope the weather stays fair," Sophie said anxiously. "Is this considered fair?"

"I don't know, but you're quite right—in England, we'd stay indoors with Mama, and be bored," Lottie replied.

"How are we supposed to even see anything, let alone shoot it in all this fog?" Sophie complained. "The wet grass will quite ruin my boots."

"You should have worn sturdier ones," Lottie said. "I wore my riding boots—see?"

Sophie sniffed. "But these match my gown. They're hand-dyed to match perfectly. What will I wear if they're ruined?" She shifted the dainty bow quiver on her shoulder. Even the quiver matched her boots, and the fletching of the arrows matched the feathers in her jaunty little cap.

"D'you suppose one of the gentlemen would lend me a gun and teach me how to shoot?" Lottie asked.

Sophie looked horrified. "Good heaven, Lottie, you can't mean it! A gun?"

Lottie raised her chin. "I do mean it. My father forbids it, which makes me all the keener to try."

"My father says archery is the only suitable type of shooting for a lady."

"But have you ever shot at anything other than a target? A grouse or a pheasant, perhaps?" Lottie asked, eyeing the decorative little bow.

"Of course not! Whatever for? We have groundskeepers and huntsmen to do that."

"For the adventure of it."

Sophie looked more horrified by the idea of adventure than she'd been at the thought of shooting something. "Adventure? Why, you bold creature—what on earth has gotten into you, Lottie?" She nodded to where William was walking ahead of them with Caroline. "Just what would your fiancé say to *that*?"

Lottie sniffed. "William doesn't care for adventure, or for excitement of any kind. He doesn't even like to dance. Nor does he engage in manly sports like boxing or curricle racing."

Sophie's eyes popped. "Curricles!"

"I had an admirer once who let me take the reins of his—it was quite thrilling. I lost my bonnet."

"I hope it wasn't an expensive one," Sophie said. "Thank heaven your William is the sensible sort. You'll be entirely safe from harm with him."

"Yes, I suppose so," Lottie murmured. "Oh, I wish I was

as brave as Caroline. I would love to have an adventure, even a teeny one, before I spend the rest of my days being entirely safe."

Sophie laughed acidly. "Don't be silly. Charlotte says she's quite ruined."

Lottie watched her aunt, chatting with William as they walked. "She doesn't look ruined. She looks . . . oh, I don't know. Happier, prettier—*alive*."

Sophie tossed her chin. "No decent gentleman of title and fortune will even look at her now, at least not as a wife."

Lottie's eyes widened as she considered what that meant. "Poor Caro!"

Sophie's smirk was tight and malicious. "So you see now what wishing for adventures will get you?"

"Perhaps you're right," Lottie murmured, staring at her aunt. Caroline threw back her head and laughed at something William said, her russet hair glowing against the mist, her cheeks flushed becomingly. Lottie frowned. She had never known her fiancé to be the least bit amusing.

Sophie caught her arm. "Of course I am—I am never wrong." She waved for a servant who carried folding chairs monogrammed with the Bray crest. "Let's sit here for a while and rest," she said, though they'd hardly been out a half hour. Lottie slipped into the seat beside her friend and watched Caroline and the rest of the party disappear through the mist.

"I must say, Caroline, you're looking well this morning," William said as they walked behind the ghillies. "Very well, in fact."

Caroline looked at him. "Don't tell me Somerson told you I was at death's door as well."

"No, of course not. I'm family—almost. They told me you had retired to Somerson Park to consider your matrimonial choices." He was staring at her with the kind of interest she had once longed for. He should be looking at Lottie that way, not her, but Lottie was sitting on the hillside with Sophie, with Brodie lounging by their feet like a big dog.

"I have," she said, turning her attention to watch Alec walking with Megan.

"Oh," he murmured, and looked almost downcast.

"I mean I have decided not to marry at all," Caroline clarified.

"Oh!" William brightened. He licked his lips, and drew a step closer to her side.

"Lottie will make a beautiful bride."

"Who?" William said like a distracted owl. Caroline raised one eyebrow and sent him a quelling look. "Oh— Lottie! Yes, of course. Lottie . . ." He said her name as if he were trying to remember if he knew a lady by that name.

"I am quite looking forward to the *wedding*," Caroline said, emphasizing the word. "My dear niece and my childhood *friend*."

He winced and bit his lip, his eyes round and sad as a puppy's. "Fr-friend?" he asked.

"Friend," she said firmly.

"Oh." This time his voice dropped an octave, heading for the depths of disappointment. "Caroline, if you're not going to marry, what will you do? Will you take a—" He turned pink to the tips of his ears. "A protector?"

Caroline blinked at him for a moment. Was he honestly suggesting that if she wasn't good enough to marry, she might consider becoming the mistress of her niece's husband? She threw back her head and laughed. "I am perfectly capable of protecting myself." She cast a glance at Lottie. "Oh, look—Lord Mandeville is showing Lottie how to shoot."

William's face went from scarlet to snow white in an instant, and he hurried up the slope to his fiancée.

"I have decided that you are quite right, Alec. Brodie is not the man for me." Megan put her arm through Alec's as they strode through the heather.

"Oh? And what's made you decide that?" he asked. He glanced over his shoulder to the place Caroline walked with William Mears, noted the high color in her cheeks, and felt a flush of desire. He swallowed a groan and concentrated on his sister instead.

"He's rather silly, isn't he? He doesn't read books. He doesn't even know clan history, and to think his grandsire used to be our grandfather's *seannachie*! Grandfather would not rest easy in his grave to think the old stories were about to be lost."

"And what do you propose we do about that?" Alec asked.

"Would it be difficult to learn the tales? Not just for telling aloud. I could write them down, keep them, pass them on to my own children—and yours."

Alec looked at her in surprise. "No, it wouldn't be difficult. I daresay there are plenty of old folk who recall the stories well enough. Are you saying you wish to be the next

MacNabb *seannachie?* It will take time to put all those stories together. Not to mention that some folk might remember the same tales differently than others."

Megan smiled. "I want to. I love Glenlorne—and it will be a long time until the London Season."

"And what if you marry an English lord?" Alec asked.

"Then he'd best be prepared to spend summers here in Scotland, hadn't he?"

Alec scanned her young face, saw the confidence in her eyes. He kissed her forehead. "Whomever you wed, lass, he'll be the luckiest of men."

She beamed at him, then shaded her eyes with her hand and looked toward the ghillies, halfheartedly beating the bushes. "I think I'll start by asking Jock," she said. "He knows everyone. D'you think he'll mind?"

Alec laughed. "Mind? I think you'll have trouble getting him to stop talking once he starts."

He watched his sister hurry down the hill.

"**O**h." Caroline found Alec leaning against a tree, staring into the woods. "Oh." She stopped where she was, feeling her skin heat. "I was looking for Megan. I thought she was with you." He put a finger to his lips and pointed. In a small clearing, a doe and her fawn were grazing. His gun stood leaning against the tree beside him. She felt a thrill as she looked at them. He waited until they moved on.

"Megan's with Jock and Leith. She's safe enough," he said.

The mist had lifted, and the sun was starting to come out. Her face was flushed with the growing heat of the day.

Alec felt his heart constrict, and he curled his hands into fists to keep from reaching for her and tumbling her here in the heather.

She blushed under his scrutiny, probably fully aware of what he was thinking. The idea that she was thinking the same thing did little to stem his desire. She turned away, her cheeks scarlet, and pretended to be interested in the view.

He looked at the woods through her eyes. The forest was cool and dark and smelled sharply of pine. Above the treetops, the old tower stared down at them. He led the way along the path, intent on guiding her back to the others before he gave in to the desire to steal a kiss, or do far more than that. They walked in silence, the mossy ground muffling their footfalls.

A hard punch to the shoulder knocked Alec backward. His teeth knocked together as the force of the blow pressed the air from his lungs. The hot spurt of blood came next, just as another bullet whizzed overhead, then the pain.

"What—" Caroline began. The next shot hit the tree beside her face. He grabbed her hand and dragged her to the ground.

"Someone's shooting at us!" she said breathlessly. "Hello!" she called to warn the hunter of his mistake.

The next bullet hit the ground beside them.

His right arm felt like lead, and he felt blood flowing under his jacket, down his sleeve, a red-hot river. He circled his left arm around her waist, hauled her against him, and dove for the sheltering trunk of a fallen tree. The exertion made his head spin, and he fought the sudden dizzy rush of pain.

"Who's out there?" she whispered, peering around, her eyes wide as saucers. "Surely it's a mistake," she said again, but yet another bullet whizzed past, and she gave a muffled cry. He scanned the dense undergrowth, but saw nothing. His gun lay where he'd dropped it, a dozen feet out of reach.

"Alec, you're bleeding!" she said, her cry soft, but still loud enough to attract yet another bullet. It thunked into the wood of the tree next to their hiding place. A wave of pain washed over him as her hands roamed over his limbs, searching for the wound, still hidden under his coat. Her expression changed to fear, and concern. Gentle as her touch was, it was still agony.

"Leave it," he said more gruffly than he intended. "It's my shoulder. A graze, probably."

She saw the blood on his hand, and cried out when she peeled back his coat and saw his bloody shirt. "This isn't a graze. We've got to get you back to the castle."

"That's three miles away, at least," he muttered.

"Then I'll go for help," she said desperately. Was it his imagination or were there tears in her eyes? They were glittering, but her chin was set in a determined point, not wobbling with fear.

"No," he said through gritted teeth. "Not with people shooting. We'll have to wait for Leith and Jock."

Caroline took out her handkerchief, and pressed it hard against the wound. He drew a sharp breath through clenched teeth at the pain. The flimsy lace was soaked in an instant. She tossed it away.

"I need to take my petticoat off," she murmured, and Alec managed a lopsided grin.

"I thought we agreed . . ." he said. She blushed.

"Don't be silly. Your very life might hang in the balance."

She stood up and began to raise her skirt. She hadn't gotten it up past her booted ankle when another shot rang out. She dropped to the mossy ground beside him. "I think they're getting closer." They lay side by side in silence, ears pricked, listening as footsteps crunched through the undergrowth.

He heard voices now, male voices. "Did you hit him?"

"I'll know when I see his corpse, won't I?"

Alec braced himself. They were coming closer. Caroline's eyes burned like firebrands as she scanned the undergrowth. "Caroline . . . stay here," he whispered. She was wearing a green riding habit borrowed from Lottie. She nearly blended into the mossy trees. Perhaps, he hoped, if he drew his pursuers away, they wouldn't see her, and she'd be safe, but she shook her head, her expression fierce, looking as protective as a mother wolf. She began searching the ground around her, digging her fingers into the leaf litter. She came up with a small rock.

A twig snapped, and she drew a sharp breath. She raised herself just enough to wind up and throw the rock into the undergrowth downhill. It bounced through the leaves, making an unholy clatter in the grim silence.

"There!" he heard the call, listened as his pursuers rushed toward the sound.

"Can you stand?" she asked, putting her arm around him. "We need to move."

"And go where?" he asked.

"There." She pointed to the old Grange. He hadn't known they were so close to the abandoned house, hadn't been here in years. It stood shrouded in ivy, locked up tight, almost invisible amid the trees that were doing their best to choke it out entirely.

"Caroline, it's locked. There's no way to get inside," he said. "It's safer to stay in the woods."

She looked at him as if he were daft, and hauled on him, trying to help him rise, though her slender frame was fragile compared to his. "Oh? The door's wide open, Laird."

Alec looked at the old house, and blinked. A few moments earlier, the door had been shut, locked tight, overgrown with vines. Now it stood wide open, and the vines beckoned in the breeze.

CHAPTER FORTY

"Three hares, a bonxie, and a badger," Leith said as they entered the kitchen. He laid them on Muira's table.

"Where's Alec?" she asked, her eyes wide.

"Isn't he back yet?" Jock said. Muira stared in horror at the bodies littering her kitchen.

Jock grinned. "I know what ye're thinking—not much meat for dinner, but when the Sassenachs stopped for a picnic, we had time to catch a few salmon and some trout for ye, Muira." He set the creel next to the bonxie.

Jock glanced at Leith, who was slathering an oatcake with butter. "I saw Alec this morning with Megan, but she came back with us."

Muira rang her hands, and Jock frowned. "What's wrong, Muira? Ye've got that look. Last time I saw it, old Jeannie MacNair died the next afternoon."

She held out her thumbs. "My thumbs prickle when evil is nigh," she said. She plucked the oatcake out of Leith's hand. "Ye've got to go and find him. Don't come back until ye do."

Jock knew better than to ignore one of Muira's premonitions. "Are ye sure it's Alec?"

"As sure as I've ever been. Go on with ye—there's no time to waste."

"I have it, Devorguilla," Brodie muttered, and held out a blood-soaked scrap of cloth. "The proof."

She stared at it in disdain. "What do you mean?"

"I found this in the woods. It's blood, so he must be dead." He broke into a wide grin, his handsome face shining. "I shot him right between the eyes."

Devorguilla put a hand to her throat. She stared at the bloody rag, then looked at Brodie. "Truly?"

"Aye. So when can I wed Sophie?"

"Did you bring me his body?" Devorguilla asked. She wanted to see it herself, to look down at her stepson's corpse and know that she'd won, that Glenlorne was hers at last.

"No, just this. Is tomorrow too soon for the wedding?" Brodie asked.

Devorguilla took the cloth in her hand. "This is a handkerchief, not a corpse. And there's no telling if the blood is Alec's or not. He might be downstairs right now, enjoying a tot of whisky." He stood, regarding her blankly. "You fool!" she cursed him.

Brodie's grin faded. "But what about Sophie?"

Devorguilla tossed the handkerchief into the fireplace and glared at him. "You won't even get a sniff of her hem if you can't make certain Alec is dead. You came back too soon.

Brodie shuffled his feet. "I can't help it. I'm in love."

Devorguilla looked at him, strong as an oak and as daft as a maypole. She had trusted everything to an idiot. He'd dropped the poisoned chalice last night, and he couldn't even manage a simple hunting accident. "All you needed to do to win Sophie was to shoot him, Brodie MacNabb, and you couldn't even do that right," she said, wishing again she'd been born a man, a laird, capable of ruling.

He thrust out his lower lip in a mulish expression. "Ye've no proof I *didn't* shoot him."

"And there's no proof you did either. We'd better go downstairs and see if he's returned yet."

"What if he's there?" Brodie asked.

"Then we'll need to try again." She pushed him out the door.

There was no sign of Alec in the hall downstairs. The ladies were enjoying tea, an English blend from Lady Charlotte's personal stock, which traveled with her. There were also cream cakes and tarts Muira had made from late strawberries. The gentlemen stood by the fireplace sipping tankards of ale or tumblers of scotch and compared the hunting in Scotland to that in England, on their own estates.

Devorguilla forced herself to smile. "Did you have any luck today, my lords?" Devorguilla asked Viscount Speed and Lord Mandeville.

"Luck?" Viscount Speed paled.

"Yes. Did you make a kill?"

The viscount went paler still. "I believe we must have, Countess," he murmured, his eyes flicking toward the door as if he were waiting for someone to walk in. He took a mournful swig of ale. It was on the tip of her tongue to ask the obvious question when Megan spoke first.

"Has anyone seen Alec?"

"Why would I know where he is?" Speed cried, shooting to his feet.

Megan raised her brows. "Someone in our party must have seen him. I was with him for a little while when we set out, but I spent the rest of the afternoon with Jock and Leith."

"The ghillies?" Devorguilla said, horrified. She despaired of ever making proper ladies of her daughters. The sooner she could take them to England, the better.

"He was in the woods," Lord Mandeville blurted out.

"Probably stalking deer, then," Megan said. "Or fishing. He's probably just forgotten what time it is."

"What if he's dead?" Brodie asked, and every eye turned to stare at him. Devorguilla closed her fists in the folds of her skirts to keep from strangling him.

"Dead?" Lord Mandeville's eyes burned like brands in his flushed face. "Whatever gave you that idea, my good fellow?"

Brodie shrugged. "He might be, mightn't he?"

"The man is scarcely an hour overdue," Somerson said, looking at his watch.

"He might have stopped in the village," Alanna whispered, her eyes wide. "To take someone a fresh fish, or a rabbit or two. He's a braw hunter."

Devorguilla pasted on a smile that felt thin and stretched. "Perhaps someone should go out and see if he's been injured. He might need help." She sent Brodie a speaking glance. "Brodie, you could go."

"Me? But I thought—" He glanced at Sophie.

"You," she insisted, and his eyes swung back to her.

"Oh," he said. "Me."

"I'll accompany you," William Mears said, and rose.

"Oh, I don't think that'll be necessary," Devorguilla purred. "Brodie knows the land, where to look."

"Then Speed and I shall accompany him. 'Tis nearly dark, and there may be wolves out there," Lord Mandeville said. "I insist."

"May I—" Megan asked, but Devorguilla sent her a quelling look.

Devorguilla smiled. "This is man's work. You will stay here."

"I shall scold Alec when he returns, for making us worry," Sophie said. "I suppose we shall have to wait dinner for him."

"Truly?" Countess Charlotte asked. She snatched the last cream bun off the plate and popped it into her mouth to stave off starvation. "Are there more buns?" she asked hopefully. Devorguilla smiled at her, and pictured her face when Alec's body was carried into the hall and laid on the long table, another Laird of Glenlorne, dead. She'd give him a glorious funeral. She'd even fake a few tears. She smiled at the thought as she looked at the clock.

She could hardly wait.

CHAPTER FORTY-ONE

Caroline helped Alec into the cool dim sanctuary of the Grange. He slid to the floor as soon as they were in the door. "Hold still," she said, kneeling beside him and tugging on his coat. He gritted his teeth, but didn't complain.

"I'm sure it looks worse than it actually is," he said, and she sent him a dubious look.

"Does it hurt?" she asked, knowing it did, if only from the pallor of his face, the beads of sweat on his brow.

"Of course it does, but allow me some masculine pride."

She ignored that and unbuttoned his shirt, aware of the warmth of his skin, the beating of his heart under her fingers. His pulse was strong, and that, surely, was a good sign. She peeled the bloody linen away from his shoulder and began to search for the bullet wound.

"Ah!" she cried when she found it.

"Is it bad?"

"Depends," she murmured. "It's in your upper arm." She tugged on him to roll him, and his breath hissed through his teeth as he bit back an oath. "I need to see if the bullet went through, or if it's still inside," she said crisply.

He forced his body forward so her probing hands could search. The room swam before his eyes.

"Ah!" she said again.

"Is that good?"

"Yes. Wherever the bullet went, it passed straight through. Have you a flask of whisky?" she asked.

"In my coat," he said, watching her. She retrieved the silver flask and opened it. The peat-strong fragrance of the whisky overcame the musty damp smell of the Grange. He held out his good hand for the flask, but she shook her head. "Here first."

He cursed as she poured it over the wound, setting it on fire. "Haven't you ever been shot before?" she asked.

"Of course not!" he said. "No one's ever tried to kill me before this, not even when I lived in London. I have been stabbed—well, nicked—with a knife, had my share of cuts and bruises, but never once . . ."

His breath caught in his throat as stood up and lifted her skirt, exposing the silken length of her shapely calf. He grabbed the flask and took a long swallow.

Caroline was aware that he was staring at her legs, but it couldn't be helped. Still, her cheeks flamed as she fumbled with the ties to her petticoat. She drew it off and let her skirt drop, aware of the bright light in his eyes.

She tore the linen and made a thick pad to press to the wound. The bleeding was already slowing. She picked up his left hand and put it over the bandage. "Press," she said, and tore another strip to bind the wound. "We need to get you back to Muira—"

There was a rattle at the door. Caroline gasped. Muffled voices spoke, and fists pounded.

Caroline gasped and tried to rise, but Alec grabbed her hand. "Don't move," he whispered.

Her heart pounded in her throat. "The door isn't locked. I don't remember closing it."

"Seems locked to me," he said, and she flinched as the thick panel shook against the bolt as a heavy body crashed against it.

He pulled her close to his side, put his good arm around her shoulders. Caroline put a hand over her mouth to keep from screaming as a face appeared in the window, an ugly splayed cheek pressed to the glass, dirty hands cupped around a glittering eye.

"Your Viscount Speed," I believe," Alec murmured. "Surely Mandeville can't be far behind." The door rattled again, but did not open.

"Hardly my Viscount Sped," she muttered.

Another face appeared next to Speed's. "Brodie," Alec said softly, and swore. "I wouldn't have thought he had the sense. I'm not surprised he missed."

"Brodie shot you? Your cousin?"

"My heir," he said dryly. "I doubt he thought of this himself."

Caroline watched the door shake, but it held fast, as if it had been locked and barred—but not by her hand. She'd left it open, she was certain, more concerned for Alec. She held her breath as years of dirt and bits of rotten plaster fell to the floor, making a fearsome clatter on the dry boards of the old floor, like hundreds of tiny feet rushing at her. She found herself curling closer to Alec, afraid of rodents and men, and everything else. He squeezed her shoulder and kissed her forehead, and she felt safer.

As suddenly as they'd come, the men left, and there was silence. It was getting dark, the last vestiges of light fading, leaving the draped furniture ghostly and white against the blackness. She shivered, and turned to Alec. He hadn't moved, and she wondered if . . . She reached up to feel for his pulse, and his hand came up to cover hers.

"I'm fine, Caroline," he muttered thickly. "We'll go once it's dark." He pulled her back against his side, kept her warm.

She fussed, feeling the bandage, checking for signs of fresh blood that she couldn't see.

"Where did you learn to bandage a gunshot wound?" he asked, his voice warm, whisky-scented, near her ear.

"My mother was sick a lot. Between governesses, I spent my days in the kitchen with the servants. One day, one of the gamekeepers tripped on his gun, and shot himself in the leg. They forgot I was there, but I never forgot what I saw. Cook rolled up her sleeves, got out the brandy, took a tot herself, then poured some over the wound. She used proper bandages, of course . . ."

"Did he live?" Alec asked.

"Yes, of course."

"Then there's hope for me, I suppose. Unless she tries again."

"She?" Caroline asked. "What do you mean?"

"Devorguilla. I have no doubt she put Brodie up to this. Probably promised him the riches of Glenlorne if he did as she said. He's going to be disappointed," he murmured. "But no matter. You're leaving all this behind, and there are other things we should discuss."

"Like what?" she asked.

"Like what do if you're with child."

She felt the shock of that rush through her. A dozen emotions followed, a whole herd of runaway horses. Dread, fear, shame, even delight. "I assure you I'm not—" She raised her chin. It was too soon to tell, of course. She resisted the urge to caress her flat stomach. "What if I am? It would hardly change anything."

"Of course it would. I will protect you, see you have money, a place to live . . ."

She laughed, and he stopped. She could feel his eyes on her. "No, Alec," she said, sobering. "I will not come back, won't interfere. My time here is done, no matter what." She was aware that her head on his shoulder belied her independence.

Alec sighed. "How I wish I'd met you in London," he said.

"You would not have given me a second glance."

"I would not have been able to look away from the first."

Caroline felt her breath catch in her throat. "Perhaps it is better not to imagine what might have been."

"I never thought I'd be Earl of Glenlorne, never wanted to be. I didn't think I could until I saw you, in the tower, imagined you by my side."

"I was here for weeks before you came home, Alec. There was no hope, no joy, no smiles. It's different now and that's because of you. You've made a good start."

"I am not the laird my grandfather was, if that's what they're thinking. I cannot bring back the days of peace and power and prosperity. Those days are long gone, never to return."

She raised her hand to his chest, drew circles with her fingertip. "Your clan wants a new beginning. You've already given them that—a pretty new countess, a handsome laird. Jock's brother has ideas for breeding a new type of sheep with better, thicker wool, Alec, and Annie MacNabb has some ideas for weaving shawls with new patterns. She saw one of Sophie's shawls. She thinks the clan could make them here and sell them in Glasgow or Edinburgh. So many others have ideas as well. Alastair MacNabb wants to build bridges. They only want your blessing, and a little money. They are willing to give Glenlorne their time, their loyalty. It's their home too. Sophie's money will do so much good."

He caught her fingertip, brought it to his lips, and kissed it. "You're a clever lass, Caroline. Did you know my grandfather was a sailor for a time? He told me about the wonders he saw while he was aboard ship. Other places, new ideas, different ways of doing things. Marvels."

"Sophie's dowry will help you do all those things, Alec," she said.

"As a matter of fact, I'm not going to spend her money at all. I have an acquaintance in London, an earl, who owns a shipping company. He's encouraged me to invest for years. I wrote to him, asked him if about shipping Glenlorne wool, investing in new ventures. He's offered to advise me. He believes my investment could do very well. I shall need money for an initial investment, of course, which will come from Sophie's dowry, but I will replace every penny, put it in trust, make my own way without living off my wife."

Caroline felt a swelling of pride, and love. "That's wonderful," she said.

"If I survive."

"The wound truly is minor," she said.

"What about next time?" Brodie is trying to shoot me, and Speed and Mandeville have some reason of their own for wanting me dead."

"They want Sophie—her dowry is many times more than mine was," Caroline murmured.

"Ah yes, there's you—if Somerson finds out I've debauched his little sister, he'll probably try to run me through."

She smiled. "No, he wouldn't shoot you himself—he'd simply pay someone to call you out," she joked. "Besides, if anyone would understand that you preferred to wed for money, it would be Somerson." She realized too late how that sounded. "I mean, he doesn't understand love." She almost bit her tongue. She had never intended to admit she was in love with Alec.

"Is that why you gave up your dowry? Does money mean so little to you?"

"How do you know that?" she asked.

"Glenlorne is an old castle with cracks in the walls, windows that don't shut tightly enough. I overheard your conversation with Somerson. You're taking a huge risk."

"I've always had money, of course, or at least I never wanted for anything money could buy. Yet I think I am happier without it. I can make my own choices, live my own life. Surely there are other folk in Scotland who wish their children to learn English."

"So you'll stay in Scotland?" he asked.

"It's the first place in a very long time that's felt like home."

"It won't be easy. Scots are suspicious of Sassenachs. Promise me you'll write to me if you need help. At the very least, let me be the brother Somerson isn't."

"I could never think of you as a brother," she whispered.

"Caroline, I have never been—"

The door swung open, and a long pool of moonlight raced across the floor. Caroline leaped to her feet, standing boldly between Alec and the intruders.

Jock jumped backward in alarm as she came forward, backing into Leith. "God a'mighty, lass, I thought you were a ghost!" Jock shifted and he pushed his tam back in relief. "Alec, lad! Are ye all right? We've been looking for ye for hours. Muira insisted something evil had befallen ye." He crouched in front of Alec.

"He was shot," Caroline said. "How did you open that door?"

Jock looked over his shoulder. The door? I didn't open it. It was standing open when we got here, otherwise I wouldn't have even bothered to look in this old place."

CHAPTER FORTY-TWO

"We're lost," Viscount Speed said grimly. "We've been circling these woods in the dark for hours. I swear I've seen that tree stump before."

"It's too dark to see a hand in front of your face," Brodie said, standing in a pool of moonlight, staring at his own palm.

"I thought you said you knew these woods intimately," Mandeville said.

"O' course I do!" Brodie said, and set off straight through a thick patch of thistles. Speed and Mandeville followed, crouched low. Brodie stopped suddenly, and they crashed into his back.

"For the love of God and all his angels, what is it now? Did you see something?" Mandeville said, straightening his coat.

"No, but I heard something," Brodie replied, swinging his gun wildly at every shadow. It ended up poking into Mandeville's bulging belly.

The Englishman pushed the barrel away with his fingertip. "Well, what did it sound like?"

"It was a terrible groaning sound," Brodie said.

"Like a person—or an animal?" Speed asked. "What kind of animals are in these woods at night, anyway?"

"Fearsome things," Brodie replied in a low voice. "Great, huge, nasty deer; furious badgers that could gnaw a man's leg off, bats—"

"Ugh. I hate bats." Speed shuddered.

"What about ghosts?" someone asked in a hollow tone.

"Ghosts?" Lord Mandeville exclaimed.

"The dead," Speed said in a hollow voice. "The *recent* dead at the very least. They walk right up and tap you on the shoulder, all gory and grim, clad in nothing but grave clothes and ashes, and when you turn—" He cried out, discovering Brodie behind him, instead of in front where he'd been a moment before. At Speed's cry, Brodie raised his gun, and nearly put the viscount's eye out.

Mandeville took out his handkerchief and mopped the sweat from his face. "Ghosts. Ha! There's no such thing, and if there were, you simply need to look it in the eye—"

"If it still has eyes to look into," Speed put in.

"You look it in the eye and say, 'Begone,' and off it goes." He waved a meaty hand.

"Is that so?"

"Which one of you said that?" Lord Mandeville asked.

"Wasna me," Brodie said.

"Nor I," Speed said, anxiously. "What's that tapping noise?"

Mandeville peered around his friend. Brodie was shaking so hard his gun was clattering against his belt buckle. He was staring into the dark above the Englishmen's heads, his face white, his eyes hollow. "Gh-ghost!" he managed, and raised his finger to point.

Speed shut his eyes and began to mutter what he hoped was an incantation against evil spirits, ill luck, and the pox. He spun when he heard Mandeville's shriek, and looked straight into the eyes of a glowing form sitting on a branch, just above his head, grinning down at them, a winding cloth still wrapped around its horrible chin, its teeth bare, the eyes sockets empty. It raised a bony hand to unwind the cloth, and the jawbone dropped onto its hollow chest.

Speed felt something warm and wet spill over his stockings, smelled the acrid scent of urine, but he couldn't look away. The horrible thing in the tree grinned, if something so horrible could be called a grin. Then it swooped forward.

"Begone," the ghost said, but by then, Speed, Mandeville, and Brodie had already fled.

"Now was that really necessary?" Georgiana asked Angus, floating up to watch the men fleeing over the hills. "It was rather undignified."

Angus rubbed his hands together gleefully. "Most fun I've had in—well, on this side of the grave, anyway. I've never liked Brodie's branch of the family, for all they're kin. Daft to a man, they are."

"And now he'll be running about the countryside telling tales of rotting ghosts in trees." Georgiana sniffed.

"Well, it did the job, didn't it? I daresay a ghostly piper standing on a hill would have been lovely, but I haven't got any pipes!"

Georgiana smiled. "Oh well, perhaps it was worth it to see Lord Mandeville barreling over the hills that way. I remember his grandmother. She choked on a candied plum at a dinner party. I daresay he won't stop until he crosses the border. He'll not trouble us further."

"Or Alec," Angus added.

"What of Devorguilla?" Georgiana asked.

Angus smiled at her. "I think we can leave her to Muira."

CHAPTER FORTY-THREE

William wandered the confines of Glenlorne Castle the next day. Alec MacNabb had been found and brought back alive, bandaged with Caroline's petticoats. The sight of him, bloody and pale, had caused Countess Charlotte to swoon, or perhaps it was the sight of Caroline in her blood-smirched gown with no proper undergarments. William had nearly swooned himself. Caroline had grown up since the last time he'd seen her in London, or fulfilled her bloom, or whatever young ladies did to go from coltish girls to lovely and desirable women.

He'd made the mistake of trying to do the chivalrous thing and catch Lady Charlotte as she fainted, and served only to provide a soft place for her to land. He'd been pinned beneath her for some minutes before the smelling salts could be found and brought to revive her, since no one could lift her. He had a bruise on his elbow, which the kind and lovely Lady Sophie had insisted upon bandaging. Lottie, who would be his wedded wife in just a few days, had been more concerned with Caroline and Glenlorne, and far too intent on hearing the gory details of their unfortunate accident to pay him any attention at all. He had noticed an unbecoming streak of willfulness in Lottie of late, which he didn't like in the least.

He'd been quivering after ten long minutes trapped under Countess Charlotte, and green-sick from the pain in his elbow and the sight of so much blood, while Lottie's eyes had been absolutely glowing. He'd have to curb that wild streak in his wife early, he decided—if he could, of course. It was obvious Somerson had not managed to do much with Lottie's mother. That's why he was prowling about the castle now, trying to decide what to say to Lottie, how to take the bull firmly by the horns, or the cow, since he was the bull in this case, and tell her exactly how he expected her to behave from this moment on. And if she refused to obey—well, that was the problem. What if she did? He had the horrible feeling that he would be the one agreeing to obey her, and that, of course, would never do. He was mild-mannered, refined, and not given to extremes of temper, adventure, or even definite decision. He expected his wife to be the same. His mother was content to sit in a corner and stitch samplers with improving messages on them. He had been raised to believe every woman should be like her, if a man's home was to be a happy one.

He wandered into the study.

There was a rustle of silk as someone rose from a chair by the window. Lady Sophie dropped her embroidery hoop on the floor.

William bowed. "My apologies, my lady. I did not know the room was occupied. Am I intruding?"

"Oh no, not at all," she murmured.

He crossed the room and bent to retrieve her needlework

at the same moment she did. Their heads knocked together, and he caught her elbow as she staggered back, one delicate hand on her forehead. He caught the scent of lavender and roses. His mother wore lavender and roses. He helped her to a chair, and picked up the embroidery. "Haste Makes Waste," the embroidered homily read.

William took the chair across from Sophie, and noticed how lovely she looked today, in a demure yet stylish gown in a more subtle shade of pink than Lottie would have chosen.

"May I offer my sincere relief that Glenlorne was not seriously harmed?" he asked.

She smiled wanly. "I was just upstairs to see him. Muira has confined him to bed, insisting he must drink some ghastly smelling herbal potion to build up his strength."

She looked anxious, and her chin quivered. He'd taken to carrying smelling salts in his pocket after his recent ordeal, and he reached for them now, just in case. "Is he very ill then, or in a great deal of pain?" William asked in alarm.

She blinked away tears, and he gallantly took out his handkerchief instead of the smelling salts and pressed it into her hand. She studied it, running her dainty fingertips over his monogram. "He seemed perfectly fine to me. He was not as—enthusiastic about seeing me as he should have been."

"Perhaps the shock—" William began, but she shook her head, and a delicate blond curl unfurled and fell across her brow. He clenched his fingers against the urge to push it back where it belonged. He couldn't bear untidiness.

"It wasn't the shock! He was studying some papers, and it seemed nothing I said could distract him from them."

"What kind of papers? The *Times*, perhaps?" He hadn't

seen a London newspaper in weeks, and if Glenlorne had one, then William would go up and pay the man a visit himself and ask to borrow it.

"No, they were documents. He said he was making plans. It's all he wished to talk about—wool prices and sheep." She made a face, and swept her hand over her gown. "I wore this dress to impress him, and he did not even notice it. He did not offer even *one* compliment in the whole five minutes I spent with him." She leaned toward him, tears dewy on her lashes, her mouth pursed to a single pink rosebud. "I ask you, am I pretty, Lord Mears?"

William blinked. Pretty? She was loveliness itself. "Very pretty, indeed, Lady Sophie."

She smiled at him, a sweet, tender smile of utter gratitude that made William Mears feel quite the hero of the tale. "I came here to measure this room—I plan to make it a library, you see, like Papa's grand library at Ellison Park—but Alec shows no interest at all in my plans. I haven't heart to measure anything. I sent the servants and the measuring tapes away."

"Do you like to read?" William asked. Reading was not good for women. It gave them ideas, desires, thoughts of things other than duty. Lottie read. So did Caroline, which more than proved his point.

Sophie tilted her head. "Read? Oh no. It hurts my eyes. But all truly elegant homes have libraries—for serving tea, and playing cards."

William brightened. "My thoughts exactly! He looked around the dowdy room, at the cold stone walls, the sparse furnishings. "I would love to hear what you plan to do in this room. I am in the process of renovating my home at Ryecroft. I have gotten as far as the wall coverings for the dining room—I have decided it must be Chinese silk, like the Prince of Wales has at Brighton."

Sophie's eyes widened like two sunlit blue pools. "Really?" she asked, clasping his handkerchief to her bosom.

"I have quite the same problem as you do. I am most anxious to return home and continue the work, but Lottie isn't the slightest bit interested in looking at samples of chintz or considering what color the morning room should be. Yellow, she says, but what precise *shade* of yellow?"

Sophie gaped. "Lottie? Truly? I thought she doted on fashion."

"As did I. I find this trip to the Highlands has affected her strangely. She tried to encourage me to go walking in the hills this morning, to consider climbing one of the higher peaks for the view—the view, Lady Sophie! And after all the exercise she had yesterday, tramping through the fields."

Sophie sighed, a sound like a refreshing breeze across a rose garden on a summer morning. "It was quite tiring, indeed. And there is a perfectly good view from the window, while one is safely indoors. I see no need to tempt the vagaries of the wind and the rain."

"Or the sun," William added, glancing out at the sunny morning.

"Precisely," Sophie said, and leaned forward. "May I confide in you, my lord?"

William leaned in as well, and lowered his voice. "Of course, dear lady. You may tell me anything, and I will keep it strictly confidential. I am the soul of discretion, I assure you."

He laid his own palm on his own breast and tipped his head toward her in a hero's pose.

She bit her lip, catching the rosy petals between her teeth. "I have begun to fear that I will not be entirely happy here."

He drew back slightly. "Really?"

She closed her eyes, and golden lashes swept her cheeks. "Glenlorne has never noticed that I am beautiful. Nor has he tried to kiss me. Not even once."

William's eyes fell to her lips. "Not even once?" he murmured.

"Shocking, isn't it? Why, I can scarcely count the number of suitors I had in London, and each and every one of them wished to steal a kiss. Oh, have I shocked you?" she asked, laying her hand on his sleeve, giving it a squeeze.

William swallowed. "Not—" He cleared the frog from his throat and tried again. "Not at all. If I were one of your suitors, I most certainly would have kissed you—after requesting permission, of course."

Sophie beamed with happiness, her eyes aglow. "Would you?"

"Yes," he said, and ran his tongue over his lips, plucking up his courage. "I'd kiss you now, if you would allow it."

She giggled and leaned nearer, puckering. "We shouldn't, of course, but what harm can a kiss do?"

He leaned closer still. "What harm indeed?"

Chapter Forty-Four

Aside from being the Crown's spymaster and one of the leading peers of the realm, the Earl of Westlake also owned a fleet of merchant ships, which traveled the globe to trade in everything from spices to exotic textiles and plants. He allowed investors to buy into his shipping ventures on occasion, and had offered such a rare opportunity to Alec. After he looked at the plans for the next several voyages, it was clear to Alec that Westlake had an eye for quality goods, and the risks had been carefully considered. By investing a few thousand pounds of Sophie's vast dowry, Alec would be able to earn a sizable return. With that money, he could invest in improvements at Glenlorne, including some of the ideas the villages had suggested to Caroline, which would generate a good income. He estimated being able to replace Sophie's money within three years.

Alec gazed out the window at the old tower, feeling hopeful that he would be able to turn over a profitable estate to his heirs when the time came for that, and he would be able to save Sophie's dowry in trust, untouched.

Devorguilla cried out as Muira stepped out of the shadows in front of her. The countess held a cup in her hand, and the liquid sloshed over her skirt.

"What's that?" Muira demanded.

"'Tis only a cup of wine for Alec. I wanted to see how he was feeling."

"Is this one poisoned too?"

Devorguilla's skin prickled. "Whatever do you mean? It's got willow bark in it, for pain." She tried to pass the old servant. Muira stood in her way.

"I'll not let you poison him the way you poisoned his father."

"Don't be ridiculous," Devorguilla said, drawing herself up to her full height. "Get back to the kitchen where you belong.

"I always wondered, but I didn't have any proof until last night," Muira said. "The wine you and young Brodie tried to give to Alec was poisoned with nightshade. I found more hidden in yer room, enough to kill a dozen lairds."

"How dare you touch my belongings!"

"Brodie told me," Muira said. "About your plan to kill Alec. He was hiding in the barn this morning, blubbering about ghosts and sin."

Devorguilla swallowed. "What do you want?"

Muira smiled slowly. "I want ye to drink that cup."

Devorguilla blanched.

Muira took a step toward her. "Or you can leave Glenlorne and never come back. If you stay—well, I know more potions than you, poisons that bring on agony that lasts hours before ye die screaming, trying to claw your own entrails out. D'you ken what I'm saying?"

Devorguilla swallowed. "But the girls, they need me. I'm their mother."

"They have Alec."

"Where will I go?" She heard the whining tone in her own voice, knew she'd lost.

Muira shrugged. "Brodie's mother is your cousin. Ye could go there. It doesn't matter, as long as you don't come back here. Ever. Or you can drink that foul brew, but I'll have your decision here and now."

Devorguilla stared into the cup. She'd watched her husband die. It had been slow and painful. While she wished that upon Alec, she had no desire to experience it herself. She looked into Muira's eyes again, saw ice-cold determination that rivaled her own. This was a fight she would not even survive, let alone win. She had no choice. "I'll go."

Angus wiped a tear from his eye as Devorguilla climbed onto the pony cart with Brodie and left. "Aren't you happy to see her go?" Georgiana asked.

"Of course I am! It's just that it didn't end the way we'd hoped, and the wedding is tomorrow. It's a matter of honor, of course—and fortune. Alec promised to marry Sophie, and he canna go back on his word. A MacNabb never goes back on his word."

"Fortune!" Georgiana scoffed. "He'll make a dozen fortunes if he follows what he's started. He's smart, but he cannot see what's truly important."

Angus looked at her sadly. "Ye canna eat love, *gràdhach*, nor can you roof houses, or feed children with it."

Georgiana tossed her head. "Love always finds a way, Angus."

"No it doesn't. Not for us, it didn't. Who's to say he won't come to love Sophie?"

"Not for us?" Georgiana set her hands on her hips. "And who's to say this isn't our second chance?" She left Angus staring at the empty shadows.

Chapter Forty-Five

Caroline was packing when Lottie burst into the room. "Happy birthday, Caro!" she cried, and dropped a wrapped parcel on the bed, and gave her aunt a hug.

Caroline smiled. "I didn't think anyone would remember," she said.

Lottie beamed. "How could I forget? My birthday is just twelve days after yours."

"You'll be an old married woman by then," Caroline teased, and crossed to the package.

"Yes, I will, won't I?" Lottie's smile faded.

"Aren't you happy?" Caroline asked, putting the gift down again.

"I thought I was. William seemed so kind and charming and—serene. Now I think 'serene' may have been the wrong word."

"Oh?"

Lottie bit her lip. "I'm horribly afraid he's just dull, and not serene at all, which makes me question if he really is charming and kind, or if I've made a dreadful mistake. He is handsome at the least, isn't he?"

Caroline's heart went out to her niece. She'd once fancied William herself as the perfect husband. Now she could not imagine anyone else but— She took a breath and stopped that thought in its very dangerous tracks. Tomorrow she'd be gone from Glenlorne, and she'd never see Alec MacNabb again. "Yes, he's very handsome," she murmured to Lottie, meaning William.

"I love to dance, but William doesn't dance. Do you see that as a problem?"

Caroline remembered the way it felt to dance on Midsummer's Eve, light as a feather in Alec's arms, her feet bare in the cool grass, her body hot with desire . . . Would she ever dance with anyone else and feel the same thrill in his arms?

"Dancing is not so important," she lied.

"And William refuses to travel, or to hunt. I wished to go to Paris for our wedding trip, now the city is open again and Napoleon is gone. He told me he gets seasick, and wouldn't think of such a dangerous journey. Dangerous! Why, my friend Anne Thorndale went to Paris to buy a whole new wardrobe, and she says it's perfectly wonderful, and quite safe. She didn't suffer even the tiniest bit of mal de mer," Lottie said. She reached for the parcel herself, and began to twirl the string between her fingers, studying her betrothal ring, a perfectly respectable if not awe-inspiring diamond hemmed in by fat pearls.

Caroline remembered the ruby ring her mother had left her, and rubbed her finger where it had once sat. She had given it to the gentleman on the street in London the night she fled Somerson House. Would she change that now, if she could go back, stay where she belonged? She knew she would not.

"You traveled here all by yourself, didn't you?" Lottie asked.

"Yes," Caroline murmured. "I'm sure you think I was foolish to flee like that. I didn't think of the dangers I might have faced." Especially if she hadn't had the stranger's advice about the Royal Mail coach, and the coin he gave her for the fare.

"Oh, I know mama says you are quite ruined, and I did think it was silly to run away at night the way you did, but look at you now—I'd say your adventures have been the making of you!"

Or the undoing, Caroline thought. She glanced at the small valise, half hidden by the open door of the wardrobe. It would hold the few gowns she'd purchased in Edinburgh, a book or two, and nothing else. She couldn't stay, couldn't watch Alec marry Sophie, promise to love and cherish her all the days of his life. She was sorry she would not be there to stand with Lottie, but she had to go. She would go to Edinburgh or Glasgow, find another job. She would write a letter to Somerson, making good on her promise to renounce her dowry, and cut her ties to her family.

Lottie squeezed the package in her hands, and the paper crackled. "Caroline, I've decided not to marry William. Just this moment, in fact. My brother George is going on the Grand Tour. He leaves next month, and I think I'll go with him." She jumped to her feet. "Have I shocked you?"

"Frankly yes. Are you sure? What will your parents say?" Caroline said.

"Well, I'll need a chaperone, of course, besides George—a companion. I thought perhaps you would like to accompany me. Oh Caroline, think of the fun we'll have. Mama can't object if you're with me, and George will be there, with his tutor and his valet."

Caroline studied her niece's flushed face, saw the spark in her eyes—determination, delight, and mischief. "Please say yes, Caro!"

Caroline's stomach tied itself into a knot. It did offer a new destination, a way to forget Alec. She tried to picture herself by Lottie's side, on a ship, or in Paris, or Italy, and saw only Glenlorne in her mind's eye. "If this is what you want," she said slowly.

The string holding the present closed unraveled in Lottie's fingers, and she looked at the parcel in her lap in surprise, as if she'd forgotten it was there. "Here I am rattling on, and this is your day, and you should be opening your gift." She handed it to Caroline. "It's a shawl," she said before Caroline had even gotten it half unwrapped. "The finest cashmere. It was for my wedding trip, but I can't bear to wear it now, and I shall buy something new and exotic in Paris or Italy. The colors will look better on you, anyway."

Caroline held up the lovely shawl. It was moss green, with a deep paisley patterned edging of gold and orange, the colors of the hills of Glenlorne. "Oh, Lottie, it's lovely, but I really shouldn't—"

Lottie snorted and snatched it from Caroline's hands, wrapping it over her shoulders. "Nonsense! You look lovely. It brings out the golden tone of your skin, and the green in your eyes. She fussed with the shawl, wrapping it over Caroline's hair, tossing the ends over her shoulders. "Oh, you look like a bonnie Highland lass!" she said. "As if you belong here."

She squeezed Caroline's hands. "I'd better go and see Mama now. She'll have just finished breakfast, and be looking forward to lunch. She's always more approachable on a full stomach. Wish me luck?"

"Luck," Caroline said. "What about William?"

Lottie turned in the doorway. "Mama's the hard part. I daresay William will simply find another bride."

Paris. Italy. The spa towns . . . anywhere, Caroline thought, taking off the shawl and putting it into the valise. "Europe." She whispered the word as she'd once whispered, "Scotland." It *was* a destination. Still, she could not rid herself of the feeling that once again, she was running away.

CHAPTER FORTY-SIX

Caroline watched Alanna gracefully cross the room with a book on her head, her spine straight, her chin high. Megan followed. Sorcha's book slid to the floor with a bang. "I shall never, ever be able to enter a ballroom like a lady," Sorcha moaned, as Caroline picked up the book with a smile. "And I'm not sure I want to."

Muira grinned from where she was sewing by the window where the light was best. She had come to tell the girls their mother had decided to pay an extended visit to a cousin for the sake of her health, and had to leave this very day, since Brodie had also decided to quit Glenlorne. The girls had been surprised, but they had the weddings to look forward to. And if they asked questions later, well, Muira was certain she would think of something to tell them.

"'Tis all right, lass, there are plenty of braw men here in the Highlands who won't find ye wanting, even if ye can't carry a book on the top of your head," Muira soothed Sorcha now.

Megan tugged her youngest sister's braid. "You have years to practice."

"She'll need every one," Alanna said unkindly, spinning in place with the book firmly in place on her head. "Sophie said she'd send for a dancing master for us, and a music teacher. We're to learn to play the piano, so we can list it as one of our accomplishments. Sophie says a successful debutante must have a long list of accomplishments."

"I'd rather read books than carry them on my head." Sorcha sniffed. "And I would rather have useful accomplishments. I can climb a tree, and win a foot race, and bake a pie."

Alanna rolled her eyes. "Useful if you're going to marry a one-legged crofter with an apple tree."

"Don't tease!" Megan said. "I daresay when Sorcha is older, she will turn out to be the family beauty and marry a prince who will adore her."

Sorcha stuck out her tongue at her middle sister, and looked barely even pretty.

"Yer face will stick like that, young miss, and I'll have to boil up a potion of roots and sheep's feet to set it smooth again," Muira said.

Jock knocked shyly on the door, looking for Caroline. "There y'are Miss. There's yet another Englishman here to see ye. He's in the den, er, library. I know Lady Sophie wants it called the library from now on."

"It's the same room it always was," Muira said sourly. "The room where the laird has always gone to drink and swear with the clansmen, out of hearing of the womenfolk. I don't know where Alec will go to do that once she's mistress here."

Jock shuffled his feet. "All the same, Lord Somerson is downstairs as well, and bid me to tell ye to hie yerself, Miss, if ye'll forgive me."

Muira folded her sewing into the basket and smiled at Caroline. "Why don't I take the lasses down to the kitchen and teach them another useful skill for a suitable wife while ye're busy? Such as how to make a proper mutton stew. To my mind, that's a far better way to win a man than dancing, reading or balancing books on yer head all day."

Caroline recognized the small man with thinning hair from her mother's funeral. He jumped to his feet as Caroline entered the room, straightening his sober black coat. Somerson rose more slowly, observing the social convention even as his eyes filled with disdain for his half sister. He hadn't spoken a word to her in days.

"Good morning, Lady Caroline. Do you remember me? I'm Mr. Rice, from Berwick. I was your father's man of business in the north, then your mother's. We met at your mother's funeral." He bowed low, and Caroline curtsied. She took in the neat stack of documents on the table and the worn leather case they'd come out of.

"Of course I remember you. How was your journey?" Caroline asked politely. She hadn't expected him to come personally.

"My journey was quite—" he began, but Somerson interrupted.

"Sit down Caroline, and let's get this over with." He turned to Mr. Rice. "I trust you brought a letter as per my instructions for Caroline to sign?"

Mr. Rice turned to Caroline. "It is my understanding from His Lordship's letter that you wish to renounce your inheritance, my lady."

Caroline glanced at Somerson, who was glaring at the man of affairs fiercely. "I am her guardian. You may address your comments to me. Caroline, sign the paper and leave the room at once."

Mr. Rice smiled politely, unafraid of Somerson. "I'm afraid I haven't brought any such letter, my lord. As Lady Marjorie's man of affairs, my business is directly with Lady Caroline now. I believe birthday felicitations are in order, my lady?"

"Thank you, Mr. Rice," Caroline said.

Somerson rose to his feet. "You may go, sir. You have nothing to discuss with anyone but myself. I am the head of this family, and Caroline is my dependent. If there is nothing to sign at this moment, then I will have my own man in London draw up the necessary documents. Good day."

Mr. Rice did not move. He instead took the top document of the pile of papers. "Not as of today, my lord. I have a copy of Lady Marjorie's will—your late mother left some very specific instructions. She left you some jewelry."

"Yes, a little ruby ring she wore every day. She gave it to me before she died," Caroline said, rubbing the finger where the ring had once sat.

"There are several other pieces, an emerald pin, a pearl necklace with a diamond clasp—"

"If they were gifts from my father, they belong to Countess Charlotte, then my own daughters, not to Caroline."

"They belonged originally to Lady Marjorie's own mother, my lord." Mr. Rice slid the document across the little table toward Somerson. "Now if you'll recall from your father's will, my lord, he did leave a number of instructions regarding

Lady Caroline's inheritance. They are restated here, in your stepmother's will."

Caroline felt her breath catch in her throat. Somerson pinned the little man with a glare that would put a bird of prey to shame. "She was hardly my stepmother. She was barely older than I was when she married my father."

"Perhaps not, my lord, but the late earl wanted both his wife and his daughter well cared for upon his demise."

"Marjorie did not suffer by my hand. After my father died, I gave her a house to live in for her lifetime," Somerson said.

Caroline recalled the gloomy, ill-repaired manor she had grown up in, as far from London as possible, with no money allotted for clothes or niceties beyond the very basics. Scarcely a month after her mother's death, Somerson had sold the place without a word to Caroline, and she had been forced to depend on the kindness of neighbors for nearly a year before Somerson summoned her to London and gave her a choice.

"Her Ladyship's will provides a specific legacy for Caroline," the man of affairs said pointedly.

Caroline looked at her half brother. His wide face was red and beads of sweat rolled down his forehead. "What does this mean?" she asked Mr. Rice.

Somerson tossed the paper aside. "It means nothing! I am her guardian. I control her money, which she has now insisted she wishes to renounce so she might be independent. She has willingly offered to sever her ties to her family, and I have agreed."

Caroline picked up the will and scanned the neatly written provisions.

"There is a clause in the will which states that if Lady

Caroline is not married by the age of twenty-three, which she is today, then she will assume control of all the moneys that have been placed in trust for her."

Caroline read the words, her eyes widening at the amount of money she was about to inherit. "What if I had wed before today?" she asked.

"Then His Lordship would have negotiated the payment of your dowry to your husband, of course. The rest of the money would have remained in your name."

Somerson got up and paced to the window. "How is this even possible? Marjorie Kirk was a penniless baronet's daughter when she tricked my father into marrying her. This is my father's money, and therefore mine, and I intend to contest the will. Where would she have gotten this kind of money unless she stole it from his estate?"

Mr. Rice patiently drew out another document. "It was a wedding present, my lord, a trust set up by the Dowager Countess of Somerson for the new countess."

Somerson turned and stormed back to the table. "*My mother?* My mother was dead!"

"I meant your grandmother, my lord, Countess *Georgiana* Somerson."

Somerson's brows crumpled inward in confusion. His face seemed to fold around the hard pinch of his lips. "My *grandmother?*" he hissed.

"Indeed. Put in trust. The funds were for any children of the union between your father and Lady Marjorie, since you would inherit the entirety of the Earl of Somerson's titles, estates, and fortune."

"As is proper. It is the law, and everything was entailed to the estate!"

"This letter was given to me to hold in trust until such time as Lady Caroline either married or celebrated her twenty-third birthday." He handed Caroline a yellowed envelope, sealed with red wax.

Somerson snatched it from her hand before she could open it.

Caroline was tempted to snatch it back, but she turned to Mr. Rice instead. "Then I have money, quite separate from my dowry, which is also mine as of today, and Somerson is no longer my guardian?"

Mr. Rice nodded. "There is a small property as well."

"She'll own land? Somerson land?" Somerson spluttered.

"The estate in question is a small house left to Countess Georgiana by an uncle, Lord Howden. It's here in Scotland, and not part of any of the Somerson holdings."

"Lullach Grange," Caroline whispered.

"Why yes, do you know it?" Mr. Rice asked.

"Yes, I know it," she said.

"Are you truly saying that my half sister—my ward—is now independently wealthy, and may live as she chooses?" Somerson demanded. "I never have to see her again, or pay her a penny?"

Mr. Rice shook his head. "Even if she renounces her ties to you, my lord, the money is rightfully Lady Caroline's. Lady Georgiana insisted on investing the money, of course, and the funds now total nearly fifty thousand pounds. Of course her dowry must also be turned over to Lady Caroline. It would not of course be a dowry, but her legacy, at this point." He looked at the records in front of him. "Twenty-five thousand pounds."

Caroline stared at Somerson."You told me my dowry was eight thousand pounds!"

He raised his chin. "It seemed enough. Both Mandeville and Speed were willing to take that amount."

She shut her eyes. "They were the lowest bidders, weren't they?"

Her half brother sneered. "Indeed they were. Who else would want you at your age? You will draft the letter for Caroline to sign, refusing the terms of the legacy," he commanded, but Mr. Rice merely smiled.

"I'm afraid that's up to Lady Caroline now." He got out a fresh sheet of paper and dipped his pen in ink and waited. "How may I be of service to you, my lady?"

"You inherited Lullach Grange?" Angus asked Georgiana. "It's on Glenlorne land!"

"I'll have you know my uncle purchased the house and the garden from your father fairly, Angus MacNabb. He had no wish to cheat anyone."

"You didna say you owned it. What if I'd torn it down, or Caroline had never come here?"

"I had no way to know, though I hoped she would."

"You woke me from my grave for nothing, to relive all the heartache over again?"

"I was alive when I made my will, Angus. I had no hope I would ever see you again, on either side of the grave. I only knew that summer we had here was the happiest time of my life. Was I wrong to want, to hope, that my granddaughter might know the joy that I did, perhaps live her whole life here, in love? I had no choices, Angus. None. I wanted to make sure Caroline had a choice."

"She has enough money to wed Alec now," Angus enthused. "Everything has worked out the way you planned it."

"Alec is still betrothed to Sophie," Georgiana reminded him sadly. "If they had no honor, no love for this place and the people who are important to them, then yes, they could wed. It wasn't about Caroline's money. Now, it isn't even about love. They have that aplenty. We simply didn't count on honor, Angus, and duty."

"Duty be damned! Does love never triumph? What will Caroline do now?"

"I suppose that remains to be seen. She has choices to make. We cannot choose for her, or we are without honor as well."

"Then we've failed?" Angus said. "All this was for naught?"

"The curse will continue," Georgiana agreed softly. "Unless they find a way to break it themselves, and I fear it may be too late for that, Angus."

CHAPTER FORTY-SEVEN

"Shall we raise a glass to the lovely brides?" Mr. Parfitt said as everyone gathered before dinner the night before the double ceremony was to take place.

"I wish to say something first," Lottie said. Alec held his breath, waiting for a tearfully romantic speech from a dewy-eyed bride, though Lottie looked remarkably clear-eyed this evening, especially when she began struggling to remove the betrothal ring from her gloved hand.

"William, I have changed my mind."

Sophie gasped in horror. Caroline stood silently, watching her niece. William Mears turned red from his chin to the tips of his ears.

Countess Charlotte frowned. "Don't tell me you wish to wed in London or at Somerson Park after all, Lottie!"

"Actually, Mama, I don't wish to marry at all. Well, at least I don't wish to marry William."

Charlotte's scream, mixed with Somerson's deeper bellow of rage, brought Muira, Jock, and Leith running from the kitchen, where they had apparently grabbed anything useful as a weapon on their way. Muira brandished a lethal toasting fork, Jock had a rolling pin, and wild-eyed Leith bore a pie, ready to throw it. He arrived just in time to soften the fall as Countess Charlotte fainted, and fell on him. The pie hit the floor and shatter, which made Muira screech.

"Here," Lottie said. She handed her ring to William, who stood looking politely stunned, staring at it. Then she reached into her pocket and took out the smelling salts obviously ready for the countess's reaction. "I thought we'd be needing these." Lottie bent over Charlotte's supine figure and waved the vial under the countess's nose, then waved them under Leith's, who was still trapped beneath her. William stood dumbly staring at the ring in the palm of his hand.

The first person Charlotte saw when she woke was Caroline, and she screamed again, and began to cry loud, noisy tears.

"I'm drowning," Leith said from beneath her vast frame. Mr. Parfitt muttered prayers as he tugged on the countess's arm, trying to raise her.

"This is all your fault! You encouraged her to do this!" Charlotte warbled, shooting hatred and blame at Caroline.

"No, Mama, it had nothing at all to do with Caroline. I just decided that marrying William was not what I wanted to do."

"What do you want to do? Are you aware of the scandal this will cause? Mears is a perfectly decent man," Somerson said. "Is there someone else?"

Lottie sucked her cheek. "Well, there's George, as in my brother George. You see, I want an adventure. I intend to go with George when he leaves on his Grand Tour."

Charlotte shrieked again, and Leith groaned, his legs thrashing beneath the countess as he struggled for escape. Alec took pity on him and helped Mr. Parfitt and Jock to lift the stricken countess and help her to a chair. "I won't allow it!" the countess protested. "Nor will your father."

Lottie hardly looked deterred. "Caroline is coming with me, and my maid, and George and his tutor and valet. It will be perfectly proper. Besides, if there's to be a scandal over my broken betrothal, wouldn't it be better if I went away for a while? I have no intention of retiring to lurk in the shadows at Somerson Park."

Alec looked at Caroline in surprise. She met his eyes for only a moment before looking away, her cheeks flushing.

"Europe!" Megan said. "How wonderful. May I go along?"

"I won't wait for you," William said. He was sitting on the settee, with the ring still in his outstretched palm. Sophie was by his side, patting his arm supportively, glaring at Lottie balefully.

"I don't expect you to," Lottie said, and gave him a sad smile. "I do wish you every happiness William, I truly do— just not with me."

Alec glanced again at Caroline, but she had slipped out of the room.

"When will you leave?" Sophie asked Lottie.

"Tomorrow," Lottie replied. "An early start."

"Right after the wedding then?" Sophie asked.

"Um, right before, rather."

Alec felt his stomach turn to iron. Caroline was leaving first thing in the morning, walking away, *running* away. He wondered if she meant to say good-bye, or if he'd just wake up tomorrow to find her gone.

"Neville, we're leaving too, since there is no point in staying a moment longer," Charlotte said. "Order the horses harnessed and have everything packed at once."

"What about supper?" Muira asked.

William shook his head. "I'm not hungry."

"Then neither am I," Sophie said.

"I have packing to do," Lottie said.

Charlotte regarded the ruins of the pie on the floor, the berries and pastry squashed and scattered like a broken heart. "Perhaps you could send a tray to my room, and I will eat while my maid packs. See to it at once."

Alec didn't bother to knock when he reached Caroline's room. He simply threw open the door and strode in, letting the panel crash into the wall with a bang. She was sitting at the desk, pen in hand, and she looked at him with her eyes wide, half rising. There were tears in her eyes, but he ignored that.

"Did you intend to say good-bye? Oh, not to me, of course, but what about the girls, and Muira, the children in the village? How long have you known you were leaving tomorrow?"

Another blush filled her cheeks. "I was writing you a letter," she murmured.

"Your resignation?" She nodded her head. "Isn't that the coward's way out? Do you have a letter for Sophie as well? She at least deserves better. She has no family here, no one at all but you and Lottie—"

"She has you!" Caroline said fiercely, sorrow turning to anger. He read jealousy in her hazel eyes, pain. He felt the same pain stab him.

"Aye, she does," he said.

"Here, you might as well have this now," she said, crossing the room in short, sharp steps to hold out a piece of paper. He took it and glanced at it.

"I don't understand," he said, feeling heat rising under his collar. "What the devil does this mean?"

"It's the deed to Lullach Grange—a wedding present. I found out yesterday that I had inherited the house from my grandmother. I cannot keep it."

"Why?" he demanded.

She met his eyes boldly, dignity warring with tears. "It would draw me back here."

"Do you hate this place so much?"

She lowered her gaze to her hands. "Quite the contrary, but I don't belong here."

He couldn't imagine Glenlorne without her. "What about the girls? What will they do without you? They adore you."

"They'll have Sophie."

Alec ran a hand through his hair. "Och, I can see it's going to be a grand wedding, with every bloody person in tears—at least the ones who are left."

"She's beautiful, Alec. She'll make a wonderful wife." There was farewell in her voice, in her eyes. His heart broke in his chest.

He gripped her shoulders. "Keep the Grange, Caroline. Let it bring you back—in a year, or two years, in five, only promise you'll come back to—" She stopped the last word—"me"—with a finger on his lips. Her skin was cool, and his mouth watered to kiss her.

Her eyes met his. "It's best this way, clean and quick. You'll fall in love with So—"

Sophie appeared in the open doorway. "Oh Caroline, I just have to have your advice about how I should wear my hair tomorrow—Lady Charlotte has commandeered every maid in the place to help her pack, and I can't bear to ask Lottie, now she's broken Wi—" She paused when she saw Alec, practically holding Caroline in his arms.

Alec watched his bride's eyes widen, saw the understanding in the pale blue depths. "Oh," she breathed, and pressed a hand to her chest. "Oh."

Caroline stepped away from him, forced a smile. "I was giving Alec my wedding gift to give to you tomorrow—Lullach Grange."

Sophie pursed her lips, still looking from Alec to Caroline and back again. She made no move to pick up the deed Caroline held out to her. Her cheeks paled to ivory, then flushed a deep shade of pink. "Then I should thank you."

Alec felt like a heel. Sophie held herself stiffly, and forced a smile. The tension, the suspicion and sorrow in this room was thick, made it hard to breathe.

Sophie wasn't stupid. She knew well enough what she'd seen, and she'd never forget it. It was a bad bloody way to start a marriage. She shook herself, smiled at Caroline, and backed toward the door. "I think—I think I shall go to bed," she said, retreating.

"Sophie—" Alec began, but she smiled at him brightly and shook her head.

"Oh no. It's bad luck for the groom to see the bride before the wedding, Alec, very bad luck indeed. Good night."

He watched her go, listened to her feet retreating down the hall, the rustle of her taffeta dinner gown, and hung his head.

CHAPTER FORTY-EIGHT

Caroline didn't sleep a wink. Once her few belongings were packed and ready to go, and she had written letters to Megan, Alanna, and Sorcha, she sat and stared out at the old tower on the hill. She traced its outlines with her fingertip, fixed it in her memory to keep her warm and remind her of happiness in the years to come. At dawn, she slipped out of her room to put the letters in the girls' rooms.

She almost ran into Sophie in the hall.

She wasn't dressed for the wedding. She was dressed for travel. Sophie let out a frightened squeak at the sight of Caroline. "Oh, Caro, you startled me!"

"Are you getting ready for the wedding so early?" Caroline asked.

Sophie lifted her chin. "I've decided not to marry Glenlorne. In fact, I'm leaving. If Lottie can do it, so can I."

Caroline's jaw dropped. "But why—" She spun at the sound of footsteps behind her, and found William creeping out of his room, dressed as well.

"Caroline!" he cried in surprise, and dropped the valise he

was carrying. He whipped off his top hat and hid it behind his back. He looked at Sophie, his face flushing.

"I suppose you've caught us, Caroline. We're eloping," Sophie said. She moved to stand with William, linking her arm through his. He put his hand on hers, and she saw Lottie's ring on Sophie's finger.

"What?" Caroline stared at them.

"I would never have been happy here at Glenlorne. I hate the Highlands, and Alec simply doesn't love me, and I can see now that he could never love me. He's honorable, and since my father left him little choice but to take me, he would have married me, despite the fact that he's in love with someone else."

William's eyes widened. "Really? Who?"

Caroline felt her face heat, but Sophie ignored William's question.

"I couldn't bear to be married to a man who did not adore me. William adores me, and I have discovered that I adore him too. We have much in common, while Alec and I—" She shrugged. "I think he'll be relieved rather than distressed when he finds I've gone."

"William, is this because of Lottie? Is your pride so hurt?"

"No, I can see that Lottie is quite right. We wouldn't suit. Sophie doesn't care a jot for adventures or long walks in the hills or views from mountaintops."

"And William understands the importance of the perfect shade of yellow," Sophie gushed. She came forward to squeeze Caroline's arm. "Don't look so stricken, Caro. I understand, I really do. I wish you only happiness, whatever happens."

Caroline felt a sharp stab of panic and guilt. "I'm leaving,

Sophie, today, with Lottie. This isn't necessary. There's nothing—" Sophie stopped her with a smile.

"If he'd looked at me the way he looks at you, even once—well, he didn't, and that's that."

"I trust you won't tell him!" William said. "If Glenlorne finds out I've stolen Sophie away, he may feel obliged to come after us and challenge me to a duel, and you know what a poor shot I've always been, Caro, and I'm even worse with a sword. Not that I wouldn't fight for Sophie, of course."

"Oh, William," Sophie breathed, and stood on tiptoes to kiss his cheek. She turned and smiled at Caroline, and Caroline saw all the happiness on her face that a bride should feel. "Do wish Glenlorne the very best when you do see him. It's quite obvious to me that adventures only serve to show us where we truly belong. William is where I belong. Good-bye, Caroline."

Caroline watched them go, stunned. Another door opened, and a small troupe of servants in Somerson livery jostled past her, bearing the boxes, trunks, and baggage they'd carried into Glenlorne Castle just one week and three days earlier.

Lottie came out of her room, and had to press herself against the wall. "Goodness, what a crush! Fortunately Mama brought only the essentials on this trip. It takes four trips to move everything she needs for the Season to from Somerson Park to the London house." Lottie said. "Are you ready to go?"

Caroline stared across the gallery, out the window at Glenlorne Tower. It seemed to ask the same question. She pictured Alec sitting in the chapel, waiting for his bride, pacing the stone floor before the altar as the Reverend Mr. Parfitt tapped his long fingers on the prayer book and mopped his brow. The villagers would be awake by now, dressed in their finest, donning MacNabb kilts, sashes, and tams and heading up the glen toward the castle behind the pipers to witness their laird's wedding.

Alec would be there when the door to the chapel opened at last, and he wouldn't understand, would never know what happened when Sophie didn't come. Caroline shut her eyes. It was all her fault.

"Caroline?" Lottie asked, her brow furrowing.

She should go. She should follow Lottie down the stairs and never look back. She took the first step, and stopped.

"I have to find Alec and tell him," she said, and ran down the stairs.

CHAPTER FORTY-NINE

Alec tugged on the sleeves of his jacket, and smoothed a hand over the MacNabb plaid of his kilt. He hadn't slept. He'd risen and dressed and gone for a long walk, climbing to the old tower and watching the sunrise, thinking of Caroline. No matter how hard he tried to replace her face with Sophie's, it was Caroline he saw—Caroline laughing with the girls, Caroline learning Gaelic from the villagers, Caroline's passion as he made love to her, Caroline's determined expression as she tore up her petticoats to bandage him. He looked up at the empty window of the tower, and remembered the very first time he'd seen her there, her red hair flying in the Midsummer wind, her expression blissful as she stared out at the valley. She'd fallen into his arms, and it had felt as if she belonged there. He remembered her by candlelight, starlight, firelight, sunlight, and rain. She'd be gone by the time he returned to the castle. Without her, the building looked as empty and bereft as the old tower.

His hands clenched in frustration. In an hour, he'd pledge himself to Sophie Ellison, promise to honor her and cherish her all the days of his life, to stand by her, to be faithful and true. Tonight, he'd take her to bed and make good on his promise. He shut his eyes. By then, Caroline would be miles away, lost to him forever. How he wished now he'd stayed in London, or gone to sea, or done anything to avoid this. He cast one last look at the window high above him, watching as a flock of skylarks burst through it, took to the brightening sky, celebrating the dawn with their cries. He trudged back down the path to the castle, going to the chapel beyond it. He passed his grandfather's grave, and his father's. He felt as if the eyes of every MacNabb ancestor were upon him, watching him, urging him to do the right thing.

And the right thing was to marry Sophie, wasn't it?

He entered the chapel, built in the days when the MacNabbs were Catholics, and since redecorated and simplified to the Presbyterian style. The wee kirk was festooned with flowers—Muira and the girls had seen to that, choosing flowers for their meanings. There were pots of garlic and chives by the door, the strong smell meant to chase away evil. Sophie would carry a sweeter-smelling bouquet of roses for love, heather for luck and ivy for faithfulness.

The inside of the church smelled like Caroline's hair, washed with Muira's wildflower soap. He shut his eyes against the craving for her, and went to sit on the altar steps, looking around him. How many MacNabbs had been wed here? Countless numbers, to be sure, villagers, clansmen, and lairds alike. It was his job to see that countless more had that chance, his own sons and daughters, the sons of his kin. The responsibility lay heavy on his shoulders.

He checked his watch. Sophie would be dressed by now,

and the girls would be putting flowers in her hair—along with the fabulous Bray jewels, of course. Mr. Parfitt would bring the ring Lord Bray had sent to put on Sophie's finger. It was huge, a diamond surrounded by sapphires to match her eyes. He put his hand in his pocket, but took it out when the door opened.

Alec looked up, expecting Sophie. He got to his feet, took a deep breath, and held it.

The morning sun caught Caroline's red hair, made it glow. The breath stuck in his throat.

"Alec!" She hurried down the aisle toward him, her footsteps sharp on the stone floor.

He resisted the urge to open his arms and catch her. He let out the breath he was holding. "Caroline," he said. He didn't get farther. A dozen questions came to mind, but he couldn't ask any of them. She stopped a few feet from him.

"She's gone, Alec."

"Who?" he asked like an idiot. Was there anyone else in the world but Caroline? Her eyes, her hair—he drank them in.

"Sophie—she left this morning, eloped with William."

It took a moment for the meaning of that to sink in. He stared at her, saw the sorrow in her eyes, the tears on her lashes. "It's my fault, of course. She saw you in my room, imagined—"

He felt a rush of relief go through his limbs.

"She imagined the worst, Alec. There isn't going to be a wedding at all."

He tilted his head. "You mean she saw the truth."

"She thought you—" She swallowed. "I mean, that I—"

He smiled. He couldn't help it. His face stretched into a

grin. Her felt as free and happy as the skylarks. "She could see that I love you, is that what you mean?" he asked. "And that you love me, and that you belong at Glenlorne, and that Glenlorne needs you?"

She shut her mouth with a snap and stared at him. He stepped forward and swept her into his arms and kissed her until her lips softened and she kissed him back. He'd been wrong—she smelled better than the flowers. She pulled back and stared at him.

"Don't you understand? There isn't going to be a wedding."

"There is indeed going to be a wedding. I don't care about marrying a fortune. We'll find a way. As long as I have you beside me, we'll find a way."

She stared up at him. The door opened behind them. Neither looked to see who it was. He dropped to his knee. "What do you say? Will you marry me, lass?"

"Yes," she breathed. "Yes, I will."

Mr. Parfitt had come to break the sad news to Glenlorne that his bride had left hours earlier with another gentleman. He shook his head as he walked past the gravestones of the little burial ground. It must be something in the Highland air. He'd never seen so many broken betrothals in his life. He'd never conducted a wedding before, being new to the clergy. He'd been thrilled, honored, and very well paid when Lord Bray hired him to escort his daughter north and see her wed as quickly as possible. He'd failed. He looked up to heaven, asked the Lord above just how he was going to explain all this to the earl—well, both earls, the father and the bridegroom.

He'd hoped for an appointment to a rich parish, and now he'd be fortunate to find a job escorting prisoners to the hangman in a London prison.

He sighed and opened the door to the chapel, and stopped in his tracks. The laird was there waiting, to be sure, but he wasn't alone, or bereft. Lady Caroline was in his arms. They both smiled when they saw him in the doorway.

"We're ready," the earl said. The clergyman tightened his grip on his prayer book.

"But—" he looked at the flushed faces of the happy couple, saw the joy in the young woman's eyes, the pride in the groom's—everything that had been missing from every single betrothed couple here at Glenlorne until now. It touched his heart. He sighed and climbed the steps to the altar. "This is most unusual," he said. The door opened again, and people began to crowd into the little church. Parfitt recognized the laird's sisters, the housekeeper, the ghillies, and dozens of other folk. They did not seem surprised in the least by the sight of Lady Caroline standing beside the laird. In fact, they grinned and nudged one another, whispering that they'd known it all along. And they smiled, as if all was right in Glenlorne and God's universe. Who was he to dispute that?

"Shall we begin?" he said, and opened the prayer book.

He did not stop until he reached the part regarding the exchange of rings. "Have you a ring, my lord? I have the Bray diamond in my pocket, of course, but under the circumstances, it seems wrong to use it now."

The laird frowned a moment, then reached into his pocket. "I have one," he said. He took out a ruby ring and laid it on the prayer book, where it glittered like a drop of blood.

"That will do nicely," Mr. Parfitt said, but the bride gasped.

"Where did you get that?" she asked.

"His Lordship just—" Parfitt began, but she was staring at the laird. He was so tall she had to tilt her head back to look at him. Her face glowed in the morning light streaming through the window behind her, turned her hair to glory.

"I hope it will do," the laird said. "I met a young lady on the street in London. She was eloping. I tried to stop her, but she insisted on continuing on her path. She was very brave, Caroline, like you. I gave her some coin for her journey, and she insisted on repaying me with her ring. I hope that she's safe."

"It was my grandmother's ring, Alec. I gave it to a kind man who offered me money and advice when I was alone and afraid. It was you?"

They stared at each other so long, and with such love that Mr. Parfitt was obliged to clear his throat. "If we might continue?"

A cheer rang from the rafters as the laird slid the ruby onto his bride's finger. Even Mr. Parfitt wiped a tear from his eye, and he wished them well and meant it as he shook the laird's hand—once Alec MacNabb had kissed his bride, of course.

The wedding party followed at once, held outside on the hillside, and every household in the village brought their own version of homemade wedding ale to toast the happy couple. The pipes came out and played merrily until sunset, and beyond. The bride danced with every happy clansman, the groom took a turn with the blushing maids and matrons, and kissed every baby in the village to ensure his own fertility while his glowing bride blushed.

Lottie sat with Alec's sisters and enjoyed the glow of her aunt's happiness, and envied her just a little. Caroline's adventure had ended just as it should have—she belonged here in Scotland, at Glenlorne, by Alec MacNabb's side.

"I always knew Caroline fancied Alec." Megan sighed as she watched them give in to the encouragement of the crowd and kiss each other. The ruby ring glittered in the firelight.

"Caroline and Alec? I never saw any sign of it," said Alanna.

"She did rescue him when he was shot," Sorcha said.

"Nonsense! We'd have done the same if we'd been there!" Alanna said.

"I've seen him look at her too, the way Sorcha looks at cake," Megan said.

"Cake?" Alanna said.

"As if she's sweet and delicious and he's dying to devour her." Megan sighed.

"I think I know what you mean," Lottie said. "Like he's looking at her now."

"Aye, like that," Megan replied. "I shan't marry until someone looks at me like that."

"We shan't marry at all without Sophie's fortune." Alanna sighed. "She promised to take me to London for the Season. I suppose we're still penniless!"

Lottie frowned. "Penniless? Caroline's fortune is at least as big as Sophie's."

Megan and Alanna stared at her. "Truly. My mother was

horrified, of course, but it's quite true. Did Muira ever tell you the old tale of the English lass and the son of the Laird of Glenlorne? My grandmother—and Caroline's— told me the story once."

The girls shook their heads, and Lottie smiled and began. "It was Midsummer, and the weather was perfect for falling in love . . ."

"How do we know if the curse has ended?" Angus asked from the shadows.

Georgiana wiped away a tear. "Of course it has—look at them!" They watched as Caroline threw her head back and laughed as Alec spun her across the grass, through the steps of a reel. She'd cast off her shoes, loosened her hair, and was as fey and bonnie as any village lass. Alec looked at his bride with such love that Georgiana's chest hurt.

"You used to look at me like that, my love," she said with a sigh that made a nearby torch gutter.

"I still do, *gràdhach*. I never stopped loving you, never will," Angus said.

"Then why are we still here?" Georgiana asked. A young couple raced past them and bumped into Georgiana.

"Oh, your pardon. I didn't see you there," the girl said politely, and they ran on.

Georgiana turned to Angus. He was staring at the departing pair in surprise. "Did you see that?"

"Did you feel that?" Angus asked.

"*Gràdhach*—" he began, and tried to float toward her. He stumbled on a tuft of gorse, and his bonnet fell over his eyes. He righted himself and looked down at his feet, saw his boots solid and sharp, crushing a wildflower. He looked at Georgiana again, and she saw the pain in his eyes, the hope. He reached out his hand toward her cheek, and she shut her eyes and waited. His touch was as warm and real as she remembered. She pressed her cheek into his palm, put her hand on his chest, felt him solid under her fingers, the breath and blood singing under the warm wool of his plaid. She could smell the flowers too, feel the gentle night breeze on her skin. They stared into each other's eyes, saw each other the way they'd been the last night they'd met, years ago, a life and death ago. He smiled as he drew a breath of real air, then threw back his head and laughed.

He took her hand in his, kissed it, and she squeezed back. "I'd say the curse is over indeed," she said.

Angus smiled at her. "Come on," he said. "It's time to go."

Hand in hand, they walked through the heather, up the glen to the tower, until the shadows swallowed them.

Read on for a sneak peek at the next fabulous romance from Lecia Cornwall!

WHAT A LADY MOST DESIRES

Chapter One

The Duchess of Richmond's Ball, Brussels, June 15, 1815

He was the only man who had the power to stop her breath just by walking into a room.

Even now, when she hadn't seen him for over a year, the same dizzy sensation stopped her dead in her tracks on the grand staircase that led to the ballroom.

It wasn't that he was the handsomest man here. There were over a hundred other officers present, from five different armies, all equally resplendent in their dress tunics. At least half of those had fair hair that shone just as brightly as his did under the light of the inestimable number of candles that lit the duchess's makeshift ballroom. Many were as tall, or taller, and had shoulders that were just as broad as his.

But Major Lord Stephen Ives was the one man of all the men in this room, in all the world, as far as Lady Delphine St. James knew, who had the power to weaken her knees, make her heart race, and her breath catch in her throat. If she could choose one dance partner tonight, one man to escort her to supper, one man to marry—as her parents were insisting she must—it would be—

"You," she whispered to the air, her eyes fixed on his back.

He turned as if she'd shouted the word, and looked up to where she was standing on the stairs, and she felt a thrill run through her body as his eyes met hers. She read surprise, then a moment of dismay, before he smoothed his features to a flat, correct, perfectly polite expression and nodded.

The thrill in her breast fizzled and died. Nothing had changed, then, since she last saw him in London, a year ago. Still, she lowered her fan and smiled sweetly at him. He did not smile back, or show any sign of moving from where he stood. Of course, hundreds of people took up every inch of space between her place on the staircase and his position on the edge of the dance floor. It would be quite impossible to cut through the crush to reach his side.

Impossible was not a word Lady Delphine St. James endured.

She snapped her fan shut. "Excuse me," she said, pushing past a Dutch officer exchanging pleasantries with a lady in blue silk. "Your pardon," she murmured, squeezing by a red-coated lieutenant, keeping her eyes on Stephen Ives all the while. He was watching her, his expression unreadable, probably hoping she was heading somewhere else—to fetch a glass of champagne, perhaps, or to speak to her hostess.

She reached the foot of the staircase, and made a quick curtsy to the Duchess of Richmond, her hostess for the evening. "Good evening, your Grace," she said breathlessly. The duchess merely nodded. If she found Delphine's haste unseemly, she did not remark on it. Her Grace had other, much more important guests to see to, of course. It meant Delphine was free to continue on her quest. She glanced up to see if Stephen had moved. He hadn't. That was a good sign, wasn't it? She picked up her skirt and hurried.

"Why Lady Delphine, what an unexpected pleasure."

Someone stepped into her path, cutting off her view of him, forcing her to stop. She almost cursed aloud. The gentleman before her bowed, and she had a brief glimpse of Stephen over his shoulder before he rose again and blocked her view of him.

She looked at the man before her. "Oh, it's you, Captain Lord Rothdale. Good evening." He was a friend of her brother's, or rather a compatriot in Sebastian's debauchery.

"Captain Lord Rothdale? Is that any way to greet an old and dear friend?" He preened, showing off his Royal Dragoons uniform, making the gold braid glitter in the candlelight. "You called me Peter when we met at your father's home in London. Don't let the uniform scare you away, I may be one of the heroes, but I am still as tame as a house cat, I assure you." He smiled broadly at his own joke and picked up her hand, bringing it to his lips. For a moment she wondered if he intended to lick it, cat like. The intensity of his eyes on her low cut gown reminded her of a cat far more dangerous than a mere tabby. "How may I be of service this evening, Darling Dilly? You appear to lack a dancing partner."

Her jaw tightened at the sound of her family nickname on his lips. She was Dilly to her siblings, and only to them. She tried to withdraw her hand from his. He refused to let go. Instead he tightened his grip, leaned closer still, and she could smell rum on his breath. The glitter in his eyes had more to do with the amount of the spirit he'd consumed than her company, she noted. He had arrived foxed, then, since the duchess was serving champagne, not rum, which made his condition all the more shocking.

She tried again to withdraw her hand from his, but he gave her a teasing smile and held on. She felt her cheeks heat, and a scathing insult came to mind, but this was hardly the place, and if she had learned one thing about Stephen Ives, it was that he did not like scenes. She'd learned that the hard way. Rothdale stepped closer still.

"Dance with me, Dilly," he said again. "Or better yet, come out to the terrace, and I'll whisper wicked compliments in your ear. There seems to be something afoot, and rumor has it we'll be off to battle come sun-up. Don't you want to give me a proper send off?"

She did indeed, but not the kind he hoped for. She felt a flare of anger. "Please excuse me, Captain," she said in her tartest tone, emphasizing his military title to remind him where he was, and who he was. She swept a cold glance over his uniform, the uniform he was dishonoring by such boorish behavior, but he didn't move. He laughed.

"Now don't be like that. I'd like to know you better. I had no opportunity at all to enjoy your company in London. You were always out when I called. But now, here we are together at last." He had the audacity to run his fingertip down the exposed length of her bare arm, from the place where her short puffed sleeve ended to the edge of her lace glove.

Delphine enjoyed flirting as much as the next lady— in fact, she was a renowned charmer, if one was to use the polite term, but not like this, not here. She tried once more to pluck her hand free, but still he would not let go. She drew a breath, stiffened her spine. She was going to have to make a scene after all. She clenched her free hand around her fan, ready to deal him a crushing blow as she opened her mouth to rebuke him for his boorish behavior.

"Lady Delphine, I believe this is our dance."

She turned and found Stephen Ives standing next to her, and her breath stopped yet again. She shut her mouth with an audible snap.

He bowed and held out his hand, waiting for her to take it, which meant Rothdale would have to let her go. He did, releasing her fingers as if they were on fire, obviously surprised to see the major. His handsome face reddened with displeasure.

Delphine clasped Stephen's hand like a lifeline and let him lead her away.

The music began—a waltz. Stephen set his hand on her waist and swept her onto the floor. He glared over her shoulder at the captain, who was disappearing into the crowd.

"Do you know Captain Lord Rothdale? He's a friend of my brother's. He is not, that is, he and I are not—" she realized she was babbling.

His eyes remained on the captain. "I do. We are in the same regiment."

Oh. Of course he'd know him, then. Delphine felt like a ninny. He didn't add to his terse comment, or offer any pleasantries. He had rescued her from a boor at a ball, but it appeared it was now entirely up to her to change the subject. She was at a summer ball in a room filled with flowers and candles, waltzing with Stephen Ives. She wasn't about to waste such an opportunity talking about anyone else. The room was warm, but the glow she felt had much more to do with being held in Stephen's arms. She could smell his shaving soap, the wool of his tunic, the scent of the flowers as they whirled past them.

"Goodness you dance well," she tried again.

"I spent six months in Vienna. They invented the waltz."

She felt her skin heat. Where was her famous charm and glib tongue now when she needed them most? "Ah, yes. You were at the peace conference, part of the embassy. I have heard stories, of course, about all the glittering parties with the kings and queens of Europe, the Tsar of Russia, the Emperor of Austria . . ." He looked slightly bored. She swallowed. He was a diplomat, and a diplomat was most unlikely to want to gossip or repeat salacious stories about crowned heads or anyone else. "Was the congress successful?" she asked.

His lips tightened at her question. "Unfortunately not, or we would not be here awaiting yet another battle with Napoleon."

She read the seriousness in his gaze. "Will it come soon?"

He met her eyes at last, as if assessing the seriousness of her question. There were many in Brussels who doubted the battle would come at all, but she was the sister-in-law of a colonel. She kept her eyes on his.

"Within hours, I hear. The French crossed the Belgian frontier this morning," he replied.

She stumbled slightly, and he caught her against his chest for a moment, and guided her expertly into the next step. Her breath stopped again as her breasts momentarily pressed against the hard muscles of his chest. The moment was thrilling, like flying.

He set her down, utterly unaffected, and changed the subject. "How is it you are here in Brussels, my lady, especially now with the London Season in full bloom at home?" She did not miss the slight edge of disdain in his tone. He was making it clear that he thought her the same vain and silly creature he'd known in London, a woman who lived for pleasure and flattery, all sharp wit and flirtation, and no substance. She felt her cheeks heat.

"I came to Brussels with my sister, Eleanor. She's married to Colonel Lord Fairlie, as you may recall. Meg Temberlay is with us as well. We are lodging at a small estate on the outskirts of the city. It is to be a hospital, if it is necessary. We knew of course that the battle was coming. There are hundreds of men camped in our orchard, and even in the rose garden, but within *hours?*"

His eyes lit with interest at last. "Meg? Is Nicholas here?" he said, referring to Meg's husband, a mutual friend, Major Lord Nicholas Temberlay. She felt hope fizzle as he scanned the crowds, looking for them, forgetting her, even though he didn't miss a step.

"Nicholas is not in the city, my lord, and we've had no real news of him, only that he is on reconnaissance. What does that mean, my lord? Meg is beside herself with worry."

He swung his gaze back to her. Did he expect her to prattle about the heat of the evening, or the number of guests present, or any of a dozen other banalities? His look of surprise told her that was exactly what he expected from her.

He let his gaze brush over her gown, her face, the flowers in her hair before meeting her eyes and looking at her—*really* looking at her, gauging the depths of interest, her intelligence.

"I don't know. It could mean many things."

"That's what we're afraid of. *Is* there reason to worry? Surely Wellington will crush the French . . ." She stopped when his eyes darkened, her breath catching for an entirely different reason now.

"I do hope so, my lady. But the outcome of a battle is never certain," he said.

She felt a shiver run up her spine. She tightened her grip on his hand for a brief instant. "Will you—will you fight?"

"Yes," he replied.

"Then you are not here in a diplomatic role?"

"I will ride with my regiment when the order comes."

She understood a little better the terrible worry her friend Meg and her sister Eleanor felt, having men they loved in battle, waiting and worrying. Bitterness filled her mouth. She swallowed her own fear, and lowered her gaze to his chest.

"The Royal Dragoons," she murmured, staring at his tunic.

"Yes." he replied.

Delphine bit her lip. What should a lady say to a man riding off to war? She was suddenly aware this moment might be the last chance she had to speak with him, to tell him— what? That she adored him, admired him, wished he would sweep her out into the June night and kiss her? She'd allow it. She'd kiss him back. She looked up at him hopefully, but he was scanning the room again.

"Lord Ives, I—" she began, but a soldier entered and

crossed the room to Lord Wellington, his spurs and boot heels ringing a warning, louder than the music or the laughter of gay ladies, or the tinkle of champagne glasses. Conversation stopped, dancers faltered, and all eyes watched as the soldier bowed and handed the duke a note. Wellington kept his expression carefully blank, but he rose to his feet at once, and nodded to his adjutants. The Duke of Richmond led his esteemed guest to a private room and shut the door behind them. She felt Stephen tense as a buzz of speculation rose, hovered over the gaiety like a black cloud.

"Is it bad?" she whispered.

"Possibly," he said through stiff lips. "May I return you to your sister, Lady Delphine?"

She felt tears sting her eyes, and panic welled in her breast at the thought of losing him, now or tomorrow, in battle.

She forced a teasing smile. "But the music has not ended."

He colored slightly. "No, but—"

The door of the Duke of Richmond's study opened again, and a grim faced cavalry officer emerged and held up his hand for silence. "Gentlemen, finish your dances, take leave of your partners and return to your units at once."

Dismayed cries rose from the ladies. The music faltered and stopped. Stephen looked around, taking note of the officers in his own regiment. She felt the tension in his body, saw the eager light in his eyes, knew he was already on duty, and she was all but forgotten. Still he kept his hand under her elbow as he caught the arm of a passing adjutant. "What news?"

The young soldier glanced at her and bowed before replying. "Napoleon crossed the frontier at Charleroi. Lord Wellington plans to march out and engage him south of here."

Delphine put a hand to her throat. It was suddenly real, and frightening. All the past weeks of gathering troops, preparing for a battle that seemed like it would never come, or at worst, would happen somewhere else, somewhere far away. Weeks of rolling bandages they were sure would never be needed, of flirting and dancing and picnicking with handsome officers, laughing at their bravado, their brave boasts of the daring adventures they'd have when Napoleon appeared at last. Now he was here, just south of the city, close by. She looked around the room at the keen faces of the men, the tears in the ladies' eyes. Despair made her sway. Stephen took her arm more firmly, tucking it under his own.

"Come, I'll escort you back to Lady Fairlie," he said gently, giving her a brave smile.

She felt the hard muscles under his tunic, warm and alive. For once in her life—and when it mattered most—her tongue knotted. She wondered again just what to say, when she may never see him again, and he might—she closed her eyes, leaned against him for a moment.

He put gripped her hand for a moment, offering her courage. He smiled gently, yet in the depths of his grey eyes, she read something else, a shadow of something indefinable, as if the battle for him might already be lost, as if some great sorrow had brought him here, and he did not care if he lived or died, once his duty was done. That scared her most of all.

"My lord, what—" she began, but they reached Eleanor's side, and he turned his attention to her. Her sister was white faced, her lips drawn into a thin line. It did nothing to soothe Delphine to see an experienced officer's wife like Eleanor, a woman who had been through many battles before, looking so grim.

"Ellie." She took her sister's hand. It was ice cold inside her glove.

Eleanor squeezed back. "Fairlie has gone to muster his men. He says we must go at once. We're to return to the villa. Keep the horses harnessed and go north to Antwerp and home to England at once if it goes badly." She looked at Stephen. Though her eyes were dry, they were huge, filled with worry. *"Will* it go badly do you think, my lord?"

"We have an excellent commander, Lady Fairlie, and excellent officers under him, Colonel Lord Fairlie among them," he said gently. "We can hope for the best outcome with such odds, I think."

Eleanor nodded. "And yet, Napoleon's officers are every bit as fine as ours. I've heard Fairlie say so."

Stephen didn't reply to that. "If I may, I think Colonel Fairlie's advice was sound. You must leave at once if things go badly." He turned to Delphine and met her eyes, as if he expected *she* would be the brave one, would be the one get her sister to safety, instead of the other way around. "Come ladies, I'll see you to your carriage. The streets will be crowded with troops moving up, and it may take you some time to reach home, so it's best to leave now." He took Eleanor's arm, and Delphine walked next to her sister as Stephen pressed through the crowds, seeing them safely through the crush.

Outside, the yard was in chaos. Torches lit the faces of panicked horses, their eyes rolling white as yelling coachmen tried to force their way to the door to pick up their passengers. Delphine watched as Stephen gave an order to one of the Duchess's footmen, and stayed close to them, protecting them from the mayhem, keeping them safe as they waited for Colonel Fairlie's coach to arrive.

And who would keep him safe, Delphine wondered. He was still wearing dancing pumps, and surely he'd need to find his boots before battle began. He could not fight in dancing pumps, surely. She felt hysterical laughter bubble up in her throat. A dozen other officers nearby also wore their formal footwear. They could not fight, so they must stay, then, surely. Fear formed a hard knot in her throat, and she tried to swallow it, but it would not go. She scanned the crowds in the torch lit courtyard. She saw a grinning officer mount his horse, stilling the beast's panic as it capered anxiously. He reached down and hauled a lady up to perch on his stirrup, holding her close, the satin of her gown shimmering. Her arms went around his neck, and their lips met in a long, passionate kiss. Delphine should have been shocked—such behavior would have been unacceptable at any other ball, on any other night than this one, but it was right in this moment, with battle looming. She wondered how many of the men here tonight would die. She looked at Stephen, so alive, strong and vital. She memorized the way the torchlight gleamed on his fair hair, lit his eyes, flamed over the width of his shoulders, made his scarlet tunic glow. He turned and looked at her as if he expected her to speak. Her lips parted, and she stepped closer, but the coach pulled up, and Stephen helped Eleanor into it before taking Delphine's hand. "Goodnight, my lady, and thank you for the dance," he said politely. "Remember, if things go awry tomorrow—"

She didn't want to think about that. She threw herself

into his arms to stop the words, the fear, and kissed him. He caught her, and for moment he was stiff, his posture indignant, but she stood on tip toe to hold his face in her hands and kissed his cheeks, his jaw, and his lips, praying that every kiss might keep him safe, bring him back. Then his arms wrapped around her and he caught her mouth with his and kissed her back. His arms tightened around her, and she felt the sudden desperation in him, the need. He pulled her closer, and deepened the kiss, and she opened to his urging, let his tongue sweep in. He tasted of champagne, and wool, and leather—like a soldier, a warrior on his way to battle. She tangled her hands in his hair, pressed closer still, and he held her there, kissed her with all the passion she had dreamed of.

"Delphine St. James!" her sister cried. "What are you doing? Get into this coach immediately!"

Stephen pulled back at once, and met her eyes, his gaze was hot, surprised. He stepped away, and bowed stiffly, the proper and correct diplomat once more, the officer, the gentleman. "Goodbye, my lady, he said, and took her hand in his, and squeezed it, a thank you, perhaps—or forgiveness for her forward behavior. Her heart throbbed in her chest, and she was on the verge of tears.

"You will be safe," she whispered, making it a command.

"Of course," he said. Did he sound sure? She couldn't tell.

His eyes swept over her. "English daisies," he murmured looking at the flowers in her hair. "How very . . . English. I used to pick them when I was a boy, carry them to my mother, my sister, even the cook."

She plucked one loose and held it out to him. "Take this one from me, for luck."

He stared at the small pink blossom for a moment. "Thank you." He closed his hand over it.

He helped her into the coach before she could say another word, and shut the door, his eyes on hers as the coach lurched forward.

She fought with the latch, lowered the window and leaned out so she could watch him walk away. One last gleam of torchlight lit his scarlet tunic, before the shadows swallowed him.

"I will see you again," she whispered. "You will come back."

Suddenly it hardly mattered if he admired her or not. She only wanted him to live.

Still want more? Keep reading for a look at

THE SECRET LIFE OF LADY JULIA

CHAPTER ONE

London, October 1813

When she looked back on the events of her betrothal ball, Lady Julia Leighton blamed it on the champagne.

Or perhaps it was the heady scent of the roses.

Or it was the fact that Thomas Merritt was not her fiancé, and he was handsome, and he'd been kind, and called her beautiful as he waltzed her out through the French doors and sealed her fate.

Most of all she blamed herself. It had been the perfect night to begin with, every detail flawlessly executed, every eventuality planned for.

Except one.

She had waited twelve years for her betrothal ball to take place, and it certainly turned out to be an evening she would never, ever forget.

She had been engaged to marry David Hartley, the Duke of Temberlay, since she was eight and he was sixteen, and as she smoothed the blue silk gown over her grown-up curves, she had hoped that David would, at long last, see her as a woman, his bride-to-be, and not just the child who lived next door.

She *was* grown up, and pretty too—a chance flirtation in Hyde Park had proven that, and she'd barely been able to think of anything or anyone else since. She wondered now what Thomas Merritt might think of this dress, as she preened before the mirror. Mr. Merritt treated her like a woman, while everyone else—David, her father, her brother—all saw her as little Julia, even if her pigtails were long since gone.

She pushed him out of her mind and practiced a coquette's smile in the mirror—the smile she meant to give David when his eyes widened with pleasure at sight of her tonight. She planned to sparkle every bit as brightly as the diamond clips her maid twined into an artful coiffure of dark curls, or the magnificent Leighton diamonds glittering at her neck, wrist, and ears. She slid her betrothal ring—a sapphire surrounded by pearls the size of quails' eggs—over her glove and stared at herself in the glass. She had been raised to be the perfect duchess, and she certainly looked the part.

"Let me see."

Julia turned, waited for her mother's nod of approval. If the Countess of Carrindale thought her daughter looked pretty, she kept it to herself.

"We'd better go down," was all she said, and "Decorum, Julia," when Julia tried to descend the stairs a little too eagerly, anxious to see the appreciation in her fiancé's eyes.

But David wasn't waiting at the foot of the stairs.

He wasn't even at the door to the ballroom, or in the salon with her father.

She felt her heart sink.

"You look well tonight, Julia," her father said, casting his eyes over the jewels, as if assessing their value against her own worth, before turning away to take her mother's arm.

She glanced up at the portrait of her bother James that graced the wall of the salon. He smiled down at her in his scarlet regimentals. If he were here, he would have bussed her cheek, teased her, told her she looked very pretty, and made her laugh, but James had been killed in battle in Spain a year ago.

She felt the familiar pang of grief as she met his painted eyes. She missed his friendship, his easy company, and his advice. Her childhood had ended with the heart-wrenching sorrow of his death. "Courage," he might have whispered now, squeezing her hand. She let her fingers curl around his imaginary ones. James had been her protector, her friend, and her confidant. She hadn't felt as safe as she did with James until— Thomas Merritt's smiling face passed through her brain. She looked down at her satin gloves. He'd squeezed her hand as well, but it hadn't felt the way it did when James touched her, or even David. It felt, well, intimate, admiring, the kind of caress a man gives a desirable woman.

She felt her cheeks heat at the memory of the encounter in the park, and gave the painting a pleading look. Would James have been horrified at her behavior? No, he would have done the same thing himself, had he been there.

Thomas Merritt was a complete stranger to her. She had never seen him at the balls and parties she attended, and she really should not have even deigned to speak to him without a proper introduction. If he'd been a proper gentleman, he would have walked right past her, ignored the fact that she was standing alone in the middle of Hyde Park with tears stinging her eyes, but he'd stopped, and pressed his handkerchief into her hand, and just in time to rescue her from the curious eyes and prying questions of Lady Fiona Barry, the *ton*'s worst gossip.

She'd been prattling too much, perhaps, about the details of the wedding, and David was looking bored, which made her try all the harder to amuse him. He'd seen some people he knew across the park and stopped walking, taking her hand off his arm and stepping away. "Wait here, Jules. There's someone I wish to speak to," David had said. She'd caught his sleeve.

"I'll come too, and you can introduce me," she said, but he'd shot her a look of irritation. "Surely I should know your friends, David. They might be guests in our home some day and—"

"It's business, Julia," he replied sharply, plucking his arm out of her grip. "Be good and wait here, and I'll buy you an ice at Gunter's on the way home."

Stunned, she'd watched him walk away, leaving her behind as if she were an annoying child.

"I would have promised you diamonds," a voice said, and she'd turned and regarded the stranger by her side. He was watching David's retreating back.

"I beg your pardon?" she said, though she didn't know him, and knew she should not speak to him at all. He could be anyone, or anything. But he smiled at her, his eyes warm, and her breath stopped.

"To wait, I mean. I would have promised you diamonds,

or something infinitely better than a Gunter's ice, unless of course you prefer those to jewels. Even then I wouldn't have left you alone in the first place, not with every man in the park watching you with such obvious admiration."

She held her tongue and glanced around. The park was indeed filled with curious eyes, and all of them no doubt wondering why she, Lady Julia Leighton, was without an escort.

"It's quite all right," he said. "Think of me as your protector until your brother returns."

"Fiancé," she murmured.

His brows shot upward toward the brim of his hat, rakishly tipped on dark curls. "I see."

Embarrassed anger filled her. "Do you? And just what do you imagine you see, my lord—"

"'Mister' will do. Thomas Merritt," he said, giving his name and bowing. "And you are?"

"The Duke of Temberlay's bride-to-be!" she snapped, rising to her full height. She still barely reached his nose, even in the tall, lavishly feathered bonnet she wore. There was amusement in his eyes, which was not the impression she'd hoped for.

"Forgive me, Duchess. At first glance I thought perhaps you were a younger sister he finds annoying, or a cousin he'd been instructed to squire about for a bit of fresh air, against his own choice. He treats you as if—"

"It's none of your affair how he treats me!"

He put a hand under her elbow. "Ah, but it is, as your temporary protector. I cannot leave the most beautiful lady in the park all alone, especially when she is on the verge of tears."

It was exactly what James might have said, and that only

added to her desire to cry. She blinked back tears. "I never cry!"

He pressed his handkerchief into her hand. "Of course not. Shall we stroll along the path a little way? Lady Fiona Barry is heading this way, and I hear she can smell tears from a hundred yards." He took her arm.

Julia's stomach froze. *Fiona Barry?* This was disaster! She would report everything to her mother, then to everyone else in the *ton*—David's absence from her side, the lack of a proper escort, and of course the presence of the handsome stranger by her side.

"Laugh, my lady," he murmured, leaning under the edge of the feathered bonnet.

"I don't think I can," she admitted.

"Then I shall make you smile. I will promise you diamonds and pearls," he said.

"I prefer emeralds," she murmured.

He looked down at her, his eyes moving over her face and her elegant new moss green walking gown. "Yes, I can see that they'd suit you very well indeed," he said, his voice low, seductive, something in his gaze suggesting he was imagining her draped entirely in emeralds and nothing else at all. She felt heat surge through her body, and she couldn't help but smile.

"There now, that's better," he said, but his eyes remained on hers. He had gray eyes, glittering and dangerous, filled with the kind of male admiration she'd never seen directed at her before this moment. She'd been wrong. *This* was where childhood ended, with the first look of male appreciation a girl received. She liked it very well indeed. Her spine turned soft for a moment, and she had the oddest desire to lean into his strong shoulder.

"Good morning, Julia," Fiona Barry said as she approached. Julia's spine stiffened to attention at once, and she tore her gaze from Thomas Merritt's handsome face. Fiona was examining the gentleman as if he were a cream cake and she was starving. "And who is this? Do introduce me, my dear."

"This is Mr. Thomas Merritt," Julia said. Even her voice sounded more adult, husky and soft. "Mr. Merritt, this is Lady Fiona Barry, a dear friend of my mother's."

He bowed over Fiona's hand. "Good morning, Lady Barry. A pleasant morning for a walk in the park, is it not?"

"Indeed," Fiona said. "But where is Temberlay, my dear?" she asked Julia. "I was sure I heard your mama say you'd gone walking with him this morning when I called."

Julia felt her face heat. Fiona could also sniff out lies. "He's just—"

"He's been called away for a moment, and he asked me to escort Julia," Thomas Merritt said smoothly.

"I see. And will you be attending the betrothal ball on Thursday?" Fiona asked, accepting the explanation, lost in Thomas Merritt's dazzling smile.

"No," Julia said hurriedly.

"I wouldn't dream of missing it," he countered, and smiled down at her, turning her knees to water again, squeezing her hand ever so slightly.

Fiona grinned, baring her teeth like an aging hound scenting prey. "It is an event not to be missed. The Countess of Carrindale gives the most marvelous parties, and her dear daughter's betrothal ball will surely be the event of the Little Season, surpassed only by her wedding." She sighed like a bellows. "I remember you in leading strings, Julia. It is hard for me to imagine you all grown up and about to become a duchess, my dear."

Julia felt Thomas Merritt's eyes on her once more, warm and appraising. He squeezed her hand yet again. "Forgive me, but I've remembered an appointment I cannot break, Julia." Even her name sounded honey-sweet from his lips. "I'll leave you to chat with Lady Barry."

He kissed her hand, and she felt the warmth of his mouth through the lace of her glove. It flowed through her limbs like whisky. "It was a pleasure," he said, looking into her eyes, and she could see that he meant it, that he was stepping away with regret. Her tongue wound itself around her tonsils, making speech impossible. And then he was gone, walking away without looking back, his long legs eating up the cinder path until the trees swallowed the sight of him. She suppressed a sigh of regret, just as Fiona heaved one of her own.

She let Fiona tell her the latest gossip without even hearing it. She felt like a woman. Not a lady, or a bride, or the daughter of an earl. A woman.

It felt like stepping into the heat of the sun on a cold day, and she wanted more.

"Julia! Did you hear me? It's time to go in. We all miss James," her mother said, and Julia realized that she was standing in the salon, staring up at her brother's portrait, and seeing not his face, but Thomas Merritt's. "You are the future now, Julia. Your son will not only be Duke of Temberlay, but also the next Earl of Carrindale." She didn't want to think of the fact that she was simply the conduit for the next generation of the peerage.

"Temberlay has waited long enough," her father added gruffly, barely glancing at his late heir.

He hadn't spoken James's name since the news of his death came, and he was no doubt pleased the wedding would take place at last. The nuptials had been delayed while her family mourned, but men without heirs to succeed them were ever anxious about the future, though David hadn't objected to the delay. How could he when his own brother, Nicholas, was a captain in the same regiment as James? Every man in the regiment had escaped certain death thanks to her brother's heroic self-sacrifice. She was proud, of course, but she wished—just a little—that he had found another way to save the others, so she might still have her brother with her now, tonight, when she needed his reassuring arm to lean on.

Julia drew herself up straight. She was a woman now, a lady, and a duchess-to-be. She could and would stand on her own two feet. She cast one last glance at James, and pushed the image of Thomas Merritt's appreciative smile out of her mind. She would soon see the same look on David's face.

"I'm ready."

She followed her parents into the ballroom, brilliantly lit with a thousand candles. Jewels glittered, regimental badges gleamed, champagne sparkled, and her betrothal ring shone brightest of all.

David didn't even notice her entrance. He was deep in

conversation with a group of gentlemen as Julia approached, just a trifle irritated by his inattention tonight, of all nights.

"Good evening," she purred, and dipped a curtsy. The gentlemen bowed.

"Oh, hello, Jules," David said with a vague smile. He dropped an absent kiss on her forehead—the kind of kiss her brother might have bestowed on her. David didn't tell her she looked pretty. Nor did his eyes light with pleasure, or anything else. In fact, he looked away from her, swept the ballroom with a bored glance, and took a glass of champagne from a passing footman without offering one to her. She reached for her own glass, and David's eyebrows quirked in surprise, as if he thought her still too young for wine. She gave him her practiced coquette's grin and sipped.

Her mother beckoned them to the receiving line, and David took her glass and set it down with his own before he offered his arm. "Shall we?" He led her to her mother's side and stood with his hands clasped behind his back as they waited for their guests to arrive. Julia watched the cream of the *ton* descending the stairs like an invading horde, drew a shaky breath and pasted on a welcoming smile.

Lady Dallen swept in like an ill wind, examined Julia's necklace through her lorgnette, and wished her happy in a dry tone before going to stir things up in other corners of the room.

Lord Dallen slapped David on the back and said he looked forward to playing cards tonight, once "this betrothal business" was concluded, as if Julia was an interruption to the evening, and not the reason for it. David, damn his eyes—she borrowed one of her late grandmother's favorite and most forbidden phrases—looked extremely pleased by his lordship's invitation. In fact, he gazed at Dallen with the kind of appreciation *she* had hoped for. If that was the way to his heart, she would have to learn how to play cards before the wedding. Her mother would hardly approve, but what else was a bride to do?

David didn't enjoy poetry, or music. He didn't read or hunt. They would have to spend their evenings at Temberlay castle doing *something*. She felt a blush rise at the other idea that came to mind, but she was an innocent, and he had never so much as hinted at the physical aspects of marriage that would transpire between them after the vows were said. Why, she'd learned more about that from a single glance into Thomas Merritt's glittering gray eyes.

"David, my mother has agreed to allow me to waltz this evening," she said, leaning into his shoulder, brushing against him in the most unsisterly way she could manage in her parents' ballroom.

He patted her hand and smiled vacantly at her. "I don't know how to waltz, Jules."

Her heart sank to her ankles.

"Then perhaps—" But she didn't have a suggestion. She folded her tongue behind her teeth and turned to smile at the next guest. Her heart stopped dead in her chest.

"Thomas Merritt," he said in a dark voice, as if they'd never met. He bowed over her hand, his grip warm through her glove, his eyes never leaving hers, filled with a mischievous, knowing, intimate stare. The heat in that look set her heart beating again, very fast. He smiled, a slow, dangerous grin, and his gaze roamed over her. *His* appreciation was perfectly obvious. Her heart climbed higher still, and lodged in her throat, making speech impossible. A lock of dark hair fell over his brow, and she clenched her fist against the urge to brush it back. He did so himself in a polished gesture as he stepped away.

He was the handsomest man she'd ever seen. Her imagination hadn't played her false. He was just as she remembered him from their brief encounter. She let her eyes linger on the lean length of his legs, the breadth of his shoulders under the black wool of his evening coat as he walked away. She dared to guess that *he* waltzed . . . among other things.

He glanced back and caught her looking. She felt heat rise over her cheeks, and she made a small sound of dismay as he grinned at her again.

"Pardon?" David asked, glancing down at her.

"Nothing," she managed. She snatched another glass of champagne from a passing footman and took a long restorative sip. The bubbles were almost as thrilling as Mr. Merritt's wicked smile.

She watched him out of the corner of her eye. He did not go into the card room or join the other guests. Instead, he leaned against the wall insouciantly, in her line of sight, and watched her. She felt her composure slip. Suddenly her gown felt too tight, too low-cut, and the room too warm.

She sent him a scathing glance, meant to discourage such behavior, squelch it utterly, but he had the audacity to wink at her. It made her stomach wobble and her knees weak. She plied her fan, hid behind it.

Had he come to reclaim his handkerchief? It was upstairs, hidden in her drawer.

"Stand up straight," her mother whispered. Julia stiffened, but with more annoyance than grace as the waltz began and David disappeared into the card room, arm in arm with Lord Dallen.

"D'you suppose they'll take a house together by the sea for the summer?" he quipped, and she turned to find Thomas Merritt beside her, watching David and Dallen go. He was so tall she had to look up to meet his eyes. "May I have this dance?" He extended his hand as if he was already sure of her acquiescence.

A thrill rushed through her. There was something about this man that warned her to say no, to run for the safety of her mother's side, but she was a grown woman. Surely the tingle low in her belly at the look in his eyes proved that well enough.

"Thank you." She took his hand and let him lead her out.

He waltzed smoothly. "You look beautiful, by the way," he said, as if he knew she'd craved the compliment, exactly the way she'd needed a protector in the park. Did he intend to make a habit of rescuing her?

"Thank you," she said again. She was acutely aware of the heat of his hand on her waist, searing through the layers of silk and lace. He made a perfectly proper touch feel intimate, as if they were alone. She felt a tingle of something unexpected course through her as his eyes dropped to the slopes of her breasts and lingered before he met her eyes again.

She *felt* beautiful.

"Does His Grace realize just how lucky he is? I wondered that the other day when we met."

"Of course he does," she said tartly, and felt her skin heat. How bold that sounded.

"You're blushing, but you shouldn't. A woman should be aware of her worth." His gaze flicked over her jewels. "Beyond the value of her jewelry, of course. I'd be willing to wager you've been betrothed for a very long time, or it's an arranged match, perhaps, since he already behaves like you are an old married couple, bored by familiarity."

"We have known each other since—forever," she said breathlessly. Why did every word out of her mouth make her sound like a ninny?

He quirked an eyebrow upward. "Forever is a long time. I suppose when someone looks constantly at a familiar object, no matter how lovely it is, they cease to see its beauty."

Exactly so. David would always see her as the child he'd grown up with. She imagined their wedding night, how awkward that was going to be. She stumbled.

Mr. Merritt caught her, lifted her, twirled her through the air and took the next step before he set her back on her feet. For an instant her breasts were pressed to his chest, her heart pounding against the hard muscles under his shirt. His hand spread wide on her waist, supporting her, and his thumb brushed the underside of her breast. Another rescue.

She swallowed a gulp of heady surprise.

"You look flushed, my lady. Perhaps some air?" he asked, glancing toward the French doors that led to the terrace.

She looked out into the velvet darkness of the late spring evening. She should refuse. It was against all the rules she'd been taught. But she was an adult, almost a married woman, and she nodded and let him waltz her out onto the terrace.

"Would you care for some champagne?" he asked, and

stepped inside to beckon to a passing footman. He took two glasses and brought one to her.

She watched the bubbles dance in the light that spilled from the ballroom.

"Shall we drink to your happiness?"

"I am happy."

"Oh, I didn't doubt it for a moment," he drawled in a tone that suggested he doubted it very much indeed.

"David is simply—" She hesitated. What? Kind, titled, stiff? Her grandmother's nickname for him came to mind. Dull Duke David.

"Oh, I know. He is handsome, rich, and safe."

"Safe?" She met the mischievous glitter of his eyes in the shadows. He laughed.

"Interesting you chose that word out of the three."

"Well, of course he's the other two things as well—and more. I suppose he's safe, too. Who would harm him?"

He tilted his head. "I meant he's a safe choice of husband. Not likely to do anything unexpected or in the least shocking." He sipped his champagne. She watched his throat work above the edge of his cravat, his skin dark against the white linen.

Dull Duke David, she thought again, and pushed the idea away. "Such as?" she said, made bold by the wine.

He studied her for a moment, reached to caress her cheek, then ran his thumb over her lower lip. "Such as waltzing you away into the garden to steal a kiss, which I have wanted to do since I met you in Hyde Park. But then, I'd bet that even his kisses are safe. Do they set you on fire?"

"I—" She began a tart response that it was none of his affair how David kissed her, but she had no idea. He had only ever offered dry pecks on her cheek or forehead. His lips were always cool. She stared at Thomas Merritt's well-shaped mouth. She'd wondered what it might be like to kiss him too. In fact, the idea had occupied her thoughts far more than it should have over the past two days.

He held up his champagne and stared into the amber depths. "A woman should feel like there are stars coursing through her blood when a man kisses her properly. Even if it is the simplest brush of his lips on hers, she should feel it in every inch of her body." He stepped closer, leaned in. "Is that how His Grace's kisses make you feel? Breathless, hot, desired?"

Could a kiss really feel like that? Suddenly she wanted to kiss a man who could never, ever resemble a brother.

Or her fiancé.

She lifted her face to his, stood on tiptoe, her mouth watering. "Show me," she said.

He didn't need a second invitation. He took her glass, set it on the edge of the balcony, cupped her face in his hands and lowered his mouth to hers. His lips were warm. She could taste the champagne on his breath, smell the soap he used, the scent of his own skin. A thrill of pure excitement ran through her, curling her toes. She tightened her fingers on his arms.

He didn't pull back. His lips shaped to fit hers, moved over her mouth expertly.

Oh my.

Her hands crept up to touch his face, to draw him closer. With a sigh, she kissed him back.

He licked the seam of her lips, and she drew back in surprise. He merely shifted his attention, laid a dozen kisses along her jaw, down her throat, blazing a trail of fire. She tipped her head, gave him access, permission. Above her the stars did indeed glitter.

He put his hands on her waist, spanning it, and drew her closer. She slid her arms around his neck, pressed against the warm length of his body. He nibbled a particularly delicate spot under her ear. "Oh," she sighed, shivering. Her eyes drifted shut but she could still see the stars.

He captured her mouth again, nipped at her lips until she drew a breath and opened. He tangled his tongue with hers. He tasted of champagne. She moved closer still, marveling at the way her hips fitted to his, how her curves perfectly accommodated his angles. His heat radiated through her clothes. More. She wanted more. She pressed her tongue against his, experimenting. He gave a soft groan, and his hands slid up her back to cup her neck and tilt her backward, deepening the kiss.

Oh, she did indeed feel breathless, hot, and desired!

Something tickled at her brain, the tiny part that could still think. She should step back, move away, go inside, but she could not stop kissing him. How had she ever lived without kisses? She hadn't even known such sensations existed. It was like the first sip of champagne, the heady tang of summer berries purloined from the garden, the sweetness of honey and wine and cake all in one. Surely this was what her grandmother had meant when she told her romantic stories, whispered them in her ear so her mother couldn't hear, of kisses such as this, bestowed on a princess in a tower by a lover who dared to climb the vines to her bower.

He pulled away, and cool evening air rushed in like sanity. Julia opened her eyes and stared at him. He was staring back, just out of reach, his face in shadow, breathing hard as if he'd been running.

"I think we'd better stop." His voice was an octave lower than it had been. It vibrated over every aroused inch of her flesh. Good sense returned like a dash of cold water. She should be ashamed—scarcely a dozen feet away, her guests were dancing, drinking, celebrating her betrothal to another man.

Dull Duke David.

She didn't know what to say. Her lips still tingled, and despite the chill of the spring evening, her body burned.

"I'll go back inside. You'd better slip in later," he murmured, looking over his shoulder now, scanning the crowd for curious eyes, worrying far too late if anyone might have seen them. David could call him out and shoot him for the liberties he'd taken. Would he shoot her too?

He was far too busy playing cards.

Mr. Merritt bowed, backed away. The light hit him, illuminated the copper lights in his dark hair, the silhouette of his lean body—the body that only moments earlier had been pressed against hers—then he stepped inside with a single regretful glance at her and was gone.

She put a hand to her lips, swollen and soft.

She needed a mirror.

She needed a cold bath.

Julia picked up her skirts and hurried along the terrace to the French doors that led into the library. She slipped inside and leaned on the cool glass for a moment. The room was dark and empty. Light from the street spilled through the windows, painting long golden rectangles on the floor.

Her heart slowed. The library was a place of sobriety and decorum. Somewhere beyond the double oak doors the party continued. She could hear laughter, voices, and music. She crossed to the mirror but could not see anything in the darkness. Was she different now? Disheveled? Did she look wanton? She smoothed a careful hand over her hair, checked for loose curls, touched her swollen lips, felt the tingle on her cheeks where his rougher skin had grazed her.

Of course she was different. She'd been different the moment she met Thomas Merritt, and now—

She perched on the edge of one of the armchairs that smelled of cigars and her father's hair oil. With nervous fingers, she tucked back a strand of hair. In a moment she would have to walk back into the ballroom, and act as if nothing had happened, but her heart was beating against her ribs like a caged bird.

She jumped to her feet when the door opened.

The light from the hall raced across the room, blinded her for a moment. Was it her mother, looking for her, or David, perhaps? Would they be able to tell what she'd been doing in the dark garden with the handsome stranger? Guilt tightened her gut even as resolve stiffened her spine. She had received many lectures in this particular room, standing on the carpet before her father's desk. She clasped her hands behind her back, as she always did, ready to face the consequences, whatever they might be.

Thomas Merritt stepped into the silence of Lord Carrindale's library and waited for his eyes to adjust to the dark. He had come to the lavish betrothal ball for one reason, and it wasn't to wish the couple happy.

He had no idea when he met Julia Leighton in the park that she was Carrindale's daughter. She'd been a lovely, distraught lady in need. He should have walked away, but he couldn't. Not when he saw the tears in her eyes. When Fiona Barry had said Julia's name, mentioned the betrothal ball, the very ball he had every intention of attending anonymously, he should have taken it as a warning.

From that moment, things had gone awry. For one thing, the countess was not wearing the magnificent tiara he'd come to steal, which meant it was most likely still in the safe. And for another thing . . . He glanced up at the shadowed portrait of the grim-faced Earl of Carrindale and grinned.

I've been kissing your daughter.

That was the other problem—the luscious lips of Lady Julia, the bride-to-be, Carrindale's unexpectedly lovely daughter. He'd noticed the stunning necklace she wore, of course, and the matching earrings, and then he saw the woman behind them, and the jewels had paled by comparison. She was even more beautiful than he remembered from their brief encounter.

Fool! He wasn't a natural thief, didn't find it easy, and the distraction didn't help.

Thomas wasn't the kind of man who lost himself in a simple kiss. He wondered how far he would have let it go if sanity hadn't saved him. And what if he'd been caught with

Julia in his arms? Would Carrindale have called the watch, or simply had him spirited away to a watery grave in the stinking Thames? The earl would certainly not insist that she marry a rogue like him when she had a duke in hand.

His pedigree was good enough, though not as high as the Duke of Temberlay's, or would have been had his brother not disowned him for his sins. He was plain Mr. Merritt now, a man who made his own way in the world without family ties to help or hinder him. This adventure would gain him only a memorable kiss, perhaps a stolen tiara—and one of Julia's diamond earrings, a souvenir of the encounter. It rested in his breast pocket now.

He licked his lips to refrain from taking it out and looking at it, and tasted champagne. He'd never kissed anyone like Julia Leighton. None of the rich widows, the bored *ton* wives, the milkmaids or whores he'd known compared. He marveled at Temberlay's stupidity in not knowing how lucky he was. What kind of man could resist the delectable charms of a woman like Julia? They had been betrothed for years. Surely by now Temberlay had claimed his right to touch her, bed her.

He shook his head, freeing his mind from that image, so he could find the damn safe and get the hell out—

The rustle of silk caught him by surprise.

She stepped out of the shadows. A mixture of fear and unexpected pleasure kept him rooted to the floor.

"How did you know I was here?" she asked him. "I thought—"

He knew what she thought, that he'd left the ball—which he would have if he'd had any sense at all—and she'd never see him again. She would have wondered about her lost earring longer than she'd remember him. Suddenly the diamond bob weighed heavy in his pocket, and he could feel it against his breast like biblical guilt.

Though shalt not steal. Not kisses, or jewels.

But a man had to eat.

He caught another hint of her perfume—it was on his clothes, would stay with him for days. Violets. It was a sophisticated, unusual scent for such a young woman. It spoke of hidden depths, secrets. Most debutantes wore lavender or rosewater.

"I—" He was lost for words. He glanced at the small landscape painting on the wall behind her, which probably hid the safe. For some reason, men like Carrindale always chose to hide their treasures behind nondescript art that wouldn't otherwise have a place in their elegant homes. He could hardly stride to the picture, take it down, and ask Julia for the combination to the safe.

He supposed in other circumstances a gentleman—or even a rogue like him, if he had any sense—would bow, make a joke of his inexplicable presence in this dark room, say he mistook the door for the way to the jakes, and take his leave before there was trouble.

But he was already in trouble. He couldn't take his eyes off her, the way the faint light outlined the shape of her neck and shoulders, the shadowed vee between her breasts, the ghostlike shimmer of her gown. The glitter of her jewels paled before the gleam of her eyes. His mouth watered.

"I—" He tried again, but she gave a desperate little sigh

and rushed toward him. He opened his arms, caught her. Her lips landed on his, and it began all over again.

He was powerless to resist. He wanted this woman. He couldn't recall a time when he hadn't been in complete control with a lover. He never lost himself to passion. Women were a means to an end, for physical gratification or gain. He offered them pleasure, took what he wanted, and left before they could beg him to stay.

But it was different with Julia, and he couldn't begin to say why. Perhaps because she was forbidden to him, belonged to another man. Was it the thrill of stealing something he otherwise couldn't have? No, it was the lady herself—beautiful, trusting, half innocent, unconsciously seductive. She'd set his blood on fire with a simple stolen kiss in a dark garden, and now—

He knew exactly what she wanted.

Him.

It wasn't rescue this time. It was plunder. She was making soft sounds as she sought his mouth, pressed her lips and her hips to his. He lifted her into his arms, carrying her the few steps to the deep leather settee, laying her down, his body on hers, as desperate as she. Her arms tightened, pulled him nearer. He was wrapped in her perfume, mesmerized by her eager kisses. She let him raise her skirts, slide his fingers up the silk of her calves, thighs, hips.

Her hands fumbled with the buttons of his shirt, then fell away as he found the wet center of her.

"Oh," she sighed, and his fingers played over her, bringing her pleasure before he took his own. She gripped his lapels, pulled him down against her as she cried out, her body bucking against his fingers. He caught the sweet whimpers in his mouth.

He reached for his flies, opened them expertly with one hand as he kissed her, unable to get enough of her mouth.

She gasped as he entered her, and tensed beneath him. She was tight, almost too tight.

Nervous, no doubt. He should have locked the door, but it was too late for that. He was beyond reason, beyond stopping, but she didn't ask him to. She gripped his shoulders, her nails digging into his flesh, right through his shirt, a sweet, sharp, sensual pain.

He didn't last long. One last, long thrust, and he filled her, felt the hot rush of release.

He fell against her, stunned. He stroked her face, kissed her gently, still buried inside her. He couldn't read her expression in the low light.

What the hell had he done?

He moved off of her, turned away and used his handkerchief to clean himself before he fastened his clothes.

She sat on the settee, arranging her own clothing, trying to fix her hopelessly disheveled hair.

"Oh no, my earring! Well, my mother's, actually. I've lost it! She'll lecture me for an hour on carelessness, heedless behavior, and—" She began to laugh.

"What's so funny?" he asked.

"Heedless behavior!" she said. Her laughter faded. "I should not have—"

Nor should he. Not here, not now. The stakes were too high. He sighed. He wished he could afford to leave here empty-handed, with nothing but the memory of a lover that finally made him feel something, even if only for a moment. The diamond in his pocket would feed him for a week, the Carrindale tiara for a month, and Julia's necklace for half a year.

She was searching the floor for it, and he almost relented. Taking her hands in his, he pulled her close for a moment, distracting her. Desire surged again. What the devil was the matter with him? He did *not* allow his feelings to get in the way of his survival. He hadn't even realized he *had* feelings until now. He kissed her gently, making it farewell. She pulled away.

He braced himself for tears, accusations, but she simply said, "You should go. The French doors lead to the garden, and there's a gate that leads to the mews and the street."

"Yes," he agreed.

"I shall go upstairs. I'll send my maid down to mama to say I have a headache."

There was no mention of Temberlay. Had the duke even noticed she was gone, that she'd been absent from the ballroom for nearly an hour? Thomas glanced at the ormolu clock on the mantel.

Less than an hour.

He straightened his rumpled cravat as best he could and bowed over her hand. Her fingers coiled around his for a moment, as if she could not bear to let him go. He pulled free gently and let himself out.

It wasn't until he'd reached his lodgings that he saw the blood on his handkerchief. How could he have been so stupid?

Lady Julia Leighton had been a virgin.

CHAPTER TWO

Thomas waited outside Carrindale House in the rain until he saw Julia get in the coach and drive away. He followed her to Bond Street, watched her alight and go into an exclusive modiste's shop. He watched through the window as she tried on a gown of sapphire blue silk. The shop assistant spread a lace veil over her dark hair, and a bitter taste filled his mouth. Her wedding gown. He clenched his fists and stepped away to wait for her to emerge.

"Why Lady Julia, how pleasant to meet you here so unexpectedly," he said brightly, as if he had merely chanced upon her in the street. He watched her pale cheeks bloom like roses, saw fear war with curiosity in her eyes.

She dipped a curtsy and turned to her maid. "Wait in the coach. I'll be along in a moment." After the girl complied, she whispered to him, "What are you doing here?"

"I found your earring," he said, and taking her gloved hand in his dropped it into her palm. It was the only excuse he had come up with to see her again, returning what he'd stolen. Well, half of what he'd stolen. "It must have gotten tangled in my clothing when we—" She shot him a wide-eyed look of horror, and he fell silent. "Are you—well, my lady?" he asked stiffly, resisting the urge to touch her flaming cheek.

She glanced at the earring and closed her hand on it. "You've rescued me yet again."

There were a million things he wanted to say—apologies, offers of marriage, confessions of feelings he had no right to, everything from concern to—affection. He'd call it that.

"Someday I shall have to return the favor," she said.

"I came to see if—" But she tilted her head, and even if her blush betrayed her embarrassment at what had passed between them in the darkness of her father's library, she schooled her expression into the same polite look of interest she'd given Fiona Barry in the park. She did not need him, after all. She was stronger than she looked. He felt admiration for her. She would make a magnificent duchess.

He took her arm and escorted her the few steps to her coach. "So when is the wedding to be?" he asked.

"January. At Temberlay Castle."

They reached the vehicle, and he let her go and bowed. "Then I shall wish you well," he said. "And happy."

She lowered her gaze. "I am . . ." She paused, and he watched her throat bob as she swallowed the lie. "Thank you," she managed.

He kissed her hand, felt her fingers tighten on his for an instant. He let her go and walked away, resisting the urge to look back. Whatever the future held for him, it did not include Julia Leighton.

ABOUT THE AUTHOR

LECIA CORNWALL lives and writes in Calgary, Canada, in the beautiful foothills of the Canadian Rockies, with five cats, two teenagers, a crazy chocolate Lab, and one very patient husband. She's hard at work on her next book.

Visit www.AuthorTracker.com for exclusive information on your favorite HarperCollins authors.

Give in to your impulses . . .
Read on for a sneak peek at four brand-new
e-book original tales of romance
from Avon Books.
Available now wherever e-books are sold.

RESCUED BY A STRANGER
By Lizbeth Selvig

CHASING MORGAN
BOOK FOUR: THE HUNTED SERIES
By Jennifer Ryan

THROWING HEAT
A DIAMONDS AND DUGOUTS NOVEL
By Jennifer Seasons

PRIVATE RESEARCH
AN EROTIC NOVELLA
By Sabrina Darby

An Excerpt from

RESCUED BY A STRANGER

by Lizbeth Selvig

When a stranger arrives in town on a vintage
motorcycle, Jill Carpenter has no idea her life
is about to change forever. She never expected
that her own personal knight in shining armor
would be an incredibly charming and handsome
southern man—but one with a deep secret. When
Jill's dreams of becoming an Olympic equestrian
start coming true, Chase's past finally returns to
haunt him. Can they get beyond dreams to find the
love that will rescue their two hearts? Find out in
the follow-up to *The Rancher and the Rock Star*.

"Angel?" Jill called. "C'mon, girl. Let's go get you something to eat." She'd responded to her new name all evening. Jill frowned.

Chase gave a soft, staccato, dog-calling whistle. Angel stuck her head out from a stall a third of the way down the aisle. "There she is. C'mon, girl."

Angel disappeared into the stall.

"Weird," Jill said, heading down the aisle.

At the door to a freshly bedded empty stall, they found Angel curled beside a mound of sweet, fragrant hay, staring up as if expecting them.

"Silly girl," Jill said. "You don't have to stay here. We're taking you home. Come."

Angel didn't budge. She rested her head between her paws and gazed through raised doggy brows. Chase led the way into the stall. "Everything all right, pup?" He stroked her head.

Jill reached for the dog, too, and her hand landed on Chase's. They both froze. Slowly he rotated his palm and wove his fingers through hers. The few minor fireworks she'd felt in the car earlier were nothing compared to the explosion now detonating up her arm and down her back.

"I've been trying to avoid this since I got off that dang horse." His voice cracked into a low whisper.

"Why?"

He stood and pulled her to her feet. "Because I am not a guy someone as young and good as you are should let do this."

"You've saved my life and rescued a dog. Are you trying to tell me I should be *worried* about you?"

She touched his face, bold enough in the dark to do what light had made her too shy to try.

"Maybe."

The hard, smooth fingertips of his free hand slid inexorably up her forearm and covered the hand on his cheek. Drawing it down to his side, he pulled her whole body close, and the little twister of excitement in her stomach burst into a thousand quicksilver thrills. Her eyelids slipped closed, and his next question touched them in warm puffs of breath.

"If I were to kiss you right now, would it be too soon?"

Her eyes flew open, and she searched his shadowy gaze, incredulous. "You're asking permission? Who does that?"

"Seemed like the right thing."

"Well, permission granted. Now hush."

She freed her hands, placed them on his cheeks, roughened with beard stubble, and rose on tiptoe to meet his mouth while he gripped the back of her head.

The soft kiss nearly knocked her breathless. Chase dropped more hot kisses on each corner of her mouth and down her chin, feathered her nose and her cheeks, and finally returned to her mouth. Again and again he plied her bottom lip with his teeth, stunning her with his insistent exploration. The pressure of his lips and the clean, masculine scent of his skin took away her equilibrium. She could only follow the motions of his head and revel in the heat stoking the fire in her belly.

He pulled away at last and pressed parted lips to her forehead.

An Excerpt from

CHASING MORGAN
Book Four: The Hunted Series
by Jennifer Ryan

Morgan Standish can see things other people
can't. She can see the past and future. These
hidden gifts have prevented her from getting
close to anyone—except FBI agent Tyler Reed.
Morgan is connected to him in a way even she can't
explain. She's solved several cases for him in the
past, but will her gifts be enough to bring down
a serial killer whose ultimate goal is to kill her?
Find out in Book Four of The Hunted Series.

Morgan's fingers flew across the laptop keyboard propped on her knees. She took a deep breath, cleared her mind, and looked out past her pink-painted toes resting on the railing and across her yard to the densely wooded area at the edge of her property. Her mind's eye found her guest winding his way through the trees. She still had time before Jack stepped out of the woods separating her land from his. She couldn't wait to meet him.

Images, knowings, they just came to her. She'd accepted that part of herself a long time ago. As she got older, she'd learned to use her gift to seek out answers.

She finished her buy-and-sell orders and switched from her day trading page to check her psychic website and read the questions submitted by customers. She answered several quickly, letting the others settle in her mind until the answers came to her.

One stood out. The innocuous question about getting a job held an eerie vibe.

The familiar strange pulsation came over her. The world disappeared, as though a door had slammed on reality. The images came to her like hammer blows, one right after the other, and she took the onslaught, knowing something important needed to be seen and understood.

An older woman lying in a bed, hooked up to a machine feeding her medication. Frail and ill, she had translucent skin and dark circles marring her tortured eyes. Her pain washed over Morgan like a tsunami.

The woman yelled at someone, her face contorted into something mean and hateful. An unhappy woman—one who'd spent her whole life blaming others and trying to make them as miserable as she was.

A pristine white pillow floating down, inciting panic, amplified to terror when it covered the woman's face, her frail body swallowed by the sheets.

Morgan had an overwhelming feeling of suffocation.

The woman tried desperately to suck in a breath, but couldn't. Unable to move her lethargic limbs, she lay petrified and helpless under his unyielding hands. Lights flashed on her closed eyelids.

Death came calling.

A man stood next to the bed, holding the pillow like a shield. His mouth opened on a contorted, evil, hysterical laugh that rang in her ears and made her skin crawl. She squeezed her eyes closed to blot out his malevolent image and thoughts.

Murderer!

The word rang in her head as the terrifying emotions overtook her.

Morgan threw up a wall in her mind, blocking the cascade of disturbing pictures and feelings. She took several deep breaths and concentrated on the white roses growing in profusion just below the porch railing. Their sweet fragrance filled the air. With every breath, she centered herself and found her inner calm, pushing out the anger and rage left over from the vision. Her body felt like a lead weight, lightening as her energy came back. The drowsiness faded with each new breath. She'd be fine in a few minutes.

The man on horseback emerged from the trees, coming toward her home. Her guest had arrived.

Focused on the computer screen, she slowly and meticulously typed her answer to the man who had asked about a job and inadvertently opened himself up to telling her who he really was at heart.

She replied simply:

You'll get the job, but you can't hide from what you did. You need help. Turn yourself in to the police.

An Excerpt from

THROWING HEAT
A Diamonds and Dugouts Novel
by Jennifer Seasons

Nightclub manager Leslie Cutter has never
been one to back down from a bet. So when
Peter Kowalskin, pitcher for the Denver
Rush baseball team, bets her that she can't
keep her hands off of him, she's not about
to let the arrogant, gorgeous playboy win.
But as things heat up, this combustible pair
will have to decide just how much they're
willing to wager on one another . . . and on
a future that just might last forever.

"Is there something you want?" he demanded with a raised eyebrow, amused at being able to throw her words right back at her.

"You wish," Leslie retorted and tossed him a dismissive glance. Only he caught the gleam of interest in her eyes and knew her for the liar that she was.

Peter took a step toward her, closing the gap by a good foot until only an arm's reach separated them. He leaned forward and caged her in by placing a hand on each armrest of her chair. Her eyes widened the tiniest bit, but she held her ground.

"I wish many, many things."

"Really?" she questioned and shifted slightly away from him in her chair. "Such as what?"

Peter couldn't help noticing that her breathing had gone

shallow. How about that? "I wish to win the World Series this season." It would be a hell of a way to go out.

Her gaze landed on his mouth and flicked away. "Boring."

Humor sparked inside him at that, and he chuckled. "You want exciting?"

She shrugged. "Why not? Amuse me."

That worked for him. Hell yeah. If she didn't watch herself, he was going to excite the pants right off of her.

Just excitement, arousal, and sexual pleasure. That was what he was looking for this time around. And it was going to be fun leading her up to it.

But if he wanted her there, then he had to start.

Pushing until he'd tipped her chair back and only the balls of her feet were on the desk, her painted toes curling for a grip, Peter lowered his head until his mouth was against her ear. She smelled like coconut again, and his gut went tight.

"I wish I had you bent over this desk right here with your hot bare ass in the air."

She made a small sound in her throat and replied, "Less boring."

Peter grinned. Christ, the woman was tough. "Do you remember what I did to you that night in Miami? The thing that made you come hard, twice—one on top of the other?" He sure as hell did. It had involved his tongue, his fingers, and Leslie on all fours with her face buried in a pillow, moaning his name like she was begging for deliverance.

She tried to cover it, but he heard her quick intake of breath. "It wasn't that memorable."

Bullshit.

He slid a hand from the armrest and squeezed the top of her right leg, his thumb rubbing lazily back and forth on the skin of her inner thigh. Her muscles tensed, but she didn't pull away.

"Need a reminder?"

An Excerpt from

PRIVATE RESEARCH
An Erotic Novella
by Sabrina Darby

The last person Mina Cavallari expects to
encounter in the depths of the National
Archives while doing research on a thesis is
Sebastian Graham, an outrageously sexy financial
whiz. Sebastian is conducting a little research of
his own into the history of what he thinks is just
another London underworld myth, the fabled
Harridan House. When he discovers that the
private sex club still exists, he convinces Mina
to join him on an odyssey into the intricacies of
desire, pleasure, and, most surprisingly of all, love.

It was the most innocuous of sentences: "A cappuccino, please." Three words—without a verb to ground them, even. Yet, at the sound, my hand stilled mid-motion, my own paper coffee cup paused halfway between table and mouth. I looked over to the counter of the cafe. It was mid-afternoon, quieter than it had been when I'd come in earlier for a quick lunch, and only three people were in line behind the tall, slim-hipped, blond-haired man whose curve of shoulder and loose-limbed stance struck a chord in me as clearly as his voice.

Of course it couldn't be. In two years, surely, I had forgotten the exact tenor of his voice, was now confusing some other deep, posh English accent with his. Yet I watched the man, waited for him to turn around, as if there were any significant chance that in a city of eight million people, during the middle of the business day, I'd run into the one English acquaintance I had. At the National Archives, no less.

At the first glimpse of his profile, I sucked in my breath sharply, nearly dropping my coffee. Then he turned fully, looking around, likely for the counter with napkins and sugar. I watched his gaze pass over me and then snap back in recognition. I was both pleased and terrified. I'd come to London to put the past behind me, not to face down my demons. I'd been doing rather well these last months, but maybe this was part of some cosmic plan. As my time in England wound down, in order to move forward with my life, I had to come face to face with Sebastian Graham again.

"Mina!" He had an impressive way of making his voice heard across a room without shouting, and as he walked toward me, I put my cup down and stood, all too aware that while he looked like a fashionable professional about town, I still looked like a grad student——no makeup, hair pulled back in a ponytail, wearing jeans, sneakers, and a sweater.

"This is a pleasant surprise. Research for your dissertation? Anne Gracechurch, right?"

I nodded, bemused that he remembered a detail from what had surely been a throwaway conversation two years earlier. But of course I really shouldn't have been. Seb was brilliant, and brilliance wasn't the sort of thing that just faded away.

Neither, apparently, was his ability to make my pulse beat a bit faster or to tie up my tongue for a few seconds before I found my stride. He wasn't traditionally handsome, at least not in an American way. Too lean, too angular, hair receding a bit at the temples, and I was fairly certain he was now just shy of thirty. But I'd found him attractive from the first moment I'd met him.

I still did.

"That's right. What are you doing here? I mean, at the Archives."

"Ah." He shifted and smiled at me, and there was something about that smile that felt wicked and secretive. "A small genealogical project. Mind if I join you?"

I shook my head and sat back down. He pulled out his chair and sat, too, folding his long legs one over the other. Why was that sexy to me?

I focused on his face. He was pale. Much paler than he'd been in New Jersey, like he now spent most of his time indoors. Which should have been a turn-off. Yet, despite everything, I sat there imagining him in the kitchen of my apartment wearing nothing but boxer shorts. Apparently my memory was as good as his.

And I still remembered the crushing humiliation and disappointment of that last time we'd talked.